HARD LINE

The Complete Jack McMorrow Mystery Series by Gerry Boyle

1. Deadline
2. Bloodline
3. Lifeline
4. Potshot
5. Borderline
6. Cover Story
7. Home Body
8. Pretty Dead
9. Damaged Goods
10. Once Burned
11. Straw Man
12. Random Act
13. Robbed Blind
14. Hard Line

HARD LINE

THE FINAL JACK McMORROW MYSTERY

GERRY BOYLE

ISLANDPORT PRESS

ISLANDPORT PRESS

Islandport Press
P.O. Box 10
Yarmouth, Maine 04096
www.islandportpress.com
info@islandportpress.com

First Edition: June 2024
Printed in the United States of America.

ISBN: 978-1-952143-89-2
Library of Congress Control Number: 2024932052

Dean L. Lunt | Editor-in-Chief, Publisher
Shannon M. Butler | Vice President
Genevieve A. Morgan | Editor
Emily A. Lunt | Book Designer
Cover photo courtesy of Dmitrii Iakimov/Shutterstock

For those who have gone before, especially Joseph R. Foley (1926-2023), who always kept McMorrow on his bookshelf. And for Vic, whose encouragement kept me typing all those years ago.

———————◆———————

Heartfelt thanks goes to Genevieve Morgan, my partner in crime at Islandport Press. Through five novels, her wise counsel, perceptive editing, and steadfast support have kept McMorrow and his creator on the right path—not always an easy task.

And when he had opened the fourth seal, I heard the voice of the fourth beast say, Come and see. And I looked and behold a pale horse: and his name that sat on him was Death, and Hell followed with him. And power was given unto them over the fourth part of the earth, to kill with sword, and with hunger, and with death, and with the beasts of the earth.
—Revelation 6:7–8

She walks these hills in a long black veil.
She visits my grave when the night winds wail.
Nobody knows, nobody sees.
Nobody knows but me.
—Lefty Frizell, "The Long Black Veil"

PREVIOUSLY, IN *ROBBED BLIND*

Zombie

There was something about the Blade Runner *chick, the way she looked at him like she could see right through his mask. Then the bell went off. She had a thing for him, most def, trying to keep him there, Mr. Zombie and all that. Pretending she thought he was a jerk, but not really. That's how some babes played hard to get. Say one thing, mean the opposite. No means yes. You got rough with them and they went crazy.*

He'd follow her home from work, knock on the door. She'd be surprised, of course, but he'd step inside, close the door, grab her and plant a juicy one on her mouth. Feel her pretend not to like it but then she'd give up. Just melt. She'd say, "I didn't know Zombie delivered."

A good feeling to have a new plan. He'd have to move on those other guys who were sniffing around, the cop giving her rides home. The other guy, the reporter, the two of them having heart-to-hearts. That guy was old, no match for Zombie. Look what happened to the last guy who tried to take on Zombie. One shot, went down like a bag of rocks.

Jack McMorrow

I called Roxanne at the hotel, heard the girls in the background.

"Jack, how's the story?" Roxanne said.

"Pretty much finished," I said. "The madness is winding down."

"Good."

"When are you coming home? You need to extract yourself."

"Tomorrow," Roxanne said. "I love you."

"Likewise." I said.

We rang off. I smiled. It had been this way for all these years with Roxanne. No matter what the chaos, the reunion—a melding of our mouths and bodies and spirit—eclipsed it.

I sat on my couch, in the dark with the phone and the guns. Reality check: One psycho dead, another with an ankle bracelet and a heart condition. Progress. But there were more psychos out there. Like Zombie.

My phone buzzed again. Stephanie Dunne.

—YOU'RE GHOSTING ME JACK. DON'T DO THIS. WE'VE GOT THE BIG CLIMAX. THOUSANDS OF LISTENERS PRIMED AND READY.
—AND IT'S THE FREAKIN' DYING PUNK ROCKER WHO OFFS THE MURDERER!! AND YOU WERE THERE!!
—WE ABSOLUTELY, POSITIVELY HAVE TO TELL THIS STORY!!!!

I knew Dunne wanted to finish our crime podcast. It was a great story. Sex. Murder. Drugs. Revenge. But I just couldn't do it anymore. I decided the world would never know the true story of Sparrow and Riff, Raymond and Germaine, Mumbo and Twinsey. The reporter who'd spent his life telling stories was keeping this one to himself.

I sat back down. The house creaked and the woodstove ticked. I picked up the Glock from the table, eyed it, put it down. Saved my life a few times—and then ended my career. Live by the gun, die by the—

A crash, breaking glass. Back of the house.

I grabbed the gun and ran through. Flames on the other side of the door to the deck. I grabbed a fire extinguisher, started to loop around through the shed. Realized I was being flushed out. Too late.

The shotgun clapped. I raised the Glock and fired at the muzzle flash. I felt the second shot hit, white-hot on my chest, my neck.

Went down on the snow, my gun lost in the darkness. No pain, but I could feel something hot and liquid spreading out across my shirt.

Blood.

I put a hand over my neck. Blood trickled through my fingers, flowed down the top of my left wrist and hand.

I heard footsteps in the woods.

Walking, not running.

Coming closer.

And closer.

HARD LINE

1

I could see the holes, centered in red splotches, the edges slightly raised like the rim of a volcanic crater. There were five of them at the top of my left arm and shoulder. That left thirteen out of sight.

Or so they told me.

"Somebody up there like you or what?" the ER doc said. "I mean, no arterial damage. A little higher? The neck? Carotid, subclavian arteries? Could have bled out before they got there. Who was it that responded?"

"Prosperity Volunteer Fire Department."

"Bless their hearts."

Her name was Dr. Goode. She'd breezed in, gray bangs straying over her mask, told me that being shot was the luckiest day of my life. Now she moved my shoulder around in its socket, paused as her phone buzzed in her pocket. She slipped it out, tapped the screen with a latexed finger.

"Woohoo," she said.

"Hit me with more good news."

"Dr. Ahmadi says we can just leave the pellets in."

"All of them?"

"Yup, the whole kit and caboodle. Take my word for it. You don't want somebody probing around in there with forceps if you don't have to. Be like those guys who look for stuff on the beach with the metal detectors and shovels."

I turned my head, felt a tug on the IV. I looked up at her from the table and grimaced. She looked to the nurse, a bearded guy with a canoe tattooed on his right forearm, and said, "Let's wrap him up."

"What if they're lead?" I said.

"He looked at the film," Goode said. "He says they're steel, judging by how perfectly round they are. Lead pellets tend to distort. Steel doesn't. In any event, prevailing practice now either way is to leave them, especially in soft tissue. Risk of blood poisoning is way overblown."

"He sees a lot of this?"

"Bird hunters. I don't know how you mistake a man for a partridge, but hey. And he did medical training in Iran and studied the effect of bullet wounds where the bullet was left in place. Don't suppose they found the gun."

"Or the shell? I don't know," I said.

The nurse asked me to sit up. I did. Winced. Gasped. He ran the tape across to my neck. Another strip down the left side of my back.

"So," the doc said, "neurovascular status is good. Full range of motion, though it'll hurt like a son of a gun for a week or two. We gave you a couple mils of morphine through the IV. Something to get you home. Called in a scrip for Percocet. And I'd go with ice and ibuprofen."

The nurse went to a cabinet, slid a drawer open. "Our slings are gray or black," he said.

"Black," I said. "I'll be able to sneak up on people in the dark."

He looked at me, then took out a black sling made of heavy cloth, looped it over my head, and slipped my arm into the opening. I gritted my teeth.

The doc was texting again. "Telling Dr. Ahmadi we're discharging you with your hardware in place," she said.

My hardware. It took me a moment. Shotgun pellets.

"Thanks," I said.

"Live to fight another day," the doc said.

"Got that right."

Another look, just like the one from the nurse.

"Figure of speech," Dr. Goode said.

"Sometimes," I said.

A young woman in green scrubs walked me out. I was wearing a gray zippered sweatshirt with MIDCOAST HOSPITAL over the left side of the chest, my own shirt scissored off on arrival. She hit a button and the door to the waiting room slid open. On the opposite wall, another door slid open and two Waldo County deputies stepped in, moving side by side. I thought it looked like the beginning of a square dance.

"Do si do," I murmured. The morphine kicking in?

The young woman stopped in front of them, then stepped back and retreated, like she was transferring custody of an inmate.

"Mr. McMorrow," the deputy said. She was the muscled one from Jason's arrest, her name tag reading D. Jackman. The other deputy was a skinny, sandy-haired kid with the faintest excuse for a mustache. Maybe he was earning a Scout badge.

"Can we talk?" Jackman said.

I nodded.

She motioned to the row of chairs along the wall and we sat, me in the middle. My shoulder was throbbing from the inside out, a new experience. The reel rewound—the times I'd been punched, kicked, bludgeoned, nearly drowned. Hit with sticks, and gun butts, and wrenches. Androscoggin, Scanesset. Lawrence, Mass. I'd had bullets whiz by my head on my own property. Hidden from hooters in a tree in a Franklin County swamp. Coyote and Bobby. I'd carried a gun, associated with people who routinely carried two.

But I'd never been shot.

It hurt to move. It hurt to stay still. I shifted in my chair, winced. Nobody asked if I was okay.

"Detectives will be in touch, but we need a preliminary statement," Jackman said. She had her phone out, a notebook and pen, too. She asked if I minded if she recorded it. I said no. Being a podcaster, after all. She said to tell them what happened. I did.

The sound of breaking glass, flames on the back deck. Me going out the shed door, realizing too late that this was likely what they were waiting for. The shot.

"You think there was more than one assailant?"

"I just saw the one guy. Turned out to be a guy. At first it was just a dark figure at the edge of the woods, along the lilacs."

"Did you see a firearm?"

"Heard it. Shotgun. That shot missed."

"Distance?"

"Forty yards, give or take."

She wrote in her notebook. The kid had his suspicious face on, like maybe I'd shot myself in the back with a shotgun for attention.

"Second shot?"

"Came just after I fired at the first muzzle flash. Second shot, he'd moved to the left, maybe five feet. I was turning, diving right."

"You missed."

"Yeah. He didn't."

"Your shoulder."

"Yeah. I'd say number-five shot. Maybe -four. Judging by what they said about the penetration. They left them in."

More scribbling. On the arm of the chair, her phone was recording, ticking away the seconds. I thought of T. S. Eliot. Prufrock. *I have measured out my life with coffee spoons. I know the voices dying with a dying fall.*

The morphine for sure.

"Was the shooter running away when you heard the footsteps?"

"No, walking toward me. Like after you shoot a deer, you approach it with caution, make sure it's dead."

"They can spring up," the kid deputy said. "Hooves are wicked sharp."

We'd found common ground.

"Then what happened?" Jackman said.

"I'd lost my gun in the snow. He came up, stopped."

"Did you see his face?"

"Black balaclava, black sweatshirt with the hood up. Military-type boots, black trousers tucked in."

"And then?"

He had the shotgun pointed at me. He jacked in a shell, mostly for the sound effect, would be my guess."

Jackman waited.

"Did he say anything?"

"He said, 'Back the fuck off.' "

"Did you say anything back?"

"Told him to go eff himself."

A flicker of eyebrow, maybe a bit of a smirk.

"And?"

"He said, 'If it were up to me, I'd kill you right now.' "

I moved my shoulder, lifting my left arm up with my right.

"And you said?"

"What makes you think I said anything?"

"Wild guess."

"I said, 'Who is it up to, you pathetic loser?' "

Jackman was writing. The kid deputy grinned. I'd won him over.

"He pointed the gun at me and then he lowered it, turned around and left. Walked back into the trees, headed east. I'm sure you can follow his tracks."

"Truck parked five hundred yards down the road," D. Jackman said. No houses that side for a half-mile.

"So, you're hot on his trail," I said.

"It went pretty cold, which is one reason we're here."

There was a pause. A nurse was escorting a grizzled, gray-bearded guy through the sliding doors, his boots scuffing on the tile floor. The doors shut, which left us alone for the million-dollar question.

"Who would want you to back off?" Jackman said.

I thought about it.

"Let's see. There's this guy Jason Stratton and his paramilitary buddies. Also, the guy robbing the stores in Clarkston. I've been writing about that. Maybe associates of this guy, goes by Mumbo. He killed Raymond Jandreau there."

"And then was killed," Jackman said. "I heard. Anyone else?"

"That's all I can think of. That's going back almost a week."

She looked at me.

"No moss growing on you, Mr. McMorrow."

The kid looked puzzled, didn't know the expression from Instagram. Jackman stopped recording, folded her notebook shut.

My phone buzzed a text:

—YOUR RIDE IS HERE.

I said, "We done?"

They stood.

I heaved myself up, winced and gritted my teeth. The pain was sharp when I moved, like somebody stabbing my shoulder with a pitchfork. I took a breath and the three of us stepped through the door, down a beige-bricked corridor and through a revolving door to the ER entrance.

The deputies' SUV was parked to the left, exhaust hovering over it like a rain cloud. We paused, then saw a truck come in the driveway entrance, headed in our direction. They saw it, too, and kept walking. The big Ford pickup pulled up.

I crunched through the snow crust, opened the passenger door. Reached up with my good arm and heaved myself in.

Clair looked at me, shook his head, and said, "God almighty, McMorrow. Can't leave you alone for a minute."

2

We caught up on the ride home, the roads deserted and dark, chunks of salt reflecting the headlights like diamond dust.

Clair said Mary walked over after she saw the lights, texted him to say I'd been shot. He was in Kingfield, after crossing the border at Coburn Gore on his way home from Montreal.

"You okay?"

"I'm okay. Sore. Foggy from morphine."

"Lucky."

"Yes."

"Any idea of who or why?"

"Militia guys playing soldier, maybe. A buddy of this piece-of-crap boyfriend of the mom of one of Sophie's friends."

"What'd you do to him?"

"Got him locked up."

"That all?" Clair said.

"Also knocked him down and rubbed his nose in it."

He nodded. I shifted in my seat and my shoulder burned.

"Where are Louis and Marta?"

Where indeed?

Marta had vanished a year ago, snatched by a Montreal biker gang, business associates of her late boyfriend, a money launderer. Louis and Clair had grabbed her off the street in Canada, brought her back into the United States with a fake passport. She was back to collect her million dollars in dirty cash.

"Mary's taking care of Marta. She's sick. Fentanyl withdrawal."

Like nursing a rattlesnake back to health.

"No Suboxone?"

"She decided to try to ride it out, get back on her feet quicker."

"What's Louis doing?"

"He went to pick up the dog."

We drove, crossing the flats west of Belfast, a dark gloom of frozen marsh on both sides.

Maine was mostly unsettled, I thought. Humans clinging precariously to the edges.

I looked out, finally said, "How'd it go up there?"

"Fine. She was in a truck with Lambert and another guy."

"How'd you get her?"

"Clear-out grenades at a traffic light."

"Huh. Military stuff?"

"You can buy them on Amazon. Louis popped the door, threw them in. Driver panicked, hit the gas, rammed the car in front of him."

"Hard to get good help," I said.

"Yes. Easier to ride around on a motorcycle, looking tough."

"So that was it?"

"Pretty much. Airbags went off. Louis grabbed her and off we went."

"Huh. No shots fired?"

"Nope. He made the grab, I drove. Louis is good at preplanning."

"No problem getting back into the country?"

"He had fake US passports for the two of them. Mr. and Mrs."

"Where did he—"

"Canadians fought in Iraq, a few of them, though they don't admit it. Did hostage rescue. Louis made some calls and had the cash. Anyway, a little chitchat and they waved us through. Left a lot of nice guns behind in Montreal, but other than that . . ."

"Another walk in the park," I said.

We were quiet.

Clair drove on, his face looking older and wearier in the dashboard light. The headlights waggled when we hit a bump. All else was darkness.

"Humiliating the head of an outlaw motorcycle club," I said.

"Hell hath no fury," Clair said.

"They'll come after Louis?"

"Somebody will. We figure they'll call in favors down here. Hard for them to cross over into the States because they're mostly felons."

"How long?"

He shrugged. "A few days, maybe? Hard to say."

"Marta, our Helen of Troy," I said.

"She'll be tucked away."

"And Louis will be what? Holed up down there waiting?"

"He knows his woods. Beefing up the surveillance. Some amazing thermal-imaging stuff out there. Makes my war look like muskets and hatchets."

I thought about it.

"Still, Louis against a whole crew?"

"He was First Battalion, Seventh Marines. First wave into Baghdad, house-to-house for days. Second deployment after that, clearing towns all along the Euphrates. Dismounted urban patrols, is what the military calls them. Clearing houses, killing insurgents before they could kill you."

I pictured it, Louis kicking in doors.

"I wouldn't want to be them," Clair said.

"What if they come after you, too?"

"I'll call you," Clair said. "While you're distracting them with probing questions, I'll go out the back."

I smiled through the pain.

He drove, big arm on top of the steering wheel like he was at the helm of a ship.

Snow squalls were coming at us from the northwest, small hard flakes streaming into the light like swarms of bugs. As we slowed and climbed the ridge, I briefed Clair on Jason and Zombie, Blake and Sparrow, Riff and Mumbo.

"Good to know you've been keeping busy," Clair said.

We crested the ridge, hard snow spattering the windshield like shotgun pellets. On the winding descent into the valley, the headlights picked up the center line of the road, the big V8 holding our speed down.

"What's your play with this Jason fella?" Clair said.

"Like you said, I'll go see him, ask probing questions."

"Need your trusted photographer, you being semi-hurt and all? I'll dust off my Hasselblad."

I smiled.

"No," I said. "You'll be busy with Marta and Louis. I'm good for the moment."

He drove. I shifted again, trying to find a comfortable position.

"Want some advice?" Clair said.

"Do I have a choice?"

"No."

He paused.

"You writer types are too much heart. In combat, or anything close to it, you always have to be three, four steps out. Think tactically, and above all, maintain self-control."

"Gotcha. Maybe I'll bring an extra thick notebook, smack him over the head."

He smiled, and for a moment I could see the skull under his skin, a glimpse of mortality. The morphine again?

We rolled up to the end of the drive, turned in, and stopped by the road. Clair started to unbuckle his seat belt and I waved him off. "I'm good."

And I was, sort of.

I got myself in. After twelve hours, the house was cold, smelling like smoke and gasoline. I lit a fire in the woodstove, went outside to inspect the damage. The window of the sliding door dirty but intact. Broken glass on the deck, a torn label that said captain morgan. A scorched wall, black up to a foot below Sophie's bedroom window. She was away with Roxanne, and Tara and Tiffanee, but he hadn't known that. Jason's little protégé could have set the house on fire, cedar shingles burning up the wall.

Sophie caught in the fire. My beautiful girl.

I felt rage reignite, turn to a slow burn.

He was a dead man.

With my phone light, I went back outside, walked around the house to the shed, slipped under crime-scene tape strung from the shed door to the shrubbery, then down the drive toward the road. I followed my own tracks, starting to fade with the new snow. There was an indentation where I'd fallen, a few blood spots still showing, tracks of feet and knees from the EMTs.

I shined the light toward the lilacs and the trees beyond, saw the tracks that came out into the open, then doubled back. My shooter.

If it were up to me, I'd kill you now.

A fatal mistake.

I went back inside, where the fire was going strong. I turned the damper down, went to the refrigerator, and took out a Ballantine, the last one. Thought of the morphine and put the ale back. I went to the chair in the study and sat down heavily. Landed on my shoulder and got a jolt. Or eighteen of them. Leaned forward and took off the sling. Held my phone with my left hand, close to my belly. Texted Roxanne:

HEY BABY. HOPE YOU'RE DOING OKAY. SOPHIE TOO. WE'LL TALK TOMORROW.

NIGHT HERE WAS A BIT EVENTFUL. SOMEBODY STARTED A LITTLE FIRE ON THE DECK, TOOK A SHOT AT ME BUT I'M FINE.

JUST A LITTLE BIRDSHOT. HE RAN AWAY. KNEW WHEN HE WAS OUTMATCHED!

LISTEN, I THINK YOU SHOULD STAY DOWN THERE ANOTHER NIGHT.

SOME POOL TIME FOR THE GIRLS AND I CAN CLEAN THINGS UP HERE.

THANKS. LOVE YOU.

PS: CLAIR IS BACK. WILL TELL YOU MORE.

HE AND LOUIS ARE FINE, TOO. ALL IS WELL.

I gingerly eased myself up from the chair, got the Ballantine Ale after all. Came back, popped it, settled into the chair. The morphine wasn't covering up the pain, just making it seem like my shoulder belonged to somebody else.

A swallow of ale and a glance at my watch. It was 3:48 a.m., and my mind was whirling.

Another few sips and I wasn't thinking anything at all.

I woke up at 7:30, still in the chair, the fire cold. Forgot for a moment about the shoulder and tried to get up, felt like I'd been jabbed. I eased back, slipped my arm back in the sling, reached the phone from the arm of the chair.

Roxanne.

6:09	CALL ME.
6:14	JACK, ARE YOU THERE?
6:31	JACK, I'M WORRIED. CALL ME ASAP.
6:48	JACK, FOR GOD'S SAKE. ARE YOU OKAY?

There were eleven missed calls.

I called back.

A half-ring and Roxanne said, "Jack, what the hell? I've been calling. For God's sake, you say you've been shot and then you don't answer for three freaking hours? Do you know how worried I've been?"

"Sorry. The meds. And I was tired."

"I was about to call Clair."

"He gave me a ride home from the hospital."

"They let you go home?"

"It's not that big a deal. Like a BB gun."

"Are you kidding me? Shot in our own yard? And someone setting the house on fire? I mean, this is nuts, Jack. And a shotgun is no BB gun."

"The pellets are like BBs, in this case."

"Like, how many? Did they take them out? Can you get around?"

I explained the prevailing medical practice, said I had full mobility, didn't say it hurt like hell.

"It really turned out fine," I said. "Missed my face, so I can still be an L.L.Bean catalog model if newspapers totally tank."

The first silence. I took the opening.

"House needs some cleanup. Fire didn't really catch. Deck was wet. Wall's a little singed, but I can fix it."

"Jason?"

"He's on home confinement with an ankle bracelet."

"His soldier friends—they're still out there?"

"Police are on it. Don't worry."

"Yeah, right," Roxanne said. A pause. "I'm glad Clair's back."

"I'm in good hands."

"What about Louis and what's-her-name?"

I told her. Marta at Clair's and Mary's detoxing. I skipped the part about the vengeful biker gang guy. One thing at a time.

"How's Sophie?"

"Fine. She and Tara went with Tiffanee to get takeout for breakfast. I get the feeling that most of the time, Tara and Tiffanee are joined at the hip. It's kind of weird."

"Just the two of them," I said. "Against the boyfriends."

"Right," Roxanne said.

"I'd play it down with her. The fire thing."

"More than you have already?"

"I think you can head home later today. Maybe dinnertime? Give me time to clean things up."

"They have Sunday rehearsal at six-thirty. It's blocking and stage movement."

"Sunday?"

"You know Mr. Ziggy."

"Guy should get a life."

"I know."

"And they still—"

"Yes, they want to go," Roxanne said. "Maybe good to get back to normal."

Normal. Was this it?

"Maybe that would be good."

There was a pause. I said I loved her. She said she loved me, the in-spite-of-it-all part implied and understood. And then she was gone.

I scrolled down the texts until I hit an old one to T. Tinkham, aka, Tiffanee, me asking her if Tara could stay for dinner. She'd said yes, but like it was sort of a big deal, Tara being away from her.

—I CAN COME GET HER AS SOON AS YOU'RE DONE.

Now I texted:

HEY, TIFFANEE. QUICK QUESTION.
WHAT'S JASON'S AUNT'S ADDRESS?
SAVE ME HAVING TO CALL THE COURTHOUSE.
HOPE YOU'RE HAVING FUN DOWN THERE.

I sat back. The phone buzzed, Tiffanee always on her phone. Like mother, like daughter.

—RITA STRATTON, HIS OLDER SISTER. LIVES IN THIS
LITTLE BLUE HOUSE UP ON A HILL NEAR THE WALMART.
—WICKED BITCH. ALL NICEY-NICE TO YOUR FACE BUT STAB
YOU IN THE BACK.

Literally or figuratively?

I closed my eyes, took a couple of deep breaths. Pulled myself up with my right arm and slowly unfolded until I was upright. It didn't hurt when I stood still.

The house still smelled like smoke. The morning was cloudy, a low gray sky holding in the cold and damp.

I walked to the window and looked out. The broken glass on the deck was under an inch of icy snow. Maybe if it warmed up it would be easier to shovel, get rid of it.

I walked to the kitchen, filled the electric kettle and snapped it on. Then I went to the stairs, made my way up one step at a time. I grabbed for the railing with my left arm and gritted my teeth. Went to the bathroom and took off the hospital sweatshirt, my boots, dirty jeans, and socks. I stepped into the shower, pushed the showerhead so it aimed at the wall. Put a towel on my shoulder and back to cover the bandage, eased in, and let the hot blast spray the rest of me. Dropped the soap and started to bend to get it and got a jolt, like one of those electric dog collars.

I let the soap lie.

Drying off, I dabbed the shoulder where the bandage was damp. That hurt, too. I walked to the bedroom, took underwear, socks, and a T-shirt from the bureau, jeans from a shelf in the closet. Dressed, working the T-shirt on slowly, the bandage clinging. Cinched my belt and went downstairs to put on my boots. Grunted as I tied the laces, gritted my teeth as I straightened. Pictured Jason's face when I showed up at his door. Mr. Tough Guy when he was going after Tiffanee, screaming at Tara, playing war games with his nut-job buddies.

Sending someone to shoot me up and burn my house? Don't think I'm going to sit at home like an invalid.

I smiled darkly, said, "I'm back, you cowardly bastard."

On my feet, I went to the hooks next to the shed door. A black Carhartt jacket. I wrestled it on, grimacing as I reached my left arm through the sleeve. Took a breath. Then selected a hat with the original Betsy Ross flag on the front, a souvenir from a trip to DC with Sophie. I hoped it would give me the look of a True Patriot, or at least the social media version.

I headed to the closet, to the back of the top shelf, took the key off the hook above my head, opened the safe. Took out a Glock 26, on loan from Louis, smaller than my 19. Snapped the clip in and out, put the gun in my jacket pocket.

"I'm coming, Jason," I said.

When I went out to the truck, I left the sling on the table.

While the truck warmed up, I searched on my phone for Rita Stratton, Augusta, Maine.

The Internet said she was fifty-eight, lived at 2 Royal Ave. There were no other residents listed. I searched the address on Google Earth and found it on the back side of the big-box stores on the north end of the city. I dropped down on the house, and sure enough, it was a small, blue vinyl-sided ranch with a one-car garage. In the photo, the lawn was mowed. There was a small white Nissan in the driveway. The side yard was fenced, like for a dog.

I reached for my seat belt, awkwardly clipped it in with my good arm. Took a deep breath, let the jolt subside. Put the truck in gear and turned it around, spinning the wheel with my right hand, my left acting as witness to the proceedings, not much more. At the end of the drive, I checked my watch. It was 8:02.

Royal Avenue was part of a development on a ridge north of the downtown, uphill from the tenements of Sand Hill that once housed the city's millworkers. The mill was gone now, and this neighborhood was home to the next generation: State workers, nurses from the hospital. We don't make anything anymore to speak of, but everyone still needs a driver's license, still gets sick.

I found the house at the dead end, Jason's jacked-up truck pulled to the side of the driveway, the same white car in the open garage. There was the same dog fence encircling the side yard, the mown lawn covered with snow. Tiffanee had said Rita got an insurance settlement from an accident and didn't have to work. Lots of time to tend to her jail-sprung nephew.

I drove by slowly, saw the flicker of a television in the front room. Jason watching Netflix? Nothing too suspenseful for his struggling heart?

Stopping in the middle of the street, I backed up, pulled into the single-lane driveway, and parked. If Rita needed to get out to do errands, she'd have to wait.

I got out of the truck, saw a woman flash by the big window to the left of the front door. She moved away and I walked up the shoveled path to the door. There were three steps to a stoop, a doorbell on the left. I stepped up and pressed it. My finger was still on the button when the door swung open.

A woman looked at me through the glass of the storm door. Dark short hair frosted with silver. Gold hoop earrings and lots of makeup, eyebrows that looked tattooed on. She looked at me, waiting.

I nodded. "You Rita?" I affected a faint Southern accent.

There was no response, just the stare.

"Friend of Jason's."

I leaned closer, glanced back at the street like somebody might be listening.

"From the farm."

Acknowledgment, just in her eyes, and then she said, "You on the list?"

A millisecond to process that. The no-contact list. Tiffanee. Tara. Jack McMorrow.

"No," I said.

"What's your name?"

"Johnny."

"Johnny what?"

"Just Johnny from the farm. He'll know."

She gave me another long look, then reached for the door handle. Opened the door and leaned forward to look out at the street.

"Come in. Cops have been driving up and down. Bastards won't leave him alone."

She went back inside, and I wiped my boots on the mat and followed.

The room was neat. Two stuffed chairs and a couch, all matching. Fake flowers in vases. Framed photos on a brick mantel: three dogs and a guy. Jason, ten years and thirty pounds ago. Hair cut short, the mullet poking out from behind his ears. Even then, a pout like he'd been wrongly accused.

Rita saw the direction of my gaze. "Before he met that first woman. Oh, didn't she make his life hell. Girls today, they got it all figured out, I tell ya."

She went into a hallway to the left, opened a door. A small white dog bounded out, yipped as it circled me. She called back, "He's okay, Remy. He's a friend of Jay's." The dog stopped barking, sniffed my boots. I leaned down and gave him a pat. He was soft like he'd been shampooed and blown dry.

I was patting when she came back, the dog sniffing my other boot.

"Jay's in the shower."

"I can wait."

Rita motioned to the chair. The dog jumped up on the couch, settled on a blanket with a monogrammed R.

"Coffee?"

"Yes, ma'am," I said.

Rita moved to the kitchen, adjoining the living room. I followed. She started on the coffee, filling a carafe with water, pouring it into the coffeemaker.

"Jay will be glad to see somebody. Stuck here with me all day and night. That bitch, excuse my French, really put the boots to him. Makes up all these lies and looks all helpless, and of course the cops believe her. I think they take a course in this now, these girls. First one he was with, oh, they bought her story hook, line, and sinker. Cost Jay his business, his truck, his house. Guys can't win. You married?"

"No," I lied.

"Smart. Jay's mom, her first husband Bart, he died. Got cancer and then got hit by a car. I think he did it on purpose, being a big coward. Good riddance. Then she hooks up with Roland and he starts in with the strap on Jay, gonna be the big boss dad, you know? Brandy, she wouldn't stick up for her own son, so I did. Went over there one day, backed that guy up against the wall, said, 'You're not gonna touch that boy again because he's coming with me.' And we left. Lived with me for two years, until he graduated high school."

"Good for you," I said.

She watched the coffee drizzling into the pot, said, "I couldn't let that go on. He was a good kid. System's been rigged against him ever since, though. I mean, this last one. He goes to get his girlfriend—useless from what I can tell, but anyway—she's there crying on somebody's shoulder, the way they all do. Guy at the house gets in his face, pulls a gun. Jay's got a right to defend himself. I mean, this is America, right? At least it used to be. So who do they arrest? Jason. Make up all this crap. I mean, this is a guy with a heart problem. What, are they trying to kill him with all this stress?"

She filled a mug, handed it to me.

"Cream?"

"Black's fine."

I lifted the mug. It had a picture of the dog on it. I sipped.

She looked at me, said softly. "Well, good for you guys to try to do something about it."

A knowing look.

"Thank you, ma'am."

"Rita. Oh, I tell you, some of these cops are bigger criminals than the criminals. We got a good lawyer, though. Got me my settlement. He's gonna sue the pants off these people, see how they like it."

"Sounds like a plan," I said.

"I told Jason you're here. He'll be up in a minute. I can hear him moving around down there. That bracelet thingy is a pain, I'll tell you. Listen, I gotta get the laundry."

She left the kitchen, went down a hallway deeper into the house. I heard a washer door open as I walked back to the living room. The dog gave a muffled yip, then closed his eyes. He opened them when a door rattled open, and Jason came out of the hallway and one step into the room. And stopped.

"What the—?"

"Hey, Jay," I said. "How's the ticker?"

His mouth was open, eyes narrowed.

"You can't fucking be here."

"Well, I am, so we might as well make the best of it. Rita made coffee." I held up the mug. "Nice lady. She sure likes you."

"Get out."

"Nope. I mean, you could try to toss me out, but it'd probably just keep ending the same way. And you with a bad heart."

"I'll call the cops."

"Go for it. Rita hates them, seeing as how they pick on you. Maybe she'd get into it with them, you could both have cuffs on."

He moved two steps closer. Thinning hair askew. A two-week beard, bare patches between mustache and chin. Jeans, a white T-shirt, white socks. The monitor was on his left ankle.

"What the friggin' hell do you want?"

"To talk. Off the record. I'm off the clock."

A dryer door slammed shut, and there was a whirring sound. Rita came down the hall, through the kitchen, and into the living room. She smiled.

"You boys have lots to talk about, I'll bet."

"Just catching up on farm business," I said, the accent again.

Rita raised her tattooed eyebrows. "Don't need to say another word. I'll leave you alone. Besides, Jay knows I can keep a secret." She looked at him, winked, bustled back out.

"She could have stayed. I could have told her you had somebody try to burn my house down, take a shot at me with a shotgun."

No reaction, not a flicker, then a belated, "I got no fuckin' idea what you're talking about."

"My fault for missing him. It was dark, but still. No excuse. I even had the nineteen, more accurate than this little twenty-six."

I slipped the Glock from my pocket, then back.

"Outside," I said.

"No."

"Then we'll talk here. The three of us."

I smiled. He hesitated, then turned, said, "There's a deck out back."

I followed him down some stairs to a walkout basement. There was a foldout couch in the corner, unmade. A big TV on one wall, a game console on the arm of the chair in front of it. Empty cans of Miller Lite on the floor.

"Alcohol? Tsk, tsk."

He took a fatigue jacket off a hook by the back door. Put it on and stepped into a pair of tactical-looking boots. Opened the door and clomped out onto the deck, leaving footprints in the inch of snow. I followed. We stood. I looked out at the view, snow-topped rooftops terracing a valley, the State House dome standing tall in the distance.

"Jeez, Jason. You can see right into the halls of power. All those people down there, conspiring against you."

He stared, stone-faced.

"What?" he said.

I turned back to him.

"Your buddy could have burned my house down, with my family in it."

"Don't know nothing about that. Besides, from what I hear, you got lots of people hate your guts, so don't try to pin this shit on—"

I took two steps closer.

"I'm not trying anything. I'm telling you. And your friend. He told me to back off, but I'm not backing off at all. I'm coming after you and your fake soldiers and your uniforms off Amazon. And if any of you come near my family or my house again, my associates and I—they're real military, by the way—will pick you off like it's a goddamn video game."

I moved closer. He took a step back, against the door.

"You're making a big mistake, asshole," Jason said. He raised his arms, clenched his pudgy fists.

I slipped the gun out and up, pressed the muzzle to his forehead. Felt my left shoulder throb.

"Only one big mistake here, my friend, and you already made it."

I pressed the muzzle into his skin, hard. Held it for a long ten-count, until he swallowed. Lowered the gun. It had left a red-rimmed circle, like a brand. Or a bull's eye.

"I won't miss," I said.

He stared at me with a cold, burning hatred.

I turned and walked back through the door, slipped the gun back in my pocket on the way up the stairs. Rita was in the kitchen and I turned, thanked her for the coffee.

"Not a problem," she said. "I hope you guys had a good talk."

"Oh, we did. Still have some unfinished business."

On my way through the living room, the dog growled.

3

The sun came out at noontime, warming the south side of the house. I was on the deck, awkwardly scraping up snow and glass and bits of char wire-brushed from the lowest course of shingles. With my right arm, I shoveled the mess into a trash can. As I was scraping the deck, I saw Louis's truck—a big black Chevy three-quarter-ton—roll slowly by.

Checking on the patient.

I went back to the deck and, left arm back in the sling, sanded the outer layer of scorched wood off the cedar. Looked up and surveyed the wall, which with the bare wood looked oddly new but less like a fire scene.

I dragged the barrel back to the shed, stepped outside. The yellow crime-scene tape fluttered in the sunshine. I walked over, untied it from shrubs and tree limbs, and laid it on the ground. No need to totally freak Sophie out. That done, I started down the path to Clair's house, where a woman was withdrawing from fentanyl addiction, and my friends were prepping for an attack by an armed biker gang.

Maine, the way life should be.

Louis's truck was parked by the house, Clair's big Ford by the barn. Mary's Kia SUV was in the garage attached to the back of the house. The gang was all here.

I went to the back door and knocked, waited. A curtain moved in the kitchen window, and then the security chain rattle, and the door shuddered open. Louis looked at me and nodded, his expression somber, like I was walking into a death watch. He held the door open and I stepped in, and he closed the door, re-hooked the chain. The big dog came over, sniffed me at his head level, above my waist. Sat back down, at ease.

"You think they'll come here?" I said.

"Better safe," Louis said, and he turned back, leaned in and gave me a guy-hug, and I winced.

"Ah, sorry."

"No problem. A little tender."

His hair was long, and he'd grown a beard, so he looked like an undercover drug agent. His black T-shirt was faded and there was a new tattoo on his neck, an eagle snatching a shadowed human figure.

"Birdshot can be more painful than a gunshot. Multiple entry points."

"I'll take it over a bullet," I said. "How is she doing?"

He turned and looked in the direction of the front hall of the house, where the main staircase led to the second floor.

"Eighteen hours in," Louis said. "Already pretty sick."

"How long?"

"Seventy-two hours to peak, then over the hump."

"What is it now?"

"Abdominal cramping, nausea. No vomiting yet. Agitation getting worse. Toughest woman I've ever met, and she says she's afraid."

"Of what?"

"Hard to say."

"Mary with her?"

"Yes. She's been great. I know she doesn't like Marta particularly."

"Doing it for Clair," I said. "Who's doing it for you."

Louis nodded.

"Semper Fi," I said.

"Right. Extends to you as well."

"Thanks."

"Understand you had a run-in with some home-grown soldiers."

"Amateur hour. But they still have guns. And a propensity to violence, as they say."

"Don't we all," Louis said.

"How much do you plan to be around here?"

"You want me to be?"

"I'm not sure."

"Whether I'm an asset or a liability?"

"Right. Do I want bikers *and* Jason's buddies on my tail?"

"I'm not worried about any of them," Louis said. He folded his sinewy arms, muscles like braided metal. I saw a bulge above his boot, the butt of a handgun.

"Lambert's posse will come to Sanctuary first," Louis said. He looked at me, held my gaze in that way he did. I shifted my gaze to the dog, also locked onto my eyes, then back. "There won't be a second. They came after your family; and they took my family, too. Jack. Marta's all I got. Nearly killed her, left her sick. So, different enemies, but we're both in the same place."

"Take no prisoners?"

He looked away.

"In the war, there were times when there were rules. And then there were times when you moved to another level. You protected your guys. It was your only priority."

"Kill or be killed," I said.

"Yeah. It wasn't something you chose. It was thrust upon you."

A Louis phrasing, faintly formal.

"Funny thing is, these paramilitary types think they're doing the right thing," I said. "Fire-bombing my house, shooting me. Government is corrupt, cops are crooked, media lies. They must supply their own law and order."

"Woe to those who call evil good and good evil," Louis said. "It's in the Bible. Isaiah."

"I didn't know you were a believer."

"I take my wisdom where I can find it."

There was a wail from upstairs, like someone giving birth. Then a clang, like something metal hitting the floor.

"Water bottle," Louis said, reading every sound.

He took a step toward the stairs, stopped, and turned. I thought he was going to tell me to be careful. Instead, he said, "Be tactical, Jack," and continued on up toward the wailing, the gnashing of teeth. I stood alone in the kitchen for a moment, listened. Marta was crying, a first. I started up the stairs, my left arm gingerly leaning on the railing. Marta's cries had morphed into sobs, then silence as I came to the top, turned into the hallway. Clair was coming out of the guest room, the water bottle in hand. He closed the door behind him, approached, and said, "He's holding her hand."

We stood there as the door opened and Mary came out carrying a bowl and towels. I caught a glimpse of Marta on the bed, Louis sitting on a chair beside her, his hand on her shoulder. She was wearing a T-shirt and gym shorts, her body looking small and shrunken amid the rumpled sheets. Mary closed the door as Marta let out another long wail, a guttural cry of abject misery.

The three of us went downstairs to the kitchen. Mary continued to the laundry room, where we heard water running in the sink.

"Never heard her cry before," I said. "Not even when she talked about the boyfriend, tied to a chair and sliced and stabbed."

"Tough kid," Clair said.

"Tough, or cold and calculating? Didn't cry when the boyfriend was killed. Managed to grab the cash on her way out the door."

"Louis loves her."

"And you know what they say about love and blindness," I said.

Clair shrugged. Semper Fi extended to the lover of his fellow Marine.

"You're going to keep her here?"

"Until she's better."

"What if they come looking for her?"

"They won't get close. Any more than anyone will get close to Roxanne and Sophie."

He went to the refrigerator with a slight hobble, favoring his right knee. I looked at him, the muscles starting to hang loose on his big frame, maybe lost a few pounds hanging around Montreal with Louis.

He took out a big bottle of orange-colored Gatorade, said, "For when the vomiting begins. Says on the Internet that follows the abdominal pain."

Clair Varney, RN.

"After Louis goes home, there's only two of us," I said.

"Only?" Clair said. "Don't underestimate yourself." He gave me a squeeze on my good shoulder, started for the stairs.

I stood for a moment, and Mary came out of the laundry room and headed back up, carrying the bowl of water and an armload of fresh towels.

"Good luck," I said.

"To you as well," Mary said.

The unmarked black Explorer was idling in front of the house. As I walked toward it, the guy at the wheel looked up from his phone. I approached and he shut off the motor and got out. Stocky, big shoulders, short salt-and-pepper hair. Round face over a trim goatee, nose bent slightly to one side like a boxer.

He said, "Was just texting you."

His New York accent brought me back to my childhood. He lifted his jacket, showed the gold badge clipped to his belt. Dropped the jacket and looked at me in that in-your-face way that New York detectives have. Police buzz cut, gray at the temples, some gel on top.

"Dave Strain, Waldo SO."

"Jack McMorrow, no affiliation."

For the first time in thirty years, I couldn't add *New York Times*. I felt strangely naked and empowered at the same time. The rules had fallen away.

Strain nodded.

I led the way up the drive, through the shed and into the house. Took off my jacket and hung it on a hook. He took his parka off and I led him to the kitchen table. Hanging his jacket on the back of a chair, he pulled the chair out. He was wearing jeans and a soft blue-and-green-plaid shirt, a gold chain showing. Somehow, New York had turned into a country gentleman cop.

"Coffee?"

"Yes, please."

I went to the counter, took the coffee off the shelf, and spooned it into the basket on the machine. Poured in water and hit the button. The machine started to gurgle. Then I filled the kettle and turned the burner on.

When I turned back, Strain had moved toward the study, was eyeing my books.

"You like history," he said. "Me, too."

"Just finished one about the Crimean War."

"Old-school slaughter."

"Yes," I said. "Now we do it with drones."

"We don't see blood much anymore," Strain said. "Not sure that's a good thing. You see somebody with holes in them, innards spilling out, kind of makes you think."

"Unless you're the shooter."

"I don't know. First-timers, some of them, it used to hit some of them hard. Taking a life and all that. Nowadays, not so much. Video games."

We stood watching as the coffee dripped, and then the machine hissed and beeped. I took two mugs from the shelf, filled his. Put a tea bag in mine and added hot water from the kettle.

"Milk?" I said. "Sugar?"

"Half-and-half?" Strain said.

Fussy. I went to the refrigerator, took it out. Maybe he'd also like a nice warm scone.

He took the carton from me, poured it carefully. Motioned to me and I shook my head. He went to the refrigerator and put the half-and-half back, scanning the shelves. I thought, Doesn't he need a warrant?

We took our mugs and sat. Sipped.

"Nice," Strain said. "Where you get your coffee?"

"Tandem in Portland. My wife's thing. They send it in the mail."

"Good for her. First thing I did when I moved up here, find the best coffee place in Belfast. It's my only vice since I quit the booze."

"When was that?"

"Fifteen years, four months, nine days. Morning they found my son dead of alcohol poisoning. Fraternity initiation. They did cocaine so they could keep drinking."

"I'm sorry," I said, glancing at the empty Ballantine Ale can on the counter.

"It's okay," Strain said. "My problem, not yours."

He didn't miss much, a good skill for a police detective.

Another sip and he said, "Twenty years, Newark PD. Patrol for three, detective division for seventeen. After a while, it was like those guys who clean the beach every morning, you know what I'm saying? Pick up the trash, rake the sand. Next day, do it all over again. Same trash, same sand, different day."

I thought, What was with beach similes? He kept going.

"Got a hunting camp over in Brooks. Roberts Hill."

"Oh, yeah. Marsh Stream runs along the north side. Big bog. Good birding."

"Right."

He said it quickly, like he didn't care for the interruption.

"Retired here—I'm divorced; it's a cop thing—got away from the Jersey rat race. Hunted that first fall, I get a nice buck. Eight points. Not a monster but pretty good. And then I'm like, Now what? Next day went down to the sheriff, said, 'I'm available.' Hired me on the spot."

"Good for you."

"Yeah, has been. But you know, it isn't Andy in Mayberry, like some of my buddies in Jersey were thinking. Same problems, just a different scale."

"I know. Meth, fentanyl."

"Exactly. Which brings me to our business."

He took a long sip of coffee, held it in his mouth a few seconds before swallowing.

"That really is good. What'd you say the name of the place is?"

"Tandem."

"Got it. Anyway, I read Officer Jackman's report. The fire, you exiting the house, somebody shoots at you, you shoot back."

Another sip.

"Then the litany of possible suspects. All the folks you said might have it in for you."

"Yes."

"We'll track down our jailbird, rattle his cage. Maybe one of his buddies. Maybe somebody on the cell block knew somebody who knew somebody who would take a shot at somebody for a coupla grand."

"Don't forget the fire," I said.

"No. Class A felony, that alone."

Strain sipped, held his mug in two hands and said, "All due respect, Mr. McMorrow. I mean, I did my due diligence. You're a smart guy. Writing for the *Times*. Not the *Post*, but not bad."

I smiled. A New York joke. It had been a while.

"And you've got a lot of experience with crime and criminals. I googled you, and the stories—you'd think you were in Springfield/Belmont. That's in Newark."

"I'm familiar with it. I grew up in New York City."

"Okay, so you'll know where I'm coming from when I say your account of the circumstances of the shooting set off my bullshit-o-meter. Not off the scale. Maybe five out of ten, ten being total crap."

I took a swallow of tea, looked at him.

"Really."

"Let's consider your past few days. This Zombie freak robs that place in Clarkston and smacks the clerk girl with a gun, even though she gives him the money. Interesting. Why did he do that? Did he know her? Was he looking for something else? Maybe she's dealing out of the store, gets behind on her payments. He's sent by her supplier. And you're first on the scene."

He took a breath, like the long list was making him tired. I waited.

"A guy's found dead down in Clarkston, tied to a bed and tortured. Nasty stuff. Place ransacked, somebody looking for something, obviously. You find the body."

"I was there for a story. Both instances."

He held up a hand to stop me.

"A known drug dealer is killed, also in Clarkston. More people tied up. This time, one of the victims fights back, the dealer is killed. Yay—one less mouth to feed in jail. But my point is, where are you? Right there again. Jack McMorrow, Johnny on the freakin' spot. You don't find the body. You witness the whole thing."

"I knew the people at that apartment."

"My point exactly. Fraternization that maybe goes beyond the normal practices for your profession."

I sipped. He did the same.

"In Jersey, I saw a few of you journalist types—not a lot, but more than handful—go over to the dark side. More TV people than newspapers, but whatever. I mean, I get it. Hey, it's exciting. The money, the cars, the girls. You're schlepping along making forty K, and these guys are wearing Gucci T-shirts and Rolexes, driving friggin' Bentleys."

"Not many Bentleys around here," I said.

"Now we get to the crime in my jurisdiction, here at this house—an armed confrontation, a shot fired. Said to be related to a domestic dispute, but I'm not so sure. I just know that you're the shooter. And drugs are rampant in this area. Then Mr. Twelve-Gauge comes around, doesn't kill you when he could have. Just wings you. Delivers a warning, but for what, we're not sure."

Another drink of coffee.

"So here we are," Strain said.

I smiled. My shoulder ached. He looked around the room. The fire. The books. One of Sophie's drawings hanging on the wall. Pokey in his stall, head hanging over the gate like an inmate.

"Nice place. Cozy."

"Thanks."

"Your wife work?"

"Not at the moment. She's finishing her master's degree. Social work."

"Good for her. You get paid by the story, right?"

"Yeah. I'm a freelance journalist."

"What's the last story you wrote?"

"A piece about one of the robberies in Clarkston."

"I found that. It was short. What else?"

"It's been a little while."

"Family money?"

"No."

"So you keep this place going on what, a few hundred bucks a month? I mean, how does that put food on the table?"

"We don't spend a lot. And every few weeks, I get a check for a bigger story."

"What, a couple of grand?"

"I also cut wood."

"No shit. I thought you were a little rugged for a reporter. Most of you are kinda flabby."

I waited.

"You get my point, right? Drugs here are no different from Jersey. I mean, I spent the day at grand jury last week. Every single case was connected. Dealing fentanyl. Cooking meth. And you know what drugs always lead to? Money and violent crime. So, logically, you know what you're connected with? Violent crime and drugs."

"I write crime stories. Hard to do it from a distance."

Strain took another sip.

"I'll give you that. But let me ask you—do you know who shot at you?"

"I told your deputy, Jackman. He was wearing a mask."

"He talked to you, you said. Never heard his voice before?"

"No."

"It wasn't a warning? As in, pay up or next time we take out your whole family? Kidnap your kid?"

I thought of Jason, my gun barrel pressed to his head.

"No," I said.

"Hey, if you're in too deep, Mr. McMorrow, this is the time to 'fess up. We can help you."

"You're going in the wrong direction, Detective."

He stood up, took a last drink of coffee.

"Maybe, but I doubt it," Strain said.

He put his parka on, walked over and put his empty cup in the sink. Took a card from his pocket and placed it on the counter. Turned back to me.

"My cell's on there. Call, text. Anytime. I mean it."

I nodded.

"How's the shoulder, by the way?"

"Fine," I said.

"See," Strain said, smiling, "that's not the whole truth, either."

And he walked out the door, pulling it shut behind him.

The cop didn't look so tough out of his uniform, showing up at her house, all sad and serious like his best friend just died. Not a lot of laughs, that guy. She needed a good time, as in a few hours in the sack. Show her what Zombie could really do. He'd have her begging for more.

The parking lot was great for surveillance. Shithole bar, people coming and going, drug deals and sex in the backseats. Sometimes he used his mom's Corolla, today mixing it up with his dad's old Silverado, his mom keeping it in the divorce, saying, "It's mine now." His dad saying Screw it, ain't worth fighting for an old beater truck. Besides, his new girlfriend, she had money. Office manager for a dentist. She bought him a new Ram, showed how desperate she was to land a guy, her not being hot at all. Pathetic.

It was like doing surveillance of a store, watching who came and went at the house, writing the times in his notebook, figuring out the routine. That cop around a lot last couple of days. What, was he on vacation? He didn't stay over, maybe weirded out by the old guy with the long hair. They kissed on the porch when he left. Hard to watch, but he wouldn't be just watching for long. Once you go Zombie, you never go back. He smiled to himself, wrote that in the notebook.

But this afternoon's different. The cop doesn't show at his regular time, usually around two p.m. Then she leaves, walking. Army boots and leggings, that cute skinny butt.

He pulls out, follows, thinking maybe she's going to work early. But she only goes to the store around the corner, buys a half-gallon of milk, walks back home.

Fifteen minutes after that the cop rolls up in his pickup, but he doesn't go in. She comes out, they talk, her leaning in the window on the passenger side. And then she kisses her fingers, reaches in and touches his hand.

Give me a break. But that's okay. That might be all he gets from this chick ever again.

Should he stay or should he go? That was a song from the olden days, he couldn't remember who. Then the decision is made for him. The old guy comes out, same goofy hat on backwards, thinking he's cool in his black leather coat. He's all happy, like he won the lottery or something, and he heads for the bar, walks right past the truck. Goes in with the alcoholics, standing at the door when the place opens at noon. Comes out five minutes later and gets in a car with some other old fart and they leave.

Which means it's party time.

He reaches down to the floor, picks up the mask and the gun.

4

It was a little after four when I heard a pickup roll in. I dried the last dish, holding it down on the counter because of my shoulder, put the towel down and went to the window. It was Brandon Blake, out of his Clarkston police uniform and a long way from his boat in Portland Harbor. He got out of his truck, started for the door. I opened it before he knocked.

"Hey," he said.

"Hi there."

I swung the door wide, and he stepped in.

"What brings you to the hinterlands?"

"Heard you got shot," Blake said.

"Just a flesh wound," I said.

"Good to hear. If I'd known, it would have saved me a trip."

He smiled. From Blake, a rare joke.

I led the way to the kitchen, said, "Coffee? I'd offer you a beer but there isn't any."

"I'm good. Had some on the ride."

He stood, looked around.

"Nice place."

"Considering it's not a boat?"

Blake smiled. Seemed relaxed, like a weight had been lifted.

"I took a couple weeks' leave. Gotta sort things out."

A police officer involved with a woman who robbed a weed dealer, taking a cash delivery from his own patrol partner. Some sorting there.

"I'm sure. How's that going?"

"Okay. We're still together if that's what you were going to ask."

"Good, I guess. How's Sparrow?"

"Fine. Riff gets his first dose of Sovaldi today. He was getting better just thinking about it. Went to the pharmacy himself."

Eighty grand for four months' worth of pills. Raymond's money and the weed robbery proceeds coming in handy.

"Nice. Maybe it's part placebo."

"Right. Many physical illnesses have a big psychological component."

We stood. He shifted on his feet, looked down at the puddle spreading from his boots.

"Hey, sorry. I can wipe that up."

He was very neat, from living on a boat.

"It's fine. I have to do a cleanup before Roxanne gets home anyway."

"How's she?"

"Good. Well, okay."

"Your daughter?"

"Sophie's good, too."

He nodded, said, "I have a question for you. A journalist and all, you see all kinds of situations."

It was suddenly awkward. I said, "Sit down."

He did, stuffing his hands in the pockets of his Carhartt.

"So," Blake said, then paused. "I'm just trying to decide—"

"You can't continue to be a cop. Not if you stay with Sparrow. Even if you're not with her."

He looked at me.

"I know how you do police work. You believe in it. You don't do it halfway."

He frowned. "I can't. Fake it, I mean."

"And you can't turn her in."

He looked at me for a beat, shook his head.

"No. I'm in love with her."

I waited, feeling the dam in him about to crumble.

"What she did, it was for him. It was getting the money somehow or watch him die. I mean, she was working her ass off, all that OT at the store. Taking care of him. Then she gets robbed, her head split open. Even with all that, she was still only thinking of her dad. She's all he's got."

"And vice versa."

"Not really," Blake said. "Not now."

"Because she has you."

"Right."

He took his hands out of his pockets, laid them on the table in front of him.

"It was weed money. They probably already made it back. Nobody got hurt. I mean, Salley was up and running in a minute. And of all the people to take that hit—the guy was double-dipping, lying to his supervisors, having sex while he was on duty."

I waited for the rationalization to end. Blake shook his head.

"I think you know this. It's your career or your girlfriend," I said.

"Yeah."

"And you've made your decision, I think."

"I can't be a corrupt cop."

"So quit. Live with it. Live with her. Do something else."

"It's all I've ever done."

"You're what, twenty-five?"

"Yeah."

"A lot of life ahead of you. You'll find the next thing. What was it I just read about Millennials? Their average stay in a job is three years."

"Right."

There was a long pause, and then he said, "Another thing."

"What?"

"You want to write about this, don't you."

"Part of me does."

"A big part."

"Yes."

"But you won't because—"

"I'm too close to it," I said. "I'm in the story as much as you are."

"Seems like kind of a cop-out. For both of us."

"Yeah," I said. "It is."

"How do you live with that?"

"I've got other things to do. You will, too." I got up, said, "Come on. Some people I want you to meet."

I put on my jacket and went out the door, Blake following. I led the way around the shed and out back, started down the plowed path to Clair's barn, glimpsing prints of Sophie's boots. He walked behind me through the second-growth woods, birches and poplar, then into the hemlocks and pines. Chickadees and titmice tumbled along beside us, a flurry of olive-colored goldfinches. And then we were into the clearing, the lights of Clair's barn showing on the far side of the field. We continued, and I saw lights on in the house, too, the back bedroom where Marta was suffering.

I looked away, held the barn door open for Blake and went inside.

Clair and Louis were at the workbench, backs to us, a fire going in the stove. We approached and they turned.

"Guys, this is Brandon. Brandon, Clair and Louis."

Hearty handshakes all around. Clair said he'd heard good things about him, his work in Clarkston. Blake seemed to wince a bit, the elephant in the room his shooting of the kid in Portland. But he thanked him, said he'd heard good things about Clair and Louis, as well.

"Brandon's taking a break from the PD. Came up to tell me not to be a wimp just because I got shot."

"Lost cause," Clair said to Blake. "You gotta remember you're talking about a professional typer."

He smiled.

"Clair and Louis just got back from Canada," I said. "They went up to help a friend."

I looked to Louis.

"She's sleeping, finally," he said. Then to Blake, "Withdrawing from fentanyl. Some people shot her up, deliberately got her addicted."

I could see Blake harden. "Nice. You went and rescued her?"

"Took her back, is how I like to see it," Clair said.

"What happened to them?"

"Nothing, yet," Louis said.

We turned to the bench, moved closer. There were cardboard cartons opened, equipment laid out. Rifle scopes, binoculars, goggles.

"Night-vision?" I said.

"Thermal," Louis said, picking up a rifle scope. "This is a four-by-forty, and I also got a one-by-ten. If it's warm, it shows up plain as day. Used a lot by serious hog hunters down south. Feral hogs move and feed after dark."

He handed a scope to Blake, reached for another carton, like Q showing Bond the latest gadgets. Took out a pair of binoculars, then another. "These are thermal, too. This one is night-vision. Light up a car or truck or a human like they're on fire."

He handed them to us, and we passed them back and forth. The pieces were black and heavy and solid, high-tech made only for killing.

"Got a raccoon or something cleaning out the bird feeders at night," Clair said. "This could be the ticket."

"Make our old Starlights in Iraq look relatively primitive," Louis said.

We handed the stuff back to Louis and he started to put it back in its cases.

"Already set up new surveillance at the gate, along the road perimeter, approaches to the cabin."

"And you have the dog," I said.

"Yes," Louis said. "There's always the dog."

We stood, Blake folding the cartons shut. Clair walked over, opened the stove door, and put in a chunk of ash—daytime wood when you were there to keep stuffing it in. Oak and maple for longer burns. When they both turned back, Blake said, "So you expect these people to come down here?"

"Or send somebody from here," Clair said.

"I suppose you can't just call the police."

"They'd be there in time to clean up afterward," Louis said. "Wrap the place in crime tape and declare it under investigation." He looked at Blake. "No offense."

"None taken," Blake said. There was a pause, and then he said, "When is all this supposed to happen?"

"Could be a couple of days. Could be a couple of weeks," Louis said.

"It'll take time to organize," Clair said. "And Louis lives deep in the woods. Some reconnaissance required."

"Sanctuary," I said. "It's more than just a drive-by."

Blake nodded. There was a ping and Louis slipped his phone from his jacket pocket, looked at it and said, "She's awake. I'd better get up there."

He told Blake it was good to meet him. Likewise, Blake said, and Louis and Clair both left the workshop and started for the house.

Blake looked at me, said "Whoa."

"Both ex-military."

"I don't know about the 'ex' part. Who are the bad guys?"

"Outlaw motorcycle club based in Montreal. They're connected to a club in Mass. Plunderers."

We walked to the door, stepped outside, started back down the path.

"And this woman—"

"Marta."

"—is Louis's girlfriend?"

"Yeah. High school sweethearts recently reunited."

"When you're in law enforcement you keep up on this stuff. There was probably fifty thousand dollars' worth of gear on that table. Not to mention the guns. I'm guessing he's not using his dad's old deer rifle."

"No."

"Where'd he get the money?"

"Inherited it," I said. "And the five hundred acres his cabin is on."

We walked. Blake said, "So he must really be into her to do all this. Go up and grab her, gear up for some sort of armed assault."

"Yes," I said. "But we all do crazy things for love."

As we walked, he looked over at me, smiled.

"I guess we do," Blake said.

We followed the path across the field, into the woods. It was dusky dark, the snow glowing the way it does as the light wanes. As we approached the house, I thanked him for coming up. He said he was glad I was doing okay, thanked me for listening.

"It's what I do best," I said.

"You know, I may have some time on my hands if somebody needs to be spelled up here occasionally. Maybe if Riff settles in, I could bring Sparrow. Get her away from the house. If these meds really help him, he bounces back, maybe she could start to back away. We'll just have to take it one day at a—"

This time it was his phone, buzzing in his pocket. He took it out as we rounded the corner of the shed. Peered at it and tensed.

"He was there," Blake said.

"Who?"

"Zombie. He came to her house."

Blake sprinted for his truck. I called after him, "Where is he now?"

"He left."

"Is she okay?"

"Yes. I mean, he didn't hurt her."

"Should I call 911?"

He shouted back, "No, I got this. I'll call you."

The motor revved and tires spun in the snow, and he backed out, slammed the pickup in gear, and fishtailed down the road.

I stood at the door to the shed. Mind racing. Zombie in Sparrow's house.

What did he want? Did he rob her again? All that weed cash. Why take such a massive chance? Was he nuts? Pushing the limits as the rush of the robberies wore off? Maybe he wanted to really show up the police. *I not only can rob stores, I can drop in on the victims.*

I had to talk to this guy, write this story. First-person. But if not for the *Times*, then for what outlet? Dunne and her podcast? Had I fallen, or was this just the new world order?

I started for the door, the pain in my shoulder stabbing through the Percocet.

Zombie's story. Who was he, really?

So this is how it went down.

I came in from the side, waited until there were no cars, nobody walking. Put the mask on and went up the steps. Rang the bell and waited, like a trick-or-treater.

I heard steps, saw something move in the window, to the left. I smiled, then realized she couldn't see it. Stupid me. Waited for a ten-count, then I just turned the knob. And it was open, like she wanted me to come in. So I did.

It was a hallway that was really warm, the way old people like it. My grandmother's apartment—I still remember how it was like a friggin' sauna.

I went to the first door on the left. I had my hand on my gun in my pocket, but I wasn't gonna shoot her. More like just in case somebody else was there. Not that I was gonna shoot anybody. Just buy some time.

But nobody else was there, just the girl, sitting in a big chair, hands in her lap. Barefoot, legs crossed. Camo tank top (hot!).

She looked at me, not all panicky or anything. More curious.

I go, "Hey."

She goes, "You wear that thing all the time?"

I say, "No. Just on Zombie business."

Good line. It just came to me, too. It was like that, everything working out just perfect.

I said I was sorry I hit her. It was bad of me. And I said I was sorry I shot the guy in the store. It was totally self-defense.

She understood. She wanted to know why I was a robber.

I told her it was exciting, all the planning, the execution. Like a video game on steroids.

We just talked, like a first date. I asked for her number, and she gave it to me. I texted her right there, heard her phone ding. And then I had to go, the Zombie clock running. I kinda tried to kiss her good-bye but the stupid mask got in the way. Still, she didn't wig out. She sort of let me, right on the lips. Yowza!

She said her name's Sparrow, like the bird.

She's wicked cool and very hot.

This could be the real deal. I'll be seeing her again.

5

I was still standing at the door when Roxanne's Subaru wheeled into the driveway. She drove up, slid to a stop beside me. They all got out: Roxanne and Sophie, Tiffanee and Tara. Sophie gave me a hug, said, "Been worried about you, Dad."

"Nothing to worry about."

I gave my shoulder a whirl, smiled through the pain.

"See? Good as new."

"Who was it?" she said, as they gathered around.

"I don't know. Somebody having a very bad day."

"Will they catch him?" Tara said.

"I'm sure. Police are good at that."

"I hope they lock his sorry ass up," she said. Caught herself. The language. Grinned.

I smiled. "Me, too."

Roxanne gave me a kiss, then stood back.

Tiffanee said, "I'm glad you're okay, Jack."

And then Roxanne smiled, turned to the girls and said, "Pee break. Then we've got to go."

I looked at her as they hurried past me, Tiffanee, too.

"Rehearsal. In Lisburn. I think we should just go on with our lives. For the girls. You think it's safe here?"

"Yeah. I think they think they sent their message."

"Who? Jason?"

"One of his buddies, most likely."

"What did the police say?"

"They're considering all possibilities."

"Like what?"

Then Tiffanee came back out, said, "I went first. Pulled rank as a grown-up."

She went to the back of the car and opened the hatch, grabbed the girls' backpacks and her bag, one of ours, borrowed when they left after Jason was hauled off. "They want to change," she said, and went back inside.

"Trip back up okay?"

"Until we were coming down the dump road, just before we turned in. This truck came screaming around the corner. I thought he was going into the ditch."

"Blue pickup?"

"Yeah."

"Brandon Blake," I said.

"From Clarkston? What was he—"

"Heard I got shot. Came up to check in, I guess. We were talking when Sparrow texted, said Zombie was at her house."

"The robber?"

"Yes. A few minutes ago."

"My God. What was he doing there?"

"I don't know. He left and she's fine. I don't know any more. Blake just took off."

"Do you think you should go?"

"No," I said. "Place will be swarming with police. Besides, I don't have a story, remember?"

She took my left arm, and I winced. She took the other, said, "Are you all cut up?"

"Small holes."

"Did they take them out?"

"No," I said. "You'll be waiting for me at airport security."

I smiled.

"Let's go to the play thing," I said. "I missed you."

Lisburn was a half-hour drive, and the girls chatted in the backseat, Tiffanee dozing beside them. Roxanne drove and I rode, well, shotgun. The seat belt pulled on my shoulder, and I slipped it under my arm.

"They didn't give you a brace or anything?"

"A sling. It doesn't help with the healing. Gets in the way."

She shook her head. When I glanced over, she looked weary, lines spreading from the outside of her eyes like sidewalk cracks. Roxanne, Clair—it was going around.

The rehearsal was just over the bridge from Belfast. It was in an old theater that had been for movies but had sat empty since VCRs came out. Now a community theater group had taken it over, cleaned up the bat and pigeon droppings, and—through the largesse of a summer person whose yacht had moored in the harbor—renovated the stage and dressing rooms, refurbished the seats.

The Dog Island Players, another of Mr. Ziggy's side gigs, were putting on *Annie.* Mr. Z was directing and he'd tapped Tara Tinkham for the title role, and Sophie McMorrow for Pepper, the tough orphan. A few inches to the right, and Sophie would have been halfway there.

I parked down the street in front of a shop where dusty antiques were aging. The girls climbed the snowbank while we walked back to where a path had been shoveled around a fire hydrant. We caught up and went inside, last ones in.

Parents and kids had filled the lobby, starting to file into the theater proper. The child actors were all girls, mostly attractive, or at least interesting-looking, wired and stagey. The parents were hovering, stage moms and dads aggressively lining up, ready to shove their kids up to the next rung on the ladder to stardom.

I considered our group: Sophie and Tara, dropped in here almost by chance, plucked from Prosperity Primary by Mr. Ziggy. Tiffanee and Roxanne, road-weary, one with a boyfriend facing multiple charges, the other with a husband filled with shotgun pellets.

It had been a hard-knock few days for us for sure.

We took our seats in the third row, the first two filled with earlier arrivals.

I shifted in my chair, trying to take the pressure off my left side. I was half-turned, saw a young guy leading four other adults, two men and two women. The young guy was tall, dressed in black jeans and T-shirt, short pull-on boots, dark hair swept back. Big but slightly doughy, with pale arms, biceps with no definition. Mr. Ziggy. He took the stairs to the stage two at a time, waited for the others to take their places beside him.

They did, all of them smiling like they were ready to take a bow.

Mr. Ziggy said, "Welcome. This is so exciting. I can't wait for you all to meet each other and begin this amazing journey." He beamed, a smile that lit up the back rows.

"Look around at each other," he continued. "You know what you are? You are the lucky ones, because you made the cut. And because you're all actors. And acting since the time of the Greeks has been one of the most awesome things you can do. I mean, become someone else, somewhere else. Travel to different worlds, not for, like, a minute, but for hours. Where else can you, like, leave your world behind for another identity? Become someone else entirely. Not act like them. *Become* them. Enter their minds and bodies. Invent them from your imagination, the magic of your creative minds."

He was breathless, then recovered.

"Think of it. It's like time travel, right? And we are the time travelers, all of us here."

Who was this guy—an itinerant drama teacher in rural Maine, giving a theater TED Talk?

I looked at Tara and Sophie. Smiling but a little wary, this all new to them. Then over at Roxanne. I gave her a bit of an eye roll, she gave me an elbow back.

Mr. Ziggy was introducing the other people onstage. Pauly, who would play Oliver Warbucks. Randi "with an I," was Lily. Jonathan was Rooster Hannigan. Opal was Miss Hannigan. They bowed slightly to the kids' applause. And then there was a rustle offstage and a woman came in leading a small black dog. The crowd oohed.

"Meet Sandy," Mr. Ziggy said.

My phone buzzed in my jacket pocket.
I took it out, held it low. A text. Blake.

—Sparrow's OK. Seems like he just wanted to talk.
—More later.
Good. Thanks.
Police all over it?

Roxanne leaned closer. I held up the phone. She read the messages and nodded.

Mr. Ziggy had moved on to introducing the cast to each other, calling them up to the stage, saying "I've seen you work. You're all stars." A bunch of smiling orphans: Molly, Kate, Tessie, July, and Duffy. Then Pepper, played by Sophie McMorrow.

Sophie got up, eased down the row, climbed the stage, and joined the line.

Roxanne reached over and took my hand. Our moment of pride. There was applause but it quickly subsided. One kid was left in the seats.

"And last, but certainly not least, meet Tara Tinkham," Mr. Ziggy said, and all eyes turned.

Tara smiled, blushed. She looked at Tiffanee, who said, "Go ahead, girl. Get up there." Tara hesitated, then, with a last push from her mom, rose out of her seat, eased her way past us, all eyes on her. I looked around, the other parents smiling and clapping, but inspecting her closely. I thought of crows around roadkill, heads cocked, ready to pick away.

She was making her way to the stairs. Tall for her age, leggings and salt-encrusted suede boots, the kind lined with fake sheepskin. Her sweater was a little too short, showed a band of bare white back at her waist. She pulled the sweater down and it pressed against her chest. Clumping across the stage, Tara started for the end of the line, but Mr. Ziggy reached out, took her by the shoulder, and turned her to face the audience.

"Our Annie," Mr. Ziggy said.

More applause.

Tiffanee wiped away a tear, the first I'd seen from her. No crying after the armed confrontation, but this—

Mr. Ziggy was saying he'd first met Tara at Prosperity Primary School. She acted and sang and danced.

"I knew right away she was right for this part," Mr. Ziggy said. "I asked her if she would join us, and Tara said yes. Woohoo!"

More clapping. Mr. Ziggy still had his hand on Tara's shoulder, like an uncle who won't drop the handshake. I glanced at Roxanne and she was watching him intently. Then he let go and Tara made her way to the end of the line of orphans, stood there with her hands on her hips. Confidence seeping in?

Mr. Ziggy thanked us. He said he'd be e-mailing the link to the doc that had the rehearsal schedule. He thanked us for our support, and promised this production would be an experience we'd look back on the rest of our lives. "And you will smile," he said.

The guy was good. What was he doing here?

He and the other adults trotted off the stage, through the theater.

The girls joined their parents, and we all made our way out to the lobby, where the grown-ups in the cast were standing in a row like a receiving line, Mr. Ziggy at the far end. Parents shook hands, chitchatted, and went out the door into the cold. We introduced ourselves, heard that Pepper was the motherly orphan and a very important role. But it was Tara who got the most attention, everyone saying they'd heard so much about her.

Tiffanee looked pleased but surprised. She said, "I know she can act up at home," and everyone chuckled.

And then it was Mr. Ziggy—handsome like a TV actor, perfect teeth, a thousand-watt smile—giving Roxanne a quick Euro hug. She half-stiffened. Then he said he was so excited to work with Sophie, that she was so smart and mature, she was just right for Pepper.

And then he gave Tiffanee a longer hug. Tiffanee looking a little squirmy, in her world, not used to being hugged by men unless it was for a purpose. Good thing he didn't try to kiss her on both cheeks.

He unhugged her, gave me a handshake with his soft hand.

I said, "So where are you from, Mr. Ziggy?"

"Oh, you can call me John," he said.

"And the Z? What does that stand for?"

"Zwiefelhofer. It's a mouthful for the kids."

"Gets pretty garbled?"

"Oh, yeah. Wiffletush. Zargenpuff. Mr. Ziggy—way easier."

"Right," I said. A beat, and I said, "So were you a child actor yourself?"

"Since I was, like, three. I was one of the Three Little Kittens. I meowed a lot."

He grinned. I smiled back.

"Ha. Where was that?"

A hesitation, like I was giving him the third degree. "Seattle area. But my parents got divorced when I was young, so I moved around a lot. My mom remarried; my dad moved to Europe—he's German—but I still saw him. I kept a backpack ready to go."

"And always did theater?"

Roxanne gave me a tug. "He'll interview you all night," she said.

"A journalist?" Mr. Ziggy said.

I nodded. "More or less."

"Awesome. Do you do theater reviews?"

He leaned closer, clasped my shoulder. I winced. He didn't notice. "We'll talk," he said.

A little patronizing, for a young guy. I smiled.

Roxanne started for the door, Sophie, Tara, and Tiffanee already outside. I held back, said, "Tara and Sophie are best friends."

"Right. They're just so sweet together."

"Not your typical actor kids."

"No, but that makes for the best theater, right?" Mr. Ziggy said. "They're so fresh. Some kid actors—by this age, they're like seasoned pros. You don't get the rawness and innocence that great theater requires. But when you get it right—and I really feel like we're gonna do that here—it's just magical. Kids have all these feelings inside them that we don't let out. Do this, do that. Go to school, go to soccer, do your homework—we kind of drum out all that imagination and empathy."

"I see."

Mr. Ziggy was still going.

"And when you find that diamond in the rough, it's just totally amazing. I mean, when I met Tara—she's just so real. I'm like, 'Wouldn't it be awesome to do *Annie* with someone who's really had a hard knock or two? I mean, most of these kids are, like, totally coddled. So I'm, like, 'What if someone could *really* feel Annie's loneliness, her disappointments. 'Cause they've lived it."

He looked around, leaned closer.

"I mean, her mom's partner's in jail, right?"

"Sort of. Out on bail."

"Well, that has to be hard on a young girl, all that trauma."

I shrugged.

"I don't know. He's not her dad, and he's a jerk. I think she's just glad to be rid of him."

It caught him, but he recovered.

"Right, but still, it's like theater vérité. Tara and her mom, I mean, they have this, like, amazing authenticity."

Roxanne came back through the door, held it open, motioned for me.

I made my excuses to Mr. Ziggy and joined the rest of them in the car, where the girls were huddled over Tara's phone, looking for the other orphans on TikTok, Instagram.

"Oh, my God," Tara said. "She's a wicked good dancer. I'm going to have to practice like crazy."

"You'll be fine, honey," Tiffanee said.

"But look at her, Mom," Tara said, turning the phone.

"Mr. Ziggy will help you. Don't worry."

I was on my phone, too, Blake texting me.

—SHE'S WITH DETECTIVES. NO PRINTS—HE HAD GLOVES ON.

—GOT A VEHICLE DESCRIPTION. OLD BLUE TRUCK.

—Sparrow's not good with vehicles. No plate.

I asked Blake what Zombie wanted.

—Got a thing for her. Probably acting out some fantasy. She recorded it.

God, I thought. Audio gold. Dunne would give her left arm.
Just then singing erupted from the backseat. The girls.
The sun'll come out tomorrow . . .
Where could Zombie be? Home in Clarkston? His parents' basement?
Bet your bottom dollar that tomorrow, there'll be sun.
Tara, belting it out, full of enthusiasm, a little off-key. Was Idina Menzel always spot-on in *Wicked*?
I looked over at Roxanne, leaned a little closer.
"Mr. Ziggy. Talk about over the top."
She glanced at me, said, "I know."
The girls kept singing.
"Is he for real?" I said.
"I don't know. Parents were eating it up."
"Blinded by the teeth."
A beat. Roxanne thinking, and then she said, "The hand on the shoulder. It went on too long."
I shrugged. "Maybe he's just a theater guy. They're demonstrative."
We drove on, Tara singing, throwing herself into the part already.
Just thinking about tomorrow, clears away the cobwebs and the sorrow . . .
Sometimes a little flat, sometimes a little sharp, but delivered with authentic enthusiasm.
What did he see in her?
I looked over. Almost imperceptibly, Roxanne was shaking her head.

6

Tiffanee's Jeep, parked in our driveway covered with snow, didn't start. She knocked and came back in, said it was a crappy battery, that she'd asked Jason to replace it but he never got to it. Would I, could I give her a jump?

I said sure, went out to the truck, jockeyed it around and hooked up the cables. It started, coughed, stalled. She tried it again and it started, coughed some more, idled roughly. We looked at it dubiously and I said, "Why don't I follow you home."

"But Roxanne—after what happened. Do you think—"

"I'll call Clair."

I did and he picked up, said, "What sort of mess have you gotten yourself into now?"

I explained. He said he'd be there in five. And he was.

Roxanne and Sophie gave him hugs, a palpable relief settling over them. What was I? Useless? No. I just wasn't Clair. He sat by the woodstove, kept his jacket on. Roxanne asked how Marta was doing and he said she was sleeping, exhausted by vomiting.

"She's sick?" Tara said.

"Tell you later," Sophie said. The motherly orphan for sure.

Sophie and Roxanne stayed, Clair with them, his jacket on, covering up something. I knew he'd gone to a shoulder holster, said it was easier on his back than the waistband. I said I'd be right back. He said to take my time.

I grabbed a battery charger on the way out of the shed, put it behind the seat. Climbed and reached the Glock from the floor and put it on the seat beside me. Tiffanee backed up, caught the snowbank and powered through. I drove out behind her, her taillights clouded by blowing snow, followed her across Prosperity to the top of the ridge, turned west toward Thorndike.

Her road was drifted, no tracks through ripples of white, like sand on a dune. I thought it was good that it was winter, that in Sanctuary the bikers would leave tracks wherever they went. I channeled Louis and Clair: outflank them from the road side, follow them in toward Louis's cabin. Somebody in the woods outside the cabin, somebody cutting off their retreat . . .

What we'd think about while Mr. Ziggy was onstage. A different sort of blocking.

And then we were there, the house illuminated by a white floodlight above the barn door.

We parked and Tiffanee shut off the Jeep, tried to start it again. It wheezed a few times, then clicked. I went to the truck, took out the charger, said she should leave it on overnight. She said there was an extension cord in the barn, so I walked over, slid the big door open a foot, went inside. I felt for a light switch, found it, and flicked the lights on.

The place was filled with old farm equipment. A tractor with spiked iron wheels and a metal seat, a 1950s stake truck, tires flat. Rusty plows and harrows and bailers, stuff stacked on top of them, the piles shifting every few years when someone went looking for something.

A perfect place to hide.

I found a cord and outlet, plugged it in. Went back out and popped the hood on the Jeep. I connected the charger, eased the hood back down. Went inside, where the lights were on and Tiffanee was sliding a frozen pizza into the oven. Tara had gone elsewhere.

"Twenty minutes, Jack?" she said. "Hungry?"

"Gotta get back," I said.

"Sure."

"The charger is on. Just disconnect it and unplug it in the morning. Call if it doesn't start. I think it was just too drained to run the fan and the lights and whatever."

"Thanks," Tiffanee said. She turned and stood, put her head back and sighed.

"Heck of a few days," I said.

"Yes. But he's gone now, the asshole. I keep telling myself that."

I thought how easy it would be to cut the cuff off, come back here. You can do a lot of damage if you don't care about being caught.

I hesitated, said, "You should still lock up. Keep your phone handy. Do you have any kind of weapon?"

"You kidding? I've got some of his. He couldn't carry them all when he left."

She turned and led the way out of the kitchen, through a den, and into another room, a hasp on the door, the frame splintered.

"Jason forgot the combination," she said. "He had to knock the lock off with a hammer."

She opened the door, turned on the light. There was a television and a saggy striped couch. On the couch were three gun cases, one short, two long. She unsnapped a long case, and I looked inside. It was a short-barreled rifle with a pistol grip. There was a box of nine-millimeter ammo with it.

"Close quarters," I said. "For home defense." Or storming a government building.

Tiffanee opened the other cases. Two handguns, a .40 caliber Ruger, and a .45 Smith & Wesson revolver, a short-barreled version of the big gun Jason had brought to my house.

"I'm thinking I could keep one of these by my bed," she said, picking up the .45.

"Make sure he doesn't use it on you," I said.

"My idea is to string pots and pans across the doorway to the kitchen. He hits that and I'll be ready."

"You're comfortable with guns?"

"Shit, yes. Grew up on the farm. Got my first deer when I was ten. Went rabbit hunting with my gramps. My uncle ran bear camps."

"Don't shoot Tara through the wall," I said.

"Not a problem. She's gonna be in here with me."

Tell Mr. Ziggy about *that* hard-knock life.

She shut all three cases, picked them up from the couch, handed me the long one.

I followed her back to the kitchen, passed through to a hallway and upstairs. The place was cold but musty, heat blowing dust out of creaky air ducts. At the top of the stairs we turned right, went to the first door and stepped in. There was a queen-size bed with shelves in the headboard. The bed was unmade and there was a remote by the pillows, a big TV on the wall across from the foot of the bed. The floor was covered with a shaggy blue carpet, like fur on a Muppet. There was a bureau with drawers open, underpants hanging from one, socks from another, a brassiere on the floor. Leopard print.

I looked away. Tiffanee said, "Excuse the mess. We left in a hurry."

I went over the sequence in my head. Tara arrives at our house, fleeing Jason. Twenty minutes later, he rolls up. He sits in his truck for a few minutes, his rage building. I pull up, we have our confrontation. He's arrested and hauled off to jail, where he has his heart problem. Gets released to his aunt's house. He hadn't been back.

"Where did he keep stuff about his militia buddies?" I said.

"Not here in the house," Tiffanee said. "He didn't trust us. Besides, he came here just to eat, sleep, and have sex. Then it was just to eat and sleep. As my gram used to say, the bloom came off that rose."

She was putting the nine-millimeter handgun on the shelf at the head of the bed.

"Then where?" I said.

"I don't know. In his truck? I didn't want to know about his stupid games. There's a shed out in the pit, has a stove. Used to be where my gramps, when he was driving the loader, would go to get warm, get out of the rain. Jason called it 'the command post.' "

"Anyone been there since they all pulled out last week?"

"I don't know. No tracks at the gate, which is locked."

"Is there another way in, other than this road?"

"You'd have to bushwhack from the main road, a couple of miles. There's a good-size stream, mostly frozen. There are fast parts where the ice stays thin. Unless you know, it all looks the same."

"Can't picture our boys from Massachusetts doing that."

"No. They mostly like to drive around in their big trucks."

She placed a tissue box in front of the gun, took the other guns out of their cases and slid them under the bed. She was kneeling there when Tara came into the room, said, "Mom! My God, your underwear!"

"I think Sophie's dad's seen women's underwear before," Tiffanee said.

"A time or two," I said. "In the laundry."

Tara shook her head and left. Tiffanee stood up, said, "There. Now we're all set."

We stood there, the underwear still strewn, and I felt a flicker of awkwardness, being in the bedroom, alone with a woman who wasn't my wife. She must have felt it, too, because she said, "Don't worry, Jack. I'm gonna be sleeping alone for a good long time."

I said, "I'm not worried about that."

"Roxanne got a good one," Tiffanee said.

"Thanks," I said. "Sometimes she's not so sure."

We both smiled, Tiffanee pulling at the sheets to make the bed. I was turning to leave when she stood suddenly, said, "One more thing."

"Sure."

"I almost hate to say this. Being her mom and all. And it's not like I'm not wicked proud of her. But do you think Tara's that good? For the play, I mean."

"Mr. Ziggy thinks so. He's the expert."

"I don't know. All those acting types. Why Tara?"

I hesitated. "They're always discovering new talent," I said. "Like Marilyn Monroe. Her real name was Norma Jeane Mortenson. They found her working in a bomb factory in California."

Tiffanee tugged at the sheets, then the blankets.

"Huh," she said. "I suppose it's okay. I just hope he remembers she's never done this before. He's gonna have to go easy on her."

I felt a tremor, the words taking on another meaning. I pictured Mr. Ziggy with his hand on Tara's shoulder. Tara naive and a little awkward, earnest and trusting. Roxanne's words, "It went on too long."

Tiffanee came around the bed, stood and faced me. She was smiling. "I shouldn't even say this, but wouldn't it be, like, wild if acting turned out to be Tara's thing? I mean, this kid from Prosperity, Maine."

She turned back to the bed, tugged again at the quilt.

"She moves to LA. We have a house with a pool. She goes to the studio or whatever, I sit out there with a cold drink."

She gave a little laugh.

"They all come from somewhere," I said, turned to go. Turned back.

"Just keep talking with her," I said. "Make sure she's okay. Stay close to her every step of the way."

I was in the truck. Clair answered on the second ring.

"All quiet," he said.

"How 'bout at your house?"

"No news is good news. Besides, I'm in the front room. Can see the road, up and down. Nobody coming or going."

"Can you give me an hour more?"

"Depends. You drinking beer and watching TV?"

"Going to a shack in the pit they call 'the command post.' "

"Sounds like time well spent," Clair said. "I'll hold down the fort."

Six inches of new snow lay on the plowed road to the pit. I drove past the entrance, pulled into a wide spot in the road three hundred yards up, and parked. Walked back, with a flashlight, gun, and a Leatherman from the console of the truck. I passed the gate, walking in the center of the road where the plow had scraped the pavement clean. Fifty yards back, I jumped the snowbank, crunched across an overgrown field at a 45-degree angle toward Tiffanee's house. When I reached the barn, I turned 90 degrees, cut into the woods.

It was birches and poplar at first, second growth where the pasture was shrinking, then oaks and hemlock. I moved quickly, breaking through the crust but only for a few inches. When I saw the opening of the road, I followed it from the trees, keeping well back. No tracks showing if someone drove in.

It was a quarter-mile to the pit, the path marked by heavy equipment rusting in the woods, trees growing up through it. An excavator, the bucket buried in the earth. A bulldozer, both its tracks missing. A dump truck, windows smashed. All of them were pocked by bullet holes, big ones, like they were casualties of some ferocious battle. The trees got smaller and thicker. I eased my way through, using my right arm to push the branches back, then came out at the edge of the pit.

It looked like a crater, the remnant of some long-ago meteor strike. The walls had been gouged out over the years the pit had been operating. There were small trees clustered like mountain goats on the slopes. The bottom of the hole was strewn with more abandoned equipment, other stuff that was new: fences in short lengths, like for an obstacle course. Piles of boulders. Targets staked out across the flattened, snow-covered ground.

I walked across, shined the light. Saw a life-size human figure, the torso and head riddled with bullets. Another with the chest stabbed like it had been bayoneted. Still another with a softball-size hole left by a shotgun blast. Double-aught buckshot.

If they were ever attacked by an army of cardboard cutouts, Jason's buddies were ready.

I crossed the pit, flicking the flashlight beam side to side. Shell casings reflected the light back, and I bent down to pick up the first half-dozen. They looked like rifle cartridges. The last one was long and thick, like something from a machine gun on a Humvee. I put them in my pocket for my panel of experts.

And then I saw the shack, set close to the far wall and edged by small trees, grown up over a decade or so. There was a single window, the glass half broken out. The door was closed, with a hasp held by a piece of tree branch. I yanked it up and out, pushed the door open. I stepped in and shut it behind me. It creaked like they do in the movies.

I scanned the room with the flashlight. There was a small woodstove, a steel chimney pipe extending to the roof. A stack of branches and limbs beside the stove, pieces of broken pallets. Chairs, the kind with aluminum frames and plastic webbing, were set in a semicircle, at the center of which was an overturned wooden crate, like a desk.

The floor was littered with cigarette butts, bent beer cans, and ripped twelve-pack cartons. Bud Ice. PBR. Convenience-store coffee cups, crushed mini bottles of Fireball Cinnamon Whisky. Empty pizza boxes, a beef jerky wrapper, a smashed Skoal can. If you couldn't outfight these guys, maybe you could outlast their hearts.

There were outlines of gun butts in the dirt floor, mouse tracks: tiny paw prints, the Nike swoosh of dragging tails. All of it faced a wall where a whiteboard had been screwed on, the writing on it smeared.

Circling the perimeter of the room, I played the light over the studs and bare boards. There was graffiti everywhere, hearts and initials, obscenities gouged with nails and knives. Donnie had been there. Slick, too. Most of the markings were old and faded, until I came to the wall with the whiteboard. A nail for scrawling hung on a piece of twine. The gouges there were mostly fresh, the newly bared wood lighter than the dirt-stained boards.

> PATRIOT LEGION . . . DIE DHHS . . . RISE UP NOW . . . LIBERTY OR DEATH. . .
>
> RUN, DICTATORS, RUN . . . WE'RE COMING FOR YOU . . . BLOOD AND SOIL . . .
>
> TAKE IT BACK . . . COLD DEAD HANDS . . . FUCK YOU GOVERNER . . .
>
> IMMIGRATE THIS . . . SIC SEMPER TYRANNIS . . .

Thus always to tyrants. Somebody said it. John Wilkes Booth?

I looked closer. What did all of this tell me? They were armed. They were shooting at targets and climbing over fences. They hated government, people of color, had some plan to fight back against what they saw as oppression, threats to their rights as true Americans.

I ran the light over the whiteboard, made out a few random words:

TEAM 2 . . . EN MIES . . . HOTL ST . . .

I looked closer, wet my cold finger and ran it over the smears. Some ink came off on my hand. Below the HOTL ST and to the right, the darkest smears.

CO S . . . REP TER . . . D H BI H

I stared at it, a different sort of word jumble.

COPS . . . REPORTER . . . DHHS BITCH

If Jason hadn't been back here since his arrest, then there had been some earlier discussion of enemies. Police, of course. A reporter. A DHHS bitch. Apparently, someone had gotten the message. He carried a shotgun and a bottle of gasoline.

I circled the room again, opened the woodstove door, closed it. Could you get prints out of this place? Would Detective Strain bother?

Turning back, I returned to the whiteboard wall, the gouged slogans. The walls were boards nailed on studs, no inner spaces. I closely examined one of the boards, screwed in place. The Phillips screw heads were gashed, like the screws had been well used before they were put in place here. Or they hadn't used the right bit. Or were they screwed on and off?

I took the Leatherman out, snapped it open. Flashlight in my teeth, I drew the screws out slowly, the bit slipping. One . . . two . . . three. The last screw was the toughest, but it finally started to turn. I eased it out, holding the board in place with my good shoulder. Lowered it to the ground, turned it around.

Grinned in the darkness.

There was a torn piece of PBR carton duct-taped to the back. I peeled the tape, turned the cardboard over to the blank side. It was a list, written in pencil: STRYKER, MADDOG, TOMAHAWK, WARRIOR, NOMAD, ARCHANGEL, SNIPER, HORSEMAN, JAVELIN, RYDER, CRISPUS, BAZOOKAJOE, BLACKHAWK, CITIZEN, REBEL, GUNNER, PILGRIM, P.REVERE . . .

Four of them—STRYKER, HORSEMAN, CITIZEN, and NOMAD—had an asterisk sort of mark after the name. Three names had been erased, leaving gray scuffs. There were twenty-two left. They were all run-on, like they were used digitally. Some sort of messaging platform. Signal? WhatsApp? Something more clandestine? How tech-savvy were these guys? The nail and the pencil suggested not very.

I took a photo, taped the cardboard back onto the board. Something for Detective Strain to consider, or would he find that this implicated me, too? I screwed the board back on, the last screw head stripping. I used pliers to slowly wrest it back in place. Forty minutes gone.

I surveilled the room one more time, shone the light up at the ceiling. There were old phoebe nests stuck to the rafters, creosote stains on the boards around the chimney, spiderwebs in the corners.

I left, closing the door behind me, stepping out into the light. The clouds had splintered, and the moon was dodging between them. I crossed the pit in my own tracks, shadows showing by the rusting hulks. Then I was back in the woods, leaning into the brush with my right shoulder, standing straighter as I came out into the big trees.

And stopped.

I saw headlights, faint through the trees from the direction of the road, then brighter. There was the sound of crunching, tires on ice, and the headlights swung in. Two, then four, as more lights were switched on, then the white glare of a light bar.

I moved behind a tree, watched as the truck crunched closer, stopped near the gate.

The lights went out and I heard a door open. I walked closer, moving from tree to tree.

A single dark figure detoured around the gate, started down the road. I watched as he passed, dark clothes, a baseball cap. My assailant? Could be, but impossible to tell for sure, from a shadow. He moved deliberately, stopping every twenty feet and looking back and into the woods. I froze behind a hemlock, waited until the sound of his footsteps on the snow faded as he neared the pit. He'd find the tracks at the shack in a few minutes. Hustle back? Call for backup? He must have seen my truck, then discovered there were no tracks showing at the entrance.

I started for my truck, staying in my own footprints. Quieter than crunching a fresh trail. When I came out of the brush and into the field, I moved slowly, trying to see if someone was waiting in the truck. The windows were tinted; I stopped, watched for a sign of life. The glow of a phone. A cigarette being lit.

Nothing.

I moved closer, swinging out toward the road, then turning to walk in the truck's tracks. I eased the gun out, walked slowly. Still no sign of anyone, just a couple of ticks from the cooling motor. And then I was close enough.

It was a black Dodge, lifted, big tires. There was an American flag sticker on the back window, the version with the circle of thirteen stars. Betsy Ross.

I moved to within five feet of the back bumper, hunched down. It was a Maine plate, nothing unusual. I snapped a photo, the flash bouncing off the snow. I listened. Nothing from the pit. Nothing from the truck. Nothing from the road.

I turned and backtracked, followed the tire tracks to the road, then the road to my truck. Got in and started it, drove slowly down the center of the road, the ice reflecting the gray light of the moon. I rolled slowly up to the intersection, didn't touch the brakes, didn't want any lights at all. I turned right, drove a mile, pulled off onto an opening cleared for a woodyard. I sat, lights off, motor idling, and texted the plate photo to Blake. The caption:

SORRY TO BOTHER YOU. HOPE EVERYTHING STILL OK.
A FAVOR: WOULD YOU, COULD YOU, RUN THIS PLATE FOR ME?
CARETAKER AT THE TRAINING CAMP. LOTS OF BULLET HOLES, SOME BRASS THERE. LOOKS LIKE AFGHANISTAN AFTER A FIREFIGHT.

I turned back, headed for home, but as I was approaching the road, I slowed. Turned in. Drove back the way I had come. Tiffanee and Tara were there, alone.

I was a hundred yards in when I saw lights on the right, in the field. He was turning around. The lights went out.

I continued past the turnoff, saw the vague black shape of the truck backed into the edge of the brush. I kept going, was almost to the farmhouse when I saw the shape move. He crossed the field with lights out, pulled onto the road, and turned away. I slowed, turned my lights off. Made a U-turn and started back. I could see his taillights now, moving fast. I kept him in sight, saw him turn. He went right, headed west. I reached the intersection, turned to follow him, but he was gone.

I drove a mile, then another. House lights showing from deep in the woods. Christmas lights on a trailer, half the string on the ground. No sign of the truck. It could have pulled down a driveway, parked behind a farm shed. He could have watched me pass him and continued on.

I pulled over, killed the lights, watched the rearview.

Headlights flared on, then swung away. Then I saw taillights that faded fast, the truck accelerating. He was headed east at a high rate of speed, as the cops would say.

I couldn't catch him. I wasn't sure what I'd do with him, there on the side of the road, if I did.

7

Clair was standing in the front-room window when I pulled in, headlights showing him as a shadow. I wondered if he'd stood there the whole time or made rounds of the house. I wondered if he and Roxanne had talked, Clair normally being our resident voice of reason.

But he had a mysterious woman at his house, stolen back from bikers, in the throes of opiate withdrawal. We, on the other hand, had only had a run-of-the-mill shooting, a sad attempt at a firebombing. Who was the voice of reason now?

I stepped in and he met me in the kitchen, which was warm, the woodstove well fed.

"All quiet?" I said.

"Yeah, you?"

"Yes. Well, sort of."

I told him about the shack in the pit, the guy in the truck who had just missed me.

"Knows you were there looking around," Clair said. "And that's not exactly you backing off."

"So word will go up the chain, or whatever structure they have."

I took out my phone, showed him the photo of the list.

STRYKER, MADDOG, TOMAHAWK, WARRIOR . . .

"No sign saying No Girls Allowed?" Clair said.

"Not that I could see. But it was dark."

"I'm seeing a lot of pinkie swears."

"And big guns."

"Not the best combination."

"No."

There was a pot of rice and beans, tomatoes, and peppers on the stove, still warm, a bowl of shredded asiago on the counter. I looked to Clair.

"Already partook," he said.

I scooped some onto a plate, sprinkled the cheese on top. As I began to eat, Roxanne came downstairs. She was wearing sweatpants and a fleece, her pre-bedtime outfit. Her face was drawn, her eyes tired. She said, "Everything okay out there?"

"More or less."

"Tell me about the less," she said.

I did. The Jeep making it home, Tiffanee and Tara okay. Then the shack and the writing on the board. DHHS. Bitch. Reporter. The pickup, the guy going into the pit, coming back out.

"Can they just go there?" Roxanne said.

"Not if she tells them they can't," Clair said. "Put up a No Trespassing sign, tell the police there have been unauthorized people on her property."

"And what would they do?" she said.

"Sit on the place, maybe," I said. "Except there's a shortage of deputies. A couple of them cover a few hundred square miles."

"Seven hundred and twenty-four," Clair said.

There was a pause. I took a forkful, chewed and swallowed.

"So, Tiffanee has some of Jason's guns. And ammo. She put a handgun on her headboard, a rifle under the bed. She said she has a plan to string up pots and pans in the kitchen as a warning system."

"Oh, my God," Roxanne said. "Poor Tara. Maybe they should stay here."

"Tiffanee's a gamer," I said. "Pretty tough. I think she wants her life back."

"Sounds like a plan," Clair said. "Until it isn't."

"What if they do the same thing to her that they did to you? With the fire?"

"Depends on whether they think she's talking," I said. "I got the impression Jason kept his activities to himself. She didn't allow them in her house, didn't want to have anything to do with it."

"Unlike you, who's just plain nosy," Clair said. Another pause, and then he said, "Depends on whether they think Jason's domestic mess is their fight. Doesn't seem to rise to the level of revolution, but who knows? Guys like this don't tend to like strong women."

"Maybe Jason's a liability," Roxanne said. "Sitting in jail."

"Some prosecutor trying to flip him," I said.

"Calls in the ATF," Clair said.

I thought of Strain, his detective hunches about me. Kept eating, then said, "What if Jason is just a flunky? They let him in because he had the facility. Somebody else really calling the shots for this consortium."

"Then the order to warn you off or whatever didn't come from him," Clair said.

"The guy in the truck," I said. "Blake's on it."

I finished dinner. Clair said he was going to head home, spell Mary on Marta duty. She was near the peak of withdrawal. Maybe tomorrow would be a better day. He stood down.

Sophie was in her room, needed some alone time, Roxanne said. She was exhausted, was going to bed. I said I understood that she'd gone above and beyond with Tiffanee and Tara. It had been a long stretch. She asked how my shoulder was, and I said it was fine.

"I want to see it," she said.

"You don't believe me?"

I unbuttoned my shirt, shrugged it off. I started to pull my T-shirt over my head, and she assisted. She was behind me and said, "Oh, God, Jack. Will they go away?"

"In time. Or maybe I'll just have to wear a shirt at the beach."

She ran her fingers over the wounds. I said, "There's eighteen, right?"

She counted.

"Yes. But a couple are sort of overlapping. If you count them as two, it's nineteen."

I turned to her, said, "Some people get tattoos."

She smiled, leaned closer and kissed me on the cheek.

"I still love you," Roxanne said.

"Good thing. T-shirts are tough all by myself."

Another kiss, this time on the lips. Gentle.

She held me, her head on my good shoulder. Leaned closer to whisper in my ear.

"You know that rule we have?"

"Which one?"

"Guns stay in the safe."

"Oh, yeah."

"Forget it. If they come back, I want you to be ready."

"I will be," I said.

"Locked and loaded," Roxanne said.

And with that, she took her phone from the table and went up to bed.

I went out to the shed to get more firewood, enough for the morning. I tucked the small Glock in my waistband. Came back in and stacked the wood in the stand by the stove. Right-handed, one piece at a time.

I finished, felt like drinking a beer but remembered I'd had the last one. I'd get more in the morning. Did anyone other than criminals deliver to Prosperity, Maine?

I put two chunks of wood in the stove—red oak, good until morning—then sat down in the chair and watched the flames. Fifteen feet away, the wall had been scorched, the flames dying with the gasoline. Had that been the intent? A little bit of a scare? But the shot, fired in the dark—he hadn't known whether I'd take that blast in the face. If they tried again . . .

But would they try again? And if so, when? Wait for me to let my guard down, return to normal? But if I were asking questions, talking to the police, a delay would just give me more time. Of course, if they killed me, it would only make my case.

I hoped Jason wasn't in charge. He wasn't big on the long view.

The fire flickered. I had the lights out and the moonlight was brighter outside, the clouds sailing on to the east.

I got up, went to a window on each side of the house, looked out. It was still, dark, silent. I went to the hallway, got my jacket, and went outside. The temperature was dropping and only the brightest stars were visible. Sirius, Betelgeuse, and Procyon, the Winter Triangle. My dad had driven with me all the way from Manhattan to Montauk one February day to wait for night and see the stars. He was a scientist, studying bugs with an unflinching eye, and all his life retained his childlike wonder for insects, stars, the power of a hurricane.

It was an innocence I'd lost along the way, one eye on the sky, the other on the dark woods, the mean streets. I let that thought creep in, then chased it away. Walked slowly down to the road, hugging the shadow of the bones of the lilacs. Close to the road, I stood still and looked both ways, listened. I heard the winter woods creaking and snapping, the faint thrum of a tractor-trailer on the main road, a mile north.

No headlights. No movement. All was well.

I walked back to the house and went inside, locking the door behind me. Crossing the kitchen, I shut the damper on the stove, drank a glass of water, went upstairs. There was a dim light from the bathroom. Our door was shut, the room dark. Sophie's door was closed, the lights out. I started to walk past, heard her talking.

I stopped. Listened. She was having a conversation, but if Roxanne was asleep, then with whom? Tara was home, and Sophie didn't have a phone. I patted my jeans pocket, felt my own. Roxanne had hers when she went up the stairs. Did she give it to Sophie?

I moved close to the door, heard her say, "But it's, like, why would orphans always be so smiley?" And then she laughed, and I knocked once, opened the door.

She was in bed, shoved her hand under the covers.

"Hey," I said.

"Hi, Dad."

"Sorry I had to go."

"That's all right. You had to help them out."

"Tara's all set now, right?"

"Yeah. I mean, as far as I know."

I moved closer, saw a faint glow through the sheet.

"Is that who you were talking to?"

She looked at me, didn't answer. We'd taught her to always tell the truth.

"Do you have your mom's phone?"

"No."

She caught herself, said, "I don't."

"Then what? Tin cans attached by strings?"

A blank look, before her time. Then she took a breath, eased her hands out from underneath the blanket, and put a phone to her ear.

"Gotta go. Yeah . . . Talk to you later."

She lowered the phone, looked at me.

I looked at the phone. "Whose is that?"

"Mine."

"Where did it come from?"

"Tara. She gave it to me. So we can talk. We have a lot to talk about, with the play and everything."

"I'm sure," I said. "Where did she get it?"

"Just an old one from their house."

"May I see it?"

She held the phone out and I took it, stepped to the doorway, and turned on the light. Sophie squinted, pulled the covers up to her neck.

I looked at the phone. It was a Motorola, one step up from a burner. The screen was cracked, and the case was scraped. I flicked the screen on, and a few apps popped up.

"Does her mom pay for it?"

"No. It's one of the prepaid ones. I bought a month's worth."

"With what?"

"The credit card."

"The one for emergencies?"

"Yeah."

"Huh. Was this one?"

"Well, sort of. I mean, we really need to talk, Dad. Tara getting this part is a big deal and she's gonna need support. I mean, she's gonna need more than her mom."

I looked at the apps more closely. Weather. Maps. A couple of messaging apps: WhatsApp. Signal.

"And this was in Tara's house?"

A hesitation, then, "Yes."

"I mean, in a drawer?"

Another beat, then, "I don't know."

"Do they have a bunch of used cell phones just lying around?"

"I don't know. At least this one, I guess."

"Was it her mom's?"

Sophie didn't answer, which meant no.

"Jason's?"

It had been at least a year since Jason had moved in, so it would stand to reason that—

"Dad, I didn't do anything wrong. It was in the trash. Tara said Jason threw it at the wall because it was, like, dead, and the battery wouldn't charge. Nobody even wanted it."

"Tara took it out of the trash."

A nod.

"Who got it to work?"

"Lizzie. She's in our class. She's like a genius when it comes to computers and stuff. Tara brought it to school and Lizzie took it home and fixed it. Something was, like, loose inside. So now it works."

"Tara didn't think to give it back to Jason?"

"He'd freak that she took it out of the trash. You know Jason. Tara's afraid of him. One time he was drunk, and he said he was going to spank her for lying to her mom, and they got in a big fight. Then Tara's mom came home, and Tara told her what he said, and he said he was just joking. But he wasn't."

"I'm sure," I said. I turned the phone in my hand.

"And Tara's mom took her side and Jason called Tara 'Little Bitch' and her mom 'Big Bitch,' and then all three of them got in a fight. Jason pushed her mom and was saying mean things, like she was fat, and she was lucky to have him, because hot girls hit on him all the time. And Tara's mom was like, 'Fine, go with them, you a-hole.' And he said he would, and he stomped around and threw some stuff. She told him to leave, and he said it was his house, too, and he called her more names, and said she could leave if she didn't want him around. So, Tara and her mom came here, and then Jason came here with his gun, and you came home, and he got arrested."

End of play-by-play.

"They must be glad he's gone," I said.

"Uh-huh. Tara hates his guts. She says he's the worst boyfriend her mom's ever had."

My daughter—not so long ago a little girl, as innocent as she could be with Roxanne and me for parents. But we tried to keep some sort of line between our work and Sophie. Now the world had come knocking.

"Well," I said, "maybe he'll go to prison and that will be the end of it."

There was a pause. I looked at the phone. Sophie looked at me. I could feel her sensing an opening.

"Dad, I'm twelve, for God's sake. Nobody I know doesn't have a phone. It's making me look like some sort of freak. I mean, it's not like we're Amish or something. You and Mom are on your phones all the time, and here I am, cut off from the universe in the middle of nowhere, like we live on a desert island or in a cave or—"

"Okay," I said.

She stopped talking.

"You're right. You need a phone. We'll get you one, your own, not some busted-up, hand-me-down burner. I don't think you want to be using this, anyway, if it was Jason's."

She paused. Switched gears.

"Wow. Great. That was easy."

I looked at the apps, Signal and WhatsApp. "So, Jason doesn't know the phone is working?"

"No."

"Does Tara's mom know you have it?"

"No."

We were quiet, and then I said, "We'll get you a phone tomorrow. Go to the place in Rockland. You can pick one out."

"Awesome, Dad. Thanks."

"And I'll hang on to this one."

She nodded.

"How do you get into it? Do you know the PIN?"

"Tara did. One seven seven six. Like the Revolutionary War."

"Huh. Did she guess that?"

"No, she was standing behind him one time when he put it in. I told her about the war part."

I shut the phone down, then powered it back on. Entered 1776 and I was in.

Sophie looked at me, said, "So you think there are clues or something on there, right? I mean, that's why you caved."

"No, that's not—"

Then I had to smile.

"I could do what you do, Dad. Talking to people and figuring things out," she said. "And you write stories sometimes, too."

I looked at her, thought of all the things she could do with her life. Scuffling around with bad people, doing some good in fits and starts, dragging your family into one mess after another. Sophie could do better.

"You can do whatever you set out to do," I said.

I kissed her on the forehead and left the room, closing the door behind me. Went back to the study, opened the damper on the stove. The blue-green flames flickered faintly, then erupted into orange. I sat back in the chair in the firelight, woke the screen on the phone.

There were only three rows of apps: weather, maps, calendar, notes, a compass. I opened the notes and it was blank. I opened the calendar. Maybe it would say FIREBOMB MCMORROW HOUSE. It didn't. The other apps were for messaging, WhatsApp and Signal, both encrypted.

I opened WhatsApp. For status, there was a thumbnail of a bull's-eye target, peppered with bullet holes. Jason was nothing if not understated. I went to chats. Nothing. Ditto for calls, communities.

That left Signal, which opened to chats. Nothing. There were two groups: Level 1 and Level 2. Level 1 had five members. The icons were guns and flags. Don't Tread on Me. Confederate. 1776. Betsy Ross flag. A hand giving the OK sign. White supremacists.

I clicked through, and there they were: the names from the shack. STRYKER, HORSEMAN, CITIZEN, and NOMAD. And a phone number for each.

Level 2 was the whole group from the shack list, with phone numbers listed. There were no conversations visible. I went to settings, security, disappearing messages. They were set to be erased after an hour. Nothing had come in. I wondered if Jason had told his buddies he was in custody, that the phone was AWOL. They'd have to find another way to communicate.

But what? A new Signal account on another phone? His aunt's phone?

All sorts of ways, but the numbers for the group's members wouldn't change. And I had them. Was one of them the bomber?

I went to the counter, got my phone, set Jason's down. I photographed the list of names and numbers. That much I had. If there were incoming messages, I'd see them. And Jason could communicate with his crew.

Or I could.

8

"So, you're going to give it to the police, right? That detective?"

We were at the breakfast table. I was having toast and tea. Roxanne was having plain scrambled eggs. Sophie had wolfed a blueberry muffin and juice, then had gone back upstairs to take a shower, get dressed. Her own phone. A big day.

"I should," I said. "He'll think it's one more piece of evidence in his case against me."

"Tell him where it came from."

"And throw Tara under the bus?"

"Everyone's under the bus in this one, Jack," Roxanne said. "He'd have the list."

"Okay, I will."

"When?"

I hesitated.

"This isn't you against Jason, mano a mano. Let the police handle it, Jack. They're the experts."

She stopped. I didn't answer.

"I'm worried about you," Roxanne said. "It's like you're, I don't know, a little out of control. This guy's got nothing to lose, but you do. A job—"

"Sort of."

"You'll get back into it. You always do. But you have a family. Me. Sophie. Our life together. You can't let these people take you down with them, Jack."

"I won't."

"I'm serious."

"So am I," I said. "Don't worry. Have fun with Sophie. Get her a nice phone."

"We're going to get lunch, do some clothes shopping. She's been such a good sport during this whole thing. It's a lot for a twelve-year-old."

"It is. But she's tough."

Roxanne leaned over, took my hand. "That's the thing, Jack. I don't want her to have to be tough. I want her to have a normal life, do normal things. I don't want her to be part of—"

She hesitated.

"This stuff that you do. These people you write about."

"I didn't invite Jason here. I didn't go seeking him out."

"I know. That was just circumstances or whatever. But the girl at the store—"

"Sparrow."

"Raymond, dying that way. I heard her telling Tara you were the one who found him, how he was tied up, the bag over his head."

"You can read about that stuff all day on the Internet."

"But it's not part of your life, not part of your dad's life."

"What if I were a cop?"

She took her hand away, gave a short sigh. "I just think—"

Sophie came clattering down the stairs, swung around the corner, and trotted into the kitchen.

"I'm ready."

She was wearing leggings tucked into brown suede boots, a black sweater that came to her hips. Her shiny dark hair was tied back with a print scarf, and she was wearing a flat-brimmed fedora.

"Nice hat," I said. "That new?"

"Mr. Ziggy had it at school. For plays. He said I could borrow it. He gave Tara this cool feather boa. He said she looked like Gene Tierney. That's a girl. We looked it up."

Roxanne and I exchanged glances. Sophie said to her mom, "Let's go. I want to get there before you change your mind."

"Strike while the phone is hot," I said.

"Exactly," Sophie said.

Roxanne was up, put her plate and coffee mug in the sink. They put on their jackets—Sophie, a short puffer, Roxanne a pea coat—and Sophie went out the door.

"Have fun with our budding actress," I said to Roxanne, but then Sophie was back.

"Clair's coming," she said. "With Marta."

We froze.

"You guys go," I said. "Just wave and pull out. I'll talk to them."

We went out to the driveway, saw Clair and Marta rounding the corner of the shed, the end of the path through the woods. Marta was holding Clair's arm, and wobbly on her feet. Roxanne looked grim as she and Sophie got in the car, backed up with Sophie still reaching for her seat belt. Roxanne buzzing the window down. They spoke for a few seconds, Roxanne smiling, Marta holding on to Clair's arm. Then Roxanne backed the rest of the way out, drove off staring straight ahead, no smile at all.

I waited. They walked up. Marta looked ten years older than the last time I saw her, thin, and drawn. Her hair was longer, straw straight, washed-out brown instead of the dark lustrous waves from before. Her eyes were sunken behind makeup that looked like it had been scrawled on with a crayon. A woman who had been kept in a cage.

"Hey, Jack," she said. "Been a long time. How are you doing? Heard you got shot."

"Birdshot," I said. "Worse things. How are you doing?"

"Better."

"She's over the hump," Clair said.

"Good," I said. "Come in. I'll make coffee."

Marta moved forward, Clair stayed put. I stepped closer and he said, "Pickup went by three times. Old copper-colored GMC three-quarter-ton. Gonna take a ride around."

"Okay."

"Could you just keep an eye on her for a little while? Mary needs a break and I'd like to have her with some protection. Just in case."

"Sure. You think they've found her?"

"Don't know."

"But if they show up?"

"The whites of their eyes, Jackson. The whites of their eyes."

He grinned, and he seemed older, too. Thinner face, more teeth showing. He started for the path, a careful sort of gingerly walk.

Clair, who'd navigated the jungle with a twenty-pound automatic rifle and a sixty-pound pack. Airlifted in, wending his way through the jungle. Shooting his way out. I remembered a story he'd told about hanging below a helicopter, his bear hug holding a wounded Marine onto a swinging ladder.

"Life or death," he'd said. "It was all the time."

I watched him walk along, slowly and carefully. Time was catching up. With all of us.

I turned, saw Marta waiting at the shed door. I went over to her. She took my arm, and I led her through the shed and into the kitchen and sat her down. She slumped, a shadow of the woman I'd known before. That woman had been tough, mysterious, sexy in a predatory sort of way. She'd sunken her teeth into Louis and he'd gone down hard. The drugs had stripped that allure away, like flesh off a skeleton.

"Tea, Marta?"

"I'll try it," she said.

I remembered reading something about avoiding caffeine while taking Methadone. I found a stale decaf tea bag—a misguided attempt at quelling my insomnia—and a regular one for me, and put the kettle on. Then I walked to the closet and opened the safe. I took out the Glock 19, the bigger one, snapped in a fifteen-round nine-millimeter clip.

Tucking the gun in the back of my waistband, I went back to the counter, poured water from the kettle into two mugs, brought them to the table. I put the decaf in front of Marta, the other mug—and the gun—in front of me. Then I went to the fridge and took out the milk carton, poured some into a pitcher.

"Thanks," Marta said. She glanced at the gun. "For both."

"You're welcome," I said. "How are you feeling?"

"Great."

"It's all relative?"

A weak smile.

"Right."

She held up the mug, her hand shaking, ripples on the surface of the tea. Sipped.

"So," I said.

"Here we are," Marta said.

"Home again, home again," I said.

"I could always talk to you, Jack," Marta said, mustering the searching eye contact, the faint pout, the seductive half-smile. A weak imitation of her former flirtatious self.

"I'm a professional listener," I said. "But I also ask a lot of questions."

She looked at me, hesitated. Her skin was blotchy, her eyes bloodshot.

"Ask away."

"Where's the money?"

She sipped the coffee, buying time.

"My money?"

"The million."

"It is mine, you know. I earned it. My cut from Nigel."

The Brit. Where it all began. Marta holed up in Nigel's villa in the Caribbean when Lambert's hired guns came to call. Nigel left dead, tied to a chair. Marta escaping with all the cash she could carry.

"He thought I was happy to be an ornament in his big house. Didn't know I was on the clock the whole time."

"I wonder if he got it while they were killing him, and you were long gone."

She shrugged. "We'll never know, will we."

"So where is it?"

"It's here."

"Buried in the woods?"

"Something like that."

"Did you expect to be gone so long?"

Marta smile slipped to something rueful. "No."

"So, you torched the car, stripped off your clothes. Had stuff to change into, guy's clothes. Figured you'd shake them."

"I almost did."

"What went wrong?"

Another sip, the hand steadier now.

"You know how in the movies they dig a grave in, like, ten minutes? Six feet deep, sides all neat and square."

I waited.

"It wasn't like that. The woods, all those trees. The ground was full of these big roots. I had a little shovel, the kind that unfolds. It was Louis's. It took me, like, a half-hour to dig a hole big enough for the bag. When I came back onto the road, I was gonna hitchhike out. You can guess who picked me up?"

"Bikers looking for their money. Which you never gave up."

"I never cracked."

"So then Toronto."

"A fancy strip club. It's called Forbidden. Snake owns it, among other things."

"Lambert."

"Right. It's all for laundering drug money."

"I heard you were trafficked."

"Sort of. It was like a brothel, really. Connected to a hotel."

"You worked there."

"Yeah. I did it for a month there, somebody always watching. I didn't run. Snake finally figured I really didn't have the money. Brought me to Montreal and added me to his harem."

"And the drugs started."

"Even that didn't break me," Marta said. "When I got high, I thought about Louis. How he'd ride in and save me. Clair, too. I knew I could depend on you guys."

"Not me," I said. "Them. Leave no one behind. It's a Marine Corps thing."

She lifted the mug, two hands. Her fingers were bony, nails unpainted.

"But now they'll be coming to get you back," I said. "Or kill you. It's a problem."

"You all can handle it."

"Maybe. But why should we have to? Ever since you came to Maine, we've been cleaning up your messes. All the lies and half-truths, it's all for you," I said, thinking, And now you are putting everyone in danger: Louis, Clair and Mary, me and Roxanne and Sophie.

"You're a user, Marta."

She looked at me over the mug, eyes narrowed.

"I think of it as more coming to the aid of a damsel in distress," Marta said.

"You're not my idea of a damsel. You're tough and shrewd and selfish. You just play the part when it's convenient for you. To hell with the consequences for everybody else."

Marta sipped, looked away from me, said, "That's cold, Jack. You know what they did to me. I had to be tough. I wasn't going to let them break me."

I looked at her, the ice in her veins, the hardness in her eyes. I wondered what had turned her into this, what hurt had hardened her like steel.

"Louis is very capable. Look how he got me back."

"And so is Clair. But he's getting older."

"You're no slouch."

"I have a family. I don't want these people anywhere near them— not on my road, not in my town, not near my friends."

"They won't come here," she said. "They'll look for me at Louis's place."

"They're like dogs. They just follow the scent wherever it leads."

"When I'm a little better, I'll leave, if that's what you want."

A pause. No reply in this case was a reply. She got the hint.

"I don't want to be a problem for your little family."

The last two words were dismissive, patronizing, condescending.

I drank my tea. Put the mug back down. Looked at her square.

"I have Roxanne and Sophie. Forever. All you have is a bag of dirty money, buried in the woods someplace. When you run out of people to use and throw away, you'll end up alone."

She looked hurt, like she might tear up. A ploy for sympathy, or had I struck a deeper nerve?

"I have Louis," Marta said. "He loves me."

"You don't deserve him. Already bailed on him once, remember? You got in the door and wrapped him around your little finger," I said. "But your powers of persuasion are fading fast."

She gave me a cold, lethal look, no more tears.

"Not a thing you say to a woman, Jack," Marta said.

"True fact," I said, and my phone buzzed. A text. Clair. Call me.

I got up, walked to the stove, tapped the phone.

"Hey."

"Need you for a few minutes. That truck is backed into the woods, quarter-mile west, on the right. Two of them."

"Okay."

"I'll circle around behind them in the woods. You pull up, use your gift of gab. 'Hey, guys. Seen a big dog? He wandered off.' Or whatever. Distract them enough for me to come up alongside."

Cautious for Clair. There was a time when he would have had them on the ground without taking out his gun.

"Got it. What about Marta?"

"Stick her upstairs, close the door. This won't take long, one way or the other."

Which is what I did. Held her arm as we went up the stairs. She was light as a skeleton.

I put her in the spare bedroom at the front of the house. It had a big closet that runs along the eaves. Her hidey-hole.

"Go in there if you hear anyone come in who isn't us. I'll call out to you on the way up the stairs, so you know."

She smiled. "See, Jack. You can't be mad for long."

"This is for Louis and Clair. If it were up to me, I'd send you packing."

But she was already surveying the room. For Marta, it was just another hideout, one of many.

The truck was backed into the opening of an overgrown logging road, big tires and four-wheel drive slamming it through the snow. I passed it. Stopped. Called.

"You set."

"Ten-four."

I backed up, parked in front of them. Got out with a big smile, started for the truck. Two guys, beards, one with long hair, the other with shaved stubble. The truck had Maine plates, an empty plow frame, chain dangling. Dents and rust.

Clair was moving in the woods behind them. They were putting something down, reaching. I saw Clair coming closer, fought off the urge to just pull my gun.

I smiled, called out, "Hey, guys. Sorry to bother you, but you been here a while? I'm looking for a black dog, part Lab, part something else. Big."

I picked the passenger side, saw that guy's head turn to look at the floor, then back at me.

The window came down, pot smoke billowing out. I said, "Good dog, but when he gets it into his head, off he goes. He booked it down the road headed this way."

The long-haired guy on my side. Something on the seat beside him, covered with a black plastic bag. He shook his head. "Nah, ain't seen nothing. Probably he went into the woods. I had a dog once, he—"

Clair was on the driver's door, yanked it open, gun pointed.

"Out," he barked.

The driver had his hands up. My guy lunged for something on the seat and I reached through the window, got my good arm around his neck and pulled, a fiery stab in my left shoulder. He flung an elbow back. Clair had his guy by the jacket, dragged him out of the truck.

"Fuckin' A," that guy said, as Clair flung him onto the snow.

I popped the door, opened it, dragging the guy with me. Jolting pain in my shoulder, a glimpse of a handgun on the seat where the plastic bag had been. I let go to get my arm out of the window opening and he came around, skinny, jeans falling off his butt. He started swinging. I blocked one roundhouse, another jolt, was tripping backwards, about to block another, when Clair came around the front of the truck, gun leveled at the guy's head.

"On the ground," he said. And the guy stopped. Said, "What the fuck?" but dropped to his knees. Panting, I moved behind him, patted him down. A box-cutter in his jacket pocket. Gave him a shove onto his belly. Clair's guy had gotten up and Clair moved toward him, gun out, and he dropped back down. "You fucking cops?" he said.

I leaned into the cab, took out the handgun. A junk .380.

"This your gun?" I said to my guy. He shook his head, quick and hard. Telltale for a felon, him not knowing if I was some sort of cop.

I snapped the clip out. Tossed the knife, the clip, and the gun onto the snow.

Clair was leaning into the cab from the driver's side. He flipped the seat forward, snapped it back. Looked at the rear cab window. Decals: a Bangor tattoo parlor, a marijuana leaf, Harley-Davidson, the standard orange and black.

He went to his guy, ordered him up, shoved him around with his buddy. Pushed him onto the front of the hood, told him to keep his hands out. Then he went and did the same with my guy. They turned their heads to watch the gun, and Clair said, "What are you doing here?"

"Nothin'."

"You in a club?"

"What, like snowmobiling?" my guy said.

"No, bikers," Clair said.

They shook their heads.

He pointed to the Harley insignia.

"Came with the truck," the driver said.

Clair leaned in, took a wallet from the driver's back jeans pocket, flipped it open, pulled out a driver's license. "Monroe. What are you doing here?"

"On our way to Waterville," the driver said.

"You drove by three times."

"Looking for the right spot," my guy said.

"Can't a guy pull over just to smoke a joint anymore?" the driver said.

Rousted for smoking weed beside the road. What was the world coming to?

"Turn around," Clair said.

They did. I moved to the gun, clip, and knife. Picked them up and walked back to Clair, showed him the gun, the knife.

"Low-budget," I said.

"Who the hell are you?" the driver said, getting his confidence back now that he was probably not going to be shot.

"You don't want to know," Clair said.

"Sure, I do," the driver said.

"Out of your league, bub," I said. "And this is private property."

"You can't just go pointing guns at people," my guy said, "throwing them on the ground."

"Can and just did," Clair said. "Get in your truck and go."

He tossed the wallet, minus the driver's license, in the driver's window, where it landed on the seat. I threw the gun, clip, and knife in the truck bed. The boys huffed a bit, then climbed back in, muttering, gave us their best death stares. The starter wheezed, and the motor sputtered and then roared, blue smoke billowing into the woods. There was a grind from the gearbox, and then the truck swerved past mine, lurched over the snowbank, and spun its way back onto the road. As they drove off, my guy flipped us off out the window.

Face saved.

"Thanks," Clair said.

"Just like we knew what we were doing."

I smiled.

"How's your shoulder?"

"Okay. I'm supposed to be using it."

"Interesting physical therapy."

We stood. The edge of the woods was spruce and pines, draped with snow.

"They weren't Canadian," he said.

"But no way were they just a couple of lost stoners. Had to pretend they were surprised to see us."

Clair slipped his gun back into his pocket, and we walked back onto the road. Lingered for a minute, the way guys do beside a truck. There was the *kik-kik-kik* of a pileated woodpecker from the woods, the closer scold of a blue jay.

"Kids and women did surveillance for the VC," Clair said. "Had eyes on everything. You're seeing it in Ukraine, old ladies texting locations to the guys with the mortars."

"Okay."

"So . . . if you were this guy Snake, and you were going to send somebody to poke around looking for Marta or Louis—or me—would you have them roll up in their colors?"

"They'd want to be surreptitious."

A pause, both of us thinking. Clair reached into his jacket pocket, took out a license. He glanced at it again. Handed it to me.

Our guy: Lucas Sawtelle, 1556 Jackson Road, Monroe, Maine. DOB 8/7/88. Five-eight, 140 pounds. He was looking at the camera sullenly, like he'd just been arrested. I handed it back.

"He wasn't lying about the town."

"No, but still too easy," Clair said. "I mean, I'm old. You're a reporter."

"But a tough one."

"All relative. But no, they rolled over for us, didn't even really act all that surprised. They knew who we were. I think if we hadn't found them, their next move would have been to knock on the door. One of 'em, probably. Say their truck stalled out. Or the battery was dead.

Could we hook a chain on, give them a pull start? Or their phone died, could we call their buddy?"

"And they look around," I said. "See what vehicles are there. One truck, or two? Any sign of Louis? A woman's voice?"

"Am I here?" Clair said. "If so, do I open the door a crack? Do I open it at all? Who are you? If Marta's here, what's the layout? How do you get upstairs? Where are the outbuildings? Are there dogs? Cameras?"

I considered it. Clair kept on.

"So if the former is true, we gave them a chunk of intelligence already. We're armed. We are patrolling. We'll take the offensive. Not sitting ducks."

"But we're not Louis."

"No," Clair said. "An old guy with a bum knee and a writer with a bunch of shotgun pellets in his shoulder."

I grinned.

"Don't sell us short."

He took a step. "Marta's safer in Sanctuary."

"Even with Louis out there on his own?"

"He won't be on his own," Clair said.

I looked at him, the realization sinking in. Clair was staying with Louis, even if it was their last stand.

"No man left behind?" I said.

"No man left alone," Clair said, and he started down the road, limping in the snow. Stopped, turned. Looked at me sideways. Hesitated. I had no idea what he was going to say next.

"Jackson," he said. My full name in Clair-speak. It got my attention. "You're the toughest reporter I know." I waited for the punchline, but it didn't come. He just gave me a thumbs-up and continued on, like it was something he needed me to know before it was too late for him to tell me.

9

I called up from the stairs. "It's Jack." I reached the top and went into the spare bedroom. The closet door was ajar.

Marta was on the bed, a quilt pulled over her. She looked up at me and I could see she was shivering, her skin a whiter shade of pale. Like the song says.

"You okay?" I said.

"Shakes," she said, her teeth clattering. She tried to throw the quilt off, but it caught on her boots. I leaned down and fished it off. She was holding a small vase in her right hand. It was from the closet.

"Wasn't going easy," she said, and smiled, her teeth clattering.

I helped her to her feet, and she fell into me. I steadied her, said, "It was nothing. Couple of guys pulled into the woods to smoke pot."

"You sure?"

"Yeah."

"The clubs, they have these tentacles. One's connected to another, connected to another. They all owe each other favors. It's like a web."

"Local yokels," I said. "Their gun was a piece of junk."

Marta held my arm on the way down the stairs, where Clair was waiting in the kitchen. He brightened when he saw her. Had she wormed her way into his heart, too? Giving him one more person to protect? He had his own daughter, a banker in Charlotte, North Carolina. She came to visit once a year with her husband, who was in private equity. Both were very good-looking, and they drove a new Mercedes SUV, bored teenagers in the back. I was there one time when they arrived, got out of the car and watched them look around like they were in that movie, *Deliverance.*

"You seem better," Clair said.

"Thanks for looking out for me," Marta said.

"Neighborhood watch," Clair said.

"I'll get out of your neighborhood soon."

"Don't worry about that. You have to get on your feet first," he said. He looked toward me.

"We'll head back."

"Up to you," I said, but they were already at the door. She took his arm, and they went out through the shed, me following. I said to Clair, "I'm headed for Clarkston, see Sparrow and Blake."

"When are the girls back?"

"Dinnertime."

"You?"

"The same."

"If you're held up, call me. I'll keep an eye out."

Outlaw bikers. Jason's militia. Zombie on Sparrow's porch. Raccoons raiding the bird feeders. No rest for the weary.

Sitting in the truck at the house, the motor running, I took out Jason's phone, opened Signal and the group list. With my phone, I took photos of each contact page. Texted them to Detective Strain, the number on his card.

FOUND THESE ON A PHONE THAT BELONGED TO JASON—HIS GUN BUDDIES.

How was that for cooperation? I put the truck in gear, started down the road.

The phone beeped. I stopped. Strain.

—WHERE R U?

Told him I'd just left home, headed south.

—Lake St. George parking lot, 25 minutes.

I opened the console, stuck Jason's phone at the bottom of some old CDs, napkins from the Irving in Belfast. Drove out to the turnoff, headed up to the main road, and turned right, climbed the ridge. At the top, I could see bristly hills to the northeast, pastures showing as sheets of white, like blankets set down for a picnic. Beyond the hills was Monroe.

A project for another day, and no cops for that one.

I wound my way south and east, past farmhouses in varying stages of decay, roads named for ridges that were named for people who were long dead. The same for the corners where the road turned, the hills it wound through. It was like the towns here were cemeteries, the tough people who had hacked out a living from this cold ground reduced to unread names on a Google map. And we'd be less than that one day, gone and soon forgotten.

I rolled up to the main road, Route 3, took a right, turned off into the parking lot by the boat ramp, backed into a space, and turned off the motor. No sign of Strain.

I sat in the truck and waited, like I was there for a drug deal. Looked out on the lake.

It was quiet, midmorning on a Tuesday. There were four-wheeler tracks leading from the ramp to the fishing shacks, lined up like cabanas on the white expanse. Tracks returning. A few fishermen stood on the ice in big boots and jumpsuits, like lunar explorers on some snowy moon.

I looked at my watch. It had been thirty-five minutes. I was considering how long I'd wait when the black Explorer rolled down into the lot. Stopped. Backed into the space next to me.

Strain motioned to me and I got out of the truck, opened the door of the SUV. He tossed a briefcase into the backseat and I sat. He had a coffee in his lap.

"Stuck behind Ma and Pa Kettle," Strain said. "Didn't get that in Jersey. Everybody down there's in a hurry."

He looked out at the lake. "You fish?"

"When my daughter was younger. There's a pond in our woods. We'd catch the same sunfish over and over."

"Ice-fishing . . . never got into it. I mean, I'll sit in a tree-stand for hours. Watching, listening, you know? But standing there waiting for a fish to bite, nothing to see? I don't drink, so I was bored out of my mind."

"It's a social thing. Go out with your buddies."

He drank some coffee, put it down. I felt the shift. Time for business.

"You got buddies, Mr. McMorrow?"

"Not really. A couple of friends."

"Your neighbor there. What's his name?"

"Clair Varney."

"Tough son of a bitch in his day, I hear."

"Pretty tough now," I said.

"How old is he?"

I calculated. Clair had said he was twenty-one in 1970 when he moved from First Company to Third. Two close friends had been killed.

"Seventy-three or -four."

"What, like some special forces guy?"

"Vietnam. Marine Corps. Force Recon."

"Huh. That was a long time ago."

"Yes."

"My guy said your buddy acts like he's still in the Marines."

"I don't think you're ever really out."

He considered that, raised the cup, sipped. He wore a pinkie ring, a ruby set in gold. A New Jersey thing.

"I also heard you two work together sometimes."

"You hear a lot."

"It's my job. Word is that you play it pretty close to the edge. Firearms and such."

I thought of Clair, his truck loaded like an armory as he set off for Canada.

"It's Maine," I said. "Most people have a gun in the house."

He nodded, like I had him there.

"These names on this phone. Where is it?"

"Where's what?"

"The phone."

"I gave it back."

"To who?"

"To whom?" I said. "A source."

"A source? You writing a story about these guys?"

"Considering it. 'Maine farm turns into militia training ground.' "

"Except all you got is a bunch of guys running around playing soldier," he said.

"And maybe one of them taking a shot at me."

"Maybe," Strain said.

Another truck pulled in. Two guys got out, camo parkas and rubber boots. They looked at us suspiciously, wondering what we were doing there if we didn't fish. DEA? Private investigators doing a workers' comp case? Weirdos?

"So this phone."

"Yes."

"You got it from somebody in the household, I'm assuming."

"I didn't say that."

"Girlfriend and her kid, right?"

I didn't answer.

"Domestic dispute. In her interest to see him locked up."

"I think she's more interested in him not coming back. Doesn't matter where he goes."

"But this would seal that deal. You having a thing with this woman?"

"No."

"He didn't come to your house to have it out with you, 'cause you're bonking his old lady? She good-looking?"

"I'm married. His girlfriend Tiffanee and my wife are friends, sort of. Our daughters hang out."

"Like that ever stopped anybody," Strain said.

A pause for coffee, a long gaze out at the flat, white lake.

"So who told you about all this gun-nut stuff to begin with?"

"She did. Tiffanee."

"To get the boyfriend in trouble."

I hesitated, took a breath.

"She doesn't want them there. Would you? I mean, some of the holes in stuff in that pit are big as baseballs. They aren't plinking with twenty-twos."

"There's something called the Second Amendment. I can't arrest somebody for shooting stuff up. You know there are places you can pay twenty bucks to shoot a machine gun?"

The guys in the camo were loading gear on a plastic toboggan.

"I'll look at them," Strain said, like he was doing me a favor.

"Good."

"But I gotta say, you telling me half of everything isn't helping."

"I'm telling you what I know."

He turned, leaned toward me, gave me a hard look. No more Mr. Chitchat.

"When people lie to me, I ask myself, 'What are they hiding? What's going on that they don't want coming out?' " Strain said.

I didn't reply.

"With you and your Navy Seal buddy there, I'm just seeing the tip of the freakin' iceberg." He smiled. "That's what I'm thinking. You?"

That while he was looking for my shooter, he was looking at me. That we were sitting on Marta, who was sitting on a million dollars in dirty cash. That Louis and Clair could soon be breaking the law in a very loud way. That my gut said to handle Jason myself. That letting Detective Strain in the door could be a big mistake for all of us. That the lines were blurring fast, disappearing like tracks in a snowstorm.

"What am I thinking?" I said. "Not much. Not much at all."

There were no police at Sparrow's house. I figured that meant patrol officers were gone, fanned out across the city. Dogs and handlers were packed up, having tracked Zombie from the house to the truck. Maybe coursing the surrounding streets, see if he got dropped off.

Crime-scene techs would have combed the room, looking for something DNA-worthy that Zombie might have left, thinking they might get lucky. He could have shed a hair. Picked his nose.

So, I was surprised when Sanitas answered my knock.

"Hey, Clark Kent," he said, and opened the door.

"I can come back," I said.

"No. Jolie is gonna want to talk to you."

He led the way down the hallway, past crime-scene tape that closed off the door to the front parlor. That, I presumed, was where Zombie had been during his visit. We continued on to the kitchen, where it was a full house. Sparrow and Riff at the table, Detective Jolie facing them, a notebook in front of her. Blake and a uniform cop, jackets on, were leaning against the counter.

I took my place beside Blake, who nodded. Jolie looked back at me and said, "Mr. McMorrow. How you feeling?"

"Okay, considering."

"I understand somebody up your way has a beef?"

I shrugged. "Or it was a nearsighted rabbit hunter."

"You play rough up there in the country?"

"It's going around."

She paused, changing gears.

"Maybe you can help us here."

"Want to use her as bait," Riff said.

"Not exactly, sir," Jolie said. "We just want to be ready if he resumes contact."

"The freak has the hots for her," Riff said.

"Riff," Sparrow said.

"Or a crush or whatever," Jolie said. "We can use that to our advantage. Catch him in a mistake."

"You want her to work the overnight?" Riff said. "Are you freakin' kidding me?"

"We'll be there," Sanitas said. "We aren't leaving her by her lonesome."

"He's got a gun," Riff said. "He's loony. What if he decides he's gonna off himself, take her with him?"

"Riff," Sparrow said. "I can handle him. I did it once already, didn't I?"

"We'll have eyes and ears on her," Jolie said.

"This is bullshit," Riff said. "If you'd done your job and caught this asshole in the beginning. Never seen such a goddamn cluster."

"It's my call," Sparrow said. "And I say I'll do it. What if he tries another robbery, shoots somebody? And I just sat here? I can distract him, calm him down, maybe."

"Things are just turning around for us. I don't want to blow it now."

"Mr. Calderone," Jolie said. "We'll do everything humanly possible to protect your daughter, but she's our connection to him. She can bring him out into the open. What she did when he was here was nothing short of amazing."

"Of course," Riff said. "She's got more on the ball than all the rest of you put together."

He looked at Blake.

"No offense."

Blake nodded.

Jolie turned to me.

"This is where you come in," she said. "We need something out in the media that says Zombie maybe isn't so bad. That he came to the store clerk—"

"We're called associates, like Walmart," Sparrow said.

"Right. He came to you to apologize—make him seem like he has a human side. Make it more likely he'll show himself."

"But then he'll know she went to the police," I said.

"It won't come from us," Jolie said. "We'll make a statement saying this was all news to us."

Their eyes turned to me as I considered it.

"Sparrow said she trusts you," Jolie said.

"I don't have a news outlet. The *Times* dropped me after I found Raymond. Having a gun violated some policy."

I mulled it over as their eyes darted around the room.

"Dunne and her podcast," I said. "Big social media presence. Twitter, Instagram, TikTok."

"Would she put it out there?" Jolie said.

"Are you kidding? Like raw meat."

I looked to Sparrow.

"Sounds okay."

Then to Blake.

"I'm on leave," he said. "I could stay with her."

"Us, too," Jolie said.

"Dunne it is," I said.

"What have we got to lose?" Sanitas said. "We can't let this armed nut job just roam the streets."

"Her life," Riff said. "That's what you've got to lose, you fuck this up. I was in New York once, they put out an undercover cop, bait for this guy was stabbing male prostitutes. Gonna watch him. All wired up. Sure enough, the guy jumps the undercover, drags him into an alley in Alphabet City. Some screwup, cops get there, like, a minute later."

We waited.

"The guy goes to stab the cop but the cop has body armor on. They get wrestling, and the cop gets his gun out, shoots him dead."

"Happy ending," Sanitas said.

"Sparrow ain't a cop," Riff said.

"I am," Blake said.

"She's all I got," Riff said. "I lose her, you might as well take me out and shoot me."

"So do I call Dunne?" I said.

"Yes," Sparrow said.

"When do you want to meet her?" I said.

"Asap," Jolie said.

"This sucks," Riff said, looking to Sparrow. "We didn't go through all this so I end up—"

He caught himself. I watched Blake, stuck in a room with both sides represented. His police life, his love life. He looked at Sparrow. She nodded. He said, "Let's do it."

Dunne met me for coffee at Sit, her fancy café on Porto Street. She was in uniform: jeans tucked into heeled boots, an expensive-looking leather jacket. She brought the mugs to the table. Hers was frothy, a design etched in foam on top. Mine was black, some sort of roast. Like it mattered.

After she put the mugs down, she came around to my side of the booth, leaned down and gave me a hug on my pellet holes. I gritted my teeth.

"Good to see you, Jack," she said, into my ear. "I heard about you being shot. I practically had a heart attack."

"Thanks, I'm flattered."

"I'm so glad we're back together. It was just a matter of time."

We weren't, never had been. But if her social-media life could be based on some sort of fantasy, I guess the rest of her life could be, too. I explained the situation, her role. She snapped back to business.

"I'll use a photo, back to, add to the mystery. We'll take it in a store. I know somebody. Counter stuff in the background. Scratch tickets and all that. Maybe Photoshop a Zombie in the background."

"The softer side of the Zombie robber," I said.

"God, it's so good. He points a gun at her and falls in love. She hasn't exactly forgiven him but she gets him now. And she doesn't want him to be gunned down in cold blood."

And maybe he doesn't deserve to be, I thought. Maybe it's just a thirst for attention from a kid who never got any. Maybe he was bullied and this is his revenge. I thought of Rocky, my street kid in Portland, driven out of his own home by a jealous boyfriend, a weak mom. Then I caught myself. Was I getting soft? This guy was sticking a gun in people's faces. But still . . .

"You know they still consider him armed and dangerous," I said. "It's just that he's shown this sort of vulnerability. Maybe he needs a shrink in addition to jail."

"I don't think he's nuts. I think he has a mad crush."

"We can't make her look like bait."

"No, but she's sympathetic to him," Dunne said, "which is the twist. Like those people who forgive the person who murdered their mother or brother or whatever. I just saw that somewhere. This family went to prison and visited the murderer and they prayed together. I couldn't do it, but hey."

I thought of Sparrow, all her time with Raymond. Maybe she was asking herself, What would Jesus do? And what was wrong with that?

Dunne sipped her latte. Put the mug down. Her podcaster mind was whirring. "When?"

"She's working the overnight. Ten to six."

"Place will be staked out?"

"Yes, and Blake will be in the back room."

"We need to talk somewhere in the store. The sounds of the register in the background. Or maybe I record that separately."

"How soon can you put it out?"

"Teaser for social—I mean, photo and text? A couple of hours. Produced? I'll make it rough. More authentic. Tomorrow. This is guerrilla podcasting, baby. It'll go freakin' global. Cash money, Jack. You know HBO did a series based on Serial. Netflix, Amazon, Hulu. They're desperate for content. She held up air quotes: 'Pistol Whipped: A Love Story.' Based on the podcast by Stephanie Dunne and Jack McMorrow.' Or something like that."

My mind raced: Sophie six years from college. Savings going down, down, down. Strain's question: *So how do you make a living?* More than halfway to the finish line, Jack. Was it time to be a grown-up?

I shook it off, took a last sip, got up from my chair. I'd worked for the *New York Times*. Was I selling out?

"Where you going?" Dunne said.

"Home. Some stuff going on."

"Ah. I was kind of hoping we could go up to the studio. I'm sure there are other things we could come up with. If we put our—"

She paused, her mouth open, just a crack. There was foam on her upper lip. She licked it off.

"—heads together."

Dunne smiled.

"My offer stands. There's chemistry here, even if you don't want to admit it."

"I'll call you."

"You will?"

"After I talk to Sparrow and Blake."

"Ah."

Her expression moved from flirtation to business. A flick of some internal switch. She picked up her phone.

"I'll call my photo guy."

"Great."

She looked up at me. "TikTok slide-show text: 'How do you catch a Zombie robber? . . . With a sparrow.' "

Dunne was rolling, all of it coming so fast I could barely keep up. With Dunne, with the people swirling around me. Zombie. Jason. Nut jobs playing soldier. Marta and her bikers. Was this what Raymond had been escaping from? One thing about a house full of statues of Jesus, they all stood stock still.

I keep the truck in the garage with the door closed, beside my mom's Corolla. When I'm doing jobs, I rotate between the truck and the cars, my Civic and the Corolla. My friend Trevor has a cousin who has a buddy who's a Clarkston cop. She told the cousin that they canvass the area after every robbery, looking for cars that keep showing up.

Trevor moved to Las Vegas, which kind of sucked, since he's been my best friend since eighth grade, when we both got cut from the basketball team. We were way into video games and talked about designing one where you could walk into a school and shoot the asshole coach and the snot-faced players. At first it was supposed to happen in the gym during a game, but where was the challenge in that? Instead, we thought of having the shooter look for the players around the school or maybe the neighborhood. We also looked up the names of schools where you could learn how to design a video game, but by the time we were ready to think about college, we'd kind of forgotten about basketball, and the asshole coach had gotten fired by then anyway.

We both went to CMCC, a community college. Trevor signed up for machinist track, and I went for facilities maintenance because my uncle Reny ran all the buildings for a hospital in New Hampshire and made a ton of money. Uncle Reny got me a job there, but I left after six months, after this girl who was a custodian filed a complaint about me. All I said was she looked really good in leggings, just trying to make friends, but she got all pissed off and said I weirded her out and took away her "safe space." After that the women in the office wouldn't talk to me, and then my boss said I had to take some kind of training. Screw that. I came home.

My mom got disability because she hurt her wrist working in the mill before it closed. And she gets alimony now, so it isn't like she's on me to get a job. I think she likes having me around, even if I'm in my room a lot. I take out the trash, mow the lawn and shovel the driveway, play a lot of video games. Me and Trevor still text back and forth a lot and a couple of nights a week we play video games together.

Our favorite is Armed Robbery. *You rob banks, shoot security guards and regular people, the ones who pull guns and try to be the hero. Or they shoot you.*

The more banks you rob, the better guns you get. I have a short-barreled shotgun. Trevor has a machine pistol with a laser sight, but I usually beat him. That used to piss him off, but now he's totally mellow, since he started doing gummies. I play stone sober because it's training for Zombie. Like fighter pilots use simulators.

Me and Trevor have talked about Zombie and the robberies, but Trevor doesn't know it's me. The Zombie. *Trevor's a good guy, but when he's high, the dude's a blabbermouth. Can't chance it.*

What I'd really like to tell Trevor about is this chick Sparrow, the two of us not exactly successful when it comes to girls. The fact that I—or at least, Zombie—has a hot girl like her is so cool.

The problem is, I can't tell anybody, which is part of the reason I'm putting it down here. I mean, I can't tell Trevor how we met. And I can't just take her out for coffee or whatever, like she said.

And if I take the mask off, I'm just Carl, some guy who lives with his mother.

10

I drove one-handed thirty miles northeast, to Augusta, fought off the temptation to stop and see Jason, if only to put a gun on his head again. I pictured the round muzzle mark on his forehead, smiled. Caught myself as I felt the line blurring again.

Passing the bottle redemptions, shops that sold pizza and weed, I pressed on, crossed the ice-pocked Kennebec and continued east. Grown-over pastures, leafless sumac huddled in the snow, housing developments that never went beyond the now-faded sign posted at an unplowed road to nowhere. Places I'd been on the trail of someone. As I drove, their faces flashed by. Missy Hewett. Bobby Mullaney. Tammy and Rocky. Abram and Miriam. Mick and Vincent. Mennonites and mobsters. Some were alive, a few were dead.

I always got my story, for what that was worth.

I chased them off, like loitering ghosts. The road was more or less deserted now, most people off doing productive things, like real jobs. I drove fast, eased off when an oncoming trooper appeared, watched the mirror to see if the brake lights came on. They didn't and I hit the gas again, an urgency flowing through me, like if I let up, all of it—Jason, Zombie, Marta, Mr. Ziggy—would overwhelm me, and I'd go down in a knot of flailing fists and swirling lies.

What was true anymore? How would I know it when I saw it?

Halfway to Camden, I swung off the main road, headed south. The road was icy in the shade and the truck slid, the rear end waggling. I waited for it to settle, drove on, finally saw the landmark. A boulder in the woods. I started braking, turned off onto a gravel road, halfheartedly cleared.

There was a set of tracks, and I followed it, curious to see where it led. The twisting road wound through the woods, climbed a steep hill, then ended in a rough turnaround, trees bulldozed deeper in the forest, stumps left upturned like fallen giants.

The vehicle—a truck, judging by the width of the tracks—had made a half-circle, stopped and backed up. There was a McDonald's coffee cup on the ground, a brown stain like blood. No footprints.

I turned around, headed back, slowed at the entrance to a single-lane driveway. A heavy metal cable hung on hooks on a tree, the entrance left open. The truck tracks went past the entrance, continued down the road. I followed them back to the intersection, saw that they'd turned left, headed north. I pulled out, backed up, drove slowly back to the entrance to Louis's compound, put the truck in four-wheel drive, and turned in.

There was a single set of tracks showing under a couple of inches of fresher snow. I drove on, the drive swinging left and right, up and down, rumbled across a small bridge made of tree trunks and timbers that crossed a partially frozen stream, black open water showing where the current ran fastest.

Another half-mile in, there was a second bridge over a smaller stream, and then the driveway snaked to the left, leading to a quarter-mile straightaway that ended at a log cabin. Louis's Jeep was parked to the side. There was smoke coming from the stone chimney. I drove up, parked, watched for a minute. Nobody showed. I looked left and right. There was a four-wheeler inside the shelter of a pole barn, tracks leading in and out. I glanced at the mirrors, half expecting Louis to come up from behind me. Nothing. I bent and took my gun out from under the seat, slipped into my jacket. Watched. Listened. Still nothing.

I popped the door, waited a moment, then pushed it open and got out. I shut the door, took a step toward the front porch. Heard a low growl. Stopped and turned back, slowly. Louis's dog, Friend, was standing five feet from me, his big head level with my chest.

"Hey, Friend," I said softly.

He took a step forward, growled again. No teeth showing, just 130 pounds of wolfhound, with some Lab thrown in for good measure.

"It's Jack. Long time no see."

He walked around me, a creeping sort of step, came between me and the house and turned and took up his guard position.

"Good dog," I said.

Another growl, this time a glimpse of canines fit for a lion. I wondered if Louis was home or out in the woods, how long this standoff would last.

The door opened and Louis stepped out, gave a quick whistle, said "Down."

Friend relaxed, moved to me and sniffed, his tail wagging. I scratched behind his ears. My right hand.

"I missed you, too," I said.

Louis whistled again, and the dog bounded up the steps and into the house.

"Sorry about that," Louis said. "He's a little on edge. He knows when it's time to take it up a notch or two."

"How many notches does he have?" I said, stepping up onto the porch.

"Quite a few. Some I've never seen, I have a feeling."

"This could be the time?"

"Hard to say," Louis said. "Prepare for the worst, hope for the best."

He was wearing a black ball cap, camo jacket, black jeans and boots, all very military. I thought of the militia in the gravel pit, figured from a distance they'd look kind of the same. Not up close.

Louis's eyes had the unblinking intensity I'd seen when he was in combat mode, like he was here with the rest of us but had different orders that he couldn't disclose. He shook my hand, looked out at the drive, the woods.

"See the cameras on the way in?"

"No," I said.

"Good," Louis said. He turned and I followed him inside.

It was warm, the dog already lying in front of the woodstove, his watchful eyes still on me. The boxes from Clair's barn were on the floor. Next to the boxes was a table, scopes and binoculars set out, boxes of ammunition, three handguns. There was a drone, too, a high-tech-looking thing like a miniature stealth bomber. Next to the table was a gun rack, a half-dozen rifles and shotguns lined up. I was surprised he hadn't cut openings in the walls of the cabin to shoot through. Yet.

"I saw Marta," I said.

"How's she doing?"

"Better. She said she's over the worst of it."

"Good."

"Clair said she's coming down here."

"Yes. Way easier to defend."

"I agree. And, no offense, but it makes me nervous having her around. Roxanne and Sophie."

"I understand. We don't want collateral damage."

"No," I said. "And that includes Mary. And Clair."

He'd picked up a scope, moved to the rack and took down an assault rifle. He fitted the scope and it snapped into place. He aimed it at the wall, looked through, swung it toward the stove.

"Thermal works slick," Louis said. "Great resolution."

He put the gun back, picked out a short-barreled shotgun.

"Like you never left Iraq," I said.

He snapped the shotgun slide in and out.

"Some ways I haven't."

"The war never ends?"

"Just go on to the next operation is all. And now I'm in charge."

"Is she worth it?"

His jaw clamped.

"I heard you've got this girl, a store clerk in Clarkston. You've gone to bat for her."

"That's right."

"Why's that?"

"She's a good person. I like her."

"If somebody hurt her, what would you do?"

I thought about it. "I don't know. Hurt them back."

"I don't just like Marta. I love her. It used to be I killed people because I was ordered to. I didn't even know them. It was just war. This is a no-brainer."

Another rifle, a lever-action that looked like a blacked-out Winchester. Another scope slid into place.

"I get that," I said. "I just don't want you taking Clair down with you. He's doing this for you."

"And I'd do the same for him."

He was silent for a moment.

"And for you, McMorrow."

I thought of Jason, my shooter.

Louis's phone beeped. He took it out of his jacket, looked at the screen. Smiled and held it up to me.

There was a video running, a pickup truck approaching the driveway. It drove past the entrance, toward the dead end and the turnaround.

"Once, maybe you're lost," Louis said. "Twice, you've got a problem. Same truck came through this morning, a little after seven."

I thought of our locals, parked in the woods.

"Maybe just looking for a place to do drugs," I said.

Louis shook his head. "In Iraq, you developed this sixth sense. Or you didn't. Some guys got killed, not thinking the guy with the bag of groceries had a bomb. Some guys went around just lighting everybody up."

He took a shotgun from the rack, started feeding shells into the magazine. I glanced at the box: double-aught buck. A big hole.

"Time to saddle up," Louis said, and he started for the door. The dog was on his heels.

I followed the dog, thinking I'd been about to say that Marta wasn't Clair's problem and now it appeared she was becoming mine.

Louis and Friend climbed into the Jeep, a jacked-up Cherokee with oversized tires. I got into my truck and we rumbled out of the compound like we were going on patrol in Fallujah. Louis had set his phone on a stand on the dashboard and I could see the light of the video. He drove slowly and deliberately, took a left at the road and stopped. My phone buzzed. I took it out, put it on speaker, and set it on the seat.

"Yeah."

"Just need you for some blocking action," Louis said. "I'll go in first, faster than they expect. You hang back and park sideways."

"You need me to go with you when you talk to them?"

"May not be doing much talking."

He started off and I followed. We followed the new tracks, the road winding between the walls of woods. The phone was on and I could hear the dog starting to whine. And then the road straightened, and we saw the truck coming toward us. It was a new GMC three-quarter-ton, seventy thousand dollars' worth of pickup. Massachusetts plate. They'd sent the locals to Clair's house.

Closer, we could see a guy in the driver's seat. Beard. Ball cap. I slowed, turned sideways and parked. Louis drove toward the pickup and they both stopped, head-to-head. I felt the outline of the Glock in my pocket, watched.

Louis got out of the Jeep, shotgun in his right hand, phone in the other. The dog followed and in ten steps they were at the driver's door. I got out, slipped the gun from my jacket pocket, started toward them, like I was sliding down an icy slope. Louis shouted, "Hands on the wheel," and yanked the driver's door open, pointed the shotgun. I heard the other guy say, "What the fuck?" like he wasn't sure if maybe we were cops, undercover DEA.

He was big, heavy-set, thick-necked, tattoos peeking out from the neck of a heavy black parka, like it was below zero. I was ten feet away, saw Louis lean in, shotgun still pointed. He came out with a handgun, held it out toward me. I took it. Stuffed it in my jacket pocket.

"What the hell is this?" the guy said.

Louis held his phone out. "You got a problem, call 911," he said. "Tell them you're being held at gunpoint."

The guy didn't move.

"Go ahead," Louis said.

"You out of your fucking mind?" the guy said.

"I'll call then," Louis said. "It'll take a while, but they'll get here eventually."

"I was just leaving," the guy said. "Got lost. Didn't know the road didn't go through."

"You knew that the first time you drove in."

The guy didn't answer. Louis stood there, the shotgun still pointed, like he was giving the guy another try. "How's Snake?"

The guy hesitated, just long enough, before he said, "Don't know what you're talking about."

"Wrong answer," Louis said, and he lifted the shotgun so it was pointed at the guy's face.

"Just doing what I'm told," the guy said.

"Problem is, you suck at it," Louis said.

I thought of a conversation with Clair, him saying the ideal Force Recon mission for him was dropping in, getting the intel, slipping out undetected. It isn't intel, he said, if the bad guys know you have it.

"See if you're better at this," Louis said. "Bring this message to your club, and all the way back to Snake up there in Canada. She stays here. And from now on, this road is one-way, with no way out. I've got six hundred acres of graveyard."

The guy's eyes narrowed.

"Your choice. Your funeral," the guy said, shrugging.

"Yes," Louis said. "It is."

He lowered the gun, stepped back from the door, and the dog moved up, staring like he'd locked on a bird. Louis strode to the back of the truck, turned. A muffled boom and thwack that echoed through the trees. The guy flinched but stayed in the cab. The dog stayed locked in. Louis walked back, said, "Just so you don't forget me." Swung the door shut and slammed the shotgun butt into the driver's window. It spidered in place. The guy stared straight ahead.

Louis walked back to the Jeep, the dog on his heels. They climbed in and I walked to my truck and did the same. I still had the guy's gun. I took it out of my jacket pocket. It was stainless with a wooden grip. Expensive. Maybe it came with the truck. The Sig Sauer Edition.

I put it on the passenger seat, then did a three-point turn and headed back out, the Jeep behind me. Turning into the driveway, I looked back and saw the Jeep slow and then back in, stop. Louis and the dog got out. Taking the guy's gun with me, I did the same, walked up to them. We stood and waited, and in a minute, maybe two, the truck rounded the curve and came toward us.

Louis stepped into the middle of the path, the shotgun held low at his side.

The truck slowed and stopped six feet in front him. The guy stared stolidly.

Louis said, "You can give him his gun back. He doesn't have authority to shoot us."

I took the gun out, held it by the barrel as I approached the passenger side. The window buzzed down, and I stepped closer, tossed the gun onto the seat. The window went back up and Louis and the dog stepped aside. The truck rolled past, the sound of crunching snow reverberating in the silent woods. Where the M in GMC had been, there was a baseball-size hole.

It was quiet again. A breeze puffed up and snow fell from the tree limbs above us. The dog went to the base of a tree and sniffed, found the scent of something or someone. He looked at Louis and Louis said, "Okay," and the dog bounded into the trees.

"Nothing gets past him?" I said.

"Not much," Louis said. "Best thing is he knows the difference between a human and a deer."

"And reacts accordingly?"

"A deer is fun. A human is when you go to work."

"So that was a deer?"

"Yeah. You could tell by his expression."

We stood, Louis still holding the shotgun, now cradled across his chest. He was comfortable with it, like some people would be holding a walking stick.

"Thanks," Louis said.

"Anytime."

A pause, and I said, "What's your point, goading them like that?"

"Accomplishes two things. I figure they'll come one way or the other. If that's a given, it's better for them to be angry. True in Iraq. When the enemy is most pissed off is when they're most vulnerable. Emotion clouds judgment. You're more likely to go off plan, make a mistake."

Echoes of Clair. I could see why they'd become close, why I was always on the outside looking in.

"What's the second thing?" I said.

"I wanted to give them a warning. That way, when and if it starts going down, they know what they are getting themselves into. It's off my conscience."

I thought about it, the cold calculation of a professional soldier versus the potential machismo of a bunch of biker drug dealers.

"What about *your* emotions?" I said. "What they did to Marta? What they'll do if they get her back?"

He thought for a moment. "Ideally, emotion leads to resolve, which leads to a sound plan, which leads to efficient execution."

I was in class at the Louis Longfellow War College, on a back road in Sanctuary, Maine.

"Of the plan, or them?"

"Both, if that's the way they want it," Louis said.

Stark, his words and the place. We looked down the road, which was empty and cold, a gray-white path between the dark-shouldered trees. With Louis and Clair, all the high-tech stuff, this place could become a no-man's-land for the invaders. Or not. It would only take one lucky shot.

Louis turned toward the woods, whistled. We heard branches snapping somewhere in there, the dog returning.

"Speaking of emotion. You and your shooter," he said. "I get the feeling you want this guy for yourself. No interlopers."

"Yes."

"Because he threatened your family. Came at you at your house."

I nodded. "Yup. Crossed the line."

"The shooter, or the guy pulling the strings?"

"Both."

"What's your plan then?"

I told him about the phone. The names and numbers on the Signal account. The truck at the pit. The plate number.

"I'll find him. I'll know his voice," I said.

"And then what?"

I didn't answer because I didn't know.

"Always good to know the endgame," Louis said.

"What's yours?" I said.

He flashed a rueful sort of smile.

"Live happily ever after," he said, and he turned away as the dog bounded out of the woods.

11

My phone buzzed.

—'22 Dodge Ram blk.
—Roger T. Geberth 639 Belfast Rd. Rosemont.
Thanks, I replied, adding Good luck.
—You too.

Rosemont. A small town between Sanctuary and Prosperity. I was in Appleton, five miles out of Sanctuary, headed home. Rosemont was on the way, ten miles to the north.

Some things are meant to be.

It was a prosperous little place, the nineteenth-century village nestled in a hollow near a confluence of two tumbling streams. I remembered a general store with a front porch where the townspeople sat over coffee and socialized. Years earlier, I'd pulled in to get Sophie ice cream, headed home from somewhere to the south. I remembered Sophie, no more than four, saying she liked this place because everyone was smiling.

Maybe not everyone.

I parked on the road shoulder, motor running, and looked at my watch: a little after three. Enough time and daylight left to check out this Geberth guy, and still make it home. Knock wood.

I googled him. President, Geberth Concrete Products, Thomaston, Maine. I googled the company. They made septic tanks, among other concrete things. I typed the address into the old-school Garmin suction-cupped to my windshield. Pressed go. The screen showed my destination halfway between Rosemont and Route 3, the main east–west road. Nine miles. Fifteen minutes. I pulled out, hit the gas.

I slowed as I descended the hill into the center of the pretty town, passed the store, lights glowing in the dim light of the winter afternoon, continued on through. The pink-striped route on the screen took me out of the town center, the road swinging to the northeast. There were woods on both sides punctuated by an occasional house. A farm, the big colonial house fronted by giant maples. The barn was straight, shingles new. The driveway in lined with a new cedar fence.

A couple of more houses, new and neat, the seep of out-of-state prosperity moving inland from the coast, ten miles to the east. I slowed as the distance ticked down. A half-mile. A thousand feet. Destination (the home of Jason's dirtbag caretaker) on the left.

I rolled past.

The house was on a knoll, set back and overlooking waves of lawn, now blanketed in snow. It was a big contemporary place, two stories, sided in blue, a screened porch on one end, and a spacious attached garage on the other. There was a Betsy Ross flag, with its circle of thirteen stars, flying from a pole on the north-side lawn. There was a barn off to the left, two shiny black horses eating hay from a feeder on the wall to the left of the door. The horses wore matching red jackets, like twins whose mother had dressed them alike for school.

I drove on, turned at the next driveway, and took another pass.

There were lights in the house and the barn, and from this angle, I could see cars parked in the open garage bays: a big SUV, a small convertible that could have been a Miata. No black Dodge.

I circled one more time, drove back and into the driveway and up to the house. I put on my Smithsonian flag hat, parked by the garage, shut off the motor. Walked around the front of the garage, up the steps to a landing in front of a side door.

Small dogs barked from inside the house as I approached, and a motion-triggered light went on above the door. The inner door opened. A woman stood behind the storm door, two small black-and-white dogs jumping and banging off the glass. She was in her forties, blonde hair tied back, jeans, red fleece vest, and tall brown leather boots.

"Will you just be quiet for once," she said to the dogs as she nudged them back with a boot. When she looked up, I smiled. Through the window, she said, "May I help you?"

She was pretty in a made-up sort of way. Some sort of cosmetic work had given her a frozen startled expression, which seemed appropriate for this moment.

"Hi there," I said. "I'm Jack. Roger around?"

The dogs continued to yap, standing on their hind legs, paws against the door.

"Are you a friend of his?" she said.

"We know each other from the farm, in Prosperity. Jason's place."

An *Ah* of recognition. Another of Roger's buddies.

"He's in the barn," she said, "but we have basketball. Our daughter plays. There isn't another meeting, is there?"

Impatience, then a smile to smooth it over. "I know how you boys can get talking."

I gave her a quick chuckle, said, "No, I just need to talk to him about Jason. I saw him this morning."

A look of concern. "How is he doing?"

"Good, considering," I said. "You know Jason."

She nodded. One dog flopped down and walked away.

"You can just walk back," she said.

I smiled, touched the bill of my cap, tried not to wince when the pain jolted my shoulder. I turned and went down the steps, walked back along the path. Touched the gun in my waistband more out of habit than need.

Around the end of the garage, and then across the snow-cleared turnaround to where the driveway headed for the barn. There were big mounds of snow, and then I saw the John Deere tractor used to make them. It was parked by a closed garage bay on the back side of the barn. Next to it was the black Dodge Ram.

Voices inside the barn. Not a conversation. A radio voice. Someone saying, "We didn't come from some shithole. We're here, we've always been here. We're rising up to say there is something terribly wrong with this country. And we're not going to be led. We are not sheep. We are the true patriots, descended directly from the people who—"

A podcast.

There was a door beside the garage bay, I knocked and pushed it open.

It was a big open space. A smaller tractor, a four-wheeler, and a shiny black Harley with matching saddlebags were parked in a line. I stepped in, looked to my right. A woodstove was going, a stack of wood half gone. There was a yellow Gadsden flag hanging on the wall, the coiled snake and Don't Tread on Me. Below the flag there was a table, and on the table were a phone, an American flag coffee mug, and a handgun in a holster. The radio voice was coming from speakers hung from the ceiling in the corners of the room. The guy was telling me not to kid myself; the US government was a malevolent regime. A corrupt enterprise. Selling America out to the global power elite.

I called, "Hey, Roger. You around?"

There were big barn doors on the far side of the room, and I heard a shovel scraping beyond them. I moved to the center of the room, called again. The scraping stopped. I waited. One of the doors rolled open and Roger came through, holding the shovel. He was tallish, lean and broad across the top, like a wide receiver. Tan Carhartt jacket, jeans, dark green barn boots, Chameau tag on the front. Five hundred bucks. The uniform of a prosperous gentleman farmer. His hair was sandy brown under a ball cap that said USA in gold lettering, and he had stylish stubble. Roger was a good-looking guy, a match for the woman at the door.

"Roger," I said.

He looked at me, said, "Have we met?"

We hadn't. His wasn't the voice.

"No," I said. "But we have a mutual acquaintance. Jason. I talked to him today."

He turned and leaned the shovel against the wall. Turned back. "That right?" he said.

"I'm Jack McMorrow. I'm the reporter, the one who was in the fight that got Jason locked up. Except now he isn't."

Roger gave me a long look, then walked to the table with the gun. He reached toward it but picked up the phone instead, turned off the podcast. The room went silent. Somewhere beyond the sliding doors, a horse snorted.

Roger turned back to me and I moved closer. He crossed his arms, said, "You've got two minutes."

"Somebody came to my house three nights ago, where I live with my wife and daughter, and tossed a bottle of gasoline onto the deck, with a lighted wick. Fire didn't amount to much. But when I went outside, they shot me with a shotgun."

He looked at me more closely.

"You look okay."

"Birdshot," I said.

"Lucky for you," Roger said.

"Very. But that person also put the gun on me when I was down. Said if it were up to them, they'd kill me."

"Oh."

"So I guess it wasn't. Up to them, I mean. And maybe it wasn't supposed to be an execution, but if the fire had caught, who knows?"

"I'm glad it didn't. But your two minutes is almost up."

I smiled.

"You may have to front me a minute or two."

"What if I don't want to?"

"Then you'll have to try to throw me out. That could take a lot longer than hearing me out."

He waited, the clock ticking.

"You were at the pit last night. I was, too. Those were my footprints you saw. That was me following you after you pulled out."

No answer. His arms tightened across his chest.

"The Patriot Legion. I didn't really have anything against it until recently. When I was a kid, we liked playing soldier, too. Crawling through the shrubbery with toy guns, jumping over fences. I get it. It gets you out of the house, and the guns make a great big boom. Good times. And there's plenty out there to get mad about, I agree."

A horse snorted again, kicked against the boards of a stall. Roger stood straight. The Patriot Legion must have worked on posture.

"But I'm thinking somebody gave the order to shut me up, if not take me out. *New York Times*, liberal mainstream media. My wife used to work for the State. DHHS. For Jason, at least, that was a sore point."

Roger took a deep breath, then exhaled slowly. I was trying his patience. Good.

"The problem is, I'm not seeing Jason as having much leadership ability. Not very smart, out of shape, carries a silly gun. Too many Dirty Harry movies is my guess. And he's a sloppy, nasty drunk. All you need is police coming to a domestic complaint, right?"

I paused.

"So I ask myself, what does he bring to the party?"

Roger pressed his lips together. Biting his tongue? Fighting off the urge to grab the gun out of the holster, march me out?

"Come on, Roger. Stick with me here. You have the gravel pit way out in the woods, far from the road. This is Maine. You could shoot howitzers out there and nobody would complain."

I smiled.

"If you're just using Jason for his girlfriend's property, and he doesn't rank highly in your organization, then who authorized the shooter to come out to my place? Who decided I had the ATF on speed dial? Who wanted to warn me to back off? If it was just personal, Jason pissed off because I got him arrested, he'd probably just try to have me beat up."

Roger stood still but his jaw was moving, teeth starting to grind. The horse shifted, hooves on boards. My time running out.

"No, I'm wondering if maybe it was you all. Maybe Jason played up what a potential threat we were, me pumping his girlfriend's kid for information. My wife telling his girlfriend to dump the bum, kick his buddies out. Jason brings it up at a meeting with the rest of the group. It goes up the ladder to your level, the colonels and four-star generals, whatever rank you toy soldiers give yourselves."

I paused, gave him time to say something. He didn't.

"And then somebody tries to burn my house down."

Another pause.

"And then that guy shoots me. I mean, birdshot—but still. Could put your eye out, as my mother used to say."

I turned, looked around the room.

"Nice spread, Roger. You must be turning out those septic tanks. Anyway, I'll let you go, get to your basketball game. But remember this: If I'm right, then I'm gonna find who sent that shooter to my house. And I'm gonna find the shooter, too. And if it was your Patriot Legion outfit, then I'm gonna bring this whole play army down."

Roger gathered himself up, like he wanted to go out on top.

"I've heard you out. Now my turn."

I nodded.

"The Patriot Legion isn't in the business of shooting civilians. Or burning down their houses. Or being any kind of threat to anything or anyone that isn't part of or in active support of illegitimate government. Some people might say the liberal media is part of the fraud being perpetrated on the American people, but we don't go that far. We're a paramilitary organization, not terrorists."

"Some people might disagree with that."

"Patrick Henry was called a terrorist."

His voice raised now.

"John Adams. Paul Revere and George Washington. All the heroes at Bunker Hill who had the courage to stand up to tyrants and demand their rights. Which is what we're doing now. Standing up to a corrupt, tyrannical government that is plundering this country, getting rich on the backs of people like you and me."

Not the first time he'd given this recruiting speech. I'd found the top dog.

Geberth paused, like he needed to get his heart rate down.

"Time for you to go," he said.

"Sure, and thanks for the trip down the Freedom Trail. But here's the deal. I'm going to leave you my number. If you have information—the shooter, who sent him—call me, just between us. I'll take it from there. I don't hear from you in, let's say, twenty-four hours, I just tell my whole story to the cops. They can sort you out."

He looked at me.

"What the hell kind of reporter are you?" he said.

"Freelance," I said.

I reached into my pocket for my wallet, which moved him a step toward the table, one eye on the holstered gun. I took out a business card, the one that had Jack McMorrow on one side, my number on the other. I moved to the table, too, laid it down. Nodding to him, I turned and started for the door. When I opened the door, looked back, he'd picked up his phone.

"Jason may have been right about one thing," I said. "I do have the ATF on speed dial, or at least in my contacts. Agent-in-charge in Portland. Her name's McGuire. Haven't talked to her in a while, but maybe I'll call, catch her up."

I walked out of the barnyard, past the garage.

Mrs. Roger was sitting in the SUV, the motor running. The dogs barked from the back as I strode past. She beeped the horn. Roger was being summoned.

Out of the driveway, I turned north. A quarter-mile up the road there was a half-plowed driveway to an old mobile home. The trailer was dark. There were no fresh tracks. The truck parked by the door was covered with snow. I pulled in, drove up to the house, turned around. Twenty feet from the road, I turned the lights off, sat with the motor running. Took Jason's phone from the console, powered it on, and opened the Signal app.

Already two messages in the group called Level 1:

STRYKER: CODE YELLOW. REPORTER WAS HERE.

NOMAD: Got it.
BLACKHAWK: Same one?
STRYKER: Affirmative.
SNIPER: Is Rebel on?
STRYKER: It appears negative.
CRISPUS: I predicted trouble.
SNIPER: Pilgrim on?
STRYKER: Negative. Can explain.

I looked at the phone. Was Jason's code name Pilgrim? How would I know until I sent a message? I went to the contacts, and there was no Pilgrim on the list. The conversation had continued.

SNIPER: House arrest.
CRISPUS: Went rogue.
STRYKER: Maybe take that offline.
BAZOOKAJOE: What's he want?
STRYKER: Perp's name. In 24 hours.
CRISPUS: Same guy as at the location?
STRYKER: Affirmative. Says he knows Portland ATF.
P.REVERE: Fuck.
HORSEMAN: Just coming in here. Sounds like L2 discussion.
STRYKER: Will arrange. 2200 hours. Offline until then.
HORSEMAN: Roger that.
CRISPUS: Saw this coming.
SNIPER: Liability. Like I kept saying, there were other locations. This is fucking Maine.
STRYKER: Snuff it.

Sniper did. Pilgrim (Jason?) didn't join the chat, maybe not risking it while in custody? Rebel (the shooter?) was also AWOL. Warned to stay away by Jason?

Sitting in the truck, phone glowing, I took screenshots of the Signal messages. Looked up to see an SUV approach, sat back in the shadows as it passed. A glimpse: Roger in the passenger seat looking straight ahead, his wife gesticulating as she drove. Their taillights dwindled in the distance and then disappeared, leaving me alone in the darkness.

The game was on.

I got home a little after five, drove past the house to see that Roxanne and Sophie were still out. That was good. Shopping for clothes was as safe as it got. Sophie with a phone, not so much.

Continuing down the road, I pulled into Clair's driveway, saw lights on in the barn, smoke spiraling up from the chimney. I drove past the house, parked next to Clair's truck. Got out and walked to the door. Opened it and heard nothing, no music.

I closed the door and walked into the shop. Clair was sitting on a stool with a socket wrench in his hand. His smaller Farmall tractor was on a wheel stand, a front wheel off. The room smelled of woodsmoke, grease, and diesel.

"No Vivaldi?" I said.

"You're just disappointed because it's the only classical music you recognize."

"That, and it's awfully quiet in here."

"The better to hear them coming," Clair said.

I looked to the small tool chest rolled up beside him. Wrenches, pliers, a handgun.

"That new?" I said.

He glanced over.

"To me. Kimber forty-five. It's a Shadow Ghost. Very light."

"Nice. Where'd you get it?"

"Louis. For going to Montreal."

"And returning with the package," I said.

He turned back to the wheel, lifted it onto the lugs and jiggled it into place. Picked up the wrench and threaded a nut on.

"I saw him."

"I heard."

"Louis sent the guy home with a big hole in the back of his new truck."

"Heard that, too."

I leaned down and picked the gun up. It was very balanced, felt expensive.

"Why do you think they'd send locals up here, and Louis gets a muscled-up guy in a shiny truck with Mass. plates? Might as well have been waving a flag."

Clair was on the second nut, cranking it tight.

"Because she was here," he said, without looking up. "I think they knew it. Our guys were supposed to do an initial covert drive-by, report back on the layout, whether they'd seen Marta. The guy at Louis's, he was there to send a message. 'We know where you live.' "

"When is she going down there?"

"Soon as I'm done here."

I put the gun down, walked over.

"What's the plan?"

"Louis drives out, sits on the end of the road. I drive her over, have her down behind the seats. I drive in. If it's clear, he follows, a rear-guard. He does the same at the entrance road. I go in first, he waits, then follows. I leave Marta there, head home. Louis digs in for a while, I stay close to home, like she might still be here. I'm available when he needs a flanker. Other than the dog, of course."

This was military Clair, brought back to the fore by military Louis. Old soldiers don't die, they regroup.

"When, not if?"

"Bikers are like soldiers," Clair said. "Wild Ones, Plunderers— they're all the same. A lot of them have been in the military at some point, have a strong sense of hierarchy and duty. And loyalty and pride. They'll avenge a slight at all costs. Back in the day, my Third Force guys would take on a whole bar if they felt insulted. I remember one time, R-and-R at Vung Tau. Mostly Aussie Army, and one of them said something belittling about Recon. Easier to hide in the jungle than really fight. Something like that. We left the place like a bomb had hit it. Aussie MPs had to call for backup."

He paused, gave the nut a last crank.

"That hole in the truck will draw them out," Clair said.

I thought of a movie I'd seen, an Apache fighter riding right up to a line of rifle-toting cavalry, armed with only a spear. He flipped them off in some Apache way, and turned and rode off, and they chased him into an ambush.

Clair threaded another nut on, started cranking it down.

"I think I just did the same thing," I said. Not exactly the same, but hadn't I just baited the hook?

I told him about Jason's phone, the truck at the pit, my conversations with Roger. By the time I finished, he was on to the last lug nut.

"What's your sense?" Clair said.

"The texts said somebody—I'm thinking Jason and one other—did go rogue. I'm thinking that for Roger, it wasn't a total surprise. It was like one of them had proposed it but the idea had been shot down. My guess is Roger pictures something more like sending the boys to march on the State House, carrying guns, waving flags."

"Or taking the governor hostage?"

"He has a pretty nice spread, wife and daughter. A lot to lose."

I recounted Tara saying Jason said the group was a consortium.

"Maybe they aren't entirely under this guy's control," Clair said.

He finished the last lug nut, gave the wheel a tug. Leaned down and pumped the hydraulic jack to take the axle off the wheel stand. Then he slid the stand out, lowered the jack, and the tractor eased back onto the floor. Came back wiping his hands on a rag.

"There," he said. "At least something got done around here today."

Clair put the wrenches back in the drawer of the tool chest, picked the gun up, slipped it under his jacket. A holster at his waistband. He turned to me.

"Twenty-four hours," he said. "What was your thinking there?"

"It just sort of popped out. I like deadlines."

"This Roger may think you have more of a plan."

"He seemed like the kind of guy likes to have everything spelled out."

Clair smiled.

"I think he'll have it spelled out, all right. So we have to be ready for him to either cough them up or decide you're a risk that needs to be taken care of."

"We."

"Of course," Clair said.

"You must feel like you have a lot of balls in the air," I said.

"We," he said. "I figure I'll leave around eight."

"I'll keep watch on Mary, the house. They won't know Marta's been moved."

He walked over to the stove, opened the door, and put in a big chunk of oak. Closed the door and turned the damper down. We walked to the door and killed the lights, stepped outside.

"It's a two-front war, Jack," Clair said, as I got into my truck.

"No problem," I said, pulling myself up into the seat. "I used to be pretty good working with multiple deadlines, having two or three stories going at once."

"Somebody shows up, just interview the bejeezus out of them. I'll be back by nine or so."

I started the motor, sat, and waited as Clair got into his big Ford. He backed it up to the house, then turned it in so it was hidden from the road. The house was dark and the back door suddenly swung open. Mary came out, stood on the landing, and called something to Clair. He replied and she went back inside, came out with a black duffel. He got out of the cab, walked up the steps, took it, and put it in the bed of the truck.

I pulled up, truck lights out, blocked the view from the road. Mary, still on the landing, stepped aside and Marta came out.

She was wearing a puffy, oversized, hooded parka. It was winter camo, a shapeless thing that shrouded her head to knees. She looked like a monk, her face barely visible under the hood.

I held the passenger door open, took her arm as she climbed in behind the seats, butt first, and sat on the floor.

"Bye, Jack," she said, in her Eastern European accent, and there was something haunting and final about it.

"Take care," I said, and she laid back, out of sight.

Clair climbed into the cab, grunting softly as he hoisted himself up. The truck pulled away, rolled down the drive, and out onto the road.

Mary looked at me, shook her head.

"Good-bye and good luck," she said.

"Yes."

"I just want my husband back."

"You and me both," I said, and our eyes met for a moment in understanding before she turned, walked back into the house, and turned on the kitchen light.

12

Roxanne was unwrapping sandwiches, putting them on plates. Sophie was sitting at the kitchen table, texting. Roxanne had a glass of white wine going already. She said, "Hey there."

"Dad, I'll be right with you," Sophie said, not looking up.

"How'd you do?" I asked Roxanne.

"Good."

Sophie said, "It was a lot of money, Dad, but you pay it off every month with your phone bill."

"Fine," I said. "Now I can call you whenever I want."

She said, "Lame, Dad."

Roxanne glanced at her, mouthed silently to me: "She loves it."

I smiled, looked over at Sophie, bent in concentration, only her texting fingers and the top of the fedora showing. I almost asked who she was texting, then thought better.

Roxanne took a deep breath, let out a long, silent sigh. She looked at me and I nodded. We'd crossed a line, Sophie connected to the big world.

"I got you beer," Roxanne said. "They didn't have Ballantine so I got Lake St. George. Some sort of IPA. Is that okay?"

Ballantine, more and more a thing of the past. Like me.

"Great. Thanks."

I went to the counter, gave her a quick hug, took a can from the pack, opened it. Took a long swallow. Roxanne put the sandwiches on the table, came back and picked up her wineglass. Sipped.

"How was your day?" she said.

Marta and her update. The missing money, working in a brothel. Me and Clair and the local stoners, or maybe they weren't. Strain and his doubts about my credulity. Sparrow and Zombie, setting out the bait. Dunne and the podcast, the offer for more. Louis and his intruder. Rosemont and Geberth. The Signal messages flying. Marta smuggled out in a big gray coat.

"Busy," I said.

She looked at me. "You can tell me about it later." No choice offered.

Sophie finally looked up from her phone, slid off her chair, and came over and gave me a hug. She held the phone up. The screen photo was Pokey, his best Instagram pose.

"It's a fourteen. It's amazing."

"Pokey never looked better."

"The camera is amazing and it can play back, like, twenty-six hours of videos."

"Oh, boy."

"And watch this, Dad."

She held the phone up to her face, then turned it to me. It had opened.

"Face ID."

"Cool. Were you texting Tara to tell her about it?"

"No, I called her from the car. That was Mr. Ziggy. We had to talk about costumes and lines and stuff."

"He has your number already?" I thought, this guy can call her? And we don't know what they're saying? And since when did teachers have students' phone numbers?

"Tara must have given it to him after I called her. He said he has a fourteen, too, and he thinks it's awesome."

"Huh."

Was this how he cut them out of the herd? Was he after Sophie, or was she just a way to get to Tara? Or was I imagining all of it, Mr. Ziggy an enthusiastic theater guy, nothing more?

I sipped the IPA. The phone tinkled.

"I need a better text tone. That came with it. I want Taylor Swift."

She looked at the text, said, "Sorry. Tara wants me to call her."

"Dinner's ready."

"I'm not really hungry yet, Mom. That was a massive lunch," Sophie said, and she dashed down the hall and up the stairs.

"I guess we'd better get used to it," I said. "But I still want family dinners. Phones off. And the whole thing, it still makes me nervous. There are a lot of sickos out there."

"I know. I've been looking at parental controls. You can get these apps that let you monitor what they're seeing. Texts and stuff online."

"She'll balk, big-time."

"I already prepped her. The condition for her having the thing at all," Roxanne said.

"How was she?"

"Not thrilled but realistic. She knows we've granted her this privilege. We can take it away."

I looked at her.

"Would you?"

"If it turns into some social media mean-girl thing? If she starts acting like she's seventeen, not twelve? In a heartbeat."

Roxanne went to the table and sat. I did, too, setting my beer down. The sandwiches were turkey with tomato and pesto, on baguettes. I took one, began to eat. Roxanne cut a sandwich in half.

"Mr. Ziggy texted her?" I said.

"I know."

"Doesn't this guy know about boundaries?"

Roxanne was chewing. She swallowed, touched her mouth with her napkin. I waited.

"It may be totally innocent. This is how kids communicate. I mean, he's not gonna e-mail her. It's texts. Snapchat."

"But—"

"I know," she said. "If it isn't innocent, this is how it begins. A separate channel to communicate with the child directly, excluding parents and even other kids. Talk about costumes. Then photos. Maybe in the costume."

"Or part of it," I said. "He gave Tara a feather boa."

Roxanne was holding her sandwich. She started to take a bite, put it down.

"Can you find out—"

"Whether he has a record?" I said.

"Yes."

"Don't schools do background checks?"

"Sure, but maybe somehow he slipped through the cracks. Maybe ask Brandon, maybe through his police contacts? Probably he's just fine, but—"

"He's moved around a lot," I said.

"And he hangs out with young girls. I know it's the theater thing, so it's part of his job. And the kids love him. But—"

"The buts are adding up."

We both took a bite of sandwich.

"I don't want to burst this bubble for Tara," Roxanne said.

"Better than having it blow up in her face."

"Yes," she said.

A long pause, the potential outcomes rising to the surface. Confronting Mr. Ziggy. Explaining it all to the girls. Tara crushed.

"So what did you do all day?" Roxanne said.

I took a big bite, stalling as I chewed. Where to begin? How to couch things?

Roxanne took a sip of her wine, waited.

"Okay, what?" she said.

"Nothing bad."

Kept chewing. Finally swallowed. Washed it down with a sip of ale.

"Marta's gone," I said. "Clair took her down to Louis's a little while ago. More private, more protection. You can't just drive by."

"Good. You know how I feel about her."

I took another bite, tearing at the baguette. Chewed.

"You're stalling," Roxanne said.

I shook my head. "No, it's all fine."

She looked at me, hand on her wineglass. I started in.

Marta and the cached money, the brothel, and the harem. Me saying Clair and Louis shouldn't have to clean up her messes. The guys in the truck down the road, how they claimed to be just getting high. Clair thinking it might be a cover.

I took another bite.

"Did they have a gun?" Roxanne said. A significant detail.

"Just one. An old piece of junk. Anyway, most of the people driving down this road are armed."

I kept the story moving. Strain, the detective, at the lake. New Jersey. His feeling that I wasn't telling him the whole truth.

"You're not," Roxanne said.

"I gave him enough to work on."

She sipped, pursed her lips. Not happy. I jumped in the chronology, told her about Blake getting me Geberth's name, address. My visit there. His denial.

"You just walked in there?"

"It's what reporters do. If you want an answer to something, you go knock on their door and ask."

"This isn't about a story, Jack. It's about somebody who shot you. Did you expect him to just admit it?"

"I wanted to see his reaction."

"And?"

I drank some ale. Took another bite. Roxanne was catching on.

She waited, her gaze locked on me as I chewed. I swallowed, told her about Jason's phone, the messages.

"What? She had Jason's phone?"

"I think they were just texting."

"It's not 'just' anything. And now you're getting in the middle of their crazy shit?"

"It's fine. It gives me the upper hand, like those code-breakers in England in World War II."

She didn't push back at that moment, so I plunged in. Them saying somebody was going rogue. Then I told her about the twenty-four hours.

"You gave this Geberth some sort of ultimatum?"

"I wanted there to be a deadline. Let him know I wasn't going to just go away. I want to know who did it. They offer up Jason and the shooter, then I go to Strain, say, 'These are the guys. They're all yours.' "

"What if they decide to protect all of them?"

"I think they'll want to protect this Patriot Legion outfit more than they want to save Jason's butt. They can move on, find another farm."

"What if you're wrong, Jack?"

"This guy Geberth runs a pretty big business. Manufactures concrete things like septic tanks. I think he'll do a cost–benefit, decide it's in his interest to cooperate."

"He's also running around with guns, talking about taking over the government. That's not business. That's an extremist zealot. And now you've backed him into a corner. *Us* into a corner."

I didn't have a counter to that. Couldn't undo it now.

Roxanne sipped, her face hardening. I took another swallow of ale, started again. I backed up in the chronology, to Zombie coming to Sparrow's house, their conversation. Him trying to make up to her in some weird way. The police plan to use her as bait. Dunne and the podcast. I left out her offer.

"So he's fixated on her," Roxanne said. "I'll bet he's never had a girlfriend. And this is an attractive girl who pays attention to him."

"Hard not to, a gun in your face."

"She's brave, putting herself out there."

Roxanne paused, shook her head, said, "It's all crazy, this stuff. It's coming from all sides. Part of me trusts you. I mean, it's always worked out in the past. But part of me thinks you're in way too deep this time. Clair, too."

I reached over, took her hand.

"It'll be okay. We just need them out of our lives. All of them."

"And life back to normal," Roxanne said. "But I'm not even sure what that is for us anymore."

"Sophie. Her being excited about having a phone. That's normal. She and Tara and the play."

She sipped her wine, not convinced. Slipped her hand away and took a bite of sandwich.

"I missed you," I said. "When you were away."

"Me, too."

"Awkward being with Tiffanee for so long?"

"No," Roxanne said. "I mean, she's very nice. But you know what's funny?"

"No."

"I was with her for two days, at the hotel, driving back and forth to Portland. The girls were chatting away in the back, and Tiffanee and I talked. At the hotel, sometimes the girls went in Tara's room and we'd be sitting there. Or by the pool. I mean, for hours."

She paused.

"I feel like I know her, but I really don't. It's like she only told me so much."

"About Jason?"

"Oh, she talked about him, what a jerk he turned out to be. Her previous partners. How they seemed sweet and kind until they drank. Or started doing opioids. Or cheated on her. Or whatever thing went wrong. Tara's real dad, in Texas or wherever he is, he never calls. His only contact with her is a card on her birthday, and then he just signs it 'Love, Dad.' No note."

"Why bother?" I said.

"Exactly. Tiffanee said she wishes she was like me and chose right the first time."

"Sometimes it's a crapshoot," I said.

"Right. But the odd part is that there wasn't any more. It was like her life started when she was nineteen. I asked her where she grew up and she said here and there. Her mother got divorced from her father, married a couple of more times. They moved all over the place. Ohio, Nevada, I think she said. Then when her grandmother died and left her the farm, she moved to Maine."

"She hadn't lived here before?"

"I don't think so. Maybe came just to visit? It was hard to tell. She talks a lot, but when you think back over it, there's a chunk missing."

"Maybe her childhood was miserable, all the upheaval. She doesn't want to revisit it."

Roxanne shook her head.

"No, people like to talk about their misery. This was odd."

A pause. We sat. The firelight flickered. From upstairs, Sophie's voice, louder and animated—*Well, at least you get to wear something sort of cute, while I get this raggedy old thing.*

Roxanne stopped talking, was listening.

"Why can't this stuff wait till they're at school?" I said.

"It's not a school play."

I drank.

"I still don't like it. And what's with this costume stuff with Mr. Ziggy? Isn't there a person for that? Like, they have somebody do the set and the lights? Why's the director talking about what Annie's going to wear?"

"It's community theater. Maybe they all pitch in on everything."

"How many molesters did you have to take kids from? All those boyfriends."

"I know, Jack. We'll check him out. Maybe he's gay. Maybe he's got a husband, perfectly nice normal life. Maybe he's just totally into theater. Gets an idea, gets all excited, fires a text off to the cast."

"Maybe," I said.

She hesitated, forming a thought.

"I get it. I have the same feeling. But part of me, a big part, wants something in our life that isn't about guns and gangs and robbers and all these awful people. You getting shot, and the house set on fire. Raymond killed, the other guy. Now your store girl, this nutcase robber-stalker. Louis, Clair, Marta. These guys coming here, right on our road. It's just too much, Jack."

I reached out, took her hand. "Maybe Mr. Ziggy will come back clean as a whistle. That would be one good thing, right?"

Roxanne smiled.

"Yes, it would," she said. The smile fell away. "If he doesn't, he's toast."

We sat. Roxanne took another bite of sandwich and chewed, stared straight ahead. From upstairs we heard Sophie again. Laughing, saying, "I know, right? Why can't there be cute boy orphans?"

More laughing.

"We've got to protect her," Roxanne said. "It's our job. More than Marta and this Sparrow woman and the guy with the statues. Even Louis."

"Yes. The most important job."

More laughter from upstairs.

Roxanne got up, took her plate to the counter, tossed the remains of her sandwich into the trash. I got up, did the same. Roxanne put both our plates in the dishwasher, then put Sophie's sandwich in a plastic bag and stuck it in the refrigerator.

"I've got work to do," she said, and she went to the hall and picked up her bag, headed for the living room, her place on the couch.

I still had half a beer. I picked it up, took a drink. Leaning against the counter, I ran through the conversation, the stark reality of it all, the whirling maelstrom of threat all around us. What if our suspicions about Mr. Ziggy were right? If Mary's fears for Clair were founded? If this time, we were all in too deep? What if we'd rolled the dice too many times?

And then I thought of the things I hadn't told her.

Dunne and the podcast. Louis shooting a big hole in the biker's truck.

Why leave it out? Was I protecting Roxanne, or shielding myself from her disapproval, maybe anger?

Who might get hurt as a result?

It was almost eight. Sophie came down, phone in hand. She went to the closet and put on her boots and barn jacket. I was sitting in the chair in the study, empty beer can on the floor beside me. I got up. She'd moved to the refrigerator, taken out a bag of carrots.

"Pokey," she said.

"I think Clair put her inside."

"I'll just check, make sure. I'm sure he missed me."

"I did, too," I said. "How 'bout if I come along."

She hesitated, as though that hadn't been part of her plan.

"Okay, I guess. But you don't have to."

"No, it would be good to get out."

I took my jacket from the hook, started to wrestle it over my shoulder. Sophie moved closer and gave my sleeve a last tug. "Thanks," I said, thinking it was a glimpse of the future: Sophie helping me put on a shirt, kneeling to tie my shoes. I shook it off.

We went out the back, the sliding door, the smell of the sanded cedar shingles still in the air. I said, "Forgot my phone," and went back inside. Got the small Glock from the safe, pocketed it, and hurried back out. Sophie was fifty feet down the path through the snow. I caught up and we fell into step.

"So what's the deal, Dad?" she said. "Because of the person who shot at you, I can't go outside by myself?"

She had her mother's way of cutting to the chase.

"For now," I said. "Also, I just haven't seen you much lately."

"Do you think he'll come back?"

Like her mother, not easily deflected.

"No. I think he got the message."

"From you?"

"Yes," I said.

"Did you find him?"

"I found somebody who knows him, who can tell him to cut it out."

"Did they?"

"I think they will, very soon."

We walked, the path ice-blue in the light of a half moon. Our steps crunched, the sound reverberating through the trees. I waited for Sophie's next question.

"Why can't the police just arrest him?"

"They will. They just don't have the evidence yet."

"Why don't they just track his cell phone? If he was in our yard at that time, then he's the one."

I thought about it. Why don't they? From the mouths of babes, except Sophie wasn't one.

"Do you know who it is, Dad?"

"I'm getting closer," I said.

"How long will it take?"

"Not much longer."

"And then I can be on my own?"

"Yes."

We kept walking. I watched the woods, peering through the brush, the shadows beyond the trees. Listened for anything other than the sound of our footsteps. The Glock swung in my pocket with my strides.

"So was it Jason?" Sophie said.

"No. He can't go out. I think it was one of his friends."

"Do you think they wanted to kill you, Dad?"

The words were hard and jagged, coming from my daughter.

"No. I think they wanted to warn me."

"Why?"

"I don't know. Because I ask a lot of questions."

A pause, our feet falling in unison. She was getting tall, long-legged.

"Were you scared?"

"No. I was more mad."

"Then it didn't work," Sophie said.

"No, honey. It didn't work at all."

We were at the barn, the lights still on, Clair's truck gone. The shop door was unlocked, and we went inside, clomped down the board walkway between the box stalls.

Pokey snorted. He could sense a carrot coming.

Sophie opened the gate to the stall, and Pokey moved close to her, nuzzling her jacket for the carrots.

"Don't be a greedy Gus," she said, and he raised his head and she stroked his muzzle. She was too big for him now, a small pony that had seemed gigantic just a few years ago.

Taking the bag from her pocket, a long thick carrot from the bag, she held it up and Pokey chomped half of it off, crunched it down. Then the rest of it, and she moved him back, slipped a rope around his neck, snapped it to a ring on the wall. Then she went to the cupboard, took out the brush, and started on his neck. He looked back, seemed content.

I watched, then walked to the end of the barn. Three more stalls, all empty. Haymow upstairs, manure pile below. Lots of big dark spaces. You could hide an army.

There were stairs along the back wall, and I walked up, flicked my phone light across the loft. Hay bales. Tools. A door to a boxed-in room where a hired hand had slept, back in the day. I walked across, opened the door and pushed. It swung. I scanned the room with the light. More tools. A moth-eaten blanket. A picture of a 1930s Ford truck, an advertisement from a magazine, nailed to the wall.

I backed out, closed the door. Went back down the steps, up to the stall.

Sophie had switched to another brush and was doing Pokey's mane. She brushed with her left hand, fed him carrots with her right.

"Almost done," she said. "He really needed it. Clair's good with the grain and hay but he doesn't give him the TLC. Right, Poke?"

He crunched. Sophie straightened up, gave him a last pat on the muzzle, and undid the tether. He swung around for another carrot, and she fished out one more. Pokey stood there chewing as Sophie closed the stall door, and we started back through the lighted part of the barn. Then the shop, tools on the bench.

The stove cold, the music silenced. The Kimber gone.

I fought off a feeling of foreboding, smiled at Sophie, and then we stepped out into the cold night.

"Maybe time for a horse, you think?" I said.

"Jeez, Dad. A phone, a horse. What's going on?"

"Nothing's going on. We just love you."

It came out funny, like I was hiding something. Like I could have said I was making up for lost time. Or even worse, time that might be lost in the future.

Sophie just smiled, looked at me like I might be losing it.

We left the barn, and I looked up at the house. The light was on by the back door, and lights were on in the kitchen, the den to the right of it. I thought of stopping in to check on Mary, but then reconsidered. Maybe she was finally enjoying some peace and quiet. At least cleaning up after Marta.

Sophie had started down the path ahead of me, had her phone out, a blue-gray glow. I started after her, passed the corner of the barn, the light spilling onto the snow from the workshop windows. I glanced left at the woods.

A glint thirty yards in.

I kept walking. Another glance. It still was there. Something metal. Or glass.

Sophie stopped, turned to wait for me. I caught up, stopped, and crouched, and turned toward the woods as I retied my boot. Still there. The barn lights reflecting off something.

Sophie waited while I did the other boot.

It was twenty yards in from the edge of the grassy edge of the barnyard. There was an overgrown path back there, dating back to when they'd hauled water to the barn from a spring. The path crossed a tractor trail that paralleled the road, left over from when we'd taken hardwood out of Clair's land to the north.

Sophie put her phone in her pocket, said, "Are you serious about a horse?"

"I'll have to talk to Mom, but I think it's a good idea. You could ride again, and Pokey would have some company."

We kept walking. Her phone rang, the ringtone swapped for some sort of hip-hop thing. She took it out, answered said, "I'll call you in ten. I'm with my dad."

"Tara?" I said.

"Yeah. She wants to talk about the wig."

I looked at her.

"Annie, I mean. It's like this lame fuzzy red thing. She looks like Ronald McDonald. We're gonna tell Mr. Ziggy it needs a serious update."

"Ah," I said, and we kept walking, and then we were home.

Sophie went up the steps to the deck. I said I was going to walk back and check on Mary, and Sophie slid the door open and went inside.

I went out to the road, started walking. The tractor path led to a roadside woodyard, a cleared area where we hauled the logs and stacked them. A truck came and loaded them up, took them to a sawmill. We made enough money to pay our property taxes.

The moon was reflected off the ice in the road, and I tried to stay in the shadow of the trees. At Clair's house, the lights were on, the windows of the barn illuminated, too.

As I approached the woodyard, I slowed. Stopped.

There was a car parked at the far side, nosed into the trees, motor off. I watched. No movement. Walked closer.

It was an old Subaru. Dark red, a dent in the tailgate. I approached slowly. No one inside.

I felt the hood. It was warm, but barely. I looked for tracks, found faint ones going from the car to the tractor path, more distinct on the path itself.

Snowshoes.

I followed them, putting my feet in each snowshoe indentation. A crunch, but not a loud one. I aimed for the front of each print where the footplate had stamped deeper and my steps were quieter still. Gun held low at my side, I walked awkwardly, slowly, silently. The path was lighted by the moon and the trees were dark silhouettes against the snow and sky.

A shuffle to my left, in the trees. I froze, brought the gun up. Something was moving in a stand of oaks. It was behind big trunks, and I aimed as it emerged. A porcupine shuffled out. I lowered the gun, turned back to the trail. The prints.

Started walking, until the lights of the house showed from beyond the trees. Then the lights of the barn. They were ahead, to the right. I was close, within earshot in the quiet woods.

I slowed. Stopped. I peered into the trees. The barn was just ahead on my right. I took one step at a time, pausing to listen, searching the dim woods for the glint I'd seen from the path. Took another step, then one more. Two. Stopped.

And there it was. A glimmer. I waited. Watched. Saw it again. Thirty yards. To the right of the road. I placed each foot carefully, shifted my weight gradually. The glint disappeared and I froze. It reappeared, like a twinkle in the darkness. A figure emerging where the glint was, still there when it disappeared. Ten steps. They were sitting, arms up. The glint again.

Binoculars.

They had the Varney house staked out. Looking for Marta.

13

I took one step at a time, a long pause in between. A footprint collapsed, crunched. I froze. Watched. Waited. The glint, the barn window lights reflecting off the binocular lenses. They still had them up.

A noise from the house, the back door opening. There was a silence and then the door slammed. Clair home? Mary putting the trash out? Rattling. The trash-can lid.

I started moving. Footsteps from the house, someone going up the back steps. The door shuddered open.

I was close. A guy sitting on a camp chair, the kind that folds up.

The storm door at the house slammed shut, then the inner door, a muffled thump.

He shifted. The seat creaked. Cold aluminum frame. I took another step. Squared. Raised the gun, said, "Hands on your head or I'll blow it off."

No reaction.

"Now," I said.

His arms came up slowly, the binoculars in the right hand.

"Drop them."

"Hey, they cost like three hundred bucks. Hate to get 'em wet."

One of the guys from the truck, the driver from Monroe.

"Now."

He tossed the binoculars to his right, and they landed in the snow with a thud.

I moved closer, kept the gun trained. "Hands on your neck."

He complied.

"Stand up."

It took two tries, but he pushed himself up out of the low-slung chair. He lurched as he got to his feet.

"Easy," I said. I moved close, switched the gun to my left hand. Patted him down with the right.

He smelled like cigarettes, was bigger than the guy I'd hauled out of the truck. I went down along his right side: a knife in a sheath on his belt. I lifted his jacket up, yanked it out, and tossed it onto the snow. Switched the gun to my right hand.

Left side, handgun in a holster. I lifted the jacket again, pulled the gun up and out. A small semiautomatic, Smith & Wesson. No pawn-shop junk this time. I tossed it behind me.

"On your belly," I said.

"Really?" he said.

"Down," I said. From the side, I saw him smile. A slyness, not afraid. The goofball stoners in the truck had been an act.

"Move," I said, as he dropped to his knees.

I put a boot on his back and shoved, and he landed face-first in the snow, turned his head toward me. He was still smiling. I felt an urge to kick that smile off his smug face. How do you like it now, chump? You think all this is just a big game, you piece of shit?

I caught myself. Clair's mantra: Self-control above all.

I bent down to check his boots. Sure enough, knife in the right. I slipped it out, tossed it with the first one. Checked the left: derringer in a holster strapped to his calf, the butt pointed forward, two extra cartridges in the loops. I pulled it out, slipped it into my jacket pocket. Stood, the gun still pointed.

"You expecting an army out here, Lucas Sawtelle?"

A moment of hesitation when he heard his name.

"Hey, I was a Boy Scout," he said. "You know what they say about preparation."

"From Boy Scout to drug-dealing biker bro?"

"Not that much of a leap. You still earn badges with good deeds."

One man's good deed, another man's felony. It was all relative.

"What's good about this?" I said.

"Hey, somebody snatched a big boss's old lady. We're an affiliate, got our orders. Find her so they can take her back."

"Search and rescue," I said.

"You got it. Now, can I get up? It's cold down here."

I took a step back.

"Roll over, hands still on your neck."

"You searched me. Come on."

But he kept his hands clasped as he turned onto his back.

"Sit up."

He did.

"Stand up."

He turned and knelt, then staggered to his feet. Faced me.

"Sit in the chair."

He took three deliberate steps, turned, and sat. The chair legs sank deeper into the snow.

"Where's your buddy at?" Sawtelle said.

"Coming."

"Right," he said, then grinned, turned to look at me. "A little different being the main guy, not the backup, ain't it. I remember first time I took point. These fools, construction workers outta Jersey, thought they were tough. Jumped a couple of our guys in this bar in Old Orchard, like, six on two. Cut one of our guys on the face with a bottle. The kind of cut that leaves a big scar. Very unnecessary. Anyway, we caught up with 'em at, like, three in the morning, motel off the Mass Pike. I was a prospect, this was gonna get me patched. So I was the one kicked the door in, went in first."

He cleared his throat.

"Turned out to be no big deal. Idiots were sound asleep, we busted 'em up pretty good. Boom, boom, boom with the bats. Arms, legs. And the cutter, he lost an ear. Welcome to the real world, right?"

"Enough talk."

"Oh, come on. I mean, we both know you won't shoot me. Your buddy, on the other hand. That old guy's a mean motherfucker, you could tell. What's his deal?"

"Ex-military. Special forces."

He was right. I wasn't Clair. I wasn't going to shoot him. But what to do with him? Call the police?

I looked at him, sitting there perfectly relaxed with my gun pointed at his back. It was like I'd hooked a shark from a canoe. I thought of Louis, cutting the guy from Massachusetts loose, a warning shot to the tailgate. Maybe I could put a round in the back of the Subaru?

Instead, I did what I knew how to do: spell it out.

"Get up. Go back and tell your lame-ass friends to stay away. Next time I *will* shoot you."

I picked up the guns and the knife out of the snow, stuffed them in my jacket pockets, and stood back. "Pack your crap."

Sawtelle did. The chair, the snowshoes. He held them under both arms, and we started back on our tracks, me ten feet back, the gun at my side. The moon had risen a bit and it was brighter, the snow glowing under the trees. Our footsteps crackled through the cold, silent woods.

Fifty yards in, Sawtelle started up.

"This ain't your scrap. I mean, I made some calls, this lady at the town office there. Said I was looking at buying land out here, needed to contact the neighbors. She knew your names, so I googled you guys. Nothing much online about your buddy. A couple of assault charges that got dropped. But you're a friggin' celebrity. Jack McMorrow, *New York Times*—that's big-time. Saw you wrote about that robber in Clarkston. Weird shit or what? I mean, the zombie mask? What's that all about?"

He stopped, put the snowshoes down.

"Gimme a sec."

The chair had started to unfold and he bent as he squeezed the legs back together, then whirled around and swung the chair like a baseball bat, caught my right hand, sent the gun flying. I staggered backward and he swung again, landing on my bad shoulder, pain shooting out of the pellet wounds.

Then he dropped the chair, came at me, bulled me over onto my back, landed on my legs, fell forward. One hand locked onto my throat, held me down as he threw a punch. I turned my head and his fist glanced off the side of my head. I pushed him back up, got enough space to kick him in the groin.

He grunted. Threw himself back on top of me as I rolled to my right, caught me on my side. I elbowed at his arms, grabbed his left hand, twisted. His other hand was worming into my jacket pocket, He yanked the derringer out and put the barrel to the side of my head, just like I had done only a day before to old Jason.

I went still. He did, too. He was panting.

"You should lay off the cigarettes," I said.

The gun fell away.

"And you should stick to writing stories," Sawtelle said.

"So I've been told."

We lay there like spent lovers, and then he flipped to his feet, pushing the derringer into his pocket. I got up, brushed the snow off my jacket, jeans.

"Let's call it a day," Sawtelle said. "I'm not gonna shoot you. That wasn't the assignment. You're not gonna shoot me. I mean, you're a last-resort kind of shooter. And none of us wants to bring in the cops. Am I right?"

I didn't answer.

"Exactly. So let's go. I'm friggin' cold. Don't the temp drop fast when the sun goes down?"

I walked over and picked up my gun. Took his gun and knife out of my pockets, handed them back.

He started down the trail. I followed, both of us in the snowshoe tracks. Two tired men; in another life we could have been cutting wood together, ending the day with a beer on the tailgate. I thought about Zombie, and how Sparrow had talked him down. She tried to understand him, listened to his story. What I'd done all these years as a reporter, listened to people's stories. How had I gotten here, gun out, a trigger pull away from killing?

He hiked the chair up under his arm, adjusted his grip on the snowshoes.

"What do you do?" I said, over his shoulder. "I mean, when you're not doing this?"

The reporter in me. He half-turned.

"Pipefitter. Used to chase the big money, out of state most of the time. Pennsylvania, Virginia, Alabama. Living in motels. But after a few years of that, my kids, the wife—they barely knew me. Now I stay close to home. Paper mills, when I can get it. The shipyard."

We walked, crunching down the trail, single file.

"Huh. Biker on your days off?"

"We all have jobs."

"Not the boys in Montreal. This Snake guy, I looked him up."

"Different level. That's big business."

"Drugs. Prostitution. Human trafficking. Nice people you hang with."

"Not my line," Sawtelle said. "I just ride with the club, have a few beers. My buddy there, he's an ironworker, still a prospect. We don't look for trouble, but you go after one of us, we all come down on you like a freight train."

"One for all and all for one?"

"You got it."

"Why not just ride your bike and have beers? Without the affiliation?"

He walked.

"The old lady asks the same thing. It's like this. I like order. Rules. The group being stronger than the single individual. Why I like being in a union. They got my back."

"Military," I said.

"Two years, Army. Wheeled vehicle mechanic."

"Deployed?"

"Fort Bragg, the whole time."

We were almost to the car. A faster walk when you didn't pause between steps.

"The two guys you're watching. Both former Marines. Saw a lot of serious combat."

"I figured, the old guy. These hard-core combat vets, they're a different cat. Only saw the younger guy from a distance."

"Same type, probably more dangerous. Sometimes it's like he never left Fallujah."

Sawtelle walked on for a few steps, then said, "Yeah, at Bragg we used to see the guys coming back. Afghanistan, mostly, my time. Some of 'em, the ones just left the thick of it, you could tell they weren't ready for stateside. Look at you in the bar, and it was like, 'Gimme an excuse to kill you.' I remember this one time, a wiry little guy is in the bar next to one of our mechanics. Muscle-head, twice his size. They bump, he shoves the little guy, says something stupid. That little guy moved like a friggin' weasel, put that big ape down, hands locked on his throat before that meathead even hit the ground. Our guy never even got a punch off."

We walked on. I waited, let him go over that scene again in his head.

"You've got two of them, except probably tougher. No emotion," I said. "If your higher-ups are smart, they'll find a way to walk away from this. A bunch of bar brawlers out in the woods? It'll be like target practice."

No reply. The Subaru was in sight. I waited until we came into the woodyard, walked around and stood between him and the car.

"I don't know," he said. "The two of them. I mean, you could have twenty guys going in there. Some of them bastards are mean, make me look like a friggin' minister."

"Not mean enough," I said. "You love your kids, your wife? They'll be crying at your funeral."

He frowned, looked past me. "You make a pledge to the club. You're all in. I mean, I love these guys."

"Then don't let them get hurt," I said. "Because I promise you, they will if they keep it up."

Sawtelle took a deep breath. I moved toward my truck, and he went to the car. Opened the hatch and threw the snowshoes and chair in.

Turned back to me. He reached into his pocket, and I did the same, the Glock clenched. He took out a pack of cigarettes. Shook one loose, lit it with a lighter from the other pocket.

"Crazy, huh? All over some friggin' chick," he said.

Sawtelle drew on the cigarette, the red glow flaring in the dark. Blew out smoke.

I thought of Sparrow, the cloud of steam over her head. Blake giving up his career for her, maybe. How can anyone know who's worthy of that commitment and who isn't? Just have to make a choice and let the chips fall. Louis had made his choice, and people like me and Sawtelle were dragged along.

"You got a kid," Sawtelle said. "I seen her. Wife, too. What are you doing out here, Mr. New York friggin' Times?"

I thought for a moment. He took another drag, watched me and waited. A biker playing with my head.

"Same as you, I guess," I said. "I took a pledge."

He smiled, turned toward the car.

"See," he said. "We're all the same in the end."

"Maybe."

I took a step away, then turned.

"Seriously, don't come back."

"No need," Sawtelle said. "They moved her."

14

I passed Clair's house. No truck. I pulled up to the shed, shut the motor off, and called. No answer. I texted:

> YOU OK? CALL WHEN YOU CAN.
> SOME ACTION ON THE HOME FRONT.
> ALL CLEAR.

Waited a minute. No reply. I looked at my watch. It was 9:43, coming up on 2200 hours. Stryker was about to convene his meeting.

I went inside. It was quiet as I strolled through the kitchen, down the hall. Peeked into the living room, saw Roxanne working, feet drawn up underneath her, laptop open, earbuds in. I stepped back, listened. Could hear music from Sophie's room, then the wood-thrush burble of her laugh.

I smiled, went to the kitchen. Took the Glock out of my jacket pocket, checked it for condensation. Wiped it down with a dishtowel and some alcohol, put it in the safe. Hung up my jacket and went to the study, put more wood on the fire and watched the spots of lichen on the dried bark catch spark and ignite. Ashes to ashes. Thought about Sawtelle, the pipefitter-biker-philosopher. Were we all the same in the end? Not really, but closer than we'd like to admit.

He said he had kids. Maybe a daughter, like Sophie. We could have talked about how girls change so fast, one day a child, the next day, half grown up. The divide growing, moving in their own lives. Was Tara the right friend for Sophie? Could Sophie handle the real world when Roxanne and I weren't there to protect her? What part of that real world confronted her with that dirtbag Jason? Creepy Mr. Ziggy?

The flames were licking the new wood now, leaping higher. I turned the draft down to keep it from burning too hot. That much I could control. I stepped back, eyed the fire for a moment more, took out both phones and sat.

It was 2158 hours. I opened Signal on Jason's phone. The previous conversation had disappeared, just like the settings said it should. I held the phone on the desk in front of me. The two minutes ticked off. And then I was invited to join a group: Action Force. I did.

There were already nineteen members. I ran down the icons. The group from the last conversation, minus Rebel. Was this like Judas not inviting Jesus?

STRYKER: THANKS ALL FOR JOINING IN. SOME ACTION REQUIRED.
HORSEMAN: PILGRIM PRESENT?
STRYKER: I INVITED HIM.
CITIZEN: 10-4 WITH IT.
NOMAD: AFFIRMATIVE.

I hesitated. Should Jason join in? I started typing.

PILGRIM: WHAT'S UP?
STRYKER: U MISSED EARLIER CONVO.
PILGRIM: HAD OFFICIAL VISITORS. THEY DON'T KNOCK. PHONE IS DEEP 6.
STRYKER: ROGER THAT. WE HAVE SITUATION. HAD VISITOR TOO . . . SUBJECT FROM YOUR INCIDENT.
PILGRIM: NO SHIT.

The rest of the group following along, like it was a tribunal.

STRYKER: Related to incident at subject's residence.
R u familiar?
PILGRIM: No. Was busy. S.O. Hospital. Now in Augusta,
with relative.
STRYKER: No knowledge? Fire, shooting?
PILGRIM: No. In the media?

A pause.

HORSEMAN: Short item, Bangor Daily.
PILGRIM: Missed it. Been sick, heart problem.
STRYKER: News to u?
PILGRIM: Yes.
NOMAD: I call bs.

How would Jason respond to being called out in front of the
group? I typed.

PILGRIM: F U
NOMAD: Gone under.
STRYKER: Subject looking for shooter.
PILGRIM: Can't help.
STRYKER: Maybe ask Rebel. Where's he at?
PILGRIM: No idea. I got ankle bracelet, outta touch.
CITIZEN: This cld bring unwanted attention.
STRYKER: Subject knows ATF.
PILGRIM: Guy cold-cocked me, he's a pussy.
STRYKER: Still a problem.
PILGRIM: Ain't going down for this—was in jail.
HORSEMAN: Level 2 discussion?
STRYKER: Roger that. Signing off. L2, then meet again.
PILGRIM: What about me?
STRYKER: Be in touch.

I took screenshots, the whole exchange. Went to contacts, scrolled down until I found him. Jason's partner. Rebel. A 207 area code. Maine. I did a reverse phone trace, waited as the wheel turned. No record. A prepaid phone like Jason's.

The fire had started to burn down. I got up and put in another chunk of wood, sat back in my chair. Saw Sophie trot and skid into the kitchen, take a tangerine from the bowl, and skip out. We could trace her phone location with one of those apps helicopter parents use, but that was with access to her phone. What about Rebel's? Where was he? Where had he been?

I got up, went to the window at the far corner of the room. Looked out at the moonlit snow, the draped trees. A winding line of fox tracks from the trees to the birdfeeders. Holes and mounds where the fox had dug for mice. Digging. The fox and me, both.

Police used cell-phone data all the time to pin the suspect to a crime scene, all those signals triangulated off cell towers. But I wasn't police. But I knew one.

Standing by the window, I texted Blake, asking him to give me a call as soon as he could.

Waited. The yard was still, foxes knowing when humans were sure to be asleep, those hours when night was just beginning to give way to morning. My phone vibrated.

Clair.

"Hey," I said.

"I'm outside," he said.

I climbed in. The cab still held Marta's fragrance. Shampoo?

"How'd it go?" I said.

"Fine," Clair said. "She said she was glad to be home."

"Huh. She hadn't seen Louis in years. Shows up unannounced, then, after a week, she takes off. Funny idea of home."

"I guess it's where the heart is."

"Listen to you. Mr. Romantic."

He smiled.

"Took longer than you expected," I said.

"Louis and I were talking strategy and tactics."

"You should be," I said. "They know she was here. They know she was moved. Pretty sure they know where to."

He went quiet, his way of showing surprise. I told him about Sawtelle doing surveillance. Our confrontation. His motivation. My warning.

"You think he gets it?"

"I don't know. Maybe. Two years in the Army, mechanic at Fort Bragg. Saw fresh combat vets. It comes down to how strong your sense of loyalty and duty is."

A pause.

"Yours *and* his," I said.

Clair nodded. I glanced past him, saw the butt of a gun in the side pocket of the door.

"Doesn't have to be your fight," he said.

I thought of my doubts, scrapping with Sawtelle on the snow in the woods.

"No," I said. "And all my fights don't have to be yours."

We sat quiet for a moment, two.

"But they are," he said.

"Yes," I said. "Who would have thought?"

"An old soldier and a typer."

"We have other skills. Pretty good with chain saws."

Clair smiled again. A little wistful?

"So what else?" he said. "You fritter away the rest of the night or actually get something done?"

Movement in the house. Sophie looking out her bedroom window. Clair flashed his lights. She waved, disappeared.

"She has a new phone," I said.

"Ah. Hope she isn't on it all the time. Wonder if kids ever see a real sunset anymore."

A beat, and I started in. Stryker's meeting. Jason saying he knew nothing about the attack. Me having a phone number for Rebel. Planning to ask if Blake could trace its movement.

"That would put the phone here," Clair said. "Need him, too."

"I hear his voice, I'll know."

"Text him as Rebel, or whatever he calls himself in their video game. Set up a meet."

"Yes."

"I'll back you up, apropos the earlier part of our conversation."

"Apropos?" I said. "What have you been reading?"

"*New York Times*," Clair said. "I keep a list of the big words, look 'em up later."

And then he reached over, gave my shoulder—the good one—a squeeze, like he never did.

I glanced over at him, the hard profile, the silver hair, and felt a strange sense of déja vu. Me speaking to my father on his deathbed. The apartment on East 81st. Me home from college. My dad holding my hand when he could no longer speak. I shook it off.

He dropped his hand, reached for the key.

"I should go," Clair said. "Mary."

"Right," I said. "We'll talk."

"What you do best," he said, and smiled.

I was rattled. Came into the house and put another piece of wood in the stove, all the while seeing him. The squeeze on my shoulder. Like it was over, he was looking back. I adjusted the damper, my hands yellow-orange in the glow of the flickering flames. Told myself he was just tired, it'd been a long day.

I didn't believe it.

I went to the living room. Roxanne was standing by the couch, packing up her bag: legal pads, laptop, chargers, the spine of a paperback: something about inherited family trauma. Were we a case study?

"Hey," I said.

"What's the matter?" Roxanne said.

"Nothing. I'm fine."

She rustled with her papers.

"No, you're not. Spit it out."

I paused, turned away, then back.

"Just talked to Clair. Outside. He seems off."

"Off, like what?"

"Like he's looking back on his life or something."

"He should be, at his age," Roxanne said. "Self-reflection is important."

"I know. The examined life and all that. Maybe he's just never done it with me before."

She hefted her bag, picked up her mug. I smelled herbal tea.

"We'll talk in the morning. I've got to go to bed. It's all catching up to me, I think." She moved close, kissed my cheek. A peck.

"Yes," I said. "Get some rest. It's been a lot."

"*Is* a lot," Roxanne said. "And I'm afraid I don't know the half of it."

She went to the stairs, started up. I waited, listened. Heard her clogs come off, knocking against the floor. Listened. Nothing from Sophie. Probably surfing the Internet in her bed.

I shook my head, went to the kitchen. Took out another can of ale, went and sat by the fire. Opened it and drank, feeling like I needed some sort of moment but I didn't know what it was. Watched the flames. Drank. Felt myself starting to spiral downward. What was it all for?

My phone buzzed.

Blake. Finally

"Hey," I said. "Any news?"

"Still searching. A lot of blue pickups out there."

"Too bad she didn't snap a photo."

"Next time," Blake said.

"If there is one?"

"There will be. He's circling closer."

"How's Sparrow? Riff?"

"He wants to buy a gun, shoot him on sight. She's more sympathetic. Wants to bring him in before police kill him."

"Not unlikely," I said, "if he keeps waving that pistol around."

Death by cop. The coward's suicide.

"For sure, if he puts his hands in his pockets," Blake said.

I took a drink. Felt the ale easing through me. "The plan still on?"

"Yeah. She works tomorrow night, usual shift. Ten to six."

"How's she getting there?"

"Fake Uber," Blake said. "Plainclothes driving."

"Everybody ready?

"Yeah."

"You?"

"No. Too involved, they said."

"So?"

"One block over, radio on."

I hesitated, then asked him: "When does she talk to Stephanie Dunne?"

"Tomorrow morning. I'll take her over."

"Is she getting cold feet?"

"Not for the right reasons," Blake said.

A rattle in the background, then quiet, the truck shut off.

"Where are you?"

"The house. Staying here for the duration."

I started to ask him if he was ready to shoot someone again if he had to. I stopped. I knew the answer.

Blake said, "You wanted me to call."

"Yes. A favor to ask."

I explained the situation: the Stryker group messages, me wanting to track Rebel's cell-phone data; knowing that police did it, but would it require a warrant? That could take days, weeks.

Blake listened. I pictured him sitting in the pickup outside Sparrow's house. The lights of the Red Hen.

"A burner phone," he said.

"Most likely."

A pause. "You didn't hear this from me," he said.

"Got it."

Clarkston PD had a subscription to a data tracker, he said. It followed phones, laptops, through their advertising IDs.

"You search for lawn mowers; your computer is flooded with lawn-mower ads. It's part of that. The ID shows where the device is at a certain time so advertisers can figure out where the user goes, what they do, what their interests are. They call it 'life patterns.' Something like that."

"Then I need to know this guy's life patterns. Like if he was on this road, outside this house."

Another pause.

"I can try. A few favors left to call in."

I heard the truck door open and close.

"I'll text you the number," I said.

"I'll call you," Blake said.

"Thanks. Tell Sparrow good luck. And you—"

But he was gone.

Good luck? It seemed like next to nothing. Because it was.

I sat. Sipped the ale. Turned the fire down. Picked up the Jason phone, opened Signal, went to the new group, Action Force. I invited Rebel to join. Waited, the phone on my lap. It pinged. He was in.

I closed my eyes, tried to channel Jason. Angry. Filled with self-pity. The consummate victim.

PILGRIM: Bro, we need to talk.
REBEL: Yeah. Been staying low. Heard he found Stryker.
PILGRIM: Enuf.
REBEL: Ok.
PILGRIM: I got a cuff. Fuckin sucks.
REBEL: Heard.
PILGRIM: U can't come here.
REBEL: No.
PILGRIM: I can get out, 30 minutes before they notice. Cops r bunch of fuckups.
REBEL: Ok.
PILGRIM: Round the corner, mall where Walmart is. Bookstore has a coffee place.
REBEL: Been there, for gun mags.

PILGRIM: 0900. I'LL BE THERE EARLY TO SCOPE IT, WILL BE SITTING. IF CLEAR, READING *GUNS & AMMO*. IF I'M READING TRUCK MAG, U KEEP WALKING.

REBEL: ROGER THAT.

Sitting there in the firelight, I smiled. All good news. I'd see him and, ideally, hear him. I'd have the gun magazine flying like a flag.

It was a fitful night. Every time the house creaked in the cold, my eyes snapped open, and I listened hard. Then I told myself it wasn't necessary, that Pilgrim wasn't in Prosperity. Sawtelle knew Marta was gone. Jason was cuffed in Augusta.

I woke up anyway, at 3:14: a creak and snap. At 4:35, coyotes howling on the ridge. At 5:22, a book falling from Sophie's bed. Or was it her phone?

At 6:10 I listened to Roxanne, her easy breathing. I leaned over, checked my phone. Texts.

Blake, 5:38: Call me when you can.

Sparrow: 5:59: Hey Jack. Time to talk? This podcast lady is freaking me out.

I opened Signal, half expecting Rebel to have canceled. Nothing. "Yes," I whispered, caught myself. Roxanne stirred.

I pulled on my T-shirt and jeans and moved quietly down the stairs. From the hallway, I scanned the kitchen, then the study. Went to the windows and looked out: no new footprints on the snow out back, no new tire tracks in the driveway. I put the phone on the table, went to the shed to get the ash bucket. Scooped out the cold cinders from the stove, put the bucket back in the shed. Stopped. Listened. Wind in the beeches, rattling the leaves. Chickadees in the bare lilacs.

Back inside, I checked the phone again, then built a fire: newspaper, pine kindling, pieces of a spruce log, bigger slices of dry ash. The newspaper was the *Times*. It seemed fitting to see it go up in smoke.

I watched the flames lick their way through the paper and wood, then fastened the door shut, opened the draft. Went to the kitchen and put the kettle on. Got out the coffee and the press, a tea bag and two mugs. Maybe Sophie would start drinking coffee now that she had a phone.

The water was almost boiling. There was stirring above me. Sophie's door opening, water running, the toilet flushing. Voices, then Sophie's footsteps cascading down the stairs. She trotted into the kitchen, said, "Hey, Dad. I gotta go do Pokey. That okay?"

I thought of Sawtelle, Marta gone. Clair back home. My meet with the probable shooter.

"Yeah, but take your phone."

She brightened at that, pulling on her Wellies, a knit hat. Grabbed her barn coat from the hook.

"We have to be at school early. Mr. Ziggy wants to talk to me and Tara before homeroom. Mom's gonna take me."

Me and Tara. Better than either of them alone.

"What's your ETD?" I said.

"Twenty of. I'll hurry."

And then she was gone, the shed door slamming shut behind her.

I looked at my watch. Twenty minutes to give Pokey hay and grain and water, open the door to the paddock. I had to leave by 7:30, get to Augusta in an hour, do some reconnoitering outside. Set myself up in the bookstore café.

Roxanne came down. She hurried into the kitchen, reached for her bag, pulled out her laptop.

"Morning," I said.

"Hey."

She went to the table, opened the laptop.

"What's the matter?"

"An assignment was due last night. I forgot to send it."

"Sunday-night deadline?"

"This professor has no life."

She was typing, peering intently at the screen. "Goddamn it. That's not the right version."

More typing, peering, a scowl on her pretty face.

"I'm making you coffee."

"Thanks," she said, not looking up. "Where did I put that? I hope I saved it. God, I'm late."

I poured the water. Pressed the coffee.

"Want me to take her?"

No reply for a moment, two, then, "No, I'll do it. I'm going in early. These cohort meetings. I mean, just let me do the work, you know? I did this stuff for ten years. Why do I have to drag these people along with me?"

I poured the coffee, put the mug on the table. Got out the milk, poured it in a pitcher. Set that down, too.

"Sophie seems happy," I said.

Roxanne hit send, said, "There. Take that." Slammed the laptop shut and jammed it in her bag.

"What?"

"I said Sophie seems happy."

She took a sip of coffee, sighed.

"Yes. A new-phone high. It'll wear off."

A rattle from the shed, Sophie banging through the door. She yanked her boots off, left them on the floor by the closet. Looked at her phone. "Fourteen minutes. That's a record," and trotted through.

I smiled. Roxanne was drinking coffee, eyes closed.

"Toast?" I said. "Yogurt?"

"I'll get something at school. It'll be quiet so I can work. The youngsters will still be sleeping off the weekend."

I poured my tea. From upstairs came the sound of a door slamming, the shower coming on.

"You okay?" I said.

She looked at me. "I'm fine."

"You don't seem it. Sleep okay?"

The bathroom door rattling open, Sophie's bare feet running down the hall.

"No," Roxanne said. "Bad dreams."

"About what?"

"About you."

"What about me?"

"I don't want to talk about it," Roxanne said, and then she put her coffee down, walked to the bottom of the stairs, calling up.

"Honey, are you almost ready?"

A muffled reply. The sound of Sophie throwing shoes into her closet. I went to the cupboard, took out Roxanne's travel mug, poured her coffee in. She came back to the kitchen, said, "Thanks."

"Should I be worried?" I said.

"No. It's just a dream. Everything seems worse in the middle of the night."

"Were you thinking about what we talked about?"

Clair. Louis. Marta. Death.

"Yeah," she said. "And it wasn't so good then."

"No," I said. "I'm sorry for it, the part I dragged in."

"It isn't the dragging in, Jack. It's that nothing seems to get dragged back out."

I started to say that Marta had. At least she'd left. That I hadn't invited Jason into our lives, hadn't hurt him when I could have. Maybe I should have, in hindsight. Instead, I said, "There's something we need to talk about. I'm going to—"

And then Sophie came back down the stairs, ran down the hall and into the kitchen. She was wearing leggings, black work boots, a gray sweatshirt half zipped. A scoop-necked black tank top under the sweatshirt, two buttons undone, a gold chain against the bare skin of her chest.

"You're going to school like that?" I said.

"Like what?" Sophie said, and she grabbed her backpack.

"Breakfast." I waved the yogurt container at her back.

"I'll eat at school, after our meeting," Sophie said. "Come on, Mom. Fire up the Batmobile. Bye, Dad. Love you," and she was out the door.

"See you tonight," Roxanne said, hefting her bag to her shoulder. She went by me, stopped, and turned back. Kissed me on the cheek.

"Please take care of yourself," she said.

"I'll be fine. I'm going down to—"

But she was gone, too. The hubbub of their exit echoed for a moment, and then the house was still. I went to the table, took a gulp of tea, then went to the woodstove, put in a big chunk of oak. I turned the damper down and picked up my phone, punched in Clair's number.

"What are you doing?"

"Drinking coffee, eating eggs. Talking with my lovely bride. She's going to her knitters' group. I'm going to miss her."

A beat. Not a joke.

"You?"

"Roxanne and Sophie left for school. I'm getting ready to head down to Augusta. I'm supposed to meet the guy I think shot me."

"And what? Get to the heart of his issues?"

"See his face, hear his voice. I haven't thought any further ahead than that."

"That's why you get in trouble. Don't plan for contingencies. Or exigencies, for that matter."

"Want to come along? It's a bookstore. He thinks I'm Jason. I'm having tea."

"What? The cupcake bakery was closed?"

I smiled. Waited.

"Time?"

I told him.

"Location?"

I told him that, too.

"Roger that," Clair said. "Been a long time since we rocked and rolled."

"Listen to you with your Led Zeppelin. And don't forget, we just did the two stoner bikers."

"That was a minuet, Jack. This dance is just getting rolling."

15

The direct route was 220, down to Route 3 at Liberty, then Route 3 all the way into Augusta. I drove slowly, thinking. When I reached frozen Lake St. George, I thought of what I could deliver to Detective Strain: I can't ID the shooter by sight because he was wearing a mask. But I would know his voice. Could hear it in my head: *"If it were up to me, I'd kill you now."*

I mentally anticipated Strain's counter moves: *What, you've been doing your own investigation? You're a voice expert now? Besides, he says he was with his girlfriend in Bangor.*

My counter to his counter: *I have his phone located. It was in Prosperity at the time of the shooting.*

The conversation from there: *Well, aren't you Mr. Hi-Tech Detective? How'd you manage that?*

Can't tell you, I'd reply.

Unlike editors, who understand protecting sources, cops tend to be less sympathetic.

I'd cross that bridge.

I was past the lake when cell service got strong enough to call. I pulled over, tried Blake. It went to voicemail. I tried Sparrow. It went to voicemail, too, and I left her a message to text me.

It had clouded up overnight and the sky was dirty gray, the snowbanks, too. The road from there seemed to go downhill, leading me inexorably to whatever and whomever was waiting. East Palermo. South China. Vassalboro. I hooked up with the Augusta commuter traffic headed for the hospital, the courthouse, the offices where Jason's supposed villains worked. Would they go into lockdown if he and his buddies marched on the State House? If Rebel could shoot me in my own driveway, who else would he shoot?

I was on the outskirts of Augusta—the highway snaking by houses, truck garages, former hayfields filled with gray walls of solar panels—when Sparrow called.

"Hey," I said. "How are you doing?"

"Shitty," she said. 'I'm supposed to talk to this lady in a half-hour."

"I know her," I said. "You'll do fine."

"It's not how I'll do. It's what she's gonna do with what I say."

A clink of dishes, then a faucet turning on and off. Sparrow cleaning up after breakfast with Riff and Blake? I waited.

"Brandon thinks I'm freakin' crazy," Sparrow said. "My dad, too."

"Why?"

A pause. Then Riff's voice faint in the background. I heard Sparrow's footsteps, then a door closing. It was quiet.

"Because I'm worried about him," she said. "I don't hate him, and I'm not scared of him. I'm more scared for him."

"Who?"

"Zombie. They're gonna blow him away, Jack. That's not right."

"But Sparrow—"

"I mean, I know he shot Bob at the store, but if he hadn't, Bob would have killed him."

"You don't know that."

"Sure I do. Because Bob wanted to be the hero. The brave store owner who took out the Zombie robber. Get on TV, talk about how he didn't fear for his own life, all that macho bullshit."

"So—"

"So in a way, for Zombie it was self-defense. And now he's a killer-robber because of it. And all these cops are gonna want to be the hero, too. I can just see it. Like they always do. 'Put down your weapon.' The guy doesn't do it in a friggin' second and boom. You kidding? He won't have a chance. I mean, he's barely a grown-up. Who the hell knows what's going on in his head."

I thought of Blake, the kid he'd killed in that alley. A paintball gun in the dark. Pleading with the boy to drop it. Then suicide by cop. The kid dead, Blake damaged.

"Sparrow, it was Zombie who walked in and pulled a gun," I said. "He chose to put himself in that situation. He put your manager in that situation."

I heard a sucking sound. Her vape pen.

"That's what Brandon says. I mean, I know this is a wicked trigger for him, so I hate to even bring it up. Brandon says Zombie's actions are putting innocent people in harm's way. People in the stores or whatever."

"But that's exactly right. People like you. Somebody buying milk. The police who show up."

"I know, but—"

"Sparrow, this is the guy who pointed a loaded gun at your face. Cracked your head open with it."

"He said he was really sorry for that."

I could feel myself churning.

"This is nuts," I said.

I heard her bang something. A coffee cup on a table?

"Okay, Jack. I know it sounds crazy, but I thought you might understand, 'cause you actually listen to people. And I know if you talked to him, you'd get it. He's just a fuckup, Jack. I know what that feels like. Riff thinks it was cool, me being his punk-band kid growing up, but it wasn't. I was that weird kid. I never knew what was going on in class 'cause I was gone half the time. Everybody thought I was some loser dummy."

"You're not, Sparrow. You're one of the strongest people I've ever met. Not many people would do what you've done for your dad."

A long pause. Had I convinced her?

"Here's the other thing, Jack. Raymond."

"Yeah?"

"All the statues and saints, the Blessed Virgins and Jesuses on the Cross—I mean, it was way simpler than that. He told me, 'Sparrow, it's all about Jesus, and Jesus was about forgiveness.' He said he forgave his parents for messing up his life, all their fighting. He said if they'd forgiven each other, the whole thing would have been different."

"So you're going to forgive—"

"My mom for being a junkie, ignoring me most of my life. Riff for thinking mostly about himself even when he's talking about me. All the so-called friends who dumped me when somebody better came along. This girl who cheated on me when I kind of loved her. It's all okay. I'm looking forwards, not backwards."

"That's good, but Zombie—"

"He got into this thing, Jack, and now he's in so deep he can't get out."

"Sparrow, there's no two ways about this. The guy's going to prison."

"Right. I mean, sure. I don't mean just let him go. I mean, don't just fucking execute him. That's what's gonna happen, I know it. Unless—"

Noise in the background.

"Unless what?"

Somebody knocking. Zombie?

"I gotta go. Don't tell Brandon I called you. This is just us."

And she was gone.

I drove, tried to take it all in. Raymond somehow imparting the philosophy of Christian forgiveness to Sparrow. Tough-as-nails Sparrow, telling the robber he was a loser, fighting the bureaucracy for her dad, robbing Salley with a stun gun stuck in his neck. And then the forgiveness idea kicking in when Zombie came to apologize.

Jesus.

I was crossing the Kennebec River, chunks of gray ice floating in the black water. The downtown in the distance, the gleaming State House dome. The state workers, the people headed to the hospital—all alongside my whirling sphere of trouble. Forgiveness? Not gonna happen.

The road led to the interstate, which dumped me off at the entrance to the mall. I waited for the light, then parked at the edge of the lot facing the bookstore. The store was just opening, a woman unlocking the doors from the inside, a few people waiting, some holding laptops.

They filed in, headed for coffee, romance novels. None of them looked like my shooter.

I was scanning the parking lot when a sudden glint of gold caught my notice. Across the road was a big cemetery with a cross at the center. Jesus was hanging there, keeping watch over the graves of the faithful, forgiving their sins. I felt like he'd been sent to watch me, too, to ask me what sins I was willing to forgive. Would I heed Sparrow's seeming conversion, Raymond's odd proselytizing? I felt a weird tremble, then shook it off.

I shifted back to the parking lot. Most cars were parked far from the store. Employees. Nobody sitting and watching except for me. And now Clair.

The big Ford rolled in from the back side of the lot, some delivery road. He pulled in beside me, nose of the truck in. Our windows went down.

"Morning," Clair said. "What's the plan?"

I told him my idea. I'd go in first, set up at the café. He'd sit on the door, watch for a tallish guy, rangy. Probably dressed in a way that evoked military. A camo hat. Tactical boots. We'd meet in the café. I had to see him, hear him. A few seconds was all.

"And then what?" Clair said.

I told him the rest of the plan. He made some adjustments. We bumped fists out our truck windows, and I got out, reached behind the seats for a second jacket, a black Carhartt. I put it on over my parka, added a green camo cap, REMINGTON on the front in script. It had been free with a shotgun, which seemed appropriate. I pulled the hood of my sweatshirt up.

"A little bit Michelin Man," Clair said.

"Jason's a chunky guy."

I reached back in, came out with a pair of black gloves, the fingers cut off.

"Jason's trademark," I said.

"Because you never know when you might need to pull the trigger," Clair said.

"Those cardboard targets don't have a chance."
A last pat-down. Wallet, phone, Glock. I started to turn to the store.
"Hey, Jack," Clair said.
I waited for the reporter joke.
"Be careful."

The people who'd been waiting at the door were now in the café, sitting at tables with coffee, laptops open. Another day at the office.

I went to the counter, ordered a large coffee. Thought of Jason, his belly over his belt, and added a raspberry Danish. While I waited for the coffee, I went to the magazine rack, the outdoors section. I selected a copy of *Guns & Ammo*. Moved down the aisle and picked up the latest *Four Wheeler*. Then I went back and picked up my order, moved to a seat in the corner, facing the front door. I sat, slouched down on the bench, opened the gun magazine, and bent over it.

My hood was up, my jackets zipped. I leaned on my elbows, gloves on, my face behind the bill of the cap, my head buried in the gun magazine. It was 8:40.

The minutes passed. A couple of people left, a couple more came in. A middle-aged couple having an outing. They ordered and sat. He was short, balding. Not Rebel.

A young guy alone, laptop under his arm. Tall and slim. Orange running shoes and stretchy black Adidas pants. He took off his puffy parka. A T-shirt that said *Take Back the Night*—a benefit 10K for domestic violence prevention. He took off his green watch cap. Short hair, the bangs dyed blonde.

Rebel undercover? He paid me no attention, opened the laptop.
I decided not.

I leaned back down, flipped the pages. A story about suppressors, how they let you get off more than one shot when hunting boar or coyotes. Another about the best new pistols and revolvers. There was a new Glock.

It was 8:48.

I raised the magazine on the table, the cover clearly showing. Kept my eyes on the room. Traffic through the front door was picking up. A store worker, a young guy with glasses and a name tag, came in and ordered a scone and a cup of tea.

8:52.

I turned the page. A review of a tactical shotgun with an optics mount. It was a Mossberg. Louis owned one.

8:55.

New rifle bullets that were better for long range. Grooves made for better aerodynamics. The writer tested them hunting deer in Nebraska, killed a buck at 466 yards. I turned the page. Looked up.

And there he was.

From the rear: jeans, work boots, Army fatigue jacket, camo hat. Tall and slim but broad-shouldered. The young woman behind the counter smiled at him. Some chitchat. She turned to make his coffee. I lifted the magazine, covered my face. Felt him turn, scan the room.

I waited. A machine whirred. Rebel had ordered a latte. Who knew?

Reaching into the pocket of my outer jacket, I took out my phone. Put it on the counter and opened voice memos. Hit record, slipped it under the truck magazine. Peeked out. He had his coffee. He was coming over. I kept my head down.

"Dude," I heard. "How you doing?"

Then the chair sliding out. I waited for the sound of him sitting, the cup placed on the table.

I lowered the magazine.

"Rebel," I said.

16

There was a flicker of surprise, and he stood there, frozen in place. Mouth open over an unshaven chin, hand still wrapped around his coffee, a Don't-Tread-on-Me rattlesnake tattooed on the top of his hand.

He smiled, gave a brief snort, looked around, sipped from his paper cup. Said, "I don't really like coffee. That's why I get it with all this milk."

The voice.

"Good to see you again," I said.

He hesitated, said, "You must think I'm somebody else." Put the coffee cup on the table and turned. I came out of my seat as he started for the exit, walking normally, then faster. He hit the door, me behind him, and broke into a trot across the lot.

An old Yukon, parked at the end of the row to the left. The truck sprayed flat black, the windows tinted dark. He slowed to get his keys out, skidded to a stop, caught himself against the driver's door. Yanked it open, flung himself in. Sat. Froze.

Clair was sitting in the backseat, his Kimber pressed against Rebel's neck.

Rebel laid his hands on top of the steering wheel, the snake trembling.

I closed the door, came around and opened the passenger side. There was stuff on the seat—fast-food wrappers, a bottle of Mountain Dew, junk mail, a lug wrench. For protection? I swept it all to the floor, got in. Closed the door and said, "If it were up to him, he'd kill you."

I leaned over, patted his jacket. The gun was in a shoulder holster on the left side. I yanked it out, put it on the seat beside me, door side. Said, "Let's go."

"No," Rebel said. "You won't shoot me here."

"I won't, but he might. He just found out he has a terminal illness. Doctors, you know. It's like Pandora's box. Bottom line is, most time he can do is maybe ninety days. And he's very close to my daughter, who you could have burned up."

I paused.

"Me, I'm like you. I was never in combat, tend to go a little easier. So if you're smart, you'll be home by lunchtime. Start the truck and drive. I'll give the directions."

Rebel hesitated. Clair prodded him with the gun. Rebel turned the key and the motor roared, then rumbled. He reached slowly for the shifter, put it in drive, and eased out of the space.

We drove out of the back side of the lot, took a left. Rebel drove the speed limit as we wound through a neighborhood of ranch houses, slowly descending. He was nervous, kept licking his lips. I said, "Relax. And don't give him an excuse."

He took a deep breath.

We passed the turnoff to Jason's aunt's house.

"He had to stay in home confinement, after all," I said.

Rebel tensed, and then we passed a few tenements, came into the harder side of the downtown. Warehouses, offices, stuff built for a mill that was long gone. We sat at the light, the gun still on his neck. He looked to the sidewalk, a couple of guys walking by with bags of empty cans.

"Don't even think about it," I said. "We shoot you and put the gun in your hand. You shot me but I didn't die. You came to finish the job."

The light changed. Rebel turned and we crossed the Kennebec, ice floes drifting downstream, the edges of the river frozen to the banks.

"You know how long you'd last in that water?" I said. "About fifteen minutes. That's until you're dead. You're starting to get paralyzed after five."

Then we took a right, headed south along the east side of the river. There were turnoffs—hiking trails, boat landing—and I told Rebel to go right. Clair, still silent, nudged him with the gun.

We were the only vehicle as we turned down the boarded-up arsenal, all gray stone, wooden trim weathering in the winter wind. Rebel drove faster, like he wanted to get out of this deserted place, and I said, "Slow down," and he did. We looped back up to the road, went right again. State buildings now, trucks and boats parked behind barbed wire like they'd been jailed.

And then the empty fortress of the old Augusta Mental Health Institute buildings. AMHI. Stone-block walls, peeling paint, and rusting fire escapes. All of it surrounded by a chain-link fence, as if a fence might keep the ghosts of that cursed place from escaping.

There was a parking lot there. A handful of cars, a couple of them plowed in.

"Here," I said.

He pulled in and parked facing a sign warning against trespassing, which seemed highly unlikely. I reached over and turned the key and the truck went quiet.

Rebel's hand slipped off his lap toward the door, and Clair flicked the gun barrel up and caught him in the ear.

"Aaagh," he said, reached up, felt the blood. "Fuckin' A."

"Love tap," Clair said, speaking for the first time. His voice was low and somehow, in just two words, menacing.

We sat in silence. A thin rivulet of blood ran from Pilgrim's ear to his neck, then stopped.

"Grim place," I said, looking out at the dark windows, the brush growing up along the walls. "I did a story once about the history of it. Sometimes people would escape and run down to the river and jump in, kill themselves rather than stay here."

A beat.

"We won't make you do that."

I reached down to the floor, picked up the mail. It was a flyer for a sporting goods store, addressed to Milford T. Graves II. An RFD address in Randolph, just downriver. A sale on guns and ammo.

"Buy your shotgun here, Milford?" I said.

No reply.

"You can tell me who sent you to do the firebomb and shoot me," I said. "We move on up the food chain. It's always better to cut the head off the snake."

I looked at him as he stared straight ahead. Narrow face with a long nose, jutting chin, sunken cheeks. Hair coming out from under his cap like he had his head buzzed once a year and the year was almost up.

"Was this Pilgrim's idea? Doing a little thinking on his own? He's on home confinement, so he calls you?"

He clenched his mouth shut.

"An alternate scenario. I don't think it was Stryker, but maybe Horseman or Citizen or Nomad? I went to talk to Stryker. Nice spread, by the way. Guy has some bucks. But he wasn't happy. Not just that I'd tracked him down, but the fact that what you did led me to him. If you all were in a drug cartel, you'd be dead by now. Maybe Stryker would have you chopped up and poured into a foundation."

Rebel pursed his lips.

Clair lowered the gun, rested it on top of the seat. The cooling motor ticked. Some pigeons burst out of a roosting place atop the building, circled and landed back where they started.

"What I could do is go back to Stryker, say you ratted him out. You said you're just a foot soldier. He gives the orders."

Rebel shook his head. "He wouldn't believe that. I mean, we swore an oath."

"Cross my heart and hope to die?"

"There's no rats."

"But Milford, this was a major screwup. I don't know what your overall plan is. I mean, march on the State House? Shoot up some power stations? Blow up a politician's car? Kidnap the governor?"

He didn't answer.

"But intimidating one reporter probably isn't it. And now you've got all this attention coming down on you and your boys. I think they've already decided you're a weak link, a loose cannon, going off on your own little missions."

He shook his head. "No way. I'm just defending myself. We all are. Defending real Americans against a freakin' corrupt government. This country is gonna be overrun by socialists and goddamn immigrants if people like me don't fight back. And politicians won't do shit, any of 'em, because they're all getting rich off the rest of us."

He took a breath. "My dad, his dad—they worked their asses off, dairy farming. You oughta try that, mister man. Twelve hours a day, every day, no vacation, no holidays. And the fuckin' government kept cutting the prices, hitting us with new regulations, inspectors coming in, giving all these stupid fuckin' orders, never worked on a farm a day in their lives. Then the town jacked up the taxes on the land. My dad lost the cows, lost the farm. Some out-of-state assholes got it for nothin', put houses on it. They got rich, too."

He squeezed the steering wheel with both hands.

"So you know what the old man did about it? He killed himself. Shotgun, but it wasn't no birdshot. They came to auction off his milking machines, first they had to clean his brains off the wall."

Rebel was breathing hard.

"Now we got Blacks and Hispanics pouring in, sucking up the welfare. Selling drugs."

"Most Maine drug dealers are just like you," I said. "White as the driven snow."

"Well, where do they get it from then? Mass., New York. This fuckin' state is going down the shitter."

"So, you're a racist moron. I get it. Why shoot me?"

He tensed. "You were a fuckin' problem, that's why," he said. "Asking all these questions, pumping Jason's old lady, her kid for information. Your wife working for the State Gestapo, you for that fucking lib newspaper, spreading lies. Needed you to know you were playing with fire."

"So to speak," I said. "Who gave the order?"

He went quiet, like he knew he'd said too much.

"Don't matter," he said. "Not like anybody got killed."

"Doesn't. And no, nobody got killed."

A beat.

"Yet," I said.

We sat. He took a deep breath. Behind him, Clair's gun hand was steady, like a surveillance camera focused on Rebel's neck. We sat there for a moment or two, and then Clair said, "So what are we gonna do?"

Like we were a team tackling a problem.

I looked out the window, thought of Sparrow and Raymond, Jesus, and forgiveness. I considered Detective Strain—that we could just turn Rebel over to him. He'd confessed, though a lawyer would argue that it was all inadmissible, that a gun had been pointed at his head. If they did charge him—aggravated assault, attempted arson—would they charge me and Clair for terrorizing with a dangerous weapon, kidnapping? And where would that leave Louis and Marta, Sophie and Roxanne?

And then I thought of Stryker in the horse barn—that maybe Rebel really *had* become a liability. That they'd want to cut him loose anyway. Clair looked at me. He was waiting, too.

"Let's go," I said.

Rebel did, warily, like a student driver. We circled the lot, back-tracked along the river. As we crossed the bridge, back in traffic, he seemed a little relieved, like maybe this had all just been an informational chat. Let bygones be bygones. The old guy, he was dangerous, but the reporter was all talk.

Back through the capital's downtown, with its weird mix of grand and grime. Up the hill, the Kennebec snaking along below us. Tenements gave way to a labyrinth of streets with their boxy ranch houses. I told him to turn.

Rebel did. He drove on and I told him to turn again. This time he looked at me, but still slowed, eased onto the street where Jason was locked in the house with the pampered dog, his aunt making his favorite meals.

There was a double lot next door, another ranch house with a snow-covered lawn, a wishing well with a wooden bucket hanging under a shingled roof. I wondered what they wished for. Probably not much.

I told Rebel to pull over and stop. He did. Put the truck in park.

"We're comin', asshole," Rebel said, braver now that he had one foot out the door. "All the people like you, like your friggin' Gestapo old lady, your kid. Surprised she wasn't a liberal abortion. You're the enemy. And don't think we can't find you, 'cause—"

I felt anger rise like bile, reached down to the floor, picked up the lug wrench. Held it by the sharp end, the heavy socket weighing down the other end of the steel bar. He was still going on as I pivoted in my seat, swung the wrench as hard as I could.

His right hand, knuckles, trigger finger. A smacking thud, bones shattered.

Rebel screamed. Grabbed his right hand with his left, held the broken one against his belly.

He shouted "Oh, my fuckin' God!" over and over as his face went pale. He began to sweat, beads on his forehead, under his hat. Then he was crying out, moaning, rocking forward and back.

"Don't ever come near my house again," I said. "If you do, I'll do your other hand. And then I'll kill you. Now get out."

He looked at me, panting, in some kind of shock. But then he leaned over, opened the door with his good hand, the broken hand still close to his belly. Turned and slid down.

I jumped out on my side, came around and climbed into the driver's seat.

"You got lucky," I said, throwing his gun and clip into the snow at his feet.

I shut the door, shifted into drive, and drove off slowly. Stopped in the middle of the street. When I looked in the rearview, he was picking the gun up with his left hand. He stood and shoved it into his jacket pocket, shuffled over to pick the clip up, too. Took the broken hand in his good hand and started walking slowly toward Jason's aunt's house.

We pulled out, backtracked. There was a Thai restaurant on the cross street. I pulled in, took Jason's phone out, then mine. On my phone I searched for the non-emergency number of the Augusta police. Switched to Jason's phone and called.

"I'd like to report a suspicious man in the vicinity of 58 Royal Ave. I saw him put a gun in his jacket. This was less than a minute ago. He's going into that house, where a man named Jason is on monitored release. This would be a violation of his conditions."

"Who is speaking, sir?" the dispatcher said.

"A concerned citizen," I said, and hung up, pulled back out.

The phone buzzed, the dispatcher calling back. I reached over and turned it off. Drove back up the hill. At the crest, I took a right onto the road to the mall, emerged by the bookstore. There were more customers now, our trucks sandwiched by cars. I parked Rebel's truck at the far end of one of the rows and shut off the engine.

I sat back, Clair still in the backseat, his gun put away.

"And now we wait," he said.

"See if they really want to cut him loose."

"If not, we gave the bear a serious poke."

Clair got out and came around to the front seat, put the wrench back on the floor.

We sat as people walked in and out of the bookstore. I looked out at Jesus across the way, watching over the cemetery. Clair rustled in his seat.

"Metacarpals and phalanges, nerves and tendons," he said. "Human hand is a complex piece of engineering. He's gonna be a lefty for a good long while."

I nodded. And then I told him about Sparrow, how she was thinking of Raymond and his religion, that she was worried the police would shoot Zombie, that maybe she should even forgive him.

"Makes you think," Clair said. "I mean, what kind of world do we live in? How do we want to go out."

He looked over at the graves, a strange stone encampment, the monuments lit by the low-lying sun. "Had a friend from the war. Rodney

Lane, from Houston. We called him Rambo. The book had just come out, no movies yet. Anyway, we were in the same Recon platoon for almost a year. He walked point, mostly. Tremendous soldier, great tracker, calm under fire, always thinking three steps ahead. A brother you could always count on. And smart. Read all the time when we weren't in the bush. Kierkegaard. *The Odyssey*. I remember him reading this big fat biography of Mozart. Must have weighed five pounds. Who knows where he got it. Said he was interested in the details of genius, how some minds worked in such different ways. Used to read me parts out loud."

He paused, still gazing at the cemetery.

"We stayed in touch. He even came to Prosperity once. Said it was a scene from a different time, the fields, the Amish. Said I'd escaped into a painting by Bruegel."

A beat, the point coming.

"I went to see him a while back. He's in a nursing home—memory care, they call it. Didn't remember me. Thought I was his father. Kept saying, 'Daddy, why didn't Mom come?'"

Clair swallowed hard.

"They'd given him a teddy bear, and he held it the whole time. Had a bib because he kept dribbling. Worker came in and fed him his lunch with a spoon. Talked to Rambo like he was a toddler."

Another pause. I waited.

"I don't want to go out like that, Jack. Not remembering my friends or family, my life erased from the inside. Starting to slide already, searching for words. The other day I couldn't remember 'mendacious.' Day before that it was 'tamarack.' Took me five minutes, just staring at the goddamn tree in a field. Connections slowing down.

"So what's the alternative? Hey, Mary and the kids, they're good, chunk of money set aside. All that's left is to do a little good on the way out. Leave the world a better place, kind of like we've been doing all these years, you and me. And you know what they say: You can do a lot when you're not banking on your own survival."

He smiled.

"Hey, it's a win-win," I said.

He adjusted the gun under his jacket, tugged at the bill of his John Deere cap.

"Anyway, it's been an interesting day, Jack," Clair said. He got out, leaned through the open door, and said, "Way to turn the other cheek."

17

We left Rebel's truck in the lot, keys in the visor, and split up.

Clair went from Augusta to Sanctuary to meet with Louis. More tactics, less strategy. I drove thirty miles southwest to Clarkston, pulled up in front of Sparrow's house just before eleven a.m. She was home. Blake's truck wasn't there.

I went to the front door and knocked. Waited on the stoop. The door opened.

"Hey," Sparrow said. Gray hoodie pulled up, tufts of blue hair peeking out. More than the usual black eyeliner, blue sparkly mascara.

"Hi there," I said. "Your dad home?"

"Brandon took him for a ride in the truck. They drive around, look for blue pickups."

"Hay in the haystack."

"Yeah. There's hundreds of them."

"You want them to find the one?" I said.

"I don't know," Sparrow said, and she turned and walked down the hallway. I followed.

We went to the kitchen. There was coffee in the pot and Sparrow poured me a mug without asking. Picked hers up from the table. We stood and leaned against the counter beside the row of Riff's pills.

"How's he doing?" I said.

"Good. Got on the new meds. May be just psychological at this point, but he's got way more spring in his step."

"Lifted the weight of thinking he's dying."

"He still is," Sparrow said. "We all are. Just a matter of time."

"Kind of a gloomy outlook, for whatever gen you are."

"Z. But I don't kid myself about things."

"What about Zombie?"

"What about him?"

"A guy who goes around robbing stores with a loaded gun, pistol-whips a clerk and shoots the owner—he's more than misunderstood."

"I'm not saying he's not fucked up. I'm just saying he deserves some kinda life, after prison. But he's gotta get there, you know what I'm saying?"

"Is that what you told Dunne this morning?"

"More or less," Sparrow said. "I was, like, he's still human. He's not some rabid dog."

"The next person he shoots won't get the distinction."

She sipped her coffee, looking away.

"Somebody has to break the chain," she said. "I mean, people hating, killing each other. You try watching the news? Fucking madness. But what if Jesus was right? Or Muhammad. That Gandhi dude. Whatever. I mean, it's kinda radical when you think about it. Right? What if people just, I dunno, let it all go."

I thought of Rebel, his shattered hand. We both drank coffee. I said, "How was the recording session?"

"Fine. Good. Stephanie was, like, wigging out, how much traffic it's gonna get."

"She gets excited."

"I guess."

"If it brings Zombie in," I said.

Sparrow frowned.

"I'm setting him up," she said. "In a weird way he trusts me, you know?"

"He's got a thing for you."

She shrugged. Sipped. Her lips had a dark blue line painted on the edges.

"So, what *is* the plan?" I asked.

Sparrow exhaled, like the whole thing made her tired.

"Theirs? He comes in, there's cops hiding everywhere. Cars in the parking lot. The cooler. The bathroom. Come out, tell him to drop the gun. That's where he's in so much danger. I mean, drop the gun? How fast? Does he get two seconds to think about it? What if he's kind of stunned, and they just start shooting?"

She was right. A bunch of Clarkston cops, fingers on triggers. Once one of them fired, it was over. A fusillade.

We stood there, me picturing Zombie riddled like Clyde Barrow. Sparrow thinking it would be her fault, like she was pulling the trigger herself.

"We can save him," she said.

"We? How?"

"The church. Go there. Sit and wait. I'm gonna meet him there."

"Why?"

"Because it's a safe place. I mean, even if you're not, like, religious, you get that vibe."

"Sanctuary," I said.

"Exactly."

"So then what?"

"I tell him you're good people. We talk. Or more like listen."

"To Zombie?"

"Yeah. I mean, Jack, you're the best listener I've ever met. You make people feel like you really care about what they're saying—you're taking it all in, like it's important."

"It's what I do."

"Right," Sparrow said. "So we just let him talk. Let him tell us how he got himself into this mess. You ask the right questions, like you do. I'm there to kind of be the go-between, encourage him when he gets stuck."

"And then what?"

She sipped her coffee.

"Until he's calm, feeling understood, both of us are there. And then I just level with him. Yeah, he's gonna do time. But after that, he'll have his life back. He won't be that old. He can move someplace, start all over."

"And then?"

"The two of us go with him to the police station. You're right there, and you're the press. They can't just beat the crap out of him. He'll have people—me and you, all your readers or whatever—watching. He'll turn himself in."

Sparrow looked at me from under the hoodie and waited.

"When?" I said.

She half-smiled, the blue-lined lips twitching. "Twenty minutes. I texted him. I'm bringing him to the church. You go there now, wait."

"The door?"

"I already unlocked it. I don't want to give him a chance to run on me while I'm fiddling with the key."

"Will he have a gun?"

"I don't know."

"I will. In case this goes sideways."

"It won't. Trust me, Jack," Sparrow said. "I've got this."

A single set of tracks showed in a dusting of new snow. Sparrow's. She'd stood at the door, fumbled at the lock. It was gone, the hasp hanging loose. I pulled the big door open, the hinges creaking. Stepped in and closed it behind me. Took my phone out and flicked on the light.

Dim light showing through stained-glass windows. A faint flutter high above me. Pigeons.

I walked, plaster crunching underfoot. The sound echoed. I stopped. Turned the light off. Listened. Walked to the center aisle, the altar to my right, bare like it had been looted. I continued down the aisle, smelling the sour odor of bird droppings, dust, and mold.

Halfway to the rear, I sidled into a pew. Looked back to the door, and moved farther in. Sat in the cold darkness. Looked at my phone, saw that the twenty minutes was almost up.

I reached into my pocket, felt the Glock. Waited. One minute. Two. And the door creaked open.

Sparrow came into view, hood still up. Then a guy wearing a dark baseball cap. He followed her, across the front of the church, turned and started down the aisle. She slowed and he followed suit. She saw me, and he did the same, a split second later. They stopped and she took him by the arm.

"It's okay," Sparrow said. "It's gonna be okay."

The words reverberated in the cold space.

They walked slowly down the aisle, side by side like a couple at a wedding. When they drew closer, I could see him. He was young, with a broad open face, an attempt at a beard. A blue-and-gray jacket, like you'd wear if you were on the football team. His eyes were locked on mine, hands at his sides. I kept my hands in my pockets, right hand on the Glock.

I stood as they turned into the pew, Zombie first, Sparrow's hand on his back now. They moved closer.

"Carl," Sparrow said. "This is my friend, Jack. He's good people."

"The reporter," Carl said.

"How you doing?" I said.

I held out my hand. He hesitated, then took it. I squeezed and he squeezed back. I smiled but he didn't. They turned and we all sat.

Sparrow leaned forward, looked across at me, said, "I told Carl about our plan."

Our plan?

"Okay," I said.

He turned and glanced at me, then away, his left thigh drumming on the pew.

"I told him having you along is like having a hundred thousand witnesses," Sparrow said.

"*New York Times*?" Carl said.

"Yes."

"Are you working now? I mean, what we say goes in a story?"

"Only if you want it to," I said.

"See?" Sparrow said. "He's okay."

Carl stared straight ahead into the gloom, and Sparrow and I did the same. Above us, a pigeon rustled on its roost. Dust fell like snow. We sat in the pew in silence, like we were praying. A minute passed, then another. And then Carl stirred, cleared his throat. I could smell mint, like he'd just brushed his teeth.

"It kinda started with a video game," he said. "It's called *Armed Robbery*. I play it with my buddy, Trevor. He used to live here, but he moved to Vegas."

We waited. He cleared his throat again.

"You hold up banks and shit, have different weapons. It's like you against the cops. It's pretty cool." His leg was still thrumming on the pew. His right arm moved and mine did, too, toward my gun. Carl adjusted his hat.

"I was stoned the first time I did it. I mean, it was like the game, except better, because it was real. I wasn't gonna shoot anybody or anything. I just liked walking in, the worker just freezing, giving you the money. And then you gotta get away. That was the hardest part. In my head, I got points for the robbery, then more for the getaway."

"The first time the gun wasn't even loaded, right?" Sparrow said.

"No, but when I read about all these store people arming up, I figured I'd better be able to shoot back, if I had to."

"Which you did. At Sparrow's store," I said quietly.

"Shit, that dude—it was just like the game. He reaches for his weapon, says, 'Drop it!' or whatever, but I knew he was gonna start blasting. I could see it in his face, how psyched he was. I mean, it was whoever shot first."

He paused.

"I never meant to hurt anybody. Shooting in video games is different. I know it sounds lame, but it can be confusing, you know? In the moment. Reflexes."

"Yeah," I said. "Only you hit Sparrow with the gun. Is that in your game?" I said.

Carl shook his head. He looked lost. I almost felt sorry for him.

188 · HARD LINE

"I don't know what happened then. I just kinda lost it. It wasn't her. It was, like, all these chicks that have blown me off before, and something in the way she looked at me. And the thing was, I really liked her. I mean, I still do. But then, at the store, I didn't know her like I do now. I thought she was cool, though, and I thought maybe I could even go in sometime—without the mask—and talk to her. Like, maybe I could get her number or whatever, you know? And then the way she was looking at me, I felt her, like, thinking I was some goofball loser. Not worth her time."

He took a breath, turned to Sparrow.

"You know I'm wicked sorry about that. I hate that I hurt you."

Sparrow nodded. "I know."

Carl turned to me. Behind the wispy beard, he looked like a kid. The eyes.

"I'm not making excuses, but my family is pretty screwed up. My dad left when I was eight, took off with this admin at his office. Then they moved to Auburn and it was like he'd never been with us, me and my mom. The first year he stopped by on my birthday, and then the next year he called, and after that, nothing. I mean, he was, like, eight miles away. He and Cheryl had a kid, and it was like we were erased. He's a wicked asshole, which is a hard thing to feel about your own dad." He waited for a response, then said, "Not like this is all his fault. I mean, I'm the one who did it."

"Because it was exciting?" I said.

"It was a wicked rush," Carl said. "I mean, my job is boring right now. I do data entry for this insurance company in Minnesota. But I never go there. I just punch in numbers. After a few hours, I'm brain-dead. I'm nobody. Just some guy somewhere."

"But not when you're Zombie."

"No, that's when I use everything. I mean, it's all about execution. Surveillance. Timing. When to go in. Once the mask goes on, it's game time, you know what I'm saying? You gotta know when to abort. I've been about to mask up when somebody pulls up for coffee or whatever.

That's the thing. You never know who's carrying these days. Last thing you want is a shootout."

He stopped, and I could feel his energy shifting.

"Then when I'm Zombie, in the store," he said, getting excited just telling us about it, "you gotta get the tone right. You have to be scary, but efficient. Thirty seconds max. Then there's the exit strategy, the route. More recon. Very important. This town is swarming with cops right now."

"How do you get away?" I said.

"If I told you, I'd have to kill you," Carl said, then caught himself. "Just kidding."

I waited. He looked around, said, "Parked cars. I find one that's unlocked and get in the backseat, on the floor. Just wait it out."

"What about tracking dogs?"

"Plastic bags over my boots. I read about it online. Then, I walk a couple more blocks, get in another parked car, lie down on the floor in the back. One time I rode with this guy all the way to the car-pool lot out by the highway. Never saw me." He grinned.

I smiled back. The pigeons rustled in the beams of the ceiling.

"Carl, you can do this. Do your time and be done with it, move on," Sparrow said.

Carl frowned.

"I've been thinking."

We waited. He adjusted his hat. Turned to me.

"How long a time, do you think?"

"I don't know. Depends on the prosecutor, the judge. You've rubbed their faces in it. Then you shot that guy."

He waited.

"Then again, first offense—" I looked at him. "Is it?"

"Oh, yeah. I mean, I never did anything wrong before this."

"So that, plus your background, broken home. How it started as a game, and you never meant to hurt anybody."

"So, five?" Carl said.

"No. I mean, the guy at the store could have died."

"It was self-defense."

I hesitated.

"Let's just get it out there," Sparrow said. "You've been bullshitted around enough, by your dad. I did some research. I'd say ten to fifteen."

Way low, I thought. I said, "Maybe two or three suspended. Your age and no priors." I said.

He reached for his pocket and jumped to his feet, said, "I'm not doing any fifteen years." He scrambled over Sparrow. She tried to grab his arm but he shook loose, was out of the pew and running. Halfway down the aisle, he pulled a gun out.

Sparrow was ten feet behind him, following him to the front of the church, turning left, toward the door.

"Carl, no. Stop!"

He slammed through the door, light streaming in.

She followed, and I did, too. Ten feet behind them. I saw Sparrow slamming through the gate, Carl headed for the street. There was a gray car parked there, an old Nissan. He circled it, gun in hand. Opened the door, threw himself into the driver's seat. Sparrow yanked the passenger door open, dove in. She had him by the right arm, the gun in his left.

"No, Carl. No!" Sparrow said.

He was fumbling with the key, the gun by his side. And then he dropped the key, put the gun to his head, stared straight ahead.

Sparrow sat back. I stood by the open driver's door, gun out, pointed at him.

"I ain't doing any fifteen years," he said. "I'd rather die."

"No. No, you wouldn't. You can do it," Sparrow said.

"I can't." Jaw clenched, he tightened his grip on the gun.

"You can," Sparrow said. "You're young, Carl. We're both young."

She reached over and took his right hand in hers.

I expected her to maybe say something about taking classes in prison, how he could learn a trade. It would go by fast. Instead, she said, "Carl. Would you like to kiss me?"

He turned to her, startled, the gun still pressed to the side of his head. She smiled.

"What?" He looked at her, lowered the gun.

She repeated her proposition.

Carl hesitated for a second, then laid the gun on his lap. Turned to her.

"Are you serious?" he said.

She nodded.

When he reached for her, I eased in closer, took his gun, snapped the clip out. It was a nine-millimeter Taurus. I put it in my left jacket pocket, my gun in the right.

Sparrow leaned in to make it easier and Carl kissed her, gently, on the lips. The kiss lingered and then he fell back. He let out a short sigh. Sparrow smiled.

"You are young, Carl. Even with fifteen years, you have a whole life to look forward to."

He looked at her. "You'd write to me?"

"Of course."

Carl shoved his hands in his pockets. His face was flushed. "Now what?"

"We go to the police station, the three of us," Sparrow said. "And no matter what happens after that, you remember that kiss."

He eased back into his seat.

"Maybe we'll talk on the phone."

"Sure," Sparrow said. "Of course we will."

A long pause, Carl staring straight ahead, his future unrolling in his head.

"It's gonna be okay," Sparrow said.

He thought for a moment, turned back to her. "One good thing about all this shit. I met you."

She smiled. "Yeah."

Carl drove. I rode in the back, behind him. When we got to the police station, we drove into a half-circle, stopped in front of the main door.

Carl got out of the car, took his phone, and made a call.

"This is Zombie. I'm at the front door. I'm here to turn myself in."

Cops piled out of the door, two patrol. Sanitas, of all the detectives. They had guns out.

Carl put up his hands. They swarmed him, spun him around. Shoved onto the hood of the car and cuffed his hands behind his back.

I handed Sanitas Carl's gun.

"What are you doing here?" Sanitas said.

"Bearing witness," I said. "For the record, he's got no bumps or bruises."

I held out the Taurus's clip, and he took it. He gave me a hard stare, said, "Wait here, both of you," and went back to Zombie, looking small as he stood between the uniforms.

"Inside, you fucking asshole," Sanitas said.

He took Carl by the shoulder, practically lifting him off the ground. As he was being led away, Carl turned to Sparrow and said, "I love you." And then he was gone, the door slamming shut behind him, the first of many.

We stood, leaning against Carl's car.

"That was a good thing you did," I said. "You saved his life."

Sparrow shrugged. "Somebody should tell his mom. She's gonna freak. Probably shouldn't be alone."

"You signing up for that, too?"

Sparrow didn't answer. I was suddenly cold, tucked my hands in my pockets. She let out a long sigh.

"Are you going to call him?" I said.

"I don't know."

"He'll write to you."

"Probably," Sparrow said.

"He'll expect you to be there when he gets out."

A beat, and she said, "Fifteen years, Jack. That's a lifetime."

18

There were three interview rooms in the corridor. I was in No. 3, with Sanitas. Jolie took Sparrow into No. 2. I presumed they had Carl in No. 1 with the big guns. So to speak.

I told Sanitas my story, beginning with sitting in the church alone. I said it could have ended there, with Zombie blowing his brains out. I told him how that didn't happen.

"So you played him until you got the gun away?" Sanitas said, writing on a legal pad in big round letters, like he was carving his notes onto a board.

"It wasn't me," I said. "She got him to put the gun down. By that time, I think his suicidal intentions had passed."

" 'Cause she had him in a lip lock."

I didn't comment.

He scrawled, looked up and said, "Off the record, you think she really has feelings for this loser? I mean, he busted her head with a gun."

I shrugged. "I don't know. I think she didn't want him to die for it. By his own hand, or someone else's."

"Some people would be thinking, 'Go ahead. Pull the trigger.' "

"I guess Sparrow's not some people."

He wrote something on the pad, the pen like a twig in his big fist. "Another question."

I waited.

"I know Blake is bonking her. You think he knew this was going down? That Sparrow and Zombie were talking? That she knew who Zombie was?"

"Nothing she said or he said would lead me to believe that was the case," I said.

Sanitas looked at me, said, "Right." He smiled, reached over, and ended the recording on his phone.

"Well, he's done now. Started spilling his guts before we even sat him down. Had to tell him to shut up, read him his Miranda rights. Unless a lawyer gets in the way, he pleads guilty. Attempted murder, multiple armed robberies, aggravated assault. No trial. Probably you won't even be called as a witness."

I didn't answer.

"Which is too bad," Sanitas said.

"Why's that?"

"Because you're the elephant in the room, McMorrow. The dead church guy, you find the body. Girl gets whacked in the store, you're there, too. Zombie turns himself in, you're holding his friggin' hand."

"That wasn't me," I said.

"Point is, it's always half the story, you know what I'm saying? I'd love to see you up on the stand, take that oath. The whole truth."

I waited.

"Because I think you play close to the line, sometimes cross it, whatever works for you. Sometimes I wonder which side you're on."

"I don't pick sides," I said.

He heaved himself up from the chair. I got up, too.

"Well, there comes a time, McMorrow, where you have to decide. Am I a good guy or am I a bad guy? Don't kid yourself. There's no middle ground."

He turned to the door, opened it, and stepped out. I followed and we walked down the corridor.

"Stop at the front desk," Sanitas said. "They'll give you back your gun."

He opened a door with a pass code, and left me alone.

As I passed the interview rooms, I heard Sparrow's voice, then Zombie's, him saying, "I still have the money. I didn't spend any of it. I'll give it all back."

Like that made any difference.

Outside, the rain was freezing. I decided to walk back to my truck, past halal groceries and check-cashing shops. As I walked along the sidewalks, stepped over the brine-filled gutters, I thought of Sparrow, how the gun could have been turned on her in a millisecond. Then Carl could have shot himself before I'd even gotten my gun out. I'd have been left standing there with their dead bodies.

But she'd stopped this chain of violence with an offer of affection. Faced down a gun with a kiss.

I thought of Jason and his buddies. Marta luring the bikers into our world. Louis and Clair locked and loaded, ready to do battle with the forces of evil. I felt a pang of doubt. Were we doing good or prolonging the mayhem? An eye for an eye for an eye.

Crossing the street, I felt the gun in my pocket. Shook off the doubts. Continued on.

I turned the corner, crossed the parking lot, my truck at the far end. And I saw footprints in the snow in the shadow of the church, our tracks leading to the door, and another set going in. Smaller.

I turned, followed them to the church door. It was half open. I hesitated, then stepped in. Heard a woman's voice coming from the dusky darkness.

Dunne.

"So it was here that Sparrow Aldo, Zombie's victim, the woman he struck with a gun—he even shot her boss in the chest—it was right here that Sparrow convinced Zombie, the robber who terrorized this town, to turn himself in."

I moved to the edge of the pews, saw Dunne standing at the front of the church, speaking into a microphone.

"I'm in awe. This place. That heroic deed. I mean, can I be honest with you? I'm almost at a loss for words. That Sparrow Aldo did what she did, facing down an armed robber—"

She saw me, looked away.

"—the most sought-after criminal in this city's history, convincing him to give himself up and end his reign of terror."

She started walking down the aisle. The pigeons started to flutter and she held her microphone up to the ceiling.

"This holy and haunted place was the scene of an amazing act of heroism. And you'll hear more about it in this amazing episode of *Who Dunne It?* Stay with me. Spread the word. Sparrow Aldo's story is a shining example for us all."

Dunne turned and walked slowly up the aisle toward me. Her eyes were glowing in the gloom.

"Incredible," she said.

"Yes. She's a remarkable person."

"And you were here, witness to it all."

"Who told you that?"

"You aren't the only one with sources, Jack McMorrow," Dunne said.

I didn't reply.

"Zombie infatuated with Sparrow, the store clerk he robbed and assaulted. Finds her and says he's sorry, that he'll do anything to make up for what he's done to her. So does she run to the police, call 911? No. She talks to him. She tries to understand him. And when the time comes, when they've developed a special trust, she convinces him to surrender. She even accompanies him to the police station. It's just amazing. And the icing on the cake? You were here. You were sitting in this church when it all went down."

She darted in, gave me a hug. Broke away, and looked at me.

"We'll go top ten. Did you know Spotify just made a sixty-million-dollar podcast deal? And nobody in true crime has anything like this. Nobody."

Dunne looked around.

"And this church. My God. The pigeons. The stuff crunching under your feet. I mean, the audio will be incredible."

Back to me.

"Let's talk script this week. We can create a teaser right off. Something totally atmospheric. I mean, put the listeners right here, like they're—"

"Stephanie."

She looked at me, still glowing.

"I don't know that we can talk about this, me and Sparrow. We're witnesses. He hasn't even been arraigned."

"Okay, so we delay release until after he pleads. I mean, he's confessed, right? I mean, it's not like there's some jury pool you're gonna mess up. There's just Zombie in front of a judge. The public needs to know how this happened, Jack. It's inspiring. Sparrow's courage. Not to mention, she'll be awesome on audio—on camera, even."

She paused, picturing it.

"Sexy hipster store clerk sees a masked robber as human. They fall in love. What does he look like, by the way? Not hard on the eyes, I hope. Maybe a video documentary. Or a dramatization sort of thing. We can sell it to Hulu or Netflix. I already called this agent I know in LA. Lorrie's totally plugged in."

"Stephanie, slow down."

"And you, Jack. We can market the heck out of you. I'll make some calls. I mean, forget newspapers, this Gray Lady nonsense. This will put you out there. Go right to the readers with your own blog, link to the podcast. We create this synergy, become our own media company. Oh, Jack. I know it's a lot to take in. But just leave the business part to me, and you tell the story. It's what you do best."

She darted in for another hug, coffee breath and perfume. Fell back.

"Is that a gun in your pocket or are you just glad to see me? Just kidding. I love it. I mean, talk about adding an element of danger. Even the reporter is carrying, right?"

Her phone buzzed and she held it up, peered at it in the dim light.

"Oh, it's Lorrie. Even my mini pitch—she knows we have something here."

Dunne brought the phone to her ear, smiled. "Honey! Thanks for getting back. Listen, I know you're busy so I'll just cut right to the chase. Armed robber falls in love with the woman he holds up . . . No, both of them are just kids. Early twenties. She's this gothy hipster, very sexy. He's scary until he takes off his zombie mask. Right. I mean, can't you see it?"

I turned and walked up the aisle and out of the church. The light was blinding for a moment, then gray. The roller coaster slowed but only slightly, the genie still out of the bottle. Dunne, the podcast, a potential movie. A media ruckus, when all Sparrow had wanted was for Carl to go quietly. Would he change his mind about pleading? Think Sparrow had betrayed him?

I walked to the truck, climbed in. Looked over at the church, saw Dunne come out the door, on FaceTime now, the phone held in front of her. Then she was holding it up to show the agent the church. I heard her say, "I know. I mean, can't you just see it?"

I started the motor, backed out, and drove out of the lot. It was time to head north. The world chasing me home. Again.

19

Roxanne would be on her way back from class in Portland. Maine Public Radio had news at 3:50, before NPR. They'd pick this up for sure. I wanted her to hear it from me, first.

I called her as I drove, out Porto Street. Voicemail. I asked her to call me, said that everything was fine, not to worry.

I pulled over and texted her before I reached the turnpike ramp. Same message. I pictured her phone in her bag, still on silent from class. I got on the highway, hit the gas.

The traffic was light, a few tractor-trailer rigs driving north: Walmart, Hannaford. Out-of-state pickups pulling snowmobile trailers, guys slouched in the cabs. I blew by all of them, the highway threading between snow-covered fields, empty dairy barns with billboards painted on the sides. A shiny rest stop, chain restaurants and gas pumps, a few rigs parked as drivers slept.

I was wired, images of the day replaying like a pregame highlight reel. Or was it lowlights?

Rebel screaming as his hand was crushed. Clair's unblinking gaze, his gun barrel sighted on Rebel's neck, his finger on the trigger. Our conversation in the church, Zombie's mystery falling away as the video game ended for real in the shape of a lonely, frustrated young man named Carl. Dunne's excitement, the story forming in her head, the notoriety like some sexual thing, a compulsion to be seen and heard.

It all whirled in a random jumble, like Roxanne and Sophie were the only things in my life that weren't spinning out of control. But I was spinning away from them: the church, the kiss. Rebel's shattered hand. The truth was, for a long second I wanted to do his other one. Take a shot at me now, chump.

I sped through the Gardiner tolls, the card reader blipping like a muzzle flash from the crossbar above the highway. Heavier traffic as I reached Augusta, slung across three lanes and exited, swung northeast and crossed the Kennebec River again. More black ice-pocked water. The State House dome.

My phone ringing.

Sophie. I answered with the button on the steering wheel.

"Hey, honey. Everything okay?"

"Yeah. I tried to call Mom but she never answers."

"On her way back from school. Probably forgot to turn her ringer back on."

"She's lame when it comes to phones."

"But not so lame when it comes to everything else," I said. "What's up?"

A crackle, kids' voices in the background. Then Sophie again.

"Sorry, Dad. Anyway, it's Mr. Ziggy."

"What about him?"

"He asked me and Tara to go see *Annie*. The real one."

"What? In New York?"

"No, Boston. They have these shows they put on across the country. But still, isn't that so cool?"

"I guess. But who else is—"

"He knows people who are working on the play. Like backstage. Set designers, lighting techs. And he said he can get us in to meet the actors, maybe."

I was shifting gears, grasping for this new one.

"So, what? You'd go to Boston with him?"

"Yeah, but he said he can get tickets for you guys, too."

"Oh."

"It's this weekend. I have to tell him tomorrow."

A beat as I thought about it, this weird family outing. Didn't this guy have anything better to do?

"Are you guys gonna be around?" Sophie said. "Because if you aren't, I could just go with Tara and Tiffanee."

I was still thinking. Where would I be? Back in Clarkston, explaining why I'd ended up in the pew with a fugitive armed robber? With Detective Strain, asking me if I knew how this guy ended up with his hand broken in fifteen places? In Sanctuary, waiting for an all-out assault? Listening to Dunne talk about a movie deal?

"Mr. Ziggy said his friend can get us good seats. He said we won't have to sit in the nosebleeds."

"And Tara and her mom are going?"

"Tara hasn't asked her yet. But she says probably."

The screen showed an incoming call. Not Roxanne.

"I'll talk to Mom," I said.

"Okay. I just think it would be really cool."

And she was gone. The calls were going to voicemail. The press? Other police?

I tossed the phone on the seat, felt frustration building. Cops on me from two sides, a militia nut who might be plotting revenge. Bikers converging on Louis's compound, Louis and Clair cleaning weapons, sighting scopes. And I was supposed to go all the way to Boston to see some second-rate Daddy Warbucks?

And the gnawing question: Was this guy a creeper?

Speeding out of Augusta, north toward home, frozen lakes on both sides, fields of snow slashed by snowmobile tracks.

Vassalboro, then Palermo. Church, school, library, a pole barn with cows' black-and-white heads poking out. Flashing yellow lights ahead. I slowed, came up on a tracked ATV thing towing a sled across the road. I came to a stop and the guy at the wheel gave me a wave as he crested the snowbank and dragged the sled into a field.

A snowmobile trail. The groomer.

The word lingered like a puff of smoke.

Was there another reason why Mr. Ziggy liked Tara's rough edges? She was twelve going on eighteen, in some ways more precocious than Sophie. Physically. Emotionally. Battle-hardened from Tara's tumultuous love life. All those boyfriends took a toll, left her older, wiser, a little scarred. And connected in a deep way to her mother. Fellow survivors?

Maybe that was what Mr. Ziggy wanted. A rough-around-the-edges Annie for more than the stage. Maybe he watched their TikTok dances, bathing suits and snowshoes. Maybe he watched them over and over.

I turned off the highway, headed north. Tried to shake the dark thoughts. Fought that battle into Montville. Hogback Mountain on the left, snow, and a bristle of trees. Frye Mountain on the right, the afternoon light silhouetting the peak. A beautiful place, one of my hidden treasures, but where was the joy? I slowed and looked up, tried to feel the peace that view usually gave me. Nothing.

I drove on. Imagined Mr. Ziggy, Tara and Tiffanee. Tara in the front seat, Mr. Ziggy telling them of his theater exploits, his connections to Hollywood, how Tara could make it big. Both of them wide-eyed, their tickets dangling in front of them, something for their scrapbooks. Mr. Ziggy going on. Commercials. A series, streaming on Hulu. No more back-road, falling-down farmhouse. No more scraping to get by. Warm sun, sparkling blue pool out the back door. Parties with beautiful people. Porsches instead of beat-up pickups. With Mr. Ziggy's help, they could leave their hardscrabble small-town life behind. Assuming that's what Tiffanee's life had always been.

Climbing the ridge, I remembered what Roxanne had once said: Everything doesn't have to be an investigation.

"Yes, it does," I said aloud.

I slowed for the turn, swung the truck onto the icy Dump Road. Sped down the road, tires slinging gravel. Pulled into the driveway.

Roxanne was getting out of the car. She turned and looked at me, her expression grimmer than grim.

I followed her inside. Heard the clunk as her bag hit the floor. The chink of her keys, flung onto the counter. She turned to face me.

"What the hell, Jack? I mean, what the fucking hell?"

"Was it on the news?"

"Public Radio."

I waited. She was standing there, coat on, hands on her hips. Her cheeks were flushed, cold or anger or both.

"You could have been killed, for God's sake."

"He aimed the gun at himself."

"They said he was persuaded to put the gun down. By this Sparrow, the store employee, and Jack McMorrow, a freelance journalist."

"It was Sparrow talked him down. I was just there."

"But why you, Jack? Just call goddamn 911."

"He would have taken off. Barricaded someplace, maybe killed himself, maybe killed a cop. Maybe both."

"That's not your problem."

"But it was," I said. "I mean, partly. We couldn't just let him run."

That stopped her long enough for me to talk. I told her about Sparrow asking me to wait in the church for them, because I was a good listener. The meet-up with Carl, aka Zombie. And then I told her about the kiss. As I spoke, I could see her anger begin to dissipate.

"Does she really care for him?" Roxanne said. And then, "How could she?"

"I don't know. She sympathizes, I guess. Because they're both outsiders."

Roxanne shook her head.

"It really wasn't that big a deal," I said.

A white lie.

"And now he's caught. He won't be robbing stores. He won't hurt Sparrow. He won't hurt anybody. It's over."

I moved to her, two short steps. Put my arms around her, the left one, too. She stayed stiff for a moment, then returned the embrace, put her head on my shoulder. I felt her take a deep breath and then sigh.

"I don't want to lose you," Roxanne said. "I need you. Sophie needs you."

I felt her breathing, her chest rising and falling against mine.

"There's nothing to worry about," I said.

Another white lie. They were falling like snow.

I offered to pick Sophie up at school. Roxanne got into the truck with me, like she didn't want me to stray again. We were a hundred yards down the road when I told her about Sophie's call, Mr. Ziggy, and Boston.

"Him and us and the kids?"

"That's what she said. A theater field trip."

"With the two girls. What about the rest of the cast?"

"I don't know. Maybe he could only get so many tickets."

Her eyes narrowed, her hands pressing together in her lap, fingers intertwined.

"I don't know."

"Maybe if one of us were there, we could suss out the vibe. See how he acts around them. Tara especially."

"I'd like to see what he has on his laptop," Roxanne said.

"Okay, you go, I break into his house."

She looked at me.

"Maybe not," I said.

We drove on, thinking.

"We've googled him. Nothing came up except theater stuff."

"Would it?"

"If he'd been arrested, yes."

Another long pause, the snow-covered fields flashing by.

"I did ask Brandon to run him on NCIC. The crime database."

"And?"

"I haven't heard back yet. I'll make some calls. The theaters where he worked."

"Sophie would be mortified."

"It won't be Jack McMorrow calling."

She looked doubtful.

"It'll be helpful just to listen to them. What they say about him."

"And what they don't," Roxanne said.

We mulled it over, and then Roxanne said, "I suppose if parents are there. And you're right. I could watch him, see if he seems creepy. But groomers give their targets presents, money, take them cool places.

It puts the victim at ease, and associates the older person with fun, tells the kid that this person cares about them."

The turnoff was coming.

"What if he's okay, just a little weird?" I said.

"And you know she'll be pushing hard for it. I mean, I don't blame her. It would be really fun for them to see the play done by professionals."

"Or it might freak Tara out, seeing the part played by someone who sings for a living."

"Hard to say," Roxanne said. I drove on.

As I turned onto the Belfast Road, I glanced at the mirror. A black SUV, closing fast. An Explorer. Then blue grill lights wigwagging.

I pulled over.

"What?" Roxanne said, looking back. "You weren't speeding."

I saw Strain get out, start walking toward us.

"I know him. He's a detective," I said.

"What does he want?"

"To talk. It's what detectives do."

Roxanne looked at me, her anger seeping back.

"Just once, can't we—" she said, shaking her head. The rest was left unsaid.

I buzzed the window down. Strain leaned close, nodded to Roxanne. His hands were on the door, ruby pinkie ring flashing. I could smell his New Jersey cologne.

"Mrs. McMorrow," he said, looking across me. "Pleasure to meet you."

She glanced at him and nodded.

"Just missed you at the house," he said to me.

"What's up?" I said.

"A lot," Strain said. "You have a few minutes?"

"We're on our way to pick up our daughter at school," Roxanne said.

"Go right ahead, Mrs. McMorrow," he said. "I'll just chat with Mr. McMorrow, drop him at home."

206 · HARD LINE

He looked at me.

"When we're done."

I unlatched my seat belt. Strain stepped back. I told Roxanne I'd see her at home, then got out and walked with Strain back to the SUV. Roxanne came around the back of the truck, gave me a last glance, then got in. I could see her adjusting the seat and the mirrors. I waved and she pulled away.

We got into the Explorer, which also smelled like cologne.

"Seems like a nice lady," Strain said. "She'd have to be, to put up with your extracurricular activities. My ex, she kicked me to the curb. Said police work was more important to me than our marriage."

"Was it?"

He smiled at me sideways. "Us guys don't like to admit it, but wives are almost always right."

I smiled back. Strain shut off the strobes with a switch on the dash, and drove east. The road rose to the top of Knox Ridge. When we came to the crest, he pulled into the lot of a truck garage, turned the SUV around, so we were looking out over the valley and ridges. He left the motor running.

"Pretty spot," he said. "For the boonies."

"Yes."

"Your kid won't stay here. They head for the big city, like moths to a flame."

"That's okay. I wouldn't expect her to stay here."

"No, they gotta leave the nest. My two, the boy was at Arizona State. Played baseball before he died. I told you about that, right?"

"Yes, I'm sorry."

"Yeah, well, Trevor was a shortstop. My girl, she's sixteen. Wants to skip college—sad associations after her brother. Says she's gonna move to Miami, be an influencer. Been up here twice to visit me. Says it's a friggin' wasteland."

I looked out at the snow-painted pastures, the gracefully rolling winter hills, like massive ocean waves. Strain shifted in his seat.

"What would your family do if you went away?" He asked.

I looked at him.

"Away where?"

"You know. Away. Where people go when they break the law."

A beat, taking it in. A flashback to my reporting days in New York. How they played it in the city. Sly innuendo, the meaning crystal clear.

"What law are you saying I may have broken?"

"Let me think. I mean, you've been pretty busy."

He looked out in the direction of the view.

"This thing in Clarkston this morning. I don't think they know the half of that one. Robber, victim, and a reporter meeting up. Victim is screwing a cop, who happens to know the reporter, and the robber seems to always be a step ahead. I wonder why that is?"

He paused.

"PD down there will sort it, I guess. Somebody will try to save their ass. When arrangements like this fall apart, it's usually about the money, or somebody thinking the other ones are ratting them out. Let me tell you, there's no honor among thieves. But here's where it really gets good."

I waited.

"Augusta PD gets an anonymous call this morning. Burner phone. Concerned citizen reporting suspicious activity outside an address where a guy is on home confinement. Our guy, Jason. Patrol rolls around, finds a known associate in the house. Milford Graves of Randolph, across the river. Graves has a firearm, even though he's prohibited from owning one.

"Oh, and he also has a busted hand. I mean, it's not just broken. It's all shattered to hell. He won't say how it happened—clammed up all the way to the hospital—but the lady at the house saw two subjects leave in Graves's vehicle. They'd dropped him off as a message."

A pickup pulled in and eased by. The bearded driver peered at us. I looked at the view.

"I'm thinking tit for tat, with a bonus added in. If you catch my drift."

I didn't say whether I did or didn't.

"Anyway, they found Graves's truck outside the bookstore at the mall. Detectives dusting it now, I bet, see what that turns up. Did you know they have surveillance cameras at the bookstore? I was surprised. I mean, who's gonna steal a book?"

The pickup drove by again, going in the opposite direction, the bearded guy no doubt wondering why a cop was sitting in the parking lot. Me, too.

"So, the long and short of it—you can come clean. The Clarkston thing, that's not my jurisdiction, but we'd invite them in. Hey, maybe you were just being a reporter. But associating with this Zombie character and the rest of them, and the phone call, crushing someone's hand. I mean, you're in deep there. And don't waste my time by pretending you aren't."

I took a breath, waited. The motor kept running.

"This other thing, your personal vendetta against Jason Stratton. That *is* my jurisdiction. My case. I think you believe this guy you abducted and tortured is your shooter, and you and your Rambo buddy decided to take retribution against him. Which is against the law."

He paused.

"So did you?"

"Did I what?"

"Go after this guy, bust him up. Are you the mild-mannered reporter or a vigilante, just like these militia characters? Are you a good guy or a bad guy?"

He waited.

"Clock's ticking, Mr. McMorrow."

He waited some more.

"As you probably know, judges look way more favorable at somebody who voluntarily tells the truth. And taking revenge on this schmo—that could maybe be seen as a crime of passion, if you get a good lawyer."

Strain sat, fingers playing piano on the steering wheel. After a minute of silence, he said, "Okay," put the truck in gear and pulled out. We sat side by side, not talking, all the way back to the house. He pulled in, Roxanne's car by the shed.

Strain turned to me.

"Know what I really like about this? You're not some out-of-control meth-head, kills his best friend for who knows what reason, they find him standing over the body covered in blood with a hammer in his hand. I mean, for an investigator, what's the challenge in that?"

He smiled.

"You're a smart guy, probably as smart as me in some ways. And you think you're smarter. You think I'm not gonna figure out a way to unravel your fabrications, lies of omission. It's a tangled web we weave, like Shakespeare said."

"Walter Scott, actually. He was a poet."

"Really?"

"Yeah. You can google it."

He looked at me, smiled like he was enjoying every minute.

I got out of the truck, thinking I'd try one last question. I held the door open an extra beat.

"What happens to Jason?" I said. "Did they put him back in jail for violating terms of release?"

"Nah. Heart condition and all, I guess he stays put for now. He's cuffed, but if somebody decides they don't care about the consequences, protection orders, ankle bracelets—they ain't worth shit."

I slammed the door shut.

20

My phone was ringing. I let it buzz.

I built a fire, the vibrating phone writhing on the kitchen table like a disabled bug. I watched the flames worm their way up past the kindling. When the flames were licking the log on top, I went to the kitchen and poured a Lake St. George IPA into a pint glass. One pint for clarity, two for escape. There wouldn't be another tonight.

I went to the table, picked up the phone. Six missed calls, none from my contacts. Four voice messages. I ignored all of them. Standing at the counter, I texted Clair the gist of my talk with Strain.

I didn't hit send. Put the phone down. Stared at it. Picked it up and deleted the text. If I was a criminal suspect, I'd act like one.

I sipped the ale. Felt clarity sinking in. Heard tires crunching in the driveway. Roxanne and Sophie. I walked out through the shed, pushed the door open.

Clair's truck. Clair at the wheel. I walked over to the driver's side, looked in. Marta was slumped on the big bench seat.

"Hey," Clair said.

"She's back?" Something in my stomach told me this was not a good thing.

"You can speak to me directly, Jack," Marta said. "I'm not an object."

"What happened to the plan?"

"This is the plan," Clair said. "Bait and switch."

"Why wasn't I in on it?"

"Game-time decision," he said. "Really a tactical adjustment. Louis thinks things might get too hot down there."

"They saw me go in," Marta said.

"What makes you think they didn't see you leave there?"

"Because we didn't let them," she said.

I processed it. The bikers moving on Louis's place to extract Marta. Without her there, Louis—and Clair—were free to move away from the cabin, unleash whatever firepower they deemed necessary. They could even burn the cabin down, have Marta vanish in a cloud of smoke. Again.

"You going back?" I said to Clair.

"Most likely."

"Who takes care of her?" I said.

Clair smiled. I looked past him at Marta, lying on the seat in her winter-camo parka, leggings, and black combat boots. Her legs were crossed on the seat, and she gave me a wan smile.

"I'm feeling much better," she said. "I don't need my hand held."

"They show up here, that's the last thing I'll be doing," I said.

"The barn," Clair said. "She'll stay in the bunk room. There's food and water for a week. And two exits. If necessary, she can go out through the stalls, down the stairs, out the back."

"Won't somebody see smoke from the stove?"

"Electric space heater."

"For how long?"

"Louis thinks the scouts probably came in a couple of days early. Wait too long, the situation could change. Two or three days is enough for them to get a team assembled and on location."

I must have looked skeptical.

"You can trust him," Marta said.

"I trust him," I said. "I don't trust you."

The truck was idling, lights off. I asked Clair if he had a minute and he got out, no cab light showing when the door opened. I stepped away and he followed. I told him about Strain, Graves, fingerprinting the Yukon, the security cameras at the bookstore.

"He won't talk," Clair said.

"Even if it means doing time for the gun?"

"It's his badge of honor, his sacrifice for the cause. Plus, arson is a Class A felony. He could get twenty years."

"That's their leverage on him."

Clair shook his head.

"I don't believe it. Where's the evidence? Your voice ID? But you won't even say you were with him. It ends here."

We stood. Clair eyed me.

"You okay?"

I hesitated.

"Yeah. I don't know. Seems like things are spinning a little out of control. I used to just write stories."

Clair smiled.

"Sorry to break it to you, Jack. But you haven't 'just written stories' in a long time."

With that, he clapped me on the shoulder—the good one—with his big hand. Walked back to the truck and got in. Lights off, he turned the truck around and drove out and up the road toward the barn. Marta was out of sight, never out of mind.

Roxanne and Sophie rattled in the door at 6:15, Sophie saying, "But still, isn't it kind of like Dad is a hero?"

I was in the chair by the stove.

"Hey, guys," I said.

Sophie dropped her backpack, hurried to me.

"Dad, we heard it on the news. You and that girl caught the robber."

"Well, more like she did it. I was just there."

She leaned in, gave me a hug. "Oh, my God. Your friend Sparrow must be so happy."

"I hope so. One less thing to worry about."

She pulled away, looked at me with that intense conspiratorial way she had.

"Mom said you guys kept him from killing himself."

"Hard to say what he would have done since it didn't happen. He didn't do much talking after that."

"And he was just a kid?"

"Well, by my standard. He's twenty-two. Kind of a misfit."

"That's who does these things," Sophie said. "School shootings—it's always somebody who got bullied or something. Maybe the athletes picked on him in school. This Carl, maybe this was his way of trying to get some power. People don't get how hard it is to be really unpopular at school. Kids are so mean."

"I'm sure," I said. "But there are better ways to handle that than robbing innocent people."

"What do you think he'll get?"

Her father's daughter.

"Jail? Twenty, maybe. Since he shot the man, assaulted Sparrow. Maybe a couple of years suspended because he's young, no criminal record, a first offense."

"Mom said he likes Sparrow."

"In a weird way," I said, changed the subject.

"How was school? Why so late?"

Sophie was taking off her jacket. She tossed it over a kitchen chair, and Roxanne told her to hang it on the hook. She did, saying, "Mr. Ziggy wanted to go over some lines with me and Tara. He said our parts are, like, wicked important. He wants us to start inhabiting our characters."

Roxanne was taking vegetables from the refrigerator, laying them on the counter. Then the wok from the shelf, put it on the stove and squirted in some oil. Stir-fry. She gave me a look.

"How do you do that?" I said.

"It's like when you're doing something, you think, 'How would Pepper feel about that? She's got no parents, has had to, like, fight for everything in her life. Now she lives in this place with the other orphans, and she has to keep them in line. Mr. Ziggy says each of us has a personality, and we have to make that personality shine through, even when we're just singing."

I smiled.

"Cool. So what did you do with him today?"

"We went in the theater room, read our lines to him. Tara has lots more than me, and she isn't that great a reader. So he spent a lot of time with her. He said she has to be her own Annie. They were still working when I left."

"Huh," I said. *Here we go,* I thought.

"Was her mom coming to get her?"

"Mr. Ziggy was gonna give her a ride."

More alarm bells, banging like a gong. Roxanne looked at me, eyes narrowed.

"He said he wanted to talk to Tiffanee in—what was it, Mom?"

"In situ," Roxanne said.

"In situ," Sophie said. "It means at her house. Mr. Ziggy wants to make sure Tiffanee lets Tara stay in character at home. You know, gets why it's important, doesn't think she's nuts."

"So she'll be there?" Roxanne said.

"Yeah. Tara called her, asked if it was okay. To get a ride from Mr. Z. She said it was. I think her mom really likes him. I mean, a guy who doesn't go around drunk and screaming at people. And he's been all these cool places. Tara and her mom, they've sort of never been anywhere."

Another glance. Then Roxanne dumped water in a saucepan, turned on the burner. Started chopping—broccoli, onions, and peppers. Sophie knelt on the floor, pulled stuff out of her backpack. Books. Folders. A sheaf of paper. She opened it, stood and snarled, "I said, 'Shut your trap, Molly.' "

She shoved an invisible orphan.

"She's keeping me awake, ain't she?"

There was a cold menace in her tone, her teeth bared. Nothing cute about it.

"Pepper's the toughest orphan," Sophie said.

"It would appear so."

"Annie's not so tough. She thinks her mom and dad, they're coming to get her."

"Right."

"But they're dead, she just doesn't know it. Instead, she gets invited to this mansion for Christmas. That's Daddy Warbucks. But he's not weird or anything. This was a long time ago."

"They had creepers back then, too," I said. "They just didn't believe the kids when they told on them. That's where Mom came in when she was doing her old job. She listened to the kids and got the creepers thrown in jail."

"You go, Mom," Sophie said. "Way to kick creeper butt."

Roxanne smiled, tossed the vegetables into the hot wok. They hissed.

Sophie gathered up her books and papers. As she started down the hallway, her phone dinged. She pulled it from the back pocket of her jeans, said in her Pepper voice, "Yo, Annie. How come you get to go to a mansion and I have to stay in this crappy dump?"

She laughed, turned back to me. Said, "Don't forget to talk to Mom about Boston," and was gone.

I got up and took plates from the shelf, laid them on the table. Then silverware, salt and pepper mills. Roxanne was dropping chunks of leftover chicken breast into the wok. She gave it a shake, took the tops off bottles of soy and pepper sauces, shook some in. I dumped the rice into the boiling water.

"Tiffanee being driven home by Mr. Ziggy," Roxanne said. "Are you kidding me? I mean, even if it's the most innocent thing in the world, it's just not done. Does the school know about that?"

"I don't know."

A pause.

"At least the girls are talking all the time," I said. "They don't seem to be getting any creeper vibes. Sophie would tell us, right?"

"Yes, I think she would."

She put the spoon down, turned and gave me a sudden hug. Squeezed me tightly.

"I'm glad you're here, safe and sound."

"Not that big a deal. You would have done it. Distraught guy not sure how to turn himself in."

"How did you convince him?"

"Listened to him, I guess. And Sparrow was there. She was the one who really stopped it. The last thing he said before he got taken away was that he loved her."

She eased away from me.

"They're not thinking of—"

"Charging me? No. One of the cops has all these conspiracy theories, but they won't go anywhere."

She turned back to the stove.

"Jason," she said. "He's still with his aunt?"

"As far as I know."

A twinge of guilt.

"Let's talk about Boston," I said.

The rice simmered.

"I told Mr. Ziggy I couldn't speak for you, but you had a lot going on," Roxanne said. "He said he'd heard about you. The Zombie thing."

"Mr. Ziggy listens to the radio?"

"He said it was on his news feed."

"Huh. Not as much in his own world as I thought."

I checked the rice. Roxanne gave the vegetables a stir.

"I think it would be okay for Sophie to go with Tara," she said. "Me and Tiffanee. We leave here early, go to the matinee. Come home."

"Maybe get something to eat."

"Right," she said. "I mean, seeing the actual play live will be good, don't you think?"

"Maybe. Or maybe they should do it their way. Sophie is sounding like one mean orphan."

"That's the reality for some kids," Roxanne said. "Nothing cute about it."

"If nothing else, you'll get a long look at him. What do you think you'll all talk about?"

Roxanne took the rice off the stove.

"I don't know. School? The play?"

"Tiffanee's had a hard-knock life, too," I said. "Maybe he'll recruit her."

Roxanne was back to me at the counter, spooning rice and stir-fry into bowls. She put them on the table, walked down the hallway, and called, "Sophie! Dinner!"

I went to the sink, filled the water glasses, put them on the table, got the napkins. Girding myself, I said, "Marta is back."

She froze over the table, looked at me.

"You're kidding me. Why?"

I told her about the change of tactics.

"God, I'm so sick of all this military bullshit," Roxanne said, whirling back to the counter. "We live in a small town in Maine, you know? You want to play soldier, go join up again, for God's sake. Do it for real."

She plonked the sauces on the table.

"She's going to be in the barn?"

"Yup. In the bunk room."

"Who's gonna wait on her?"

"Nobody. She has two weeks' worth of supplies. The composting toilet."

"Well, she'd better not come slinking over here. And where's she going to be when somebody is taking care of Pokey? I don't want her anywhere near Sophie, and I don't want her near me, either. Or you. I've seen her come on to you."

I looked at her. "I don't think so."

"It's her stock in trade, Jack. Wrapping men around her little finger. What Louis sees in her, I don't know. Or I *do* know what he sees. And if that's all it takes—"

"The bikers in Montreal weren't wrapped around her finger."

"Or her boyfriend, the one who got killed."

"Well, she picked the wrong boyfriend then."

There was the thumping of Sophie's footsteps on the stairs.

"I'm sorry for her troubles," Roxanne said. "But they're not ours."

And then Sophie slid into the kitchen, her stocking feet skidding on the pine boards.

"Yum."

She looked at us.

"What's the matter?" she said.

Roxanne looked to me.

"Marta is going to be staying in Clair's barn," I said. "In the bunk room."

"Stay away from her," Roxanne said.

Sophie looked at her, then me. Said slowly, "Okay."

"Your dad can take care of Pokey until she's gone."

"I don't mind doing it," Sophie said.

"We said no," Roxanne said.

"Got it, but what's going on?" Sophie said. "She's always been nice to me."

I hesitated.

"She had to extricate herself from a situation. In Canada."

"Like, she broke up with a boyfriend?"

"A little more than that," I said. "She was with some bad people. Now they're looking for her and we don't want them to come here."

"If there's any sign of anything," I said, "there's Louis and Clair and Mary. Anyone else, in front of the house, in the driveway, around the barn, in the woods—just call 911. Come in the house and lock the door."

"Well, all right," Sophie said, and unfolded her napkin, put it on her lap.

Another day in the McMorrow household.

I started the rice around, then the stir-fry. The food steamed on the plates. Sophie twisted the pepper grinder. Roxanne shook out red pepper sauce. We started to eat.

"We talked about Boston," Roxanne said. "Dad can't go, but I will. If Tara and her mom are going."

Sophie smiled, chewed, swallowed.

"Excellent! I'll tell them."

We were quiet for a minute, utensils scraping plates.

"If we're gone all day tomorrow," Sophie said, "Dad, will you be okay?"

21

They left, bright and early, Sophie looking artsy in her fedora and a pair of Roxanne's sunglasses. Roxanne looked like herself, slacks and boots and a black cashmere cardigan. I gave them hugs and kisses good-bye, felt myself hanging on extra long.

And then I made myself shake it off.

After a last wave from the driveway, I went back inside. The fire in the stove had burned through the first logs and I placed another chunk of oak on the bed of embers. Put the kettle on for a second cup of tea. While I waited for the water to boil, I went to the closet. Opened the safe and took out the Glock. I went back and made the tea, then went to the study and opened the laptop, The gun went on the desktop to my right. Pens, pencils, and a nine-millimeter. I settled into my seat, thankful that my gun hand and good hand were one and the same. Small blessings.

My phone was on the desk to my left. It buzzed every thirty seconds or so, the ringer off. Reporters, mostly, voicemails. Most started by congratulating me on bringing Zombie in, and went on to the reasons their readers, listeners, viewers desperately needed to hear my story.

They weren't good enough reasons.

I looked in the direction of the barn, which was northwest. Thought of Marta, sitting in the locked bunk room, space heater glowing. Did she bring a good book? Some knitting? Watching Netflix on her phone? I felt an urge to go over, sit down with her, try to figure out what was really going on in her head.

Fought if off. I had someone else to figure out first.

I went to the Dog Island Players website, knowing theater people are into their résumés, parts they've played, where they've played them. I clicked through to the list of artists, saw a couple of the people who had been onstage with Tara and Sophie and the rest of the cast. They were mostly smiling, some dramatically serious, like they were cops about to accuse you of a crime. They'd all done a lot of theater, most of it regional, one Off Broadway. Another had done TV, too, a show I'd never heard of. One woman had a guest spot on *Boardwalk Empire*. She was Party Dancer 6, in the first season. It was a long time ago.

The list was alphabetical. I scrolled down.

Mr. Ziggy was listed as guest children's director.

> *Mr. Ziggy (aka, John Klaus Zwiefelhofer) is passionate about children's theater and the ways it can unleash the imagination of young artists. A recent transplant to Maine, Mr. Ziggy has spent most of his career in the Northwest, where he directed and/or appeared in* Aladdin, Elf, *and* The Lion King *for regional theaters. He will bring his special brand of joy and enthusiasm to Dog Island Players' production of* Annie *in April.*

It seemed vague. What regional theaters? Where?

I googled Mr. Ziggy, John Klaus Zwiefelhofer, and theater, got hits for children's theater companies in Salem and Eugene, Oregon, and Spokane and Tacoma, Washington. I clicked through, scrolled. A younger Mr. Ziggy played Prince Anders in *Aladdin.* An even younger version played Zazu in *The Lion King.* A smiling Mr. Ziggy in a faux African suit, holding a big toucan-looking puppet.

So far, so good.

I searched again, saw a notice that Mr. Ziggy had been replaced by an understudy in the Eugene production. A few hits down, the audience was introduced to a new actor taking over the part of Zazu. The director and producers welcomed him to the cast. There was nothing about where Mr. Ziggy had gone, or why.

It petered out from there. Obits for people named Zwiefelhofer—an auto-plant worker, a homemaker—mostly in the Midwest. I scrolled on, the story of our modern lives. There was always one more page.

The search algorithm had moved to Zwiefel and Klaus: a wedding announcement for Anna Zwiefel and Anders Klaus. News that Roger Klaus had been hired as human resources director for Duluth Savings Bank. Like Mr. Ziggy, he was smiling for the camera.

And then a 2007 press release from the office of the US attorney in St. Louis. It reported the conviction of John Klaus Zwiefel, thirty-nine, of Columbia, Missouri, for fifteen counts of fraud, theft, and wire fraud. Zwiefel, who also used the aliases Johann Klaus and Kirk Ziegfeld, had scammed more than $2 million from three women in the St. Louis area.

The release said Zwiefel entered into relationships with the women, who were either divorced or widowed, and convinced them to invest in a nonprofit he'd founded to help children with malaria. Except the nonprofit was just a website, videos cribbed off the Internet, and a mail drop. Zwiefel convinced his victims to take out equity loans on their homes to fund his fake charity. In fact, he spent his ill-gotten cash on gambling, travel, and luxury cars. He got eighteen years in prison for it.

Another actor. Good money in it while it lasted. Related to Mr. Ziggy?

I got up, went to the firewood rack and took out a piece, put it in the stove. Came back to my chair. The lingering questions: Why did Mr. Ziggy leave those productions? Why did he come three thousand miles east to Belfast, Maine?

Another sip of tea, Zwiefel the scammer still on the screen.

Another search: *surname Zwiefelhofer meaning.*

The Internet spoke: *South German: Bavarian variant of Zwiebelhofer, a habitational name for someone from a farm named Zwiebelhof "onion farm" (see Zwiebel).*

The entry went on: *Zwiebel or Zwiefel is German for "onion," came to refer to a greengrocer—someone who sold vegetables.*

In the entire United States, there were 941 Zwiefels, 774 Zwiefelhofers.

Leave it to me to find one scammer. But were there two?

I leaned back, glanced at the phone, went to the missed calls. Scrolled. Halfway down the screen, Carlisle at the *Times*. I clicked on the voicemail.

"Jack, saw the AP pickup. My God, I'm so glad you're okay. That could have ended horribly . . . Listen, we've been talking. We think maybe we could interview you, send Cecile up from Boston. I mean, this Zombie thing has been an incredible saga, for you, for Clarkston, this Sparrow woman. I mean, I'm picturing an intro leading into an audio Q and A. What do you think? Give me a call, if only so I can hear your voice. I really hope we can—"

The message timed out. A Q&A. A first step back into the fold? Hey, I could tell them about the congregation of pigeons.

I got up from the desk. *Zwiefel. Zwiefelhofer.* The dad drops the *hofer*. The son puts it back on—if they were related at all.

A pang of déjà vu. Those moments over the years when I'd known I was on to something, that it wasn't my imagination running away with me. In New York with my detective friend Butch, when I realized he'd murdered the mayor. In Belfast, Maine, when Mandi and I looked at each other and I knew she was a killer. I'd let her go. In my hometown, when I realized a kid named Victor thought he was an avenging angel. He'd put a gun in my face. Roxanne had saved me.

I'd lived to fight another day. And another. And another.

And here we were.

I picked up the phone, texted Blake. If he'd come all the way to Prosperity, this would be a small ask.

Got a minute?

Waited.

—Sure.

"How's Sparrow?"

"Okay," Blake said. "Sticking close to home. Quit the job. Said she needs some space."

"I can see that."

"We both do."

"I can see that, too."

"Yeah."

I could feel him thinking. He said, "I still care for her. A lot."

"Right."

"But it's hard. It's like we're both trying to figure out who we are next. And whether there's a place for the other person."

"You'll get there."

Silence.

"Listen. There's this theater guy, at Sophie's school. About thirty, seems to have spent most of his time in the Northwest. I'm wondering if—"

"You want me to get somebody to run him."

"Right."

"What, you think he's a pedo?"

"I don't know. Nothing obvious, but Roxanne's radar is pinging. I'm suspicious of everybody."

"Huh."

"He spends a lot of time around Tara, Sophie's friend. She's the star. Annie."

"Maybe he has to, to train her up," Blake said.

"He's a little touchy-feely. Gives her rides home."

"Okay. But don't these theater people do background checks?" Blake said. "I mean, working with kids and all?"

"My bet is they were all excited to get somebody with experience. And he's Mr. Charming."

"Aren't they all."

A beat.

"I got a friend. She'll run him through NCIC. Text me his name and DOB. You check the Sex Offender Registry?"

"Nothing."

"It'll be a couple of days. My friend's fishing up north."

"Maybe I'm fishing, too," I said.

"Possible," Blake said. "But Roxanne, she's a pro. If she smells smoke—"

"John Klaus Zwiefelhofer."

"Not a stage name, I take it."

"No," I said. "But that doesn't mean the nice guy, loves kids, all passionate about theater—that it isn't an act."

"What will you do if he comes back a hit?"

I didn't answer.

"Don't touch him, McMorrow," Blake said. "I gotta say, I think you're a little out of control. May take down some bad guys, but you keep it up, you're gonna go down with 'em."

"I'm fine," I said.

"No," Blake said. "You're a lot of things. Fine isn't one."

22

Blake rang off. I sat for a moment, then left the house, followed faded gray footprints into the snow all the way to Clair's barn. Easing the shop door open, I stepped in and closed it behind me. The shop was cold, no fire in the stove. I walked carefully toward the board-lined passageway that led to the bunk room. The door was closed. I listened. Except for the creaking of the beams, silence.

Backing out, I walked toward the stalls. Pokey had his head up and out of the half-door from his box. He gave a snort and a head shake, and I moved close to him, scratched behind his ears. He nuzzled me for a treat, zeroing in on the pocket that held the carrot. If carrot smuggling became a problem, he could work for TSA.

I went into the stall, opened the lid to the grain box, started the flow of grain from the wooden chute. The box filled and I scooped some into his feed trough. He shoved his muzzle in, shouldering me out of the way. I backed out, closed the box door, and went to the rear of the barn, and climbed the stairs.

There were trapdoors along the outside wall over each of the box stalls. I opened Pokey's door, peered down to see his back, heard his snuffling as he licked up the last of the grain. The hay bales were stacked in the loft, barter payment from an Amish farmer on the ridge. We cut wood on his woodlot, took out some firewood, left the rest for the community's sawmill. He kept Pokey supplied with hay, said if Pokey ever wanted to join the Amish horse herd, he was more than welcome. That time was coming, I thought. Sophie was outgrowing the pony and didn't seem interested in moving up to a horse. Maybe if the horse could be on TikTok.

I walked across the wooden planks to the stacked bales, pulled one off with my good arm. It fell to the floor and I stooped to dig my fingers under the twine, drag it across. And saw what looked like glass. Three or four pieces. I leaned down and touched one. It was cold.

Ice.

I looked up at the roof, scanned for the stain of a leak. Water dripping onto the hay could spoil it, leave us with mounds of moldy bales good for mulch and not much else.

No stains, just swallow nests on the rafters. A pale gray lantern built by paper wasps the previous season. I scanned the floor again, took out my phone and turned on the light. More bits of ice glinted in the beam, a tiny clump of snow. I followed the trail to the far corner of the loft.

Bales had been moved in the back row, leaving a one-bale gap. The gap was against the wall, bits of loose hay strewn on the floor.

I backtracked, followed the trail across the loft. Turned to the stairs. Four treads down there was a wet spot. Then another on the floor at the base of the staircase. I peered into the dimness, caught a bit of ice or snow every six or eight feet. The trail led to the door to the workshop.

I pushed the door open, crossed to the passage to the bunk room. Three feet from the door there was another wet spot, this one in the partial shape of a boot, just the toe.

Smaller than mine.

I moved close to the door, turned my head and listened. Heard a scuffing sound, like something was being dragged. Then again. I waited for a beat, two. Then knocked.

"Marta, it's Jack."

The scuffing sound stopped.

"Are you there? We need to talk. It's important."

"Oh, hey, Jack. Just let me get some clothes on."

I heard the clump of a boot on the floor. If that was all she was wearing, it was a strange scene, indeed.

I waited. More scuffing. Then steps coming toward the door.

It swung open, and Marta stood there: hiking boots and jeans. She was buttoning the top buttons on her flannel shirt. She'd gotten some of her color back, but was still gaunt, the jeans loose around her hips.

"Just changed. I was cold. This heater, it's all or nothing. Turn it on and you start to sweat. Turn it off, in two minutes you're frozen."

She moved away from the door. I followed.

There were two wood-frame single beds, one on each side. Shelves built into the walls, stacks of Marta's clothes. A refrigerator and propane stove, small and old-school. An easy chair with a hassock in front of it. The bathroom was to the rear. That door was ajar.

"Home, sweet home," Marta said.

"Clair and Mary's kids stayed out here when they were teenagers. Get some separation."

"Where are they now, these teenagers?"

"Grown up, kids of their own, both in North Carolina. Charlotte. To them, this is the boonies."

"I wonder why," Marta said. She smiled, walked to the bathroom, a snap to her hips. She still could pack a lot into a ten-foot stroll. I got the feeling many men before me had fallen for that little hitch in her step, and she knew it. Suddenly the footprints, the ice, the whole scene started to make sense. I had been researching small-town actors up at my house when right next door, my friends were getting played by one. Only Marta should get an Oscar for this latest performance.

She pulled the door shut, turned back to me, smiling in that stealthy way she had.

I decided to play my hunch.

"What was up in the loft, Marta?"

Marta was surprised, but only for a moment. She stopped mid-stride. It was almost as if I could see her brain working. What lie would do? Or maybe no lie would be better.

"Exploring the place. I thought there might be a good vantage point."

"You try the cupola? There's a ladder. Probably see through the louvers in the shutters."

"I didn't, but I will. I don't like sitting in here, not able to see what's coming."

I considered asking her what was in the hay bales. But I didn't have to, just waited, watched her face, felt her gaze meet mine. She knew I knew, and that was enough to tear away the seductress mask, reveal the icy stare I'd seen so many times in all the grifters I'd covered over the years. Eventually, the act fell away and their ruthlessness was bared. If only for a moment.

"I was thinking," I said. "If you still have the money, I hope you keep it in a secure place. It's your ticket out, after all."

She stared, the hard look. This was the woman who'd looted her boyfriend's cash while he was being killed upstairs. The woman who'd grabbed her money and run, leaving lovesick Louis high and dry. That time, the bikers had run her down.

"When are you planning on leaving this time?" I said.

"I'll go when the moment is right."

"Does Louis know?"

Her lack of response said no.

"So your idea is to dodge the fireworks? Leave it to the boys to fight it out between themselves?"

"I don't see what possible help I'd be. I'm not good with guns."

"I find that hard to believe," I said. "I think you'd do whatever's necessary."

She said nothing, stood there in the middle of the room, faced me.

I walked past her to the bathroom door, pushed it open. There was a black duffel in the middle of the floor, wisps of hay sticking the fabric. The top was open a crack. I leaned down, pulled it open wider. Saw stacks of banded money, hundreds and fifties. The butt of a gun showed from under the flap.

Marta was behind me.

"I guess you don't have to be good with guns to carry one," I said. I turned back to her.

She had her hands on her hips, boots planted squarely. No coquettish seduction now, just defiance and anger.

"You think I wanted to be rescued, Louis riding in on his white horse? I didn't need him. I'm not helpless. I had a plan."

"And what was that?"

"One of the club guys, he was going to help me."

I waited.

"They called him Cyclops because he'd lost an eye in a motorcycle crash. It was his job to look after me. He was going to start switching in Methadone for the fentanyl, so I could get myself back together. The plan was he'd leave a window unlocked in my room. Snake had the door padlocked, windows locked from the outside. I'd get out, and Cyclops would be waiting. We'd drive east. He had friends in Quebec City."

I smiled. "Let me guess. You led him to believe the two of you could ride his Harley off into the sunset."

Marta shrugged.

"He had a serious crush. I can't help that."

"So, you bide your time, then make a break for it again. Leave Cyclops on his own. Just like you're leaving Louis and Clair to fight your battles."

"Like I said, Jack, I didn't ask them to come for me. I'm going about my business, grimy as it was, when Louis just throws a bomb in the truck, boom. All this smoke, people being hit with a club. He pulls me out. All the rest of it—the passport, bringing me back here—I had no say in any of it. It's like I'm a piece of luggage to haul here and there."

"But you set it up that way, Marta. Showing up in Sanctuary out of the blue, telling Louis you'd never forgotten him—he was your true love."

A beat.

"He was, for that time. Situations and needs change. Where I'm going, I'm not going to need anybody."

Her pretty mouth clamped shut, her chin tilted forward.

We faced each other, like kids in one of those games. First one to blink loses.

It was me.

"When these guys show up, Louis and Clair won't have what they're looking for."

"So what? They'd never hand me over."

"But when the smoke clears, if they're standing, you'll be gone. Then what was the fight for?"

"You tell me, Jack. I can't figure out you men. It's like this Russian I knew in London. He had all this art. Rembrandts, a Monet, a Jasper Johns. He showed it off when he had guests. The rest of the time, it was like it wasn't there. He didn't even like art, but having it meant he'd won. Nigel and Snake and even Louis, in a way—they never asked me what I wanted. You know what I want now? Nothing. I can take care of myself."

"Louis and Clair are trying to do the right thing," I said. "It's good versus evil."

"Oh, Christ, Jack," she said. "That is such crap. This romantic bullshit you guys invent. You know what there is? There are winners and there are losers."

"That's what you believe in?"

"I believe in survival," Marta said. "Survival of the fittest and smartest and toughest. That's it."

She moved a step closer, said, "Are you going to tell on me, Jack? Maybe they could lock me in here, too. Make sure the prize doesn't escape."

"When are you going?"

"Depends on your answer."

"I don't keep secrets from Clair. Or Roxanne."

"Then I'll go today, maybe."

"How? You can't call an Uber."

"Maybe not. But did you know the little store at the intersection, at the top of the hill, delivers? I order a sandwich, then ask the driver for a ride back. Give him a hundred bucks to take me to Belfast. Or chat up somebody getting gas. My car broke down and I have a medical appointment I can't miss. Maybe I'll tell them I'm getting chemo. I mean, I look like crap, right? I could pay them to give me a lift, then grab the bus to Boston and I'm on my way."

A beat.

"I've always loved Mexico. Have you ever been to San Miguel?"

She smiled, a look that was almost triumphant.

"Jeez, Marta. Guess you have it all figured out."

"I'm picturing an older couple, maybe going to Walmart. These Maine country people, they're all about helping strangers, right?"

"Louis did just that, didn't he?" I said.

I walked out, left her with the only thing that mattered to her.

Her bag of money.

Mary was in the kitchen when I knocked, heard her call back to me. She came to the door, unlocked it. I let myself in.

She'd emptied the refrigerator, had jars and jugs and vegetables laid out on the table. There was a trash bin close to her, and she was looking at expiration dates.

"He'll eat anything," she said. "He says, 'It's fine. You know what we would have given for bacon in the war?' I wait until he's gone, chuck stuff out."

She eyed a package of sliced turkey, heaved it into the bin. "Slimy. Problem is, there's just the two of us. And sometimes there's only one."

The words hung in the air, the implication. If something happened. If she was left in the big house alone.

"She's leaving," I said. "Marta."

Mary looked up from a saggy red pepper.

"When?"

"Could be as soon as today."

"Good. How?"

I told her Marta's plan.

"Are you kidding? I'll give her a ride, buy her ticket. One-way."

"You don't want to be with her," I said. "Just in case."

"Are you going to tell them?"

"Yes."

"I've been calling. Both of them. It doesn't go through. I've been trying for an hour."

I hesitated.

"They could be down by the bog. Not much reception there."

"Maybe," Mary said. She turned back to the fridge. "If you reach them, let me know."

"If you see her leaving, you let me know," I said.

"Roger that," Mary said.

I stood for a moment, watched her. She was a strong woman, with her muscular arms and everything else.

"Don't worry," I said.

"Oh, I'm fine. I was just thinking about when we were young, and he was out there in the jungle for days and days. Weeks would go by, and I wouldn't get a letter. We had this little house off base at Camp Pendleton, streets wound around in circles. I used to get lost, the houses all looking the same."

She smiled, shook her head.

"Getting old, this random stuff popping into my head."

I waited.

"Anyway, I knew if he'd been killed, I'd get a knock on the door. It happened all the time. One minute there would be a couple, and then there was just a widow, a wife with a big hole where half her life used to be. So, what I did is, I'd put the baby in the stroller, walk for hours. I figured if I wasn't home, I couldn't hear the knock. And if I didn't hear the knock, he had to be alive."

She shook her head, peered at the label on a carton of half-and-half.

"The crazy things you do," Mary said.

"You know, Mary, compared to Vietnam, this is nothing," I said.

She moved to the sink, poured the half-and-half down the drain. Turned to me with this sad sort of smile.

"We'd talk, the wives. Everybody had somebody in harm's way. Clair's Recon stuff, that was scary. Dropping them in, always completely outnumbered, watching some enemy base or a trail or something. Some of the other wives, their husbands were infantry, fighting all the time. There were helicopter pilots—there was a horribly dangerous job—and a couple of husbands flew fighters off of carriers. And we used to feel so bad for somebody whose husband re-upped. I remember when Clair decided to do another tour, I had the most awful feeling. I mean, you were only given so much luck. And the longer you were there, the better the chance it would run out."

She tossed the carton into the bin.

"The thing is, you and Clair and Louis, you've been in the game for a long time. Always saying everything is under control. Well, you know, Jack, it is until it isn't."

She picked up a squirt bottle, started spraying the refrigerator. Her back to me, she said, "Clair's a wonderful man. So wise, so smart, so brave. And generous. Do anything for anybody. But this is his Achilles' heel. Yours, too. You see something wrong, you won't walk away. Why not let somebody else fight the battle?"

She sprayed, started scrubbing with a cloth. I hesitated, managed, "They'll be okay."

"You know what, Jack?" Mary said, still peering into the refrigerator. "I don't think I want to do this anymore. I've done my share. After this one, I think I'm gonna tell him. Time for me to retire. You can retire with me, or not."

"What? Would you move?"

"I don't know. I'd like to be closer to the kids, for sure. North Carolina is nice in the winter. So I'm gonna tell Clair. 'You fought the good fight. Time to hang it up.' "

"But you haven't yet?"

"Hasn't been the right time, what with our patient being here and all. I mean, sure, she needed help. But now she's on her feet, and I'm done. There's a limit, Jack. Fifty-one years of keeping the home fires burning, praying he makes it home alive. I mean, who's more important? Louis? This little operator?"

She sprayed harder and leaned deeper into the refrigerator. I waited a few seconds, but the conversation seemed over, so I patted her shoulder, which felt as useless as it was.

"You take care, Mary," I said. And then I turned and left, stepped out of the kitchen, trotted down the steps.

So, after all these years, Mary had had enough. As I walked back to the barn, my mind raced through the decades. Chasing Bobby and Coyote through Lewiston. Saving a kid named Rocky from the streets of Portland but losing his buddy Tammy in Bangor. We lost Missy Hewitt in Portland, too. Clair putting a gangbanger's hand on a chopping block. Driving his big Ford through a car full of bad guys in Lawrence, Mass. Always had my back, often with a gun in hand.

Being my mentor and backup came with a price, and now he was going to have to choose.

I returned to the loft and the bale of hay I'd taken down, before I'd gotten sidetracked. Cut the twine and opened the trapdoor over Pokey's stall, pulled hay from the bale and dropped it down. It fell like dusty snow, piled on the boards of the stall floor.

Pokey clopped over and started eating, and all the while I had a growing sense of foreboding. A building unease, like something bad was coming but I didn't know when, or from where.

I shook it off, closed the trapdoor. Then I went down the steps and through the barn, glancing toward the bunk room, where I presumed Marta was finishing her packing. A million dollars and some clean underwear.

And then I was outside. I crossed the barnyard, followed the trail into the woods. When I was out of sight of the house, I glanced at my watch. It was 11:45. I broke into a jog.

The phone reception in the bog was just fine.

23

I tried them from the truck. Clair's phone didn't ring. Louis's went to voicemail. I texted them both:

HEY, GIVE ME A CALL. YOUR PHONES AREN'T RINGING.

I tried to imagine the situation that would lead to that. A cell tower had crapped out. Clair had dropped his phone and stepped on it. Louis's battery was dead and he'd left it on the charger while he went about his business.

Or they were in a firefight and answering the phone wasn't an option.

I drove down the road and out, headed east and up the ridge. The Prosperity General Store was at the crossroads and I wondered about what Marta had said, that they delivered. Or was that another lie. As soon as I was gone, she'd take Mary's car. Find it in the airport lot in Portland.

Last second, I slowed, pulled into the store lot, and parked. It was 12:30. The locals were more likely to roll in during the early morning, late afternoon. I went in the front door, waved to Sam, the owner, who was bagging groceries for a woman with a couple of little kids. He'd given the kids lollipops, and the sticks stuck out of their mouths like lizard tongues.

Sam was saying the woman should say hello to her dad for him, hadn't seen him in ages. The woman started to say something about "the dementia." I kept walking, down the bread and chips aisle, to the deli. Delia, Sam's wife, was slicing ham. I waited, then she said, "What can I get you, Jack?"

"Nothing at the moment," I said. "Just for future reference. Do you deliver? Sandwiches or whatever?"

"That we do," she said. "People got used to it during COVID, keep on asking. Hey, if they don't want to get off the couch, we'll come to them. The fee is ten dollars. They don't even blink."

I thanked her, gave a salute, left her to her slicing. Headed back up the bread and chips aisle. Stopped. Went back to the deli and grabbed a turkey on whole wheat, circled around to the cooler and picked out a bottle of water. Went back to the front of the store to pay.

The woman with the kids had left. Sam was in his store apron, Prosperity General ball cap, leaning against the cigarette rack, one of his own behind his ear. When we'd first moved to Prosperity, he'd smoked behind the counter. Now he went to the bench out front. Big changes.

"How's Mr. Jack?" he said, as I put the sandwich and drink on the counter. He picked them up, zapped them with the digital reader. It came to $9.13 and I handed him a ten. The change went in the jar, which went to the local humane society. Sam put my lunch in a paper bag, folded the top carefully.

"Heard you had some trouble up at your place," he said. "You okay?"

"Oh, yeah. Healing up just fine."

"That's good. Didn't my heart just about stop when I heard it on the scanner. Shooting. McMorrow residence. One male down. And wasn't there another one before that?"

He still had my bag.

"Yeah. Domestic thing. Boyfriend of my daughter's friend's mother. Had a fight that spilled over to our house."

"Heard a shot was fired then, too."

"Yeah."

"Nobody hurt?"

"No, all good."

I smiled. Nothing to see here, folks. Sam looked beyond me, down the aisles. Nobody coming.

"That Jason fella, he's a bad one."

So he knew.

"Came in here one time, three sheets to the wind, lugged a carton of beer up to the counter. I said, 'Sorry, son. You've had enough.' He got all up in my face, he has this right and that right. I looked him in the eye, I said, 'Mister. My store, my beer, my call. Now hit the friggin' road. And if I see you're driving outta here, I'm gonna be on the phone to the sheriff.'"

He paused.

"That got his goddamn attention. He in jail?"

"House arrest. Has some sort of heart problem, and the county doesn't want to pay for it."

"Oh, Jesus, here we go. How's the girl?"

"Tara?"

"No, Tiffanee. I think of her as a girl."

"Good person," I said.

"Oh, yeah. In and out of here all the time when she was growing up, they'd come back sometimes in the summer, stay at the farm. Nice kid. Used to give her popsicles."

Something in his tone, a hint of protective fondness, after many years. I pursued it.

"She's okay," I said. "Pretty hardened to it all, in a way."

"She's had—"

Sam looked over me as an older gray-haired woman came in, grabbed a basket from the stack.

"How's Sam?" she said.

"Good, dear. How's Dolores?"

"On the right side of the sod," the woman said, hobbling in the direction of the meat counter.

He grabbed a plastic grocery bag, hung it on a metal rack.

"She's had what?" I said.

"Oh, nothing. Just a hard row to hoe."

He turned away, looked out the window at the gas pumps. I let it float for a moment or two, eased closer, and said, "What was hard about it, Sam?"

I knew he wanted to tell me. Like so many people I'd spoken with, he just needed to feel I'd listen, and he hadn't made the first move.

"Tara and Sophie are really close friends," I said. "And Roxanne and Tiffanee are getting to be, too. If we knew, probably we'd be able to be there for her better."

Sam turned back to me, looked toward the meat counter, Dolores talking about lean hamburger.

"Okay, but you didn't hear it from me."

"No."

"You know her grandparents were Tinkhams from up on the ridge, almost to the Unity line. Whole family, hard workers and hard drinkers."

"Right."

"Her grandfather, Cluff, he kept it under control. Farming has a way of keeping most vices in check. Too much work to do, gotta be out there in the barn bright and early."

Like Rebel's dad.

Sam took the cigarette out from behind his ear, tapped it on the counter.

"Now Tiffanee's mother was their oldest. That was Sue Ann. She married Randy Winslow, from over in Freedom. Winslows got out of dairying and deep into chickens, until the whole broiler thing collapsed. Lost the farm to the bank. George Winslow, he died of disappointment, bitter, feeling sorry for himself. Randy, he was the oldest, played basketball. They had a good team back then, the school district. He was your typical farm boy, big and broad, strong as a freakin' ox. I mean, some of these other kids, they'd go up against him, was like running into a brick wall. Temper, though. Some kid would give him an elbow or whatever, and he'd give it back ten times harder. Always fouled out."

I smiled.

"I know the type."

"Think with their fists," Sam said. "So Randy, he was good with motors, growing up with tractors and all. Took mechanics at the voc school over to Waldo. He and Judy, they graduate high school, get married in the living room, burned all their bridges at the church. Pack up the truck, get the hell out of Dodge."

"Huh. No more farming."

"He'd seen how that could go sideways. Anyway, Randy and Sue Ann, they went to Connecticut. He got work in a truck garage, making decent money. So things was good for a few years. They had the baby—that's Tiffanee—and bought a house. All's well, at least on the outside."

Another tap of the cigarette.

"Well, then the old temper reared up again. Kept getting in arguments at work, then some fisticuffs, and they fired him. Bounced around with other jobs, I think. And no surprise, he took it all out on Sue Ann."

Dolores was talking to Delia in the back of the store. Sam leaned closer.

"Story I heard is over the years he got to beating on Sue Ann, cops would come. Arrest him for domestic violence, whatever they called it then. She wouldn't testify, just took him back. Start the whole thing over again."

"Hard to change that behavior sometimes," I said.

"Well, there is one way," Sam said. "A fella from Connecticut, he had a camp on Freedom Pond, used to come in here. Lawyer. According to him—"

He looked past me.

"Maybe I shouldn't get into it. Wouldn't want Tiffanee to think I'm a gossiper."

"I won't say where I heard it, Sam. But it would help us to know what's going on with her. She seems kind of lonely."

He looked at me.

"Okay. This is for her. So Tiffanee is fifteen, big girl like her dad, plays softball. This one time, Randy goes after Sue Ann, and this time

Tiffanee tries to separate them and, the story goes, Randy tells her to butt out, knocks her down. Sue Ann screams at him for hurting the girl, and he lays her right out. Come to find out, she'd had all these injuries over the years. Bruises and broken bones and a busted jaw that she didn't get treated, so it healed wrong and her face was crooked from then on. This lawyer said if there was a bone in her body to break, Randy had done it."

I waited, thought of Jason. A walking hair trigger. Sam took a deep breath.

"Anyway, Sue Ann goes wherever she goes after one of their fights. Randy sits in his chair in front of the TV. I'm picturing him tossing more beers down, but that's just my speculation."

He paused. Dolores was still talking at the meat counter.

"So," he said, his voice lowered, leaning close so I could smell his cigarette breath. "Tiffanee, she comes out of her room, they get into it again. He belts her one, she runs into her room. She comes back out, she's got a softball bat. She walks up behind him."

I waited.

"And she pulls that bat back and drives him like he was a fastball down the middle."

"Seriously?"

"Killed him dead as a goddamn doornail."

"Whoa."

"Yup."

"What happened to her?

Sam turned away. A truck had pulled up to the gas pumps. He turned back.

"Well, she's just a kid and there's all these circumstances. Lawyers said she was suffering from trauma and PTSD, whatever you call it. Probably an abuse victim herself. But still, killed him in cold blood."

"So, she was convicted? Did time?"

"Oh, yeah. Got her for manslaughter or some such thing. Gets juvenile hall for, like, two years. Of course, when she gets out, everybody down there knows she's the girl killed her own father. She and her mom leave town, knock around, Sue Ann getting jobs in dollar stores, whatever. Tiffanee moves out when she turns nineteen or so. Not long after, Sue Ann dies of drinking. End of that happy family."

"That's pretty awful, Sam."

"Yup. Anyway, then the grandmother dies up here, she leaves Tiffanee the farm. She comes back with some guy, and the child there. What's her name?"

"Tara."

"Right, she's, like, three or four, just a little girl. The dad he takes off. Then there's one boyfriend after another, none of them worth a shit from what I hear."

Sam looked up. Dolores was coming up the aisle behind me. He said, "She's a good kid. Protecting her mom was all."

He handed me my bag. Leaned close, half-whispered.

"You ask me, the bastard deserved it. What goes around, comes around, mister."

I looked it up in the truck, motor running. *Hartford Courant* archives, March 8, 2006. The headline: PUTNAM MAN'S DEATH RULED HOMICIDE. Randall T. Jones, 35, dies after being assaulted in his home.

I scrolled down. The story said Winslow was pronounced dead at the scene. Family members were being questioned. There was no danger to the public.

The follow-up, March 9 edition: JUVENILE, 15, HELD IN PUTNAM HOMICIDE. The story said the juvenile's name was not being released. Detectives from the Connecticut State Police Eastern District Crime Squad were handling the investigation.

March 11: POLICE SAY JONES DEATH FOLLOWED DOMESTIC DISTURBANCE.

March 14: JUVENILE IN CUSTODY IN CONNECTION WITH PUT-NAM DEATH. Tiffanee, still unidentified, was being held in a secure community residential program in Hartford.

A three-month gap, then this, on June 21: PUTNAM TEENAGER SENTENCED TO STATE CUSTODY UNTIL 17. Tiffanee, still unidentified, was convicted of second-degree manslaughter with a dangerous weapon. She was to be held in the same Hartford detention center. The prosecutor, Assistant State's Attorney Alicia Rodriguez, said the eighteen-month sentence was appropriate given the facts of the case, and that the juvenile defendant had no prior criminal convictions.

I put the phone down on the seat, said aloud, "So that explains it." Why Tiffanee never talked about her childhood. Why her history seemed to begin and end when she arrived at the farm, complete with family. Why she talked about visiting the farm but never said from where.

Pulling out, I went right, started south. The northwest wind was picking up, the temperature falling. Gusts swept snow from the fields and flung it across the roadway, ticking off the side of the truck like blown sand. I wanted to call Roxanne but couldn't, as she was sitting in a darkened theater with Tiffanee and the gang, watching a show about orphans. I wondered what Tiffanee thought, having half-orphaned herself. Patricide, they called it, which had always seemed to me an antiseptic sort of word for something so sad and unnatural. But then, was it more unnatural than a husband breaking his wife's jaw, repeatedly assaulting the mother of his child?

It's a violent world. We're a violent species, us *Homo sapiens*.

All of the fistfights and firefights over the years, people busted and broken, some of them good, most of them bad. All of it leading to the next one, an endless stream of hurt.

The landscape passed in a blur, trouble on all sides. Detective Strain, waiting for me to mess up. Pilgrim and Rebel, ready to fight back. Marta planning to abscond, Louis and Clair dug in to fight her battle. Or maybe it had already started?

I sped through the village of Liberty, another town named by optimists fortunate enough to not see what had happened since. Past Washington Pond, frozen white expanse like a salt flat. The road lifted and fell, twisted left and right. It was sheltered from the wind now, icy patches in the shade of spruces and firs. The truck slid left on a right-hand curve, caught in time for me to miss an oncoming log truck. The driver honked his horn. I flipped him off.

And then on to the main drag, Route 17, heading east. A couple in an old pickup, white-haired heads bobbing. Marta's old folks on the way to Walmart. I waited for a safe place to pass, blew by them on the first straight. Four miles down, went right at the gun shop, swung south. A pond on the left now, ice-fishing shacks and tiny figures, people from another world, the one without problems and crises. Not mine, where nobody was what they seemed, where there were vendettas and grudges and violence, and everyone was armed like Green Berets.

I crossed the Sanctuary line. Slowed. Took a deep breath. Said to myself, "Okay, now. What's the plan?"

South of the town of Union, the road swung southwest and started to climb. I started to slow for the turn, still came up behind a blue Dodge pickup with Connecticut plates, a blacked-out rear window. The driver braked, sped up, braked again. I eased off, was a hundred yards back when they slowed short of the road into Louis's land, braked almost to a stop. And turned in.

The truck stopped in the roadway, fifty feet in, before it reached the trees. I drove on, pulled over on the far side of the next curve. Backed up to the edge of the ditch, and reversed direction. When Louis's road came into sight, the truck was gone.

I pulled in. Stopped just short of where the truck had stopped. Saw where the four tires had settled enough to make darker marks in the gravel, before the truck continued on. Those were the tracks I followed.

The road climbed, turned north. For a mile, it ran along a ridge, woods on both sides, part of Louis's six hundred acres. Then it turned northwest, began to descend. There were frozen marshes on the right, cattails sticking out of the snow. The road made a series of S-curves and I could see where the Dodge had skidded on ice, then corrected. I couldn't see the truck so I buzzed the windows down, listened.

Nothing but the sound of my own tires crunching the frozen crust.

I was a quarter-mile from the turnoff, a single lane into deeper woods, the entrance marked by a cable bolted to two trees and an orange NO TRESPASSING sign. The cable was down when Louis was around, padlocked in place when he was in Canada. The sign remained in place.

The road curved to the right over a knoll and then continued. I eased up to the top of the crest, saw the entrance. The cable was down, but the tracks went straight. I stopped.

Turned off the motor. Listened. Waited. Thirty seconds. A minute. Heard the wind in the canopy. Nuthatches. Chickadees. Then I heard a truck door close, a muffled thud. Then a crunching noise, like somebody going over the snowbank into the woods.

They weren't lost.

I started the motor and touched the gas, eased past the gate. Stopped again and waited. The road was one lane wide here, so if the truck turned around and came back, it would meet me head-on.

I reached for the Glock, positioned it on the passenger seat. Rolled slowly forward.

And there it was, fifty yards ahead, back end to me, brake lights on, motor running. I couldn't see through the back window, had no idea who or how many were inside. I stopped. Waited. Watched. Exhaust from two pipes left clouds that hung in the cold air. Nobody showed. The truck didn't move.

I pulled ahead, turned my truck to the left, blocking the road. Stopped. Waited some more. Got out, gun close to my thigh. I started to walk slowly forward. Was halfway there when the truck's driver door swung open. A guy slid out.

An assault rifle in his right hand.

He turned—big beard, watch cap, bulky black jacket—the gun pointed at the ground. Said in a loud voice, "What?"

"Private road," I said.

"That right?" he said.

I moved five steps closer.

"You lost?"

"Who's asking?"

"I am," I said. "What's your business here?"

And then I could see it, the black bulk, the bulge. Body armor. He raised the rifle, peering through a scope. It was aimed at my face.

"Easy," I said, started to back up, still facing him.

"Too late," he said, took two shuffling steps toward me.

Another voice shouted, "Drop your weapon."

Louis.

From my left, the woods, up high. The bearded guy turned to look, first at the roadside, then up. He crouched and fired from the hip, the shot cracking. I dropped to the ground, gun up. There was a soft spit from the trees, a puff of snow at the guy's feet. He turned, dashed for the truck. I came to my feet, sprinted after him. I gained fast, the guy carrying the rifle weighed down by an equipment belt.

I leapt onto his back, rode him down, the rifle underneath him. My shoulder twisted, pain shooting through it. He twisted, tried to throw me off, and I rode up his back, grabbed his right arm, knelt on his left. He tried to roll onto his side, and I dropped, elbowed the side of his head. His left arm got loose, and he pushed himself onto his forearms, rolled right, took me with him.

I heard the clang of boots on metal, Louis coming down a ladder. The guy was on his back on top of me, trying to get to a handgun on his right side. I got my right arm around his neck, grimaced as I chopped weakly with my left fist.

He fumbled with the holster, then started groping for the left side of the belt. I slid my arm off his neck and down, felt the handle of a knife, his hand reaching for the grip. He started to pull it out.

And a rifle butt hit him on the side of the head. He went limp, blood running down his temple, into his ear. I rolled him off of me, and he came to rest on all fours. Louis stomped on his back, forced him to the ground. The guy was breathing hard, coughing.

Louis put the suppressor muzzle of the gun on the back of his head.

"Don't know how many lives you have left, my friend, but you just used one," he said.

I got up, looked for my gun. It was fifteen feet back, where I'd dropped it when I launched onto the guy. I walked over, picked it up, brushed off the snow and ice. My left arm hung, the pain radiating from my shoulder.

"Cover me," Louis said, and he slung his rifle over his back. Reached to the belt under his parka, came away with zip ties. He yanked the guy's right arm up, then the left. Wrapped a zip tie around and yanked it tight. Then another.

The legs next, yanked up. The guy was hogtied. Louis stepped back, unslung the rifle.

"You're both dead men walking," the man said.

To me, Louis said, "Could have shot him point blank, but you looked like you had things under control."

We stood there, like two hunters around a dressed deer. Louis was wearing the same camo as Marta, a helmet with goggles. The silenced rifle with a thermal scope.

"Gotta say, not a bad shot, from the hip, at a voice," Louis said. "I called, moved left two feet. He hit the tree where my head had been."

"There were two of them," I said.

"I know."

We trotted to my truck, got in. I tucked the Glock on the seat against my right thigh. Louis still had the helmet on. He folded the stock of the rifle, kept it across his lap, suppressor end toward the open window. I glanced at it.

"H and K four-sixteen," Louis said. "Picked up three of them."

I backed up, looked to the biker on the ground in the rearview camera, turned.

As if on cue, there was barking and snarling from the direction of the cabin, then a sharp rifle crack, then another and another. They were still echoing when there was a faint spitting noise. Another silenced rifle.

Clair.

Then more barking. Then nothing. I hit the gas.

Two hundred yards from the cabin, Louis said, "There," pointed into the woods to my left.

In an opening in a break in the trees, I could see a dark-clad figure. It was standing over someone on the ground. The standing person had a rifle pointed down. The dog was circling, growling, darting in to snap.

I braked, slid to a stop.

Louis rolled out, unfolding the rifle stock, ran in a half-crouch into the woods. I followed in his trail, the footprints punched through the crust. And then he stopped, moved to the side, sighted the rifle from behind a tree.

"Clear," Clair called.

We trotted to him, slowing as we approached. The dog, sensing the party might be ending soon, dodged in and grabbed the guy's leg, pulled and ripped the combat pants away.

"Get him off me," the guy shouted.

"*Stoppen*," Louis said, and the dog paused.

"Hold him," he said, and the dog went to a spot two feet from the guy's head and growled.

The biker was flat on his back. There was blood on the snow, an assault rifle six feet away, a handgun beside it.

"He's hit," Clair said. "Right hip."

Louis moved close and the guy looked up. I could see a dark braid on the snow, a neck tattoo from his flak-jacket collar to his hair. The letter P, with the round part a skull. Plunderers.

"You're fucking dead," the guy said.

"So we keep hearing," Louis said. "Roll onto your right side."

The guy looked at him and spat. Louis pointed the rifle and snapped a shot. The snow jumped next to the guy's head and he flinched. The dog growled louder. The guy took a breath, clenched his teeth. Used his arms to push himself up, then eased over. Louis leaned down. "Looks like it went through," he said.

"Missed the femoral," Clair said.

"Somebody up there likes you, dude," Louis said to the biker. "Not sure why."

The guy reached for his belt. A knife.

Clair stepped closer, aimed his rifle at the guy's back.

"Two-twenty-three, subsonic," Clair said to the biker. "Your luck will run out fast."

Louis reached behind him, pulled more zip ties from his pocket. Yanked the guy's arm back, then pushed him onto his face. Jerked the other arm out, said, "Cross 'em or I do it, and I might break one."

The guy did as ordered, and Louis looped one tie around, yanked it tight like a rodeo roper. Then another. Leaned in and unsnapped the sheath on the guy's belt, yanked a big combat knife out. He tossed the knife onto the snow with the guns, said, "Up."

"Can't."

Louis looked to me. I moved in and we stooped down, got a hand under his arms. On three, we pulled him to his knees. Took a step back and lifted him the rest of the way. He groaned, said, "Jesus Christ."

"I think he's forsaken you," Clair said.

Louis said, "Move."

We walked him back on Clair's tracks, Louis and I on each side, Clair behind with the rifle poised. The dog loped along beside us. When we got to the steps, we counted three. Lifted. Then again and again. We crossed the porch and Clair moved up, opened the big plank door. We moved him inside.

There was a cot against the wall near the woodstove, a shelf filled with medical supplies, like they'd prepared for casualties. We moved the guy over to it, turned him, pulled off his vest and jacket, tossed them to the floor. Then we lowered him down. Louis gave him a push and he fell back. The guy groaned and the dog growled again. I lifted his legs up and onto the mattress.

Stood, saw his blood on my hands.

Louis unslung his rifle, handed it to me. I took it to the front wall, leaned it next to other rifles, boxes of ammo. Louis had his knife out, smaller than the one on the biker's belt. He sliced the trouser leg open to the waist. More tattoos. The words LIVE FAST, DIE HARD running down his calf.

Louis looked at the black hole. Pulled the guy's leg up, eyed the quarter-size exit wound, red muscle, lacerated skin. I swallowed hard.

"We're good," Louis said.

He went to the shelf, took down a bottle of disinfectant, boxes of dressing, bandages, and tape. I watched as he cleaned the wound, the guy gritting his teeth, the dog showing his, too. There was surprisingly little blood flowing, and he pressed a compress on. I held out the tape and he sliced strips off, the knife blade like a razor. He wrapped the compress, took a last look. Stood straight and looked at the guy.

"You'll live to die another day," Louis said.

"Gonna kill all of you," the guy said. "That's a promise."

Louis went to the bathroom, and we heard the faucet running. Clair came over with a bottle of water, opened it. He put a hand behind the guy's neck, raised him up slightly. Tipped the bottle and the guy gulped the water down, spilling it down his chest. Clair dropped him back, where he lay panting, his braid draped across the pillow.

We stepped away.

"In over his head," Clair said. "I saw him through binoculars coming through the woods. Then there was gunfire behind him. I guess he thought he was outflanked, decided to just charge the ramparts. I was beside the house, called for him to drop his weapon."

"He didn't, I take it," I said.

"Kept coming. Called him out again. He just stops, starts shooting. Standing straight up, no cover. Looked like they used him to model targets for the range."

He glanced back.

"Figured I'd shoot below the vest, instead of above. Didn't necessarily want to kill him."

He looked at me. "What about the other guy?"

"Got a shot off at Louis in the tree stand. Tried to make it back to his truck, ended up getting wrestled down. He's hogtied in the road."

"How's the shoulder?"

"Serious physical therapy," I said.

I paused, looked at him.

"So what's the endgame anyway? Where's this all going?"

"Maybe this is it," Clair said.

"What if they keep coming, like those Russian inmates they hauled out of prison to fight in Ukraine?"

"Then they will, as they say, suffer the same fate."

Our guy was lying still, eyes closed. The dog had taken up his position, crouched on the floor, eyes fixed, like a border collie watching sheep.

Louis came back into the room. We looked to him for the next move. His house, his dog, his girlfriend. He looked at us and smiled, calm and in control. Then he glanced at the guy on the cot, walked to the kitchen counter, picked up a plate, came back. Held it out. We walked over.

"Made 'em last night."

Scones. Every good commando can bake them.

We each took one, the three of us.

"I'll make tea," Louis said. Went back to the sink, filled the kettle. Put it on the stove. The water on the bottom hissed in the flame. He came back. We stood.

"Quick debrief," Louis said, like it was just another day in Mosul. "So they sent a hit team. Two-man, not the A-team. Guy on the road, ex-military. Not highly trained. This one maybe just watched movies. They way overestimated their abilities, underestimated ours. I mean, I figured they'd drive past the gate, walk in. Maybe have the driver head back out. Turns out they were more low-budget than that. There's only one turnaround, so I set up looking down. Serious tactical error on their part."

He took a bite, said to the dog, "Good job. Way to execute."

I looked at him, all energized, another battle to fight. And he'd won the first skirmish, the enemy overmatched. We took bites of scone. The kettle hissed.

"Why now?" I said. "Why not wait until it got dark?"

"Hard to move in the woods without night vision, and they don't have any," Clair said. "You can't see, make all kinds of noise. I imagine their plan was to dig in with the cabin in sight, move in later tonight."

"What are you gonna do with him?" I said, nodding toward the cot.

"Maybe trade him," Louis said.

"For what?"

"For a face-to-face parlay, maybe."

"Will they do that?"

"If they're smart. They keep shooting, we're gonna have game wardens and State Police in here," Clair said. "Be hauling bikers off in buses, scrolling through the outstanding warrants. Better off to cut their losses, stay out of prison."

Louis turned to the stove, turned the gas off. Set out three mugs, dropped tea bags in. We watched as the tea steeped. Louis went to the refrigerator, took out a milk carton. Held it out to us.

"Two-percent?" he said.

I took the carton, poured milk in my mug. Handed the carton to Clair, who did the same. Louis held the scones out again. Clair took a half. I passed, the whole thing surreal. A wounded guy on the cot. A hogtied man in the road. An armory of a cabin. Scones.

For two of us, life was good. But what was I doing here?

"They'll need a way to save face," Clair said, chewing. "These guys have a very strong sense of honor and dishonor."

"Just don't plan on Marta having anything to do with it," I said. "She'll be long gone."

24

Louis froze, mug at his mouth. He lowered it slowly.

"What do you mean?" he said.

"Departed for parts unknown," I said. "Had her bags packed, including the one full of money."

"When was this?" Clair said.

"Two hours ago. She hid the money in the back of the barn, under the hay bales. I went to feed Pokey and figured it out. We talked in the bunk room. She told me she never asked to be rescued, that she had her own plan all along. Said she'd convinced one of the Wild Ones up there to start to sub in Methadone, clean her up enough so she could make a break for it."

I hesitated, knowing how this might land for Louis, but better a friend deliver the blow.

"With him."

The biker moaned, shifted on the cot. The dog's ears pricked and he tensed his hind legs, ready to move.

"Wouldn't have made it out," Louis said. "I saw how that operation worked."

"Not the point," I said. I hesitated, before delivering the real bad news.

"She said she doesn't want to be controlled. Not by this Snake guy, not by you, not by us."

He looked stunned. "But we're supposed to be together. Forever. She said it. It's the drugs. She's not right in the head."

"Her head seemed fine, Louis."

"How's she planning to leave?" Clair said.

I told him. The store, the bus, Boston and beyond.

"I'd say her ultimate destination may be Mexico," I said. "She mentioned San Miguel. Expat haven. But that could be a feint."

Louis took his phone from his hip pocket, flicked it on. A couple of taps and I could see the surveillance images, the same as the laptop. Military stuff he could do. It was his default, when things got rough, when he'd been deceived.

I pressed, the looming carnage seeming pointless.

"So what do you do now? With no Marta for them to find."

"Doesn't change a thing," Louis said. "They were never going to find her."

"Except when it's over, she's long gone. Who are we saving here?"

Louis sipped his tea.

"We're not doing this so she could just trade one prison for another," he said, already adjusting for the new situation. "Snake's big, ugly mansion for my cabin in the woods."

There was something in his tone, like it was a new scenario, and he was trying to convince himself. That he wouldn't miss her. That he didn't love her. That he hadn't planned for the two of them to live happily ever after. Together.

I pushed him harder.

"Then I don't get it," I said. "I mean, what's this all for then?"

Louis crossed the room, peered at the laptop, straightened up a leaning rifle. We waited.

"I find animals out here," Louis said. "Last one was a hawk, busted a wing in a fight, my guess would be with an eagle, probably tried to steal his lunch. I brought it home, got a hood on it, set the wing. Fed it for six weeks until it got strong again. When it was ready, I took the cage outside, opened the door. It looked at me for a minute. A couple of running steps and airborne. Whoosh. Like a fighter taking off from a carrier."

He paused.

"Marta's the same thing. I didn't help her to hurt her. If she wants to go, that's her right."

"But if you lose her, Snake loses her—maybe you're even already. Fight over."

Louis shook his head. "Doesn't matter," he said. "It's good guys versus bad guys."

Clair was nodding.

"Remember what they did to her, Jack," Clair said. "That place they put her, prostituting her. The drugs. Lambert was killing her slowly, from the inside out."

"There have to be consequences," Louis said. "You know that, Jack. We have to fight back or it's all lost."

I looked at my tea. Clair took a bite of scone, chewed.

Louis took another sip. "But why this particular battle?" he said, talking as much to himself as to us. "Because I know I'm on the right side, know exactly who the bad guys are. Not a flicker of doubt. Not so clear in Iraq, fighting your way through the smoke and chaos, everybody giving you the death stare, kids loaded up with IEDs."

Louis swallowed, seemed to move deeper inside his head.

"After we took back Mosul, like a day after that Hajji blew up the mess tent at FOB Marez, we're on patrol. Six Humvees, we're lead, taking AK from Hajjis, sweeping the roofs with the M240. And right in the middle of it this woman with a baby buggy comes marching toward us, right down the middle of the street. I mean, maybe it's a woman. Hard to tell, she was all wrapped up. Veil, *abaya*. Just her eyes showing. We stop, get on the speaker, tell her to move out of the way. She keeps on coming, like the guy in Tiananmen Square with the tank. We're screaming at her in English, in Arabic. 'Get out of here! Go! *Rajaeat! Rajaeat!*'"

He paused.

"Then she starts to run, right at us. Rios, he's our squad leader, he says, 'Take her out. There's a bomb in there.' Rios, he's on the fifty-cal, he says, 'Are you sure?' Rios screams, 'That's an order. Light her up!'"

Another pause. Louis took a bite of scone. Chewed.

"So Callahan does. Shreds the lady, the buggy. Looks like they'd been run over by a lawn mower."

He swallowed.

"No bomb went off. Because you know what was in the buggy? A baby. A little girl. We're freaking out, seeing the little body there in the street. I mean, how do you justify that? Nothing can make that right."

Another sip of tea. A long, deep breath. The dog turned his head, seemed to listen.

"There was an investigation. Decided Rios was acting to protect American troops. We gave more than adequate warning. IEDs had been delivered in all sorts of ways, including kids turned into suicide bombers, guys pretending to be women, women pretending to be pregnant. She could have been a walking bomb. You couldn't take that chance."

The biker stirred in the corner. I wondered where he'd served.

"But she wasn't. And then it eats at you. Did we do the right thing? Why were we there to begin with? What if we'd done nothing? The baby and mom would be alive. Did we put ourselves first? Poor Rios, they sent him off for counseling, never saw him again. He didn't join up to kill mothers with babies. None of us did."

I waited. It was the most I'd heard Louis talk in one stretch. Ever.

"So I can shoot guys like the one by the truck all day long, Jack."

"What if you both go to prison? I mean, you're not cops. I'm not, either."

"Justified deadly force," Louis said. "I believe all of these guys were about to use deadly force on me or a third person. Came heavily armed. Attempted to enter my dwelling place without a license or privilege to do so."

"Self-defense? But you could call 911 right now."

"It's about more than doing the minimum," Louis said. "Because when we win and they lose, that's a net gain for the world. No doubts, no nightmares, no lying awake in the dark. When this is over, I'll be fine. Every time the bad guys lose, it balances out some of the times it wasn't so clear."

"But why not call the police in? Because having them take care of this isn't enough of a penance?"

"This is my fight," Louis said.

"What if you end up in prison?"

"That's a risk I take. You're no different, Jack. Come on. You jump in as much as I do. Just the pen instead of the sword. Or sometimes the sword. Clair was filling me in on your payback with that guy with the code name. Would have done both hands myself, but, hey. I get you're a reporter and—"

I was sitting between two Marines who were planning for a fight that could end up with all of us dead. I had too much to lose. Roxanne, Sophie . . .

Louis's head twitched, a slight jerk. Both he and Clair were looking at the laptop.

We all moved closer. A dark-colored van had driven into view behind the black pickup. Two guys got out of the front, one on each side. They were dressed like the first two, and both drew handguns. They approached the hogtied guy, pivoting with guns drawn. Then one guy holstered his, bent to cut the zips. The other guy kept his gun on the black Dodge. And then the three of them were on their feet.

If I wanted out, it was too late.

"Let's go," Louis said.

He went to a table, picked up a flak vest, tossed it to me. I started to put it on over my jacket.

"Hang back, Jack. You're press," Louis said. "Embedded. Just like in Iraq. We sure as hell didn't want anything to happen to them."

They went to the cot, Louis slapping the guy on the cheeks. The dog was on his feet, growling softly, teeth bared.

"Up," Louis said.

They pulled the guy upright so he was sitting, then lifted him to his feet. He stood on the good leg and hopped, grunting and grimacing all the way to the door. I pushed it open and the dog led the way out, stopped. Listened. We followed, the biker's bare leg white in the cold.

"Let's put him in the back of your truck, Jack," Clair said.

I jumped down, patting the Glock in my pocket. Backed my truck up, got out and lowered the tailgate. They half-carried the guy, turned, and sat him down on the steps. Then Louis went around the side of the truck bed, yanked him in, his leg outstretched.

They went back inside, and I was left with the biker.

He looked weak, woozy, the bravado drained away. He said, "I want outta here."

"You and me both," I said.

Clair and Louis came out of the cabin, helmets on, dropping rifles over their shoulders. Louis sprang up into the truck bed, crouched like we were on patrol in Iraq. I joined Clair and we slid into the cab, me driving, and we pulled out, going fast up the road, snow spraying.

A hundred yards from the entrance, Louis knocked on the side of the truck. I stopped and he vaulted out, ran twenty yards further, the dog beside him. Then they veered into the woods.

"He's the flanker," Clair said. "Give him two minutes." He looked at his watch, and when the time was up said, "Go."

I drove, fighting off the urge to just floor it, get the hell out, leave the guy by the side of the highway. The truck crunched over the snow and gravel, and I glanced over at Clair. He had the same tricked-out assault rifle as Louis, and I knew I was seeing the former him, the one from the war, the one who'd spent days hidden in the jungle. Firefights. Skirmishes. Death and destruction. Because of skill, temperament, luck, he'd survived and come home. But the Recon Marine soldier was always somewhere inside him.

"What's the plan?" I said.

"Block the road, dump this guy. Send the message."

"Which is?"

"More of the same if they come back."

I kept driving.

"Will Louis be there for this?"

Clair nodded, looked back at our prisoner. We were close to the entrance now, fifty yards from the bikers' truck and the van. They'd hear my truck coming up the road. I slowed. Reached for the Glock, took it out and placed it on the console.

I was going home, one way or the other.

When we came to the gate, I inched the truck forward. We looked right and could see the back of the van. It was starting to move, the pickup following. I turned right. Drove ten feet and stopped, blocking the road.

We sat. Waited. After a minute, the van cab doors opened. The two new guys—the one with the beard, a shorter one with a ponytail—got out, handguns held low. They walked slowly to the front of the van and stopped. Clair clicked the safety off, got out, the rifle still across his chest, his fingers on the trigger.

I stayed in the truck, held the Glock in front of me. The motor idled.

Clair walked ten feet forward, a slow saunter. The two bikers did the same. One of them called out to the guy in the truck bed, "You okay, brother?"

The biker in the back shouted, "Yeah. Shot in the leg."

The biker on the left, the one on the camera, took two steps forward. "You shoot him, old man?" he said.

Clair didn't move. "Gave him due warning," he said. "He could have dropped his weapon, turned around, gone back the way he came. Instead, he started firing. Same with your other buddy. Not fast enough, not smart enough. Just like you."

The guy scowled, eyes narrowing at the insult. He started to raise his gun and there was the *pfft* sound again, puffs in the ground at his feet. The other guy lifted his gun. The rifle spat from somewhere in the trees, ice and gravel spraying.

They lowered their guns, looked to the woods to the right. The uphill side, the higher elevation. Another tactical error. The dog came bounding down the bank, across the road. He skidded to a halt in front of them, barking, teeth bared. They raised their guns, started to back up as Louis came out of the woods, rifle leveled, like a *Star Wars* stormtrooper. Stopped at the edge of the road.

"Drop your weapons."

They didn't, and Louis put a round through the back of the van, two feet from their heads. The ting of metal, the reverberating shot.

They eased down, crouched, put the handguns on the gravel. The dog feinted, and they backed up a step.

Louis said. "On the ground, facedown. Arms out toward me."

That coldness in his voice. Still, they hesitated.

"Could just kill all three of you," Louis said. "Plenty of places out here to stick you."

They dropped to their knees, then to the ground, chins against the gravel, eyes on the rifle and the dog, his teeth now at face-level.

Louis moved in, Clair, too. He picked up the handguns, tossed them ten feet away. They hit the snow and skidded.

Clair stepped past the guys on the ground, gripped the door handle at the rear of the van. Louis positioned himself in front of the door, gun leveled. Clair yanked the door open.

The van was empty.

They stepped back, both rifles aimed at the guys' backs. I got out of the truck, gun at my side.

"Up," Louis said. "Slow."

They did, raising themselves first to their knees, then to their feet. The fronts of their pants and jackets were flecked with gravel and snow. The second guy started to reach across the front of his jacket and Louis fired a round past his head and the dog snapped at his boot. The guy froze.

Louis told them to move. They hesitated, then started, like someone walking the plank. They shuffled past my truck, Louis and Clair behind them. The wounded guy was sitting up, shivering.

"Get him out," Louis said.

They did, pulling him onto the tailgate by his good leg. When both legs were extended, the guy groaned in pain. They lifted him off the truck, his arms around their shoulders.

"In the van," Louis said.

They started walking slowly back, the wounded leg swinging. When they got to the van, they sat him down. He scooched himself in. When he was inside, the bearded guy reached to close the van doors.

"Keep them open," Clair said.

The guy whirled around.

A handgun.

A boom, Louis falling, the guy diving into the van, the wheels spinning. Clair firing into the back of the van, hitting the swinging doors. More shots as the van lurched away and the doors swung back open.

And then we were both on the ground by Louis. He was on his side, holding his left leg at the quad. There was a puddle of dark blood on the snow, more blood dripping.

"Artery," he gasped, and Clair pulled a knife, sliced the cargo pants above the pocket. He pressed a hand on the black spot of the wound.

"Gotta tie it off," he said.

I ran to my truck, yanked the lid of the storage compartment behind the seats. Pulled out a tangle of bungee cords, shook one loose as I ran back. Clair took it, looped the cord around Louis's thigh and knotted it.

Louis watched, his face pale, skin blue-gray. His breath was ragged, rapid. His forehead was covered with sweat.

"Shock," he said.

"Lie him down," Clair said.

I did, easing his head to the ground. Took off my jacket and draped it over him. Dialed 911.

"In the truck," Clair said. "We'll meet them."

I ran back, pulled the truck up. Reclined the passenger seat, slid it back. We hoisted Louis to his feet, his head lolling. Brought him to the truck and eased him in. His head fell back.

Clair raised Louis's leg and propped it on the dash, then clenched another cord around his thigh. He slammed the door, ran around to the driver's side, and got in the back seat.

I jumped into the driver's seat and slammed the truck into gear, fishtailed, and eased off the gas, then back on. When I glanced in the mirror, I could see rifles on the ground by the puddle of blood.

"Gun in the door," Louis wheezed, his voice slurring. "My mistake, boys. Sorry about that."

"All good," Clair said. "Don't talk. We'll get you patched up."

I bounced down the driveway, the truck slaloming through the corners, following the tracks of the van. I came through the gate, slid sideways, and started toward town.

Clair was on the phone, saying there'd been a shooting, describing the van.

"Approach with caution," he said. "Two armed and dangerous. At least one with a gunshot wound."

Louis paler; his breathing more rapid.

Clair felt his neck for a pulse. He tucked my jacket around him, said, "Almost there, Marine."

I drove, gravel and snow spraying. And then we were on the pavement, driving fast toward town. After three miles, we saw blue lights approaching. A sheriff's cruiser. It skidded to a halt beside us. Then red lights, a siren. A rescue truck. Sanctuary Volunteer Fire Department.

We all braked, stopped in the middle of the road. The EMTs jumped out, two of them, ran to us. We bailed out, the gray-haired deputy approaching with his hand on his holstered gun.

"Shot in the upper thigh," Clair said. "Caught an artery. In shock."

They pulled the door open and bent to Louis. Camo. Ballistic vest. Knife on his belt.

Louis looked up at them woozily, said, "Sorry to impose," and smiled weakly.

One ran to their truck, took a gurney out of the back. She wheeled it back and they eased Louis on. The truck seat was stained with blood.

They shoved the gurney through the snow, lifted it to the back of their truck, and eased Louis in.

Clair started to climb in with him, but the deputy said, "You come with me. We'll follow them."

The deputy spun him around, patted him down. He took the knife off of his belt, and a small handgun from a holster on his thigh.

He turned to me, said, "Who are you?"

"He's just a bystander," Clair said. "Helped get Louis out here."

"Jack McMorrow," I said.

"The news guy? You witnessed whatever the hell happened here?"

I nodded.

"Detective is going to want to talk to you," he said.

I slowly reached for my wallet, picked out a business card, and handed it to him. He pocketed it and they hurried to the cruiser. He put Clair in the back and wheeled the cruiser around. It followed the ambulance, and I stood there, watched the red lights recede, and was left alone.

The woods were dark and deep, but not so lovely. I peered into the shadowed trees, so silent after the gunshots, like everything that had happened was already washed away.

If Louis died . . . for what? For whom?

To ease his guilt for a killing in a war filled with them? For a tough survivor of a woman who'd used him up and spat him out? Maybe it was more than that. Maybe both Clair and Louis had some deep-seated unspoken wish to be KIA, to be warriors to the very last moment.

I didn't. I was only press, after all.

I walked to the truck, got in. It smelled like blood, and the stain on the seat was black as ink. How to explain that to Roxanne, to Sophie? My embedded life was catching up with me, and it was following me home.

25

It started to snow on the way north, a fitful sort of squall with wind-blown dry flakes. Then stopped, then started again. Like even nature's heart wasn't in it.

I was in Montville, between ridges, waiting for phone reception. I called Strain. A preemptive strike. He didn't pick up.

I drove on, the snow swept across the road, the wind buffeting the truck. I was at the crest of a ridge when the phone buzzed. I picked it up.

"Dad, it was amazing," Sophie said. "And we got to go backstage, and Tara met Annie."

My brain stalled for a moment, then reconfigured. The other world. "No kidding. Wow."

"Tara said she was so cool. I didn't get to meet her. Just Tara and Mr. Ziggy. We didn't want to, like, swarm at her."

"Right."

"Her name's Hermione, like in *Harry Potter*? She's fifteen but she looks way younger onstage, with her hair and everything. She's from San Francisco. She does school remotely, all so she can pursue her dream. Which is to perform on Broadway. She told Tara TV is, like, such a cattle call."

There were voices in the background. Tiffanee, Mr. Ziggy.

"So everybody had fun?"

"It was awesome. We met the director after, and Mr. Ziggy invited her up to see our show."

Fat chance of that, I thought.

"Great," I said.

"And now we're going to have a late lunch."

Very big city. Away from the phone, I heard her say, "Where is it?"

Then she was back. "Legal Sea Foods. It's right on the water. Tara and I decided we want to go to college in Boston."

"Lots of colleges there," I said.

"Or maybe New York City. We could be roommates and go to shows all the time, Tara could do auditions. Mr. Ziggy said he'd take her down, maybe for April vacation. He knows all these theater people."

"I'm sure he does. I'm sure her mom would like to see it, too."

"She has to work. She said she used up all her vacation going to court about Jason."

"Ah, right."

"But Mr. Ziggy, he has these girls who are his friends that they could stay with."

"I see. You don't want to go?"

A pause. In the background, Tara laughing, rapping, *It's the hard-knock life*. Mr. Ziggy saying, "Yo, girl!"

Sophie whispered, "Mom wasn't so hot on the idea."

"Oh, okay. Hey, is she there?"

"She's driving. Mr. Ziggy is back here with us. Tiffanee is with Mom, doing Google Maps on her phone. We don't want to get lost and end up in a bad neighborhood."

Maybe Tiffanee could break out her bat, I thought.

More singing, "Easy Street." Tara holding a sustained note, only slightly sharp. She was getting better.

"Ask Mom to call me when she can. After you eat is fine," I said. I told her I loved her. She said she loved me, too. And the curtain went down.

This is what I'd risked losing, if the shot had hit me, not Louis. If the guy had gotten off more than one. Bleeding out on an icy gravel road in the middle of nowhere. No Sophie. No Roxanne. They were what I'd almost lost when the shotgun blast took me down. When the flames crept up the wall of the house.

I had to keep the bad guys at bay.

I was just south of Appleton, rolling snowy hills, the squalls blowing tumbleweeds of snow across the road. A flat-white pond on the left, down the ridge. The turnoff coming up, Route 105 to the northwest and home. I kept heading north, Rosemont pulling me in.

Unfinished business.

It was a little after four o'clock, off-season for the foundation business. I figured the chances were good that Stryker would be puttering around the shop, organizing the troops.

They were very good. I rolled up at 3:20, skipped the house and the missus altogether. The Dodge was parked by the door to the barn. The lights were on.

I put on my Smithsonian flag hat, got out and went inside.

The room was warm, woodstove going. Stryker was seated at the table on his laptop, no doubt communicating in some encrypted way. He looked up. I kept coming. He reached under his armpit, came out with a small handgun. He held it on the table, not aimed at me but not far off.

"Save your bullets," I said. "I didn't come to tread on you."

"No lug wrench this time?" Stryker said.

"No. Just checking in. I never heard back."

He paused, seemed to be thinking. How much to say? Maybe I was wearing a wire.

"My guess is they're going to be doing surgeries on Rebel's hand for months," I said. "It was a pretty good whack."

A beat.

"Kind of a sad sack, really. I feel a little bad."

I channeled Louis and Clair.

"But just a little."

A flick of his eyebrows.

"Just so you know, if you or any of the others come near me, my family, my home, I'll stop you. And that'll be the end of your little Scout troop. Nobody to play soldier with. Nobody to wear cheesy uniforms. No secret decoder rings."

He was staring at me, gaze fixed. The gun started to tap on the table.

"I don't control their every move," Geberth said.

"Well, you'd better start, General Stryker. Because I see so much as a footprint, this will be my first stop. The head of the snake. Work my way down to the tail."

He swallowed, tried to look unperturbed. Tried again, puffing up his chest, still came up short.

"Nobody comes to my home and threatens me," he said.

"Maybe nobody before today."

"I could shoot you right now."

"But you won't, because in this crew, you're the brains. And you know shooting people is very complicated, even best case. Headlines. Bad press for your business. Jail time. Civil suits. Lawyers. This spread, the horses, the pretty little family—it would all go up in smoke."

Geberth bristled, just the eyes. The family reference. Pulled himself back together. He looked at me, and his eyes narrowed like he was trying to get a closer look, figure me out.

"You got it? It's your last warning."

He looked at me, clenched his jaw. The hand tensed on the gun, then slowly relaxed.

"No wonder you got fired from the New York *Times*," he said.

"No wonder at all," I said, and turned and walked back to the door and out to the truck.

I took a long, deep breath as I left the property. Then I thought, how did he know that? Who had he talked to? Had Sophie overheard me talking to Roxanne? Sophie says something to Tara and Tara mentions it to Tiffanee? Was Tiffanee talking to Jason again?

Or maybe Stephanie Dunne? Had she tried to talk to Jason? Infiltrate a Maine militia on her own?

And then, the question that had been lurking underneath it all: Would Louis make it?

Rich kid turned soldier. What was the story Marta had told? Some drunk guys in high school trying to assault her, Louis taking them on, saving her. Then and now. Living alone in the woods according to his own code of honor. Like a sinner turned monk, trying to assuage his guilt. The Iraqi woman with the baby propelling him into yet another firefight, this time, he hoped, truly on the side of good. Riding to his lover's rescue like some white knight.

It ran through my mind in a loop as I wound my way northeast. Snow was still scudding down the road, starting to accumulate in shallow drifts, like sand on a beachfront parking lot. There was a stop sign at the Route 3 crossing and I slowed, accelerated through it. The road continued north, threading its way past frozen ponds and bogs, a ridge to the west throwing a shadow. I sped past the town of Morrill, turned west at Knox, climbed the ridge, slid down the far side.

Slowing for the turn to Prosperity, I glanced over at a truck that was stopped and about to pull out. An old Tacoma, red. Oversized tires, a hood with a scoop. A kid at the wheel. Blaze-orange sweatshirt, camo hat. He was grinning, talking. There was a woman in the passenger seat. Hair tucked into a watch cap. She was smiling, too.

As I passed our eyes locked.

Marta. It was all going according to her plan.

I coasted, eyes on the rearview, and had an urge to follow her, catch up to her at the store. Tell her what destruction she'd caused. That Louis was seriously wounded, that Clair had shot one guy, wasn't going to desert his post. In spite of her.

But then the truck pulled away, and I kept driving.

It wasn't about her. It was about atonement and duty and doing the right thing. It would be lost on her.

I went home, put the Glock in the safe (my nod to Roxanne). Restarted the fire. Sat down in the chair and watched the flames creep up through the kindling, lick tentatively at the first small chunk of wood. Thought of the fire shooting up the wall under Sophie's window. Should have done the other hand.

My shoulder was throbbing. My temple hurt where the biker had punched me, just before Louis put the gun to his head. I thought of having a beer, some quiet. But what peace would that bring? What I really needed was to be a reporter again, not a half-baked security guard.

I stood by the woodstove, called Clair. It went to voicemail.

I rang off, opened the door of the stove and stirred the fire. As I was poking, my phone buzzed.

I picked up. "How is he?"

"Hanging in," Clair said. "Lost more than half his blood."

"How much can you lose?" I said.

"And live? Two-thirds is the limit."

He said Louis was being moved from the ER to ICU. That the bullet, a .45, had pierced the artery, hit the femur, then bounced off to do more damage. Police found the van abandoned on a side road north of Sanctuary Village.

"What about you?" I said.

"What about me?" Clair said.

"Are they asking about the shooting?"

"They're asking."

"What'd you say?"

"I stood my ground," he said.

I was thinking it was way more than that—that in a way, the bikers had been lured into a trap. I thought about saying it, but decided it wasn't the right moment. Instead, I started to tell him about Stryker, delivering my message.

And then Clair said he'd spotted one of the ER docs, had to go. And was gone.

I was left wondering if my warning was an empty one, in light of what had happened to Louis. Standing there alone, I answered my own question. *No.*

The fire was going. I went to the sink, filled a pot with hot water. Grabbed rags from the bag in the closet, went out to the truck. Opened the door and leaned in, started scrubbing blood off the seat, the towels turning a dark red-brown.

After fifteen minutes, the stain remained, and I went back inside. Clair hadn't called, but was that good or bad? I went back and forth, finally opened my laptop. Went to Mr. Ziggy's LinkedIn page, started digging.

If I couldn't save Louis, maybe I could protect Tara and Sophie.

The Eugene Stage Co. had a website, the usual list of staff, trustees, recent productions. I scrolled down to *The Lion King*, then to the director's name. Jamie O'Day, pronouns: they/them. This linked back to the staff list, where there was an e-mail listed, but I went to the contact tab, found the number for the theater company's offices.

I called. It rang a few times, and as I waited for voicemail, a woman answered.

"Eugene Stage. You've reached Jamie."

She had a big theatrical voice that probably reached the back of the hall.

"This is Rick Smythe," I said. "With a *y* and an *e*. I'm calling from Maine. I'm hoping you know Mr. Ziggy. John Zwiefelhofer?"

A moment of silence. Then way more quietly, "What is this about?"

"Mr. Ziggy is working in our schools here. I'm a parent adviser to the theater department—my daughter is in the cast of *Annie*—and we're preparing to give him an award. He's been outstanding."

"Okay."

Not exactly cheering for Mr. Ziggy.

"I'm looking for anecdotes because I'm doing the award speech. It's at the theater boosters' annual dinner. We like to get them fired up, start writing checks."

I waited for a chuckle. Nothing.

"Anything that you remember that I could put in there. You know, maybe kid actors he had a profound influence on, inspired them to continue with theater. What he brought to the production. His interpretation of the part. What was it? Zazu?"

"That's right."

"And you directed."

"Yes, but it was a while ago."

"But you must have worked closely with Mr. Ziggy. Kids love the name, by the way."

"I'm sure."

"So, anything to share?" I said.

A pause.

"Your name is what?"

"Rick."

"You said you have a child in a play?"

"My daughter. She thinks Mr. Ziggy walks on water."

Another pause. I waited.

"Yes, he can be very . . . engaging."

"Oh, he is that. He's just has thrown himself into the production."

"I'm not surprised."

I waited. Silence. A pattern emerging.

"Can you be more specific? I'd like something that really sings, so to speak."

I waited. They cleared their throat. I could hear papers shuffling.

"I'm trying to think. It's been a while."

"Well, listen, I noticed he had to leave mid-production. But you still staged the play?"

"Oh, yeah. You know. The show must go on."

"Right," I said. "So why did he have to leave? Just curious. We don't want to lose him. I notice he's moved around to a lot of different theaters."

"It was his decision," Jamie said. "A personal matter, I think. I don't know that he ever shared exactly."

"So he didn't get canned." I smiled. I didn't feel a smile coming back.

"No. He just decided to move on."

"Well," I said. "If you think of anything."

"Sure," Jamie said. "Nice talking to you. Good luck with *Annie*. It's a fun show."

As I started to say it was nice talking to them, too, they hung up.

I sat back. A personal matter. Not a single anecdote. Not even faint praise.

Rick Smythe went back to work. Yvette in Tacoma said Mr. Ziggy had been part of a very strong production, but had little to say about him specifically. Our *Annie* actor was new to theater, I said. Mr. Ziggy had taken her under his wing.

"Oh, I can totally picture that," Yvette said. And that was it.

Equally awkward were conversations with Kyle in Salem, Oregon, and a briefly ebullient Aleesha in Spokane. They all wished me well, and seemed eager to get off the phone. Theater people with little to say?

It was just after six, after three on the West Coast. I got up, put another piece of wood in the fire. Still nothing from Clair. Back to the phone.

I tried managing directors at each theater. Two had assistants who took messages. In Eugene, someone named Fatima said she really didn't have that much interaction with the actors. In Tacoma, Fergus said he recalled Mr. Ziggy's name but didn't have any more specific recollections than that. And then Fergus had to go.

I sat back in the chair. Considered my next move. Heard the shed door roll open. The back door rattle.

They were home already. What happened to the late lunch?

I got up, walked through the kitchen, turned the corner.

Jason was standing there, gun in his right hand, bracelet on his left ankle.

26

"A bone to pick," Jason said.

He was slurring, weaving on his feet. His rank breath smelled of alcohol.

I grinned.

"Gee, Jason. Hope you have a designated driver. Seem like you've had a beer or two."

"Shut up."

The gun came up. The muzzle made tight circles in the air in front of my face. The closet was behind him, my gun in the safe.

"Easy with that thing, bud," I said, half-turning. "Come on in. Sit by the fire."

"Don't you walk away from me, you piece of shit," he bellowed.

"Well, if you come with me, I won't be walking away, right?"

I turned, moved into the kitchen. Heard him follow, his boots scuffing on the pine floor.

"I'm talking to you," he shouted.

"I hear you."

A shuffle of steps, a hard blow across the back of my head. The pistol.

"Turn around," Jason said.

I did. Ran a hand through my hair. Felt warm blood.

"That's for Rebel."

I looked at my hand.

"Oh, yeah. Good old Rebel. How's he doing?"

I took a step toward the sink.

"You mind if I get a towel? There's a lot of blood vessels in the scalp, and it's bleeding pretty good."

I took two steps, heard his shuffle, waited for the next blow. It didn't come. I took a towel off the rack by the sink, ran it under the tap. There was a butcher block of knives to the left of the sink. I shifted to block his view of it. Turned back quickly.

The gun was pointed at my face.

It was another revolver, four-inch barrel. Chrome with a black grip, like a G-man would carry in an old movie. I could see the copper tips of the bullets.

"Another retro gun there, Jay," I said. "A lot to be said for a revolver. So few moving parts compared to a semiautomatic, you know? I'm partial to my Glocks, but I can understand why—"

"Shut your mouth!"

A scream this time, almost primal. His eyes had narrowed to bloodshot slits and there was spittle on his lips. The gun was still circling.

"Don't wanna hear a word you say," Jason said. "Who gives a shit? Nobody's gonna say Jason took any crap. Nobody's gonna say he didn't stand up for his friends. Nobody's gonna say that a friggin' ankle cuff was enough to hold him down."

"No, it won't hold you down. That's clear. You're here. But it does set off an alarm when you leave the house. Then the GPS tracking kicks in. I mean, they'll know where you are, be coming after you."

"I don't care what they fuckin' know. What *I* know is you smashed Rebel's hand to bits. My aunt, she used to be a nurse. She said that hand ain't never gonna work right again."

"Why God gave him two," I said.

"Sit down," Jason said, "you wise-ass son of a bitch."

He stepped back, pointed at the table.

I moved toward him and he circled. I was between him and the closet alcove.

"How 'bout a beer? Got a nice IPA. Kind of hoppy, if you're into hoppy. Some people aren't. And I have to say, there's a lot to be said for a good Pilsner. I mean, a nice cold Bud. Hard to beat that."

"I said sit. You hear me?"

The gun was still raised, four feet from my head. It seemed like he was tiring, the barrel dropping incrementally, then him jerking it back up.

I pulled a chair out, sat down. The gun loosely tracked me.

"You're not gonna get in a standoff when they show up, are you?" I said. "I mean, they'll take you out. They bring in that State Police tactical unit, and man, it's like fighting an army. It's either surrender or get blown away. And they don't just shoot you once. Things explode and you're taking fire from all directions. Nobody can—"

"Shut up," Jason shouted.

I did.

"Keep your hands on the table."

I did that, too.

The gun started to lower, from my face, to my chest, to my right hand.

"This is very Old Testament," I said. "You know. Eye for an eye, tooth for a tooth. I guess you didn't think to bring a lug wrench. Not sure what I would have used if Rebel hadn't had one handy."

"Will you just shut the—"

There was a footstep in the shed, outside the door.

"They're here, Jason," I said. "That didn't take long."

He turned, the gun, too. I came off the chair, over the table, bad shoulder to his chest, knocked him backwards. He stumbled and I drove him like a football lineman, pain shooting down my arm. He hit the cupboards. Tried to bring the gun down and around, and I twisted and grabbed his wrist, smashed it against the wall.

Once. Twice. Three times.

The gun didn't come loose and we spun and fell to the floor. The gun clunked, was still in his hand. I rose to a crouch, stomped hard, over and over. I felt bones breaking, his fingers flattening against the trigger guard. I stomped and he bellowed, and the gun skittered out of his hand, just a couple of inches. I bent and punched him in the face, fell to my knees, and crawled over him toward the gun.

And then I had it and I scrabbled away, turned. He'd pulled a knife from somewhere, lurched to his knees. I rushed him again and the knife flew over me, hit the wall. I bowled him over backwards, saw the left hand against the floor. He was starting to move, and for a moment I was reared up, a boot raised to crush that hand, too. Then I thought of Clair in the truck with Rebel, my "remarkable restraint." Raymond and Sparrow and Jesus in the cemetery, all those other cheeks turning.

I kicked him in the ribs instead.

He grunted, held his broken hand close, moaned.

"You're so dead," Jason said, lay still.

"So I keep hearing."

I heard another step outside the door, walked over. Listened. Heard someone clear their throat. Cough.

I put Jason's revolver in the back of my waistband. Opened the closet, then the safe, took out my Glock. Raised the latch with my bad hand, pulled the door open.

A kid was standing there, huddled with his hands under his arms. Orange sweatshirt, camo hat.

He drew his hands from his armpits, put them up. I lowered the gun, motioned with my left hand for him to do the same. He eyed the blood on my gun hand from my head, Jason's face. Hesitated, like it might be a trick.

The arms came down. "Sir," he said. "Sorry to bother you."

"No bother."

I was just wrestling a gun away from a guy with nothing to lose.

"It's just that I tried a couple of other houses but nobody was home. I work at Prosperity General Store."

"Right."

"This foreign lady, she was from the next house down. She ordered a sandwich, asked me for a ride back to the store. But we got up around the corner, she, like, says she feels sick. I pull over, you know, in case she's gonna puke. She gets out, she's standing there, I go to see if she's okay. She says she's gonna walk a little, get some air. Gets to the back of the truck, runs around and jumps in, and takes off."

"She took off."

"Right. I mean, my phone's in there. My wallet. Everything."

"Okay," I said.

"So I just need to call the police. I been walking for, like, twenty minutes, friggin' frozen. Still, they oughta be able to find her, right? I mean, where could she go?"

Where, indeed?

He looked at me. I must have had blood on my face.

"You all right?" he said.

I looked down at my hand.

"Friend tripped and fell, cut his head. I was helping him."

I told him to go outside and wait, went inside to get my phone. Jason was sitting against the wall in the kitchen, looking dazed, cradling his broken hand in his lap like a kitten. I bent down, his gun uncomfortable in the rear of my waistband.

"Sit tight," I said.

I got my phone off the counter, went back outside. Jason's pickup was parked beside Tiffanee's Jeep. Just like old times.

I waited while the kid called. He told the dispatcher the highlights. Then he repeated his name and the story. The dispatcher asked for his location and I tapped him on the shoulder. He turned, covered the phone.

"I can give you a ride to the store."

Keep the police off my doorstep.

"Prosperity General Store," he said into the phone. "I'll be there in ten."

I went back inside, motioned for the kid to follow. He did. Jason was still sitting on the floor.

"This is my friend Dave," I said. "He fell and hurt his hand and his head. He needs to go."

"Okay," the kid said.

"Dave can't drive. Would you drive his truck?"

"What?" Jason said.

The kid looked at Jason's bloody head, the cuff on his ankle.

"You sure he doesn't need an ambulance or something?" the kid said.

"He's fine," I said. "Just needs to wipe his face. We'll follow you. He can have someone meet him at the store. Right, Dave? Maybe they can get you home before anybody knows you were gone."

He scowled. I leaned close, whispered: "If police come here, you want to be waiting for them?"

He shook his head.

I leaned down, lifted Jason to his feet. He grimaced, held his hand. I walked him to the sink. Took paper towels off the roll, wet them. Handed him the towels, and he wiped his forehead and face with his left hand.

He tossed the bloody wad into the sink. I picked it up, put it in a plastic bag, said, "Let's go."

The three of us walked outside. The kid looked at Jason's pickup, climbed up and in.

I stuffed Jason in the passenger seat of my truck, on top of Louis's bloodstain. He sat cradling his hand, exhausted, his manic drunkenness fading. I came around to the driver's side, placed Jason's gun on the floor to the left of my seat. Got in.

The pickup roared. I flashed my lights and the kid put the truck in gear, backed down the driveway, took a left on the road. I followed, the Glock in my left hand, held low.

"Who will you call?" I asked. "Stryker?"

He hesitated. "I guess."

He reached across to try to get to his right pocket with left hand. Struggled with it, and finally got his phone out. Laid it on his lap and tried to turn it on. It fell to the floor at his feet.

"We'll be there in a few minutes. I'd wait," I said.

He looked down at the floor, sank back. "What a fucking cluster."

"It's not so bad. Look at it this way: You busted out to try to stick up for your friend. You came to my house to exact some sort of vengeance. It didn't work out. I mean, you're drunk and not that good on a sober day. But it wasn't for lack of trying. Rebel will know you gave it a shot. It's the thought that counts, right?"

He stared straight ahead. "It ain't over."

I kept driving, followed the kid and the truck onto the main road, headed east. "Your call. But you know, you caught me on a good day. Getting a little soft, I guess. Been thinking about Jesus and nonviolence, and where this all leads us. What does it accomplish?"

He looked at me.

"It accomplishes me blowing your fucking hand off," Jason said.

I smiled.

"It's all about execution, Jay, and you came up a little short."

He scowled.

We drove on, quiet for a time. Then the lights of the gas-pump canopy at the store were ahead.

The kid sped up, and I followed. He pulled in, bailed out. I came alongside, stopped, shut off the motor, pocketed the Glock, and got out. The kid called on the way by, "Keys are in it," then trotted for the door.

I came around, opened the passenger door. Jason swung out, pushed himself to his feet with his left arm. He turned for the phone and I said, "I got it." Leaned past him, picked it up. Gave him a shove and said, "Get in your truck."

He walked over. Opened the door, reached up for the handle, and pulled himself up. He wavered like he might fall back, and I pushed him up and in. He was kneeling on the seat, then twisted and got his legs swung around. I took my gun out, swapped it to my left hand, jammed it against his side. Leaned in and took the keys from the ignition.

"Hey," Jason said.

"You can't drive. You're drunk."

I walked to the back of the truck, took out Jason's phone, and called 911. Said, "There's a guy in a black Chevy pickup, parking lot of Prosperity General Store. His name is Jason Stratton. He's out on bail for a bunch of violent crimes, jumped electronic monitoring in Augusta earlier today. He's drunk, and injured. Probably needs medical attention."

"Who is this speaking, sir?" the dispatcher said.

"Mahatma Gandhi. And another thing, there's a handgun and ammo in the bed of the truck."

And I ended the call. Put the phone into the bed of the truck with the keys. Snapped the cylinder open on the revolver, shook out the cartridges, and threw them into the bed of the truck. Tossed the gun back there, too.

I walked to my truck, started it, and backed out. As I rolled away, I wondered where Marta was, how long before she picked out the next chump, leaving them behind her like empty beers cans on the side of the road.

I pulled into my driveway, parked beside Tiffanee's Jeep. Sat in the truck in the dark. Texted Clair:

How is he?

I sat. Stared at the phone. It dinged.

—Hanging on.

Hanging on. Like, might not make it.

Might not make it?

Another pause. Longer. I pictured Clair thinking, then punching at the letters with his big fingers.

—He'll come through it. He's one tough Marine.

Yes, he was. How are you doing? I texted. I expected him to say fine, or okay. Or not reply at all.

—Hanging in there.

A pause. Then:

—Didn't have to happen this way.

What? That somebody should have thought of a hidden gun? Left the guy tied up in the road, then backed off? Or persuaded Louis that Marta wasn't worth it?

HINDSIGHT IS 20/20. YOU WERE THERE FOR HIM.
The message went. I waited. Hesitated, then added:
MARTA'S ON THE RUN AGAIN. STOLE DELIVERY KID'S TRUCK. FYI.

A quick reply.

—TEXTED HER. TOLD HER ABOUT LOUIS. THOUGHT HER SHOWING UP HERE MIGHT HELP PULL HIM THROUGH.

Right, I thought. Probably headed for the Mexican border, bag of money in hand.
I asked if he needed me to come to the hospital.
The phone glowed. I could see Louis's blood under my fingernails. His reply:

—NO. STAY HOME. TAKE CARE OF YOUR GIRLS. WHERE YOU BELONG.

I sat. Read it again. Did he mean I wasn't tough enough for the fight? Had my being there fouled things up somehow?
Another message.

—SHOULD NEVER HAVE DRAGGED YOU INTO THIS ONE. SORRY. ABOUT ALL OF IT.

Then:

—KEEP YOUR GUARD UP, JACK.
Another pause.
—GOTTA GO, SEE ONE OF THE DOCS.

I sat. Reread the conversation.

Had Louis getting shot shocked Clair? Had he decided this wasn't worth Louis dying for, let alone him?

I'd been swept along, too, by all the violence, coming from every corner. I'd turned into my own commando, and for whom? Smashing Rebel's hand, Jason's, too. Playing soldier with Clair and Louis, and Louis almost killed.

What story was that telling, Jack McMorrow? Want your byline on that one? What would the headline be? "Former Reporter Leaves Broken Bones in His Wake."

Cold crept into the truck cab. I felt frozen in place. A sudden crack from the woods jolted me loose. A tree branch snapping, the way they did in winter. I slid the phone into my pocket, next to my notebook and my gun. For the first time since this whole thing had started, I noticed how jarring that was.

Back home, I put the gun in the safe, cleaned the sink, wiped blood smears off the counter, droplets of blood off the kitchen floor. Made sure the furniture was back in place. Threw the sodden and bloody paper towels into the woodstove, burning the evidence.

They were still smoldering when I heard Roxanne's car pull in. I heard Roxanne say, "Would you like to come in, use the bathroom?"

I gave the kitchen a quick scan, went to check the bathroom. All good.

I came back out as they all came in.

"Hey, Dad," Sophie said.

"Hey, Soph," I said. "How was your fancy meal?"

"Good. We could see the boats and ships and stuff."

"Fun," I said, turned to Mr. Ziggy, held out my hand. He took it and we shook. His hand was soft but he grasped mine tight, looked me in the eye. I felt like we were in a play. The dad giving the daughter's boyfriend a closer look.

"Mr. McMorrow," he said.

"Jack," I said. "Thanks for doing all this."

He let go of my hand, looked to the girls. "My pleasure entirely. It was so fun. Good production, good singing, great dancing. Right, girls?"

"I kinda suck at singing," Tara said.

"No, you don't," Mr. Ziggy said. "Stop talking like that."

"Compared to them, I do. That Annie was like from a movie."

"You're like from a movie, girl," Mr. Ziggy said. "Your own movie." He took a step toward her, gave her a pat on the back of the shoulder, a little rub. "You're gonna be awesome."

"Better than awesome," Sophie said. "She was good but kind of plastic. You're real." She moved quickly to give Tara a hug.

Tara smiled.

Tiffanee, too. I found myself watching her, my gaze lingering. She caught it, and our eyes locked, held there. Her smile fell away.

"You would have enjoyed it, Jack." Roxanne said.

"I'm sure. But things to do," I said.

Bikers. Jason. The kid from the store.

"I have to pee," Tara said.

"Tara," Tiffanee said. "Where are your manners?"

"Well, I do," Tara said, and hurried down the hallway. Sophie said, "Me, too," and trotted up the stairs.

Mr. Ziggy said, "Love your place. It's so totally Maine."

Tiffanee said, "I'll start the truck," and went back outside.

Mr. Ziggy walked to the slider, watched the birds on the feeder. Redpolls.

"Look at them," he said. "They're so cute."

Roxanne looked at me, whispered, "What is it?"

"What is what?" I said, as the door rattled and Tiffanee poked her head back in.

"I'm so sorry, Jack. The battery again. Can you give me a boost?"

I grabbed my jacket, followed her out. She went to the Jeep and popped the hood from the inside. I lifted it, put the brace in place. She came up beside me. "I'll get a new battery tomorrow."

"Right," I said.

I started for my truck, but she put a hand on my arm, stopped me.

"You know, don't you," Tiffanee said. "About me."

I hesitated.

"Yes."

"I can tell when people do. They look at me the way you just did. Then they try too hard to be normal."

"Sorry."

"It was a long time ago, Jack. I was a kid."

"In a very grown-up situation," I said. "I'm not judging you."

"But now Roxanne will know. It was, like, so fun having a friend who doesn't."

"She won't judge you, either. Roxanne, of all people."

She was still holding my arm.

"Does Tara know?" I said.

She looked away. "When she was, like, eight, I sat her down. Told her the story. I wanted her to hear about it from me first."

"And how did that go?"

"Okay. She listened, said she was sorry my dad was a bad person. Never mentioned it again, like she blocked it out. But ever since then, the two of us have stuck together. I mean, we're more like friends than mom and daughter. She totally has my back. When Jason was getting bad, you know what I was afraid of?"

"I can guess," I said.

"Two things, really. That I'd lose it and kill him. Sometimes when he was asleep, I'd think how easy it would be to just get a knife from the kitchen and . . ."

She took a breath. Let it out.

"But second offense, my record. They'd really send me away. No two years in juvie."

Another long pause.

"What's the second thing?" I said.

"That Tara, she'd follow in my footsteps. Kill him, or hurt him, and then they'd take her away from me. I couldn't handle that, losing my baby. I don't think she could handle being away from me. We're all we've got, really. Each other. My mom, she drank herself to death. Friggin' coffee brandy. By the end, she was drinking like twenty hours a day, wired and blasted at the same time. I've got no brothers or sisters. I have an uncle, but he lives in Florida. I haven't seen him since I was, like, nineteen. He was totally afraid of me, like I might attack him or something."

She paused. Mustered a bit of a smile.

"That's why I was so freakin' amped when you got Jason arrested."

I hesitated. The wind blew, and when the gust subsided, I said, "He was here today. He was drunk."

Tiffanee pulled on my arm, said, "But he can't. He's got that thing on him."

"That just tells them where he is. It doesn't keep him from going places."

"What happened?"

"We talked. It didn't go all that well, but could have been worse. We got wrestling around and he got a little hurt."

"Where is he?"

"I don't know. Dropped him at the store."

"Did the police come?"

"I imagine."

"What would they do—put him back in jail?"

"That would be my guess. When he gets out of the hospital."

She looked at me, then away. Voices from the kitchen. Mr. Ziggy, Tara.

I went to my truck, maneuvered it closer. Opened the hood, took jumper cables from behind the driver's seat. Hooked them up to my battery, then to hers.

She climbed in and turned the starter and it rasped a few times, then the motor caught. She revved it a couple of times, then got out, left it running.

I was unhooking the cables from the Jeep when she sidled up next to me.

"Thanks," Tiffanee said.

"No problem."

"You know, it really messed Tara up, having Jason around. He never really bothered her, but all the screaming and yelling, calling me all kinds of filthy names."

"Not good," I agreed.

"That's why this play is so important. I mean, Mr. Ziggy—he really came along at the right time. She needs to know that all men aren't, like, all violent and angry. That some of them treat you nice, like they really do care about you."

I reached to shut the hood, said, "Does he know about Jason? About you?"

"I think Tara told him something about Jason. My story, no. But you know, he really has a way of sensing when she's down, picking her back up. He's been so good for her confidence. If I tell her she's awesome, so what? But if this guy—an actor, who's been in plays all over the country—says she's awesome, I mean, I can't tell you what that means."

I couldn't tell her, either. Not yet.

27

They came outside, Sophie and Tara hugging good-bye. Roxanne thanking Mr. Ziggy again. He leaned in, gave her a quick Euro cheek kiss. She hesitated, then cheek-kissed him back. He turned to me and shook, first with one hand, then clasped my hand with both of his.

"Thanks for allowing me the company of your lovely daughter, Jack," he said. "It was a blast."

"Thank you," I said. "The girls seem very pumped up."

"They're so amazing," Mr. Ziggy said. "I mean—I can't wait for that curtain to go up."

And then he released me, got into the Jeep with Tiffanee and Tara.

Mr. Ziggy turned to Tara in the backseat, started singing. "The sun'll come out, tomorrow, bet your bottom dollar . . ." They turned and waved like they were taking the show on the road.

We went back inside, and Sophie picked up her backpack, said, "I'm a famous actress. Why do I have to do algebra?" And then she thumped her way upstairs, singing, "It's the hard-knock life for me."

We stood. Roxanne looked around the kitchen, said, "Thanks for cleaning up."

"Sure," I said.

I went to the refrigerator, took out a bottle of Chardonnay and an ale, took out two glasses, and poured. Turned to Roxanne, handed her the glass. Leaned in and gave her a kiss of my own. She returned the kiss, held it, then pressed harder.

We broke apart.

"She'll be awake for a while," Roxanne said.

"I know."

"Oh. I thought you were romancing me."

"Always," I said. "But I thought we could talk."

She looked at me.

"What is it?"

"Nothing bad. I mean, nothing too awful."

I took her hand.

"Come sit."

We did, on the couch near the fire. Roxanne sat down first, waiting. I put another log on the fire, tapped at the damper. When I turned back, she'd drunk off a half-inch of wine. I sat beside her. Hesitated.

"Spit it out," she said.

"Louis," I said.

"What? Everything okay?"

"No. Things went wrong, right at the end."

I drank. She waited. I told her Louis had been shot in the leg, had lost a lot of blood, was in ICU.

"My God."

"Clair's there."

"What? They think he might die?"

I shrugged. "Clair said he was hanging on. That's all I know."

Roxanne was holding the glass with two hands. She leaned toward me, said, "So some guy just shoots Louis?"

"He had a gun hidden in the rear door of this van. We were letting him go. He was hurt. Clair shot him."

"God almighty," Roxanne said.

"Louis will probably be okay. He's very tough."

"No, I mean, it could have been you, Jack. Just as easily, right?"

"I was farther away. In my truck."

"But a bullet doesn't care about that. Twenty feet or two hundred feet. It goes right through a truck."

"I wasn't the target."

"Doesn't matter. Look at these little kids who get killed when some gang members start shooting at each other."

Roxanne turned to me.

"Police are looking for them," I said. "They won't get far."

"This is madness, Jack," she said.

I hesitated, said, "I know. I won't do it again. Clair won't do it again, I don't think. It sort of shocked us both. That Louis might not—"

"I don't care about Louis. He can go get himself shot. I don't care about Marta."

"Marta's gone. For good, this time."

I told her what had happened. The kid knocking on the door.

"Ding dong, the witch is dead," Roxanne said.

"Or at least on the run."

"While Louis and Clair—and you— risk your lives cleaning up her mess."

"I guess so. But I mean it—I'm done with that."

"Good. Because you're not a soldier, Jack," she said, leaning close, grabbing my shoulder. "I mean, you've always landed in the middle of things, but you're a reporter. A journalist."

"I know."

"With a family."

"I know that, too. And sometimes that leads to these situations."

"Not fighting alongside Louis."

"No, but letting people know they can't shoot me, can't threaten you and Sophie, or bad things will happen to them. Sometimes you're not given a choice."

Just then, Sophie clattered down the stairs. She grabbed a book bag and trotted back up. I drank my beer. Roxanne sipped her wine.

"There's more," I said.

I took another drink, started in. I told her about calling Mr. Ziggy's past theaters. How I said I was with a theater group and we were thinking of giving him an award.

She waited, eyes fixed on mine.

"He never stays anywhere long at all. Once he left mid-show. *The Lion King*. The director there said it was 'a personal matter.' "

"Maybe he got in a snit about something," Roxanne said. "They're actors."

"But walk out while the play's still going?"

Roxanne listened.

"But the odder thing was, I couldn't get anybody to say anything very good about him. These are theater people. Aren't they supposed to be theatrical?"

She sipped.

"A couple of them, it was like they couldn't wait to get off the phone. One said Mr. Ziggy 'could be engaging.' That was it. I talked to six people. If I were writing a story, I wouldn't have one."

"But the kids love him. He brings all this energy."

"Exactly," I said. "Why didn't I get any of that?"

"Maybe they had a falling-out about money or something."

"All of them?"

"When will you hear from Brandon Blake?"

"I don't know. But just because he hasn't been prosecuted doesn't mean he's okay. Look at all the pedo priests."

She frowned, sipped, then looked at me. Sensed there was more. Waited. The fire crackled. I cleared my throat.

"Tiffanee," I said. "I know why she doesn't talk about her childhood, why you feel like you only get so far with her."

She waited.

"She killed her father."

Roxanne froze, mouth open.

"She was fifteen. He'd been abusing her mother for years. I mean, emotionally, physically. Broke her jaw, all these other bones. Years of it. One night was particularly bad, I guess. Tiffanee got a bat, bonked him on the head. He died."

"My God."

I ran through it. Connecticut. Tried as a juvenile, convicted of manslaughter. Sent to juvenile detention, released after two years. Went back with her mother, but the mom drank herself to death. Tiffanee takes the mother's maiden name and—no surprise—moves around, has Tara. Moves to Prosperity when she inherits the farm.

"Who told you this?"

"Sam at the store. He'd seen Sophie and Tara together. Said the mom, Tiffanee, had been through a lot. He knew her when she was kid and came up here summers."

We both drank. Roxanne was looking at the fire, thinking.

"Tiffanee was afraid if things got too bad with Jason, she'd kill him, get locked up again. Or Tara would do something, get in trouble like she did."

"You talked to her?"

"Just now. Outside. She said she can sense when people know."

"Like she will with me," Roxanne said.

"I said we wouldn't judge."

"Defending her mother from a violent abuser? No."

Sophie dropped something upstairs—probably her math book.

"Do we tell her?"

"I don't know. Maybe it will come from Tara, now that Tiffanee knows we know."

The fire was reflected in Roxanne's eyes. She looked beautiful but sad.

"It's such a violent world, Jack," she said. "It's just everywhere. Clair just shot somebody, and then they shoot Louis, and we go on, just like that's normal."

"With Clair, it was self-defense."

"Sure. With the two of you, there's always a good reason. But it's still violence."

She sipped her wine. Shook her head. I waited, almost said nothing, but couldn't.

"Jason was here," I said.

"Jason. I thought he was—"

"Wearing a cuff? Yeah, he had it on. They just hadn't caught up with him yet. He was drunk."

"What did he want?"

"To vent, I guess," I said. "We talked, and after a while he calmed down."

"Huh."

"I gave him a ride up to the store. Then I called the police."

"God, there's no break from it ever. Did you tell Tiffanee?"

"Yes."

"Will he come back?"

"No. They'll lock him up this time."

"Good," Roxanne said. "Throw away the fucking key."

The F-word seemed to surprise her. She drank, a long swallow. She lowered the glass, and I said, "And another thing."

Roxanne said, "There's more?"

"As far as I can tell, Mr. Ziggy's not on TikTok. Or even Instagram."

"Well, that's good," Roxanne said. "Unless—"

"Unless it's because he's kind of laying low, doesn't want his face out there."

Roxanne mulled it over, said, "You know what else?"

I shook my head.

"These people at the play in Boston—he schmoozed with them, very charming. But I don't think he knew them. I think he just talked his way backstage. The girls—these starry-eyed kid actors from a Maine—were his ticket."

"Makes you wonder," I said.

"What else he's talked his way into."

"Or out of."

"Yes," Roxanne said. "That, too."

They went to bed early, Sophie crashing after the excitement. Roxanne sobered by the news. Only Sophie said good night.

I sat by the fire, silent phone beside me. I picked it up, put it down, picked it up again.

Nothing.

I looked at my notes, such as they were. The theater people not saying much. The list of code names for the militia. Next to Stryker, I had written, "I can't control what they do."

Two of his brothers-in-arms put out of action. Would that call for a response? Or would he call it good, cut his losses?

At 10:45, I got up, fed the fire. Picked up my phone, grabbed my jacket off the hook, and walked out through the shed and outside. The wind had diminished some, and high clouds were scudding by, moving northwest to southeast. The moon shone between them, illuminating the snow like a slow-flashing neon sign. I listened to the winter night, the trees cracking like they were breaking free from ice, starting to move.

And then a hint of headlights showed coming down the road from the east. I heard the sound of tires crunching the snow, faint in the distance. And my phone buzzed in the back pocket of my jeans.

I took it out. A text.

Not Clair. Strain.

—WHERE ARE YOU?
I told him I was home.
—ARE YOU UP?

When I said yes, he replied BE RIGHT THERE, and he was, head-lights approaching, the Explorer easing to a stop at the end of the driveway.

I walked down; the passenger window opened.

"Working late," I said.

"Hey, when you're divorced, you make your own hours. Go for a ride? We need to talk."

The radio in Strain's truck hissed. I looked back at the house, Sophie's bedroom window dark, no need to wake her.

"We won't go far," Strain said.

I got in.

He had a mug of coffee in the holder, a bag of doughnut holes on the console. He held it up, ruby pinkie ring glinting in the dashboard light.

I shook my head.

"I got a wicked metabolism," he said. "Gotta keep eating or I get weak."

We pulled out, drove toward Clair's. There was a single light on in the house; the barn was dark. No truck in the dooryard.

"So, the shooting down in Sanctuary."

"Yes."

"Not really my jurisdiction, the location, I mean. But you are."

"Okay."

I shrugged, said, "Did they catch up with the van?"

"Yeah. All out-of-staters, known members of an outlaw motorcycle club in Connecticut. They pulled into the ER at Maine Med this afternoon. Brought a guy in with a bullet wound."

"He gonna make it?"

"Yeah. He got lucky. Your buddy Louis, not so much. Word is he's touch and go."

We were past Clair's house, back in darkness. Strain took a sip of coffee, held up the doughnut bag again. I shook my head.

"Anyway, Portland PD, they take a look at the guys' van, find a whole bunch of firearms."

"Huh."

"And there's a piece of paper in the wounded guy's jacket."

I waited. The dark woods rolled past.

"Clair Varney's name is on it. And Louis Longfellow, his buddy. And directions to this Louis guy's compound in Sanctuary."

"I see."

"These outlaws aren't talking. How 'bout you?"

"You talk to Clair yet? He's at the hospital."

"Knox SO has him. I said I was needing to talk to you anyway, so I'd track you down."

A beat, Strain looking at me.

"I gotta say, you've been one busy boy. I swear, I need another officer just to keep track of what you're up to."

"Is that right?" I said.

"Kid from the store. He calls SO, tells them how some woman hijacked his truck. He met her at Varney's house. Then he walked back as far as your place because he was freezing. Said he knocked, there was a guy in there with blood on him, blood on you, too. Guy's hand was all busted up."

He popped a doughnut hole into his mouth.

"So report comes in about the stolen truck. About the same time, we get a report that one Jason Stratton is at the same store where the kid calls from. Dispatch got an anonymous tip."

He waited.

"They record those 911calls, by the way. I think it will sound almost exactly like you."

A beat.

"Where's Jason now?"

"Took him to Waldo General. His hand is pretty crunched. Wrapped it up, I guess, but he's gonna need some surgery."

"Too bad."

"He's not talking, being such a tough guy. But as a detective, I'm trained to see patterns. This guy has a beef with you, gets his hand busted. Guy in Augusta, he was at Stratton's relative's house. His hand is all busted up, too."

"You don't say."

"What I see emerging is somebody who takes things into his own hands," Strain said. "So to speak. Somebody who consorts with known criminals."

I shrugged. "So much for the ankle cuff, I guess."

"Somebody who should be a law-abiding citizen, but doesn't seem to want to cooperate with law enforcement."

"But I'm here. Isn't that cooperation?"

"Even when we talk, you don't say shit."

Aggravation coming to the surface. He pulled to the side, made a U-turn, started back.

"So you know what this is, Mr. McMorrow?"

"No, what?"

"Your last chance."

"To do what?"

"Stop playing games."

"I don't play games," I said. "I'm serious to a fault. My wife says it's a problem."

"Sanctuary," Strain said. "Where does this Louis Longfellow guy get his money?"

"He made it the old-fashioned way. He inherited it."

Strain shook his head. "More dribs and drabs."

I looked at him, waited him out.

"Okay, here's the deal. We're gonna lean on Jason hard. Got him for breaking house arrest, the firearm, alcohol. Screw his stupid heart. Five to eight hanging over his sorry head, so he's gonna talk. And then we're gonna get you for aggravated assault. Maybe times two. Start peeling the Jack McMorrow onion from there. You want to lay it out there first, it'll help you shape the narrative, as they say."

I looked out at the headlights stabbing at the dark.

"Newspapers hire people with assault convictions? I don't think so. You'll be working at Walmart, if you're lucky."

He collected himself, looked at me and smiled. Held up the dough-nut bag. This time I reached in, took a handful for Sophie. We were approaching Clair's house as Strain said, "You know this reporter thing you got going?"

I looked at him.

"I think it's just a cover. You're a vigilante, just like these militia guys. The bikers, too."

I didn't say anything.

"There's a line, and I figure you've always danced around it, dipping a toe on the bad side from time to time. But now you've gone way over."

It hit me. Roxanne's reminder that I was a reporter, not a com-batant. Clair saying he was sorry he'd dragged me into the biker fight. Louis saying I was embedded, just like the journalists in Iraq.

I took a breath, stepped back over the line.

"The woman in the stolen truck," I said. "I'd start there. Her name's Marta Kovac, but she probably has aliases. Maybe that's one, who knows? She's been romantically involved with Louis. Also, she has a million dollars of dirty money in a bag. She stole it from her ex in the British Virgin Islands. He was a money launderer. He got it by skimming off money from a biker gang in Montreal. They killed him, but in the confusion she got away with the cash. She came here a few months ago, hid out with Louis, who she dated in high school. But they caught up with her and hauled her back to Montreal, held her more or less captive. Trafficked her and got her hooked on fentanyl. Louis went up and broke her out, brought her back here. And they sent the bikers, some sort of US affiliate, to get her back again—hence the firefight."

Strain pulled to a stop at the end of the driveway. Looked at me.

"See, Mr. McMorrow?" he said. "That wasn't so hard, was it?"

I didn't reply.

"I hope your buddy makes it," he said.

I nodded.

"Because, boy, do I want to talk to him."

"Me, too," I said. "There are some things I need to tell him."

28

I stood at the end of the driveway, called Clair. Again. This time, he picked up.

"Jack."

"Anything?"

"They're giving him plasma and platelets, meds to try to get him to start clotting."

A beat.

"They think he's had a stroke."

"Oh, no."

"Still haven't gotten the wound all closed up. He's kind of shredded in there. Did patch up the artery. Amazing what one bullet can do."

"So—"

"Lost over forty percent of his blood volume, which is five pints."

"God."

"When he's stabilized, they'll bring in a chopper. Get him to Portland."

"But he's not. Stabilized."

"No," Clair said.

I heard voices in the background, hospital noise.

"Where are you?"

"Waiting room outside ICU. A couple of other people here. Brother and sister. Their dad is in there. Heart attack."

That guy has a family. Louis has Clair. And his dog. Had Marta, maybe, but she was gone.

"How are you doing?" I said.

"Okay. Seen this a few times before. A couple of stays in Evac hospitals. Long Binh, Vung Tau. I got fixed up, shipped back. For a lot of guys, it was the last stop."

He paused. I waited.

"I don't know, Jack. I think we might lose him."

"You don't know that yet. Hang in there."

"Right."

Another pause.

"We had a plan, Jack. For when they came back, with the heavy artillery. Let them drive in, we're out of the cabin, in the woods. Both sides. Thirty yards to the front. Hundred yards apart."

He paused. I heard a faint sip. Coffee.

"Call 'em out. They start shooting, we've got crossing fire from both sides, kill zone inside that triangle. Anyone gets to our flank, we're close enough to get back to the cabin. Log pile on the back side as cover for that direction. They call it an area ambush."

A beat.

"Won't need that now."

"No," I said. "Because the war's over, Clair."

Another moment of silence, then, "That's fine. I've had enough of it."

"Yes," I said.

"Louis is a good man," Clair said.

"Yes. A strong sense of duty."

"To go up there and get her. Bring her back here, knowing they'd probably come after her. He loves her, you know. Marta and the dog."

"Sorry I told him she'd bailed."

"It wasn't just about her," Clair said.

Hospital noise in the background, beeping, an automatic door hissing shut, the clatter of a gurney. I waited.

"Rather have him dead than be a vegetable," Clair said. "Same for myself."

"You're fine. You'll get through it. Come home and we'll cut wood. I think I know Vivaldi from Mozart now."

I felt him smile.

"Highly unlikely," he said.

We were quiet for a second or two, and it struck me that this was the first time I'd given Clair a pep talk. It had always been the other way around.

"It's been a heck of a run, Jack."

"Yeah," I said. "It has."

"Give my girls a hug," he said. The phone beeped and he was gone.

I half slept. Rolled over every hour to check my phone. Roxanne stirred at 3:30, awakened by the phone light. I went to the bathroom at 4:45. Nothing. I stayed up.

I made a fire in the woodstove, put the kettle on for tea. I looked at the phone. No texts. Went to my laptop and searched—*Sanctuary Maine shooting*. Nothing. The sad state of the news business.

At 5:30, I texted Clair.

ANYTHING?

Stared at the phone as I poured the tea. No response. I poured milk into my tea. Waited. Waited some more. Five interminable minutes. Was Louis gone? Was Clair planning a memorial? Would it be at Arlington?

At 6:30 I'd skimmed the news, the *Portland Press Herald* and *Bangor Daily*. Nothing about the shooting. I considered calling Mary but it was too early. If Louis was gone and she knew, she would have called. Or come running over. I pictured a parka over her nightgown. Boots and bare legs.

At 6:40, Sophie came down, chipper and cheerful. She asked how I was. I said I was good. She said she was good, too. I made her tea—lots of milk, two sugars—and she got out cereal, filled a bowl, poured the milk, and ate it at the counter as she read the news on her iPad.

Was this how she'd find out about Louis? About Clair? Maybe about me? "Maine Journalist Charged with Assault . . ."

"Shower time," she said, and trotted back upstairs. I was relieved.

Still no sound of Roxanne. I hated to wake her, the oblivion of sleep a respite from shootings, Tiffanee killing her father, Jason's threats, bikers with guns. I could envision the few seconds she'd have before it all came rushing back.

I checked the Internet. My phone. Considered breakfast but my stomach was in a knot. Made a second cup of tea instead.

And then Sophie was back. Jeans, high-tops, a baggie sweater, and the fedora. Her backpack was loaded down. I said, "I'll take you, let Mom sleep."

She said, "Great. Let's roll," and started outside. I followed, went out and started the truck. She was fitting earbuds in, said, "I have to listen to *Annie*. Mr. Ziggy says we need to immerse ourselves, twenty-four seven."

She fiddled. I got out of the truck, went back inside. Listened. Quiet upstairs. I went to the closet, punched in numbers on the safe. Took out the Glock, went back outside and got in the truck, and off we went. A new day.

Sophie was singing softly, "No one cares for you a smidge, when you're in an orphanage . . ."

I drove. The song ended. She fiddled with her phone, started singing again. "It's the hard-knock life for us," her head bobbing.

And then we were approaching the school. Sophie flicked at her phone.

"Oh, sugar," she said. "Tara's going home sick. Now we can't work with Mr. Ziggy."

I turned into the parking lot, stopped behind a school bus, red lights flashing.

She was texting, spoke as she tapped.

"She came in early for one-on-one. She's not the greatest dancer, actually. Now she says Mr. Ziggy is taking her home."

Taking her home? Wasn't that breaking every policy?

"Her mom's at work. Tara texted her, and her mom said she couldn't leave early because somebody didn't show up today, and couldn't Tara tough it out."

We pulled up, stopped. Sophie scanned the crowd of kids, put the earbuds in a pocket on her backpack. "What if we take her home," I said. "There's time, right?"

"That's okay. They already left," Sophie said. "Have a good day, Dad." She looked around to see if anybody was watching. Nobody in sight, she gave me a quick hug, and then she was out of the truck and gone.

He's giving her a freakin' ride home?

I pulled out, following a school bus, started back down the road and pulled over. At the next intersection, I signaled to turn left. Stopped. Thought for a moment. Went right.

Tara's road was four miles out, a back road off of a back road. I wasn't sure why I was going there, what I'd say if Mr. Ziggy passed me on the way back, if Tara was on the front porch when I pulled up.

A mile on, a loaded log truck pulled onto the road, diesel smoke billowing. I braked, eased in behind it. The road took a long gradual curve to the right, no passing. A chunk of bark flew off the top logs, and I backed off more.

My phone pinged.

I held it up. A text from Blake.

I held it closer, hand on the wheel.

John K. Hofer, DOB 6-7-92. Mercer Island, Wash.
Feb. 4, 2020. One count, possession of child pornog-
raphy, minors under 12, Class C.
2 years, all but 90 days suspended.

DOB matched. Mercer Island, a suburb of Seattle. Mr. Ziggy without the Zwiefel.

I flipped the phone onto the seat, edged out, hit the gas. Passed the truck on a long upgrade, the rear end of the pickup slaloming in the snow. Gripped the steering wheel, aiming for the wheel ruts in the ice.

And then the turn came up, and I took it, slid left. Sped up but ran into a minefield of potholes, slowed again. Saw a car coming up fast in the rearview mirror.

It was a blue Jeep, and it blew past me, bouncing over the broken pavement. A glimpse of a dented tailgate.

Tiffanee. She'd gotten out of work after all, must have called the school, was told Tara was headed home, Mr. Ziggy giving her a ride. The truck slammed into a pothole, bounced, and braked.

Mr. Ziggy, the overgrown drama kid, the Pied Piper of children's theater, his hand on Tara's shoulder. Roxanne had been right.

My phone dinged again, and I held it up. Dunne.

—WHEN CAN YOU MEET?

I tossed the phone down, kept driving, weaving through the potholes all the way to the intersection. At the intersection, I went left, hit the gas.

Potholes again, junk in the field, the mobile home with broken-out windows, ringed by rusting cars. The barn was in the distance. Then the entrance to the Patriot Legion training camp. The house.

Tiffanee's Jeep in the dooryard—next to Mr. Ziggy's Honda.

The side door flew open. Tara ran out, crossed the yard, running toward the road. I skidded to a stop. She was coming toward me, no jacket, no shoes, her shirt half unbuttoned.

I jumped out of the truck, called, "Tara, what's the matter?"

She swerved, trotted toward me in her socks. She was crying.

"Mr. Ziggy," she said. "He . . . he and my mom, they're fighting. Oh, my God. Oh, my God." And then hard sobs, her arms wrapped tightly around her.

I told her to get in the truck, she'd freeze. Led her to the passenger door, helped her in. Reached to the console for my phone. Left the truck running.

I ran for the house, the side door still open. Up the steps and inside, heard Tiffanee screaming.

"You son of a bitch. You son of a bitch."

Thumps, clunks, furniture scraping.

I ran toward the sound, the bottom of the staircase. Went up two steps at a time, then left. An open door. Tara's room.

Mr. Ziggy was backed up against the wall on the far side of the bed. Tiffanee was flailing at him with her fists, and he was trying to grab her wrists, shouting, "Stop it. Stop it. It's not what you think."

She landed a punch, his face, and he fell back, blood on his mouth. She was loose, swinging left, right, left, right. He saw me, bulled her away, and she fell backwards, hit her head on the floor, lay there, moaning.

Mr. Ziggy tried to dodge past us for the door and I caught him by the arm on the way by, jolting my bad shoulder. I hung onto his shirt, and it tore.

He tried to scrape my hand off, push me away. I hung on, spun him around, and he came at me with a punch, hit me in the side of the head. Hard. My head spun, my left shoulder burned. I pulled him close, smelled cologne and sweat. He tried to hit me in the head again, missed, grabbed my ear and twisted it.

"No," I said, got my right arm back, punched him in the chin. He took it, teeth clenched, eyes fixed on me in a cold, hard stare. Mr. Ziggy unmasked.

He drove me back into the wall, bigger, stronger than I thought, fueled by adrenaline. And then the hand came off my ear, and he got me by the throat, then the other hand, too. Squeezed hard, grunting, and I couldn't breathe. I raked his face with my nails, went for his eyes, but he jerked his head back, and I got cheek, neck. His grip tightened, and I couldn't breathe. Leaned down, bit his arm, felt my teeth sink in, tasted his blood.

I was choking, saw shadows, started to black out. I punched him again, aimed for the throat, but he'd dropped his chin and I hit his jaw, jarring pain up through my arm. I stomped his feet, kneed his groin. Still couldn't breathe.

Was *this* the end? Killed by a pedophile.

I got a hand under his chin, around his throat, squeezed, but his muscles were tensed. I went for his eyes again, dug my nails in.

He screamed, reached to get my hand away. I tripped him, and he fell hard on his back and I landed on him, gasping, punched his face, pressed a knee into his belly. He rolled me off, got to all fours, and Tiffanee was back up, jumped on him from behind, an arm around his neck, grunting as she pulled his head up.

He squirmed, spun, Tiffanee on his back. She was between us, and he was dragging her toward the door. I came around her, got an arm around his neck, and he dragged me, too. Elbowed me in the face, blood spurting. I punched him in the side of the neck, the ear, squeezed my arm tight.

Tiffanee shouted, "She trusted you, you filthy bastard."

She dropped her head and bit him, and he bellowed and shook her off, got to his feet. We were lurching toward the door, Mr. Ziggy dragging both of us.

"You piece of shit," Tiffanee said. "You goddamn piece of shit."

I got a leg between his, pushed him back, ran him into the wall.

He sagged, and Tiffanee was on him, kicking. Shin, knee, belly. He tried to cover himself.

"I didn't hurt her," he said, panting.

"Filthy pervert," Tiffanee said, and she punched him in the face, over and over. His face was bloody, gouged and scratched. I reached out and grabbed Tiffanee's arm. The frenzy stopped.

"I'm sorry," Mr. Ziggy said, a bloody mumble. "I know I'm messed up. My dad, he went to prison when I was a kid. My therapist said I'm trying to get back there, to when I had my family, when everything was okay. So I kind of turn into a kid again."

The gigolo scammer.

"Shut your mouth, you filthy scumbag," Tiffanee said.

"I didn't plan it. It just happened."

"Like all the others?" I said. "Eugene? Spokane? Salem? Tacoma?"

He looked at me, panic setting in.

"But I left those places. When I could feel it coming on, I left before anything happened. To protect them, I swear. Listen, I'll leave here. Just let me go."

"Before anything happened?" Tiffanee said. "Before anything *happened?*"

"I wasn't hurting her," Mr. Ziggy said. "And I really care for her. She's so pure. I mean—"

"She's twelve," Tiffanee bellowed.

She shoved me aside, grabbed him by each hip. Spun around like a shot putter, just once, and flung him off the top of the stairs, headfirst, arms waving. A beat of silence, Mr. Ziggy in the air. A *thunk* as he hit the landing, a crunch, almost simultaneous, as his head hit the wall.

He was still. The house was quiet. Tiffanee was on her knees at the edge of the stairs, panting, crying.

I moved around her, tripped down the stairs. He was on his side, head jammed against the wall. I fell to my knees beside him. His neck was twisted, head to the side, eyes open and unfocused. I leaned down, listened for breathing. Put my hand in front of his open mouth. Nothing.

Tiffanee came down the stairs, leaned down beside me.

"Oh, my God," she said. "Is he—"

"I think his neck's broken."

"You mean—it can't be. He's dead?"

I didn't answer.

"CPR," Tiffanee said.

I eased him away from the wall, so he was on his back on the landing. His head lay flat and she started compressing his chest. Mr. Ziggy stared up at us, eyes unblinking.

"Oh, dear Jesus," Tiffanee said.

She kept pumping.

Pointless, I thought. His spinal cord was severed, his brain no longer connected to the rest of him.

"Breathe, you piece of crap," she said, doing push-ups on his chest.

I felt his wrist for a pulse. Nothing.

She kept pumping. I leaned close to Mr. Ziggy's mouth. Still as a cave.

She stopped, leaned back, started up again. I watched as she rocked up and down like an oil rig. Her bloody handprints were on his white shirt.

And then, after what seemed like a very long time, she slowed. Stopped. Sat up.

"Tara," Tiffanee said.

"She's in my truck. It's running. She's warm."

"I have to go to her. My God, they're gonna take her."

She jumped to her feet.

"No, they won't," I said.

"But I killed him, Jack. I did it again. I wanted to kill him and I did. I'll go to jail. Oh, my God. They'll lock me up, Jack."

Mr. Ziggy stared up at us like he was listening, waiting to see if, one last time, I'd do the right thing. In an instant, I knew what that was.

"Tiffanee," I said.

"We can get away," she began. "I'll go to the ATM."

"Tiffanee, listen."

"Do you need a passport to get into Canada? Oh, my God, I need to pack."

I grabbed her arm. Shook it.

"Will you listen?"

She looked at me.

"I got here," I said. "It was clear what he'd tried to do with Tara. You were arguing with him, he shoved you down. I fought with him in the bedroom, then he got by me, and I tried to stop him. We wrestled around. He got loose, and I caught him in the hallway. When we got out here, we fought again, and he went down the stairs."

She looked at me.

"You were in the bedroom," I said.

"But I wasn't."

"You were."

"I threw him down the stairs," she said.

"You didn't, Tiffanee. You didn't even see what happened."

It sank in, and she looked at me, still standing over Mr. Ziggy's dead body.

"You don't have to do this, Jack."

"But I do," I said.

"They'll charge you."

"I know."

"But what about Roxanne? And Sophie?"

"They'll be okay."

"But you'll go to jail."

"I know. But not for long. Mitigating circumstances. Manslaughter, maybe plead to a Class C."

"What's the other class?"

"A."

"What would you get for that?"

"It doesn't matter."

"But Jack," she said, "you don't know what they'll do."

"It's decided," I said. "You go to Tara. She needs you. Now and for a while. I'll take care of this."

Tiffanee reached over Mr. Ziggy and hugged me, stepped over his body, trotted down the last flight of stairs. The door slammed behind her.

I took out my phone. Was about to call 911 when the phone buzzed. *Clair Varney.*

I'd call him back.

I held the phone in my hand like it was a living thing, this bearer of bad news. And then, with Mr. Ziggy still looking up at me, I called 911.

The dispatcher answered. She said, "What is the nature of your emergency?"

Where to begin?

All the king's horses and all the king's men eventually showed up. Prosperity Fire and Rescue, the same people who'd responded when I was shot. Paramedics from Belfast. Deputy Jackman and her Boy Scout partner, who was assigned to find Tara's shoes. They all went inside and gathered around Mr. Ziggy, on the off chance that he wasn't dead, after all—that I was wrong.

But I was right. His spinal cord was severed. They brought him down the stairs on a gurney, dropped the wheels, and rolled him outside. An ambulance hauled him off to Augusta for an autopsy. No lights, no siren. No rush.

Tara and Tiffanee sat in the back of Jackman's SUV. I was in the front seat of Strain's Explorer. He had his phone on the dash, recording. He read me my Miranda rights, though he didn't have to actually read them. I said I understood. He said to tell him what happened. I told my story.

Strain listened, didn't push back on any of it. When I was done, he signed off on the recording with the date and time. Turned the recorder off, and said, "I have a feeling this isn't the worst thing you've ever done, Mr. McMorrow."

"Not by a far cry," I said.

They said I could go, so I did. From the truck, I called Clair. He answered, said, "Where are you?"

I said I was headed home, be there in ten. He said he'd meet me and rang off.

I knew.

Clair's truck was parked at the end of our driveway, the motor shut off. I could hear music as I walked up. Vivaldi. Or maybe Mozart.

I opened the door and climbed up and in. He was staring straight ahead, took a moment to look over. I waited, saw Louis's dog stretched across the backseat, head on his paws. The music played.

"Requiem in D minor," Clair said.

I listened.

Strings and horns and chorale. Somber, like the truck was filled with overwhelming grief.

"Mozart died before he finished it."

I waited.

"Still, quite something to leave behind."

"It is," I said.

Clair was staring straight ahead, the inside of the windshield clouded with condensation.

"He's gone," he said.

"I figured. I'm sorry."

"Better this way. They said it was a bad stroke. He could have been paralyzed."

"I see."

"Maybe not even been able to talk."

He was trying to convince himself.

"That's not living," Clair said.

"For Louis? No."

"He was a good man. A good Marine."

A pause, Clair turned inward.

"Wasn't a simple operation. The execution made it seem that way, but there was a lot of planning, a bunch of moving parts, considerable risk."

"I'm sure."

"And he knew they'd want payback. But he was prepared for that."

Almost, I thought, but not quite.

"I should have known. Not let them open that door without clearing the van. Had a rifle barrel on that guy's neck."

"You can't blame yourself for that. None of us saw it coming."

He stared straight ahead, not hearing me.

"It's the way it happens. I saw it so many times. A guy holding off the enemy so the rest of the platoon could make it into the chopper. Someone retrieving a wounded buddy under fire. So many dying because they chose to do the right thing."

He paused.

"I'm sorry," I said.

"The good ones stand and fight, Jack. The cowards skitter away."

I waited, and then said, "Mr. Ziggy, the theater guy."

"Yes."

"He's gone, too."

I told him about Tiffanee finding him with Tara, Mr. Ziggy dying. The details, I left vague.

Clair listened, then turned to me. He smiled the saddest of smiles.

"Taking a bullet, Jack?" he said.

I thought about it, the need to hold it all so close. Even from Clair.

"You know how it is," I said. "Sometimes you have no choice but to do the right thing."

29

The first two rows of seats in Belfast Superior Court were full. If it had been a wedding, they would have said the attendees were all from my side.

Clair and Mary, Tiffanee and Tara, sitting close. Roxanne and Sophie, holding hands.

Sparrow and Riff and Blake, Sparrow in the middle, close to Blake. I'd been wrong on that one, but romance had never been my strong point.

Dunne was on the edge of her seat, phone in hand, ready to tweet. Carlisle had flown up from New York with a reporter, a woman named Westbrook who was doing the story. Mrs. Hodding, whose woodlot we cut, was sitting in the back, her walker parked at the end of the row.

A few police officers showed up, sat in the back. Strain. Jackman and the Boy Scout. Rousseau, the State Police sergeant I'd known for years. Assorted troopers and sheriff's deputies. I wondered who was protecting Waldo County.

The prosecutor, an assistant AG named McGowan, asked for three years, all but twenty-six months suspended. "While the victim is alleged to have attempted to commit what would have been a serious crime, he didn't deserve to die. If Mr. Hofer had been allowed to flee, he likely would have been apprehended and brought to justice. The defendant, intentionally or unintentionally, imposed his own sentence."

My attorney, Carol Lynn, asked for two years, all but nine months suspended. "Mr. McMorrow was defending a young girl and her mother against a serial predator. This death was a tragic accident, for which Mr. McMorrow does accept some responsibility."

The judge listened and noted that other victims of Mr. Ziggy had written to the court, describing his inappropriate behavior. And she said she considered the statements of the alleged victim in this case, and that of her mother. She wished them the best in the future.

And then the judge asked me if I wanted to say anything. I shook my head, said, "No, Your Honor." So, then she read the sentence: "Thirty months in the custody of the Maine Department of Corrections, all but twenty months suspended." She proclaimed this in her judge voice, which made it sound very official. Which it was, because I was remanded to custody as soon as the gavel fell.

When I turned, a gray-haired court deputy was there. He took me by the arm and started for the door, but he did lead me along the rail so I could touch a few hands, like a baseball player high-fiving the fans in the front row of the stands.

Clair told me to take care of myself. I told him to do the same. Since Louis had died, he'd been somber and mostly silent. He said he'd be fine eventually, but eventually hadn't come yet. When he shook my hand and looked into my eyes, it was like something was missing in his.

Brandon Blake said to let him know if I needed anything. I said I would, that we'd see each other soon. Sparrow leaned close, said, "I'd give you a freakin' medal."

And then Tiffanee came forward, Tara hanging back. Tiffanee put her hand on my arm and whispered, "Thank you."

I smiled, said, "No thanks necessary."

Last up were Roxanne and Sophie. They were crying, wiping their eyes. I told them I'd be home very soon, that I'd have lots of stories to tell at the dinner table. I said I loved them very much. Sophie hugged me, held on for a long time. Then Roxanne leaned in, put her tear-streaked cheek to mine, and whispered, "I'm with you always, Jack McMorrow."

"Same here," I said, squeezing her hand. "Forever and ever."

And then the deputy tugged my arm, and I turned and followed him, leaving all of them behind. It was time.

EPILOGUE

One of my cell mates at "the Farm" was a guy named Jorge. He originally was from Guatemala, came to Downeast Maine to work processing sea urchins. Then he married a local woman, got a better job driving a truck back and forth to New York for a lobster company. Gang members in Guatemala City abducted his youngest brother and demanded ransom, so Jorge started bringing drugs back to Maine in his lobster truck to pay them off. And then they kept upping the price. On his second run, he got caught, was sentenced to four years. He was lucky he wasn't deported.

He was a decent guy, wrote letters every week telling his younger siblings to work hard in school, learn a trade. Jorge was teaching me Spanish, and Sophie and I spoke some when she and Roxanne came to Warren for visits, usually on Sunday afternoons.

"*Hola, Padre*," she'd say.

"*Hola, mi hija hermosa*," I'd say.

She'd reach across the table and hold my hand.

Sophie would hold one, and Roxanne would hold the other. We wouldn't let go for the entire hour as they chatted away. Roxanne's new clients in Belfast. Sophie's reports from school. Tiffanee and Tara's news from Phoenix.

"Tara's doing awesome," Sophie said. "Her school is doing *The Addams Family*. She's Morticia."

Roxanne listened and squeezed my hand. Hard.

Sophie and Roxanne were on my approved visitor list. So were Clair and Brandon Blake. He had his PI license, was chasing down workers' comp fraud, locating elusive witnesses for defense attorneys. Stephanie Dunne, who also was on the list, wanted him to do a podcast with her. A day in the life of a gumshoe sort of thing. Blake was resisting but Dunne was wearing him down. She said it would lead to more and better cases. He and Sparrow needed the money if they were going to buy their own place.

The money from the pot heist was gone, spent on Riff's meds.

Dunne hadn't had to twist my arm. Our podcast was called *Inside Stories*. I was the narrator, and she produced. Every week I lined up the right resident (they don't call us inmates) to call her, tell his story, which she recorded. They were interesting guys, mostly, who also had been drug dealers and thieves, bar fighters and scam artists. Some were short-timers like me. Others had come to the Farm to do the last couple of years of longer sentences.

I looked for stories that were in some way hopeful. Dunne said the podcast was starting to take off. With all the carnage and tragedy, people needed good news, even from unexpected places.

So did I, and on this particular Saturday, I had some to deliver.

It was Saturday, the 9:45 slot. Clair was sitting at the table when the officer, a former long-haul trucker named Brownie, brought me in.

"Hey," I said.

"Jackson," Clair said, getting to his feet.

We shook hands and sat. I asked him how Mary was, and he said she was very good. The day before they'd gone for a drive to the coast, seen some foliage, had lobster rolls on a deck overlooking Penobscot Bay.

His new leaf.

"Got some news," Clair said.

"Let's hear it."

"Shooter got forty years, federal prison. Homicide, transporting weapons across state lines for the purpose of committing a crime. Three buddies got twenty for conspiracy. All pleaded."

"Did they flip?"

"Bikers' *omertà*. Never said a word. Hard to tell if it's over, with Marta and the money still out there."

I waited a moment, then slipped a piece of paper from my uniform pocket. I slid it across the table.

"I have news, too."

Clair picked up the paper, unfolded it. It was a note written in neat cursive on pale-blue lined paper. He took out his reading glasses.

Dear Jack,

How are you? I'll bet you're doing okay. You're a journalist, and now you have all of those stories in there with you. And your family waiting for you when you get out. I picture many hugs.

I'm writing to you because I know you never thought much of me. Maybe this is my way to try to change your mind. I really did love Louis, just so you know. But loving me back is a double-edged sword.

So it's true what they say. Money is the root of all evil. And it turns out you can't take it with you. Not in my case. I tried but it kept pulling me back.

I think it's cursed. Proklyattya, as we say in Ukraine. It killed Nigel. It killed Louis. I'm sorry I brought it into their lives, and yours. It's waiting at that spot where you and Clair were cutting trees down, and I drove in with Louis. You can follow my tracks and there will be another note. Sorry to play scavenger hunt, but I'd hate to lose it now, after all this.

Could someone return it to Lambert in Montreal, let him get hit with the curse. Maybe Brandon Blake could help. Tell him I'll pay him for his time. He can reach out on WhatsApp. I'm Marta91.

Thanks. For this and your help. I hope this ends all of it. And sorry again. I do hope I see you someday.

Your terrible excuse for a friend,
Marta

Clair slid the note back across the tabletop.

"Seems like she's trying to do the right thing as well," he said.

"Better late than never," I said.

"The power of redemption. I'm believing in it more and more."

"Getting soft, Marine. Can you find the package?"

"As soon as I get back. Think Blake will do the delivery?"

316 • HARD LINE

"Probably," I said. "He's bored. Better be careful, though."

"Maybe I'll go with him," Clair said.

"Back in the saddle?" I said.

He shrugged. "Don't want to be the one old soldier who just fades away."

And then we sat, not talking, our hands folded on the graffiti-scarred table. Amid the silence, my mind raced through the decades. All the road-running we'd done, skirmishes and battles, meeting hard types and soft. The days in Clair's workshop, his bits of quiet wisdom. His knocks on our door, always there for Roxanne, for Sophie, for me. And somehow we ended up here.

"We managed to do some good, didn't we," I said.

"We did, Jack. Sometimes you get lucky."

"Yes," I said. "Sometimes you do."

-30-